A NIGHTMARE MADE REAL

The instant it realized it had been spotted, the dark shape dropped to the ground and began inching along the fence inside the yard, never straying far from the shadows of the overhanging trees. At the corner of the yard it turned toward him, walking . . . stalking slowly through the wet brown grass. It was a dog—a large, shaggy-haired black dog, with eyes like bonfires in a prehistoric cave. Closer now, its low growl, the sound that first captured Luther's attention, became a snarl as it bared its impressive set of fangs.

Believing any sudden movement might precipitate an attack, Luther remained still. Now that he saw it clearly, he was stunned. He had never laid eyes on the animal before in his life, but he immediately recognized it for what it was.

But that's crazy! he thought. *It's just a myth!*

His chaotic musings cost him precious seconds and very nearly his life. Trapped between the back door and the fence that separated his backyard from his neighbors', Luther had no place to go.

The beast snarled again—louder.

Other *Leisure* books by Gary L. Holleman:
**HOWL-O-WEEN
DEMON FIRE**

UNGRATEFUL DEAD

GARY L. HOLLEMAN

LEISURE BOOKS NEW YORK CITY

This book is dedicated to the people who have made a difference in my life: my wife Kathleen, my Aunt Ann, and my best friends Glenn and Marylou. Thank you.

A LEISURE BOOK®

January 1999

Published by

Dorchester Publishing Co., Inc.
276 Fifth Avenue
New York, NY 10001

If you purchased this book without a cover you should be aware that this book is stolen property. It was reported as "unsold and destroyed" to the publisher and neither the author nor the publisher has received any payment for this "stripped book."

Copyright © 1999 by Gary L. Holleman

All rights reserved. No part of this book may be reproduced or transmitted in any form or by any electronic or mechanical means, including photocopying, recording or by any information storage and retrieval system, without the written permission of the Publisher, except where permitted by law.

ISBN 0-8439-4472-2

The name "Leisure Books" and the stylized "L" with design are trademarks of Dorchester Publishing Co., Inc.

Printed in the United States of America.

"The dark power of the malignant Tree broke down the barriers between man and animal; man and man, allowing his disciples to enter and control the four-legged beasts of the field, and to usurp the bodies of their kin. For it was only through the blood of a kinsman could the black souls take permanent root in their new home, where they lay for years festering like the pox until they were ready to move on anew."

—*The Serpent's Egg* by Joshua Kantrell

UNGRATEFUL DEAD

Chapter One

Tuesday night, on his way downstairs to the combined AA/NA meeting, Luther glanced out his office window and saw a redheaded woman on the sidewalk next to the parking lot across from the University of Memphis campus. Tall and slim, she'd stood like a fiery beacon among the river of students rushing to their cars after the last classes let out. Then, as he rolled his eyes, bored almost to tears by the balding FedEx pilot who was explaining, yet again, how the company's refusal to recognize the pilot's union had driven him to drink, Luther saw the woman staring at him from the doorway.

Of course, he couldn't really see her all that well; she was standing out of the light, and in a room full of people and cigarette smoke, she could actually have been looking at the guy in the chair next to him, or even at the pilot droning away up on the podium. Yet somehow

Luther didn't think so. For when he glanced in her direction, she dropped her eyes and inched back into the dimly lighted hall.

Luther got to his feet and, being careful to avoid the cigarette butts and discarded gum wrappers on the floor, made his way down the row of nervous knees to the table at the rear of the classroom. There, he emptied six packets of sugar into a Styrofoam cup of lukewarm coffee and took a sip. It was a new blend—mud and warm piss. With a final glance at the pilot, Luther strolled out into the hall to look around. The woman was standing in front of the bulletin board beside the elevator, pretending to read a circular advertising aerobics classes.

Luther wondered who she was trying to fool. Even with her back turned, a blind man could see she had a body that made the very idea of aerobics ridiculous. He liked the way she dressed too: a simple black-and-beige sweater dress that reached just past her knees, a pair of mid-heel black pumps, and a tiny shoulder bag with a gold chain.

Strolling down the hall, he paused and, with what he hoped was a nonthreatening smile, said, "I don't mean to pry, but were you looking for someone?"

She turned, and Luther saw that the whole left side of her face was horribly scarred. He tried to hide his shock, but like most people, he had never been very good at that sort of thing and shame flitted like a shadow across her features. She quickly shifted so that the "good" side was facing him and offered her hand.

"Doctor Shea?"

Her good side was stunning, and Luther was suddenly very conscious of his faded jeans and rumpled plaid shirt. He wiped his hand on the seat of his pants before accepting hers. "Guilty as charged, Mrs . . ."

"Alana Magnus . . . and it's Ms."

Ungrateful Dead

"What can I do for you, Ms. Magnus?" Luther asked, making a face as he took another sip of coffee.

"Is there some place we could talk?" She cast an eye at the classroom where the meeting was still in progress. "Some place . . . private?"

"My office is on the third floor—if you don't mind the clutter of a disorganized mind."

"No. No, that would be fine."

They took the antiquated elevator to the third floor where Alana allowed Luther to lead her down a dimly lighted hallway, past rows of locked doors, to his office. After unlocking the door and turning on the overhead lights, he shifted a stack of ungraded exam papers from the chair in front of the desk to the floor. Alana sat down, angled her left side to the shadows and demurely crossed her legs.

The office was pretty much the way he had characterized it: institutional-green metal bookcases overflowing with occult texts and manuscripts, mounds of magazines and yellowed newspapers, a gray metal desk supporting a dust-covered, Apple IIe computer with a half-dozen empty Styrofoam cups on top. On the wall behind the door was a photo of Luther standing with a group of smiling Little Leaguers, and a diploma (cum laude) in Paranormal Psychology from Duke University in Durham, North Carolina. Behind the desk was a window that offered a breathtaking view of the brick wall across the quad, and the sill provided a platform for his collection of venus flytraps and African violets.

Luther took a seat behind the desk and casually arranged his hands over the strips of electrical tape that were holding the chair arm's padding in check and then took a deep breath and put on his best "conference with student" face.

"So, what can I do for you?"

"Well, I don't really know just where to begin," said Alana, her eyes studiously inspecting the shine on her shoes. "Like I said, my name is Alana Magnus, and I work for Federated Department Stores as a buyer. I'm not from Memphis, as I guess you can tell from my accent. I was recently transferred here from Macy's in New York." Her voice trailed off, and she smoothed the front of her dress. "A friend of mine told me about you. She said you're the local expert on the supernatural."

Mystified by the sudden shift in direction, Luther's eyebrows formed twin arches over his ice-blue eyes. "Expert? I wouldn't—"

"You wrote those books on the paranormal?"

"Book!" he corrected. "I wrote one book. And it was just a compilation of legends and myths." He wondered why he was being defensive.

"What about that story in the *Commercial Appeal*?"

Luther remained silent for several seconds. It was too bad, for he felt sorry for the woman and had hoped he would be able to help her with whatever her problem was. Now it appeared that she was just another kook.

"Don't let these plush accommodations fool you," he said, waving his hand around the cramped office. "The university pretty much considers what I do a joke."

"I . . . I don't get it."

"Neither did I, at first. It seems one of our corporate sponsors visited the Psi Lab at Duke and then came back and laid a ton of money on the school to start one here. I was as far as the administration got. I think the rest of the grant went for new basketball uniforms." Luther rose to his feet. "Well, if there isn't anything else . . ." He was already thinking about the medium-rare hamburger and home fries he was going to order at the Belmont Grill.

The woman didn't move. "Yes, but you do know

Ungrateful Dead

about the supernatural? I mean, you do teach classes on it?"

Luther's sigh made the wind chimes in the corner tinkle like glass bells. "If you call explaining to a bunch of Star Trek junkies coated with acne cream that Bram Stoker did not write *Nightmare on Elm Street* teaching about the supernatural, then I guess I teach about the supernatural. May I ask where we're going with this?"

Alana drummed her fingers on the arm of the chair. Her nails resembled pieces of clear plastic that had been gnawed by rats.

"I may be losing my mind," she said at last.

Luther tried without any success whatsoever to fathom what was going on inside the woman's head by reading her expression. Like most people, a disfigured person—especially a disfigured woman who would have been absolutely gorgeous otherwise—made him uncomfortable. And feeling that way made Luther angry at himself. She was obviously upset, but he couldn't allow himself to be sucked in by that either, for after all, weren't most paranoid schizophrenics upset about something? He reached for his address book to give her the name of his friend, Cal Weinberg, the super-shrink.

"Unfortunately," he said, "mental problems aren't really my thing. But if it makes you feel any better, I always heard that if you're sane enough to think you're going crazy, you're probably not."

"I'm possessed!" she blurted out.

Well, he thought, *so much for that idea.*

Locating his address book, Luther began flipping through the W's.

"Aren't you going to say anything?" she asked.

"I'm going to call a friend of mine who has a lot more experience in these matters than I do. His name's Cal. You'll like him. He has a nice office; all chrome and glass. And salt-water aquariums and—"

The cold click of the pistol's safety shut Luther up like a sudden attack of anarthria.

"I know how this looks," she said. "Please say something."

"I've always found that guns tend to inhibit the free exchange of ideas."

"Look, I'm not crazy. And I'm not dangerous."

"Obviously."

"I want you to come with me; to listen to me. An hour maybe two. What could it hurt? Maybe then you can tell me what to do."

The longer Luther stared at the gun muzzle, the larger it appeared, until, at last, he forced his eyes up to Alana's face. Her eyes were clear and almost painfully green. She didn't look crazy.

They never look crazy, moron!

"Please don't make me use this," she said.

And she sounded so reasonable, he thought, for a woman with a gun in her hand.

"I don't think I could kill you, but you might never walk without a limp again."

He didn't really think she would shoot him. But then again, he would never have believed that such a big gun could have come out of such a small purse.

"What do you say?"

Luther smiled and turned his palms up. "Why not?"

She used the gun to steer him down the elevator and out to the street. The night was cold for Memphis and damp, with a drizzle that peppered their faces like slivers of liquid ice. The traffic on Central Avenue was practically nonexistent, and the sodium vapor street lights created a world of wet shadows that seemed to throb with malignant life. As they started to cross the street, Alana suddenly grabbed his arm.

"Wait!"

Luther stopped and crammed his hands into the pockets of his jeans. "What? I'm freezing. At least you could have let me get my jacket."

"Look under that fir tree across the street."

"For your information, that's a Norfolk Island Pine."

The gun burrowed into his kidney. "Skip the botany lesson, Professor!" she hissed. "Do you see that man or don't you?"

Squinting against the falling mist, Luther saw there was indeed a tall, skinny man with a beard that Rasputin the mad monk would have envied, huddled in the shadow of the tree.

"Yes, I see him."

"Thank God," Alana mumbled. "Maybe I'm not completely nuts."

"It's some homeless guy trying to stay dry."

Her laugh was bitter and without a trace of humor. "A homeless guy in a three hundred dollar London Fog raincoat? You forget what I do for a living?"

Luther looked again. "Okay, so he ripped off a lawyer to keep from freezing to death. Right now, I can't say I blame him."

"He's been following me."

Oh boy! Here we go.

"Go on," she said. "The black Z."

It was the only car remaining in the lot.

Luther looked both ways, hoping against hope to spot a cruising cop, but police cars were becoming as scarce as pterodactyl teeth on the crime-ridden streets around the university. They crossed Central and, as Luther waited for Alana to unlock the car door, he snuck a peek at the pine tree. The man was gone. Certain that the woman would make something sinister out of the guy's sudden disappearance, Luther climbed into the passenger seat as soon as the electric door lock popped, fastened his seat belt, and tried to distract her with small talk.

"So, where are we going? I suppose stopping for a bite to eat is out of the question? I haven't eaten since this afternoon, and all I had then was a salad. I know this quaint little hamb—"

"He's gone, isn't he?"

"Who?"

"Don't jerk me around. That's been his pattern. He shows up just about every place I go, hangs around, watches, and then vanishes."

"Ms. Magnus, it is a sad fact of life that like most urban areas, Memphis has an abundance of homeless people."

"He's not homeless!"

"Okay, so he was looking for someone to mug."

The Z's engine roared to turbo-charged life, and she glanced over at Luther; the good side of her face made sinister by the electric-green glow of the dashboard's digital clock.

"I can't drive and hold a gun on you, but if you try anything we might end up wrapped around a telephone pole."

Luther held up his hands in surrender and leaned back into the plush leather seat. Alana switched on the headlights.

"Jesus!"

Sitting calmly on its haunches in the cone of the headlights was a monstrous black dog. It was just sitting there in the rain, its matted fur drooping like hag's hair, and its eyes glinting red as it stared defiantly at the windshield.

Alana honked the horn and the animal bared its yellowed fangs, as if finding humor in the situation.

"Cheeky bastard," Luther muttered.

Ungrateful Dead

"People should keep their animals locked up."

"Poor thing's probably cold and hungry." *Just like me*, Luther thought.

"I hate animals."

She put the car in reverse and backed up.

The dog was still sitting there staring at them when they drove out of the parking lot.

Alana pushed the powerful sports car over the rain-slick streets with casual competence, using the gears more often than the brakes, with a single mindedness that bordered on obsession. She took Poplar Avenue east, passing the Oak Court Mall where the post-Thanksgiving–pre-Christmas decorations turned the glistening sidewalks into rivers of fire; crossing the Interstate and curving through valleys of suburban office buildings and fast-food hells. The road widened, and the streetlights stopped, and before long they entered the outskirts of Germantown—Memphis' version of yuppie heaven—and took a left down a long, pitch-black road, passing subdivisions of two-and three-story, neocolonial homes and one-story, glass-and-brick schools that the kids in the downtown projects would have given their eyeteeth to attend. At a subdivision called Plantation Hills, she followed a curved, partially paved road around a golf and tennis complex to a wide, one-story brick-and-wood house that backed up to thick trees at the end of a dead-end street. As soon as she switched off the engine, the gun reappeared in her hand.

"Good grief!" Luther snapped, breaking the silence between them for the first time in half an hour. "What the hell do you think I'm going to do? Make a break for it so I can have the pleasure of running through the rain all the way back to the campus?"

Alana thought it over for about ten seconds, then

clicked the safety on and tucked the gun into her handbag.

"Okay. Come on, let's go."

Unsure what to expect, Luther stopped just inside the front door and pretended to wipe his feet as he took a quick look around. From what he could see, the place screamed transience. The walls were oyster-white, without a scuff mark or ding, there were bedsheets over the windows, and the carpet, which was champagne-colored and smelled new, was thick enough to swallow his running shoes. Open wardrobe boxes, with expensive dresses and blouses hanging out like the stuffing in a Cabbage Patch doll, stood in the corners, and the oversized, wood-burning fireplace was full of cardboard boxes labeled "dishes." The rooms were sparsely but expensively furnished. A large beige leather sectional faced a thirty-two-inch color TV across a coffee table made out of a redwood burl, and in the dining room, under a chandelier that looked like the mother ship from *Close Encounters of the Third Kind*, was a brand-new Pentium computer and laser printer resting atop a Kmart card table.

"Nice place," Luther said.

Alana punched the rheostat on the wall to turn on the overhead track lighting, but then quickly dialed the lights down to just a notch above dismal. She dropped the purse on the sectional. "Thanks. If I ever have time to unpack, I might actually start to enjoy the place."

She turned her back and strolled into the bedroom as if he were not there. A minute later he heard a toilet flush.

Looking down at the purse, Luther considered removing the gun but then thought, *what the heck!* He sat down on the section of the sofa closest to the fireplace and wished it were full of burning logs instead of boxes.

Ungrateful Dead

Alana came back into the room buttoning a pair of cut-offs that revealed just how right he had been about her legs. She had scrubbed off her make-up, changed into a loose-fitting, powder-blue Oxford cloth shirt, and pulled her hair back in a ponytail that was so tight it made her eyes look Asian. Luther interpreted the hairdo as her way of letting him know she wasn't going to allow her deformity to affect her.

And yet she clung to the shadows.

It was an unconscious habit on her part, he thought, but a more accurate gauge of how deeply into her psyche the outer scars actually went.

In her hand was a thick, leather-bound photograph album, held together with rubber bands. She placed the album on the coffee table, opened it, and picked out a faded 8 × 10 glossy from among dozens of other black-and-white and color photos. After staring at it for several seconds, she sat down on the carpet, turned so that her good side faced him, folded her legs, and pushed the photo across the table.

It was a picture of a stunning woman wearing a hairstyle and a mink coat that had both been out of fashion for more than thirty years. She was standing behind a little girl with pigtails, braces, and a Catholic school uniform, complete down to knee socks and two-tone saddle oxfords. The woman looked angry; the little girl, bored and fidgety.

Looking up, Luther said, "So?"

"The woman in that picture was my mother."

"Was? She's dead? I'm sorry."

"Save it. We weren't close."

The combination of ice and pain in her voice made it clear that this was not a subject she wanted to chat about.

"Is that you?" he asked, noting that the little girl's face was unmarked.

"Yes," she replied, staring dispassionately at the girl she had once been. "That was taken in France on one of Mother's rare visits to my school."

"And your father?" Luther asked, curious in spite of himself.

"Never knew him. I was always told he was killed in a plane crash, but with Mother . . . I believe she made him up."

Luther smiled. "Biologically, not feasible."

She looked him straight in the eye, and her gaze was intense enough to make him drop the smile.

"It's not important." Alana placed two more photos on either side of the first.

At first glance, Luther thought the picture on the right was another snapshot of Alana, only it had yellowed and cracked so badly that the image looked like it was covered with cobwebs. In it, the little girl was sitting on an old-fashioned swing, and a man was standing behind her wearing a heavy overcoat. There was snow on the ground, and in the background was a smudge that could have been the shadow of a large dog.

The second photograph was a resume-style, studio shot of Alana sitting sideways on a four-legged stool, with her hands crossed over her knees. In this one, she was wearing a business suit and was without make-up or jewelry.

"The girl in that photo"—Alana touched the sepia snapshot—"is my mother at about the age I was when that first photo was taken. This one"—she pointed to the studio shot—"was taken six months ago when I was approximately the same age Mother was in the first photo."

Confused, Luther stared at each photograph in turn, paying special attention to the one in the middle. For the life of him he couldn't guess what she wanted him

Ungrateful Dead

to see. However, he was afraid that if he said "so?" one more time, she might take the gun out of her purse and blow his kneecaps off. He opted for what he hoped was a nice neutral comment. "Nice-looking woman."

It wasn't what she wanted to hear.

"Are you blind? Look at her hands!"

"Her hands?" Luther echoed, staring at the well-manicured hands resting on the girl's small shoulders. "What about them?"

Alana sprang from the floor with the fluid grace of a jungle cat. She stomped over to the card table, returning a moment later with a large magnifying glass—the kind his German grandfather used to read to him with. "Here! Look!"

Luther took the glass and peered at the woman's slim fingers; one of them bore a diamond ring as big as a golf ball.

Alana shoved the resume photo under the lens. "Now look!"

He looked closely at the hands folded across her knees. The nails had looked better then; long and tapered and polished to perfection. Her fingers were also long and limber looking; the well-kept hands of a concert pianist.

"You play the piano?" he asked.

Turning her back, she stared at the cold fireplace as if it were a crystal ball in which her entire life was appearing, one agonizing day after another. Her pain was so intense that Luther could almost feel it radiating from her like heat from a pot-bellied stove.

"Not anymore," she whispered. "Do you see now? You must see! I have my mother's hands."

Pity prevented Luther from laughing out loud, and yet he didn't know what to say. Alana was obviously so emotionally unbalanced that she didn't realize how she sounded. He had planned, assuming he survived their encounter, to call the cops the instant she let him go, but now he wasn't sure he could do that. More than anything he wished that his friend Cal were here.

Disturbed she may have been, but she was shrewd enough to interpret his protracted silence. She walked back to the computer and picked up a piece of paper from the table. Returning once more, she handed it to him without a word. It read: *Practice! Practice! Practice!*

"I'm sorry if I'm a bit slow," said Luther. "Is this supposed to mean something to me?"

"No. But it means something to me. When I was at school, anytime I goofed off—played hooky, didn't study, didn't practice—she always knew. I'd get a telegram, and guess what it would say? 'Practice! Practice! Practice!' It used to drive me..." Alana saw his expression and lowered her voice. "I found that in my E-mail yesterday morning."

"Let me get this straight. You were away at school in France and your mother was in this country?"

"Most of the time. She spent a lot of time in England and Ireland too, our family came from there."

"And she used to send you telegrams reminding you to practice your piano?"

"You make it sound like it's some kind of coincidence! It was more than that! She always knew!" Alana paced the room, her features tightening like a fist as she fought to control her mounting frustration. "Look, dammit, every time I got one of those damned telegrams, something always happened."

"Happened? As in..."

"My favorite doll would vanish. Or the hairbrush my great-aunt left me. Once I worked a whole semester on this story for French class." She averted her face again.

"A . . . a love story. And the whole thing, eighty pages, just vanished!"

"But why would your mother want to do that? Better yet, how could she, if she was clear across the Channel?"

"You would have to have known her to understand."

Luther nodded, recognizing the circular logic used by many paranoids. And yet he was finding it surprisingly difficult to just write her off. "Alana, could it be that somebody is pulling your chain? That the whole thing is, you know, a joke? A prank? Not a very nice one to be sure, but . . ."

She stopped pacing and glared at him as if she wanted to take an ax to his head to let in a little daylight. In her anger, Alana momentarily forgot where she was and stepped into the light, and Luther took the opportunity to study her features. It was a real tragedy. The skin on the right side of her face was smooth and flawless, the lips full. It was the kind of face that would have looked right at home on the cover of *Vogue* or *Harper's Bazaar*. The other side was a red, raw, lump of dead flesh that should have belonged to a wax doll that some careless child left on top of the stove.

She realized what he was up to and quickly averted her face.

"Damn you!" she snapped. "Come with me!"

He followed her down a dark hallway, past a large bathroom done in muted pastels, around a corner, to a bedroom whose rear bay window faced the forest. Unlike the other rooms Luther had seen, this one was completely furnished. Both the bay window, which faced east, and the double window on the north side were softened by lacy pink curtains backed by semi-transparent sheers. Between the windows hung a bamboo birdcage shaped like a Chinese pagoda. In the center of the floor was a child-size Biedermeier ensemble done in dark walnut, with a matching étagère containing a mini-orchestra of crystal and porcelain symphony instruments—from which the piano was notably absent. In the alcove between the bedroom and bath was a tiny dressing table topped with lace; on top rested a gilt-framed photograph of a very pale little girl with long auburn hair.

Alana followed his gaze to the picture.

"That's my daughter, Morna. This is her room." She walked over to the dressing table and picked up the frame. Staring at the photo seemed to relax her. "She was eight when this was taken."

"How old is she now?"

"Seventeen. I guess I should get a more current picture."

"Where is she?"

"Away at school in Bern." Replacing the frame carefully, Alana turned around, her mind still captured by her daughter's face. "She will be coming home for the Christmas holidays soon."

"And her father?"

The invisible protective curtain came down with an almost audible thud. "Dead."

"Nice room," offered Luther. It seemed like a safe enough opinion.

Alana's eyes danced over the furnishings. "Morna can't stand it. She says it makes her feel schizophrenic."

Must run in the family, he thought.

"The dark wood is too masculine and all the pink and lace make her feel like a child. She was always very precocious."

Where are the rock-star posters, he wondered. *The teen magazines? The curlers, the hair spray, the dirty sneakers?*

Ungrateful Dead

The room had all the personality of an operating room.

"Luther?" She was standing beside the birdcage. "Come take a look."

He did as she asked.

In the bottom of the cage was the badly decomposed body of a small gray cockatiel. The way its feathers were scattered around the bottom of the cage, it looked as if it had swallowed a firecracker. Luther frowned and turned away, determined not to let Alana see how disturbed he was.

"Why in God's name did you leave it there?"

She seemed not to have heard. "I got him for Morna last fall, just before she flew back to school. She made me promise to take care of him. Now she'll blame me."

Astonished, all he could do was repeat the question, "But why did you leave it there?"

"So you would know."

"Know? Know what?"

"Mother killed Morna's bird to punish me."

Alana eased back the sheet covering the front window and watched Luther climb into the cab. She continued to watch until the cab's taillights vanished around the corner at the end of the cove.

Well, she thought, he was every bit as shrewd as she had heard—definitely no fool. But then, neither was she. So far it was going pretty much the way she'd expected—he'd listened to her story; he hadn't believed a word of it, but he hadn't gone to the cops, either. Instead, he'd called a shrink.

Okay, so now she'd have to go through the whole damned story again with some fat, bald-headed moron with more degrees than brains. She'd wear a short skirt and cross her legs a lot. But in the end, Luther would help her. He had to. Whatever it took, she'd make damned sure he helped her.

Alana focused her attention on the half-completed buildings around the cove. The subdivision was new, and most of the houses were shells with bare roof-beams jutting up pale and stark like decaying corpses in some prehistoric elephant graveyard. There were no streetlights either. Not yet. Maybe in the spring.

Her eyes settled on the house at the opposite end of the street a big, two-story structure, much larger than its neighbors, with a wide driveway and lots of windows. Lots of empty, black windows. In the shadows behind the picture window on the ground floor, a tiny pinprick of light appeared . . . someone had just taken a puff of a cigarette.

Chapter Two

Cal Weinberg's one true love, other than his wife, Rachel, and daughter, Samantha, was scuba diving. If it hadn't been for his mother's heart condition, he would have become a marine biologist instead of leaving the University of Miami with an M.D. in clinical psychiatry, thus saving his mother's life and ultimately allowing her to move into a condo in Boca Raton.

Cal was a big man, with a big, wide, muscular body that had served him well when he'd played linebacker for the Hurricanes. He had a head of thick, golden hair that rippled in waves across the top of his head, piercing brown eyes, and a narrow nose with a slight hump in the middle—a souvenir of a violent collision with a running back's helmet. He liked the hump. He thought it made him look like Marlon Brando in *The Young Lions*.

Cal's office, which was located on the thirteenth floor

Gary L. Holleman

of the Godwin Building in Germantown, was a shrine both to the study of the human mind and to Jacques Yves Cousteau (the man whom Cal secretly ranked far above Sigmund Freud on the list of mankind's benefactors). One wall of the office was all glass, providing his often distraught patients a tranquil view of lush green trees and golf courses. Another wall was all books; tier upon tier of leather-bound tomes on the natural sciences, law, accounting, and psychiatry. To many of the latter he had been a contributing author. The last wall, the one on the northwest side—so that the sun would be less of a problem—was dedicated to his saltwater aquariums, the smallest of which was 55 gallons—the largest was 225. And in addition to a desk the size of an aircraft carrier and a comfortable executive chair, he had a couch.

"You should have called the cops," Cal said to Luther, as he anxiously watched his prize lionfish gobble up the goldfish he had just dropped into the tank.

"I should know better than to expect compassion from a man who feeds live fish to each other."

"She pulled a gun on you, for crissake. She pulls a gun on me, I'll slap her in jail so fast it'll make her head spin."

He dropped a second goldfish into the water and then moved to the next tank; seventy-five gallons of purple and green corals, variegated sea anemones, and gold-and-white clownfish. Plucking a morsel of fresh shrimp from the food platter he prepared daily for his "babies," Cal dropped it into the water, watching eagerly as the gaily striped little fish darted up, shredded the shrimp, and then dragged the pieces back to their tentacled hosts.

"Look at the way those little suckers work to feed the anemones," he chuckled. "They keep it clean, feed it; all in return for a safe place to live."

Ungrateful Dead

"That's fascinating," Luther muttered. "I wish I could find a woman willing to do that for me."

Cal glanced at his friend. "Maybe if you didn't walk around looking like a damned hippie bum all the time, some nice woman might take a chance on you. How long has it been since Alice dumped you? Six months?"

"Dumped? Nice, Cal. With friends like you, who needs the IRS?"

"Touché. Talk about cannibals!"

The intercom on Cal's desk buzzed.

Placing the food tray on top of the large tank, he walked over to the desk and pushed the button on the intercom.

"Yeah, Grace?"

"A Ms. Magnus is here to see you." Cal's secretary's voice oozed out of the box like spilled grits, turning Magnus into a three syllable word and making her "you" come out "ya."

"Okay. Gim'me five minutes."

Cal replaced the food tray in the small refrigerator in the closet, slipped into his Armani jacket, and checked the knot in his tie in the mirror over the bar. Turning, he looked Luther up and down. "Looking at you, anybody'd think I was being held hostage."

Luther glanced at his reflection in the mirror. He saw a slim man in his early forties, blue eyes, which after a night without much sleep looked rather hard and clinical, long hair—part brown, part gray—pulled back into a ponytail, and a gaunt, clean-shaven face. At five-eleven and one-seventy, Luther thought he still looked pretty good. The jeans he had on (which were at least clean) and black cashmere, crewneck sweater only served to make him look relaxed and scholarly.

"I don't look that bad."

"Like I said." Cal took his place in the chair behind

his desk. "I can give her five minutes, and then I'll politely refer her to Henry Stein over at the Medical School."

"I appreciate it. She needs help."

"You frigging liberals," Cal rearranged the piles of legal-size folders on his desk and then aimed the photograph of his wife and daughter at the bergère chair next to the one Luther was occupying. "Save the whales, hug the trees, kiss the gun-toting whackos."

"So sue me. Her story was too damned odd to brush off—gun or no gun."

"Hmph! Maybe I ought to have Grace frisk her before she comes in."

"Besides," Luther added, "when you see her you'll understand."

At that, the door opened.

Luther offered Alana a welcoming smile as she strode confidently up to Cal's desk, shifted her photo album from her right hand to her left, and then stuck out the right hand. She had arranged her hair so that it cloaked the scarred half of her face and had jettisoned the previous evening's conservative sweater dress in favor of a clingy, emerald-green sarong with a slit up the front that drew Cal's eyes like a magnet. Luther hardly recognized her.

Cal came out of the chair as if shot out of a catapult. He clasped her hand in both of his and greeted her with a wide smile splitting his face. "Welcome! Welcome. Please, have a seat there beside my old buddy, Lute."

"Lute?" She pointed a cocked eyebrow in Luther's direction.

If possible, Cal's smile grew even wider. "Luther and I go way, way back."

Alana sat down next to Luther, checked the arrangement of her hair and crossed her legs.

Ungrateful Dead

Cal reclaimed his seat, glanced at Luther and nodded toward the door. "If you don't mind?"

Luther started to get up, but Alana laid a hand on his arm. "I'd like Luther to stay, if he doesn't mind."

"You're sure?" Cal asked.

She nodded.

"So, Ms. Magnus, Lute tells me someone has been harassing you."

Alana recrossed her legs, and Cal's eyes bounced from the slit to her face. The good half of her mouth turned up at the corner. "First let me say how much I appreciate your seeing me on such short notice. I only hope I'm not wasting your time."

"Oh? Why do you say that?"

"I'm not crazy, Weinberg."

Leaning back in his chair, Cal made a tent out of his fingers. "Why don't you tell me what's been happening?"

Alana glanced at Luther. "It started the summer I was nine. Up until then I always spent my vacations with the nuns; sometimes in Rome, sometimes in Lourdes. But that year, out of the blue, Mother came and took me with her to Manhattan. I remember she was very agitated about something, but I was so pleased that she wanted me that I didn't want to chance ruining everything by asking a lot of stupid questions.

"When we arrived, her townhouse was full of people. I realize now that they were a bunch of weirdos and freaks, but back then I thought they were sophisticated and very avant-garde. That is, until I met Anton Gadarn.

"At the time, Anton was the latest in Mother's long line of . . . how shall I put this? Lovers isn't exactly right, for most of her beaus were overly tanned gigolos in string bathing trunks who were constantly sniffing around her wallet like dogs. No, Anton was different.

He treated her like a queen—which, as I remember, both amazed and frightened me. Then there was his appearance; he was short. I don't mean short for a man, I mean short for anyone—a midget."

Cal and Luther locked eyes for a moment.

"He dressed like a slob, always had food stains on his shirts, and wore this awful, sickeningly sweet cologne that smelled like Lilac Water only much stronger."

"How did they meet?" asked Cal.

"I don't know. She picked him up somewhere in Great Britain."

"What else do you remember?"

Alana was silent for a few seconds. "Let's see . . . that was the summer the piano lessons started. Mother always loved music, she said it reminded her of the village where she grew up."

"Village," Cal said. "Don't hear that term much nowadays."

"She used it all the time. And she loved the piano. I bet if I heard her say it once, I heard it a million times—if only she hadn't been saddled with a child, she could have been a concert pianist. You can imagine how that made *me* feel."

Cal flipped open the spiral notebook on his desk pad and, without taking his eyes off Alana, started scribbling notes.

"Also, that fall, when I returned to school, was the first time I noticed I was being followed—"

The intercom buzzed.

"Excuse me." He stabbed the talk button with the eraser on his pencil. "What?"

"Sorry to bother you. Your two o'clock is here."

"Reschedule him and cancel the rest of the afternoon.'' Cal glanced at Luther and shook his head slightly. "Go on, Alana."

"There's not much more. After that she always seemed to know where I was and what I was doing and with whom I was doing it. As I told Dr. Shea, if I did anything to displease her, things of mine—things I cared about—either disappeared or were destroyed. I stopped trying to make friends and after a while, I stopped writing or reading, or doing anything I enjoyed. This went on even after I graduated from college and..." Alana paused and lowered her eyes. "I know how this must sound... it was only after she died last June that I started to have a life."

The sunlight, which only moments before had been streaming through the windows, suddenly cooled as masses of black clouds rolled in from the west. Inside the thunderheads, bright flashes of lightning could be seen. Cal rose and went to the last window and lowered the miniblinds. He stopped at the next window to watch the storm approach.

"It sure has been raining a lot lately," Luther noted.

"Tell me about being followed," Cal said.

"After the funeral everything stopped," Alana replied. "The men vanished, and my life turned around. I got a job, bought a car and a house, and then, about a month ago, I began seeing the same three men everywhere I went. At first I tried to convince myself it was just a coincidence, and I started varying my route to and from work. It didn't help. Everywhere I went, they were there. The parking lot at work. At the supermarket... everywhere"

"Just men?" Cal asked. "No women?"

Alana cut her eyes to the shrink's wide silhouette framed like a shadow box in the window. His question had taken her by surprise, and as she considered her response, she wondered, *Could I have misjudged him?*

"The men kind of stood out." She touched Luther's arm. "Like that guy last night." When she looked back, Cal was leaning against the window sill staring at her. "I guess there could have been women, and I just missed them."

"Go on."

"That's it. They just follow me. They never try to talk to me or approach me or anything."

"You ever try to approach them?"

"No."

"Why not?"

"They would—they might hurt me."

"Why do you think they would do that?"

Alana smoothed the slit in her dress again. "I don't know. They just scare me."

"Do a lot of things scare you?"

"No. Not a lot of things."

"What things, for example?"

"I don't know. The usual things. Dark places. Spiders . . . dogs."

An explosion of light ripped the darkening sky in two. Alana gasped and threw a hand up to shield her eyes. An instant later the lightning vanished and drops of water the size of silver dollars began to pound the glass.

"Lightning scare you too?" asked Cal.

Alana lowered her hand and glared at him. The eye on her good side seemed to reflect the light like a cat's. "Yes, if you must know, lightning scares me too."

"Uh, listen," Luther spoke up. "Maybe we should—"

"Quiet, buddy!" Cal said. "What was your mother's name, Alana?" When she didn't reply, he said again, "Alana?"

"Morgana."

Ungrateful Dead

Morgana Magnus?"

"Yes."

"Hmm. And you think her spirit is trying to take over your mind?"

Alana's fingernails gouged crescent-shaped craters in the soft fabric of the armrest. "Not just my mind."

She picked up the photo album and pulled out the same set of photographs she'd shown Luther.

"Look." She spread them out on Cal's desk

Cal walked over and glanced at the pictures. "Yes, Lute told me about these. You think they prove she is trying to take possession of your body."

"Look at the hands." She pointed to the pictures.

"I see, but I don't know what you expect me to say."

Sighing, Alana leaned back in the chair. "I don't suppose you'd take my word that over the last few months my fingers have gotten longer and slimmer." Cal glanced at the resume photo, noting the ornate topaz ring on her finger.

"I can't wear that ring anymore," she said.

He was enough of a professional not to smile. "Alana, it is not at all unusual for a woman's body to go through certain changes as it matures; even a woman as young as you are."

Nodding as if she had expected that, she reached down and pulled a manila envelope from the album. "Then there's not much more we can accomplish today. Do me a favor. Keep these and I'll come back in a few weeks."

Cal eyed the envelope warily. "What is it?"

"Take a look."

He opened the envelope. Inside were two nude, full-body photographs of Alana; one front and one rear. Cal's face turned as red as a carnival balloon. "What am I supposed to do with these?"

She picked up the album and rose to her feet. "Keep them. If anything else changes, I'll have proof even you can't deny."

With that said, Alana glanced at Luther. "See you." And then she marched out of the office.

As soon as the door closed, Luther got up and went around the desk. "Let me see."

Cal turned the photographs over and placed his hands on top of them. "I don't think that would be ethical."

"Hey, I'm a doctor too! And don't forget who referred her."

"Well," Cal muttered with as much dignity as he could muster. "I guess it wouldn't hurt to have a witness to verify when and under what circumstances she gave me the photos. Here, first I'll date the envelope . . . and now the time. . . . now sign here on the back."

Luther did as instructed, and then Cal turned the photographs over.

For almost half a minute, the rain hammering the windows was the only sound in the room. Finally Luther glanced at Cal and muttered, "Nothing wrong with her body."

Cal nodded. "That would pretty much be my professional opinion, too."

Fifteen minutes later, Luther rolled his twenty-one-speed mountain bike through the entrance of Cal's building and stood under the awning. The rain was still coming down in sheets, overflowing the gutters and turning the streets into waterways. The cloud cover had pushed the afternoon into early evening, and as usual, the instant the first drop of rain hit the pavement, the morons who roamed Memphis's streets in their rolling steel coffins felt compelled to start ramming into each other.

As Luther waited for the rain to diminish, he watched

Ungrateful Dead

the flashing blue lights of the police cars and tow trucks battle it out with the blinking headlights and blaring horns of the cars not involved in a wreck. The black Z pulled up to the curb, and the tinted window on the passenger side opened about an inch.

"Want a ride?" Alana yelled.

Luther checked the sky. The clouds didn't look like they were in any hurry to go anywhere.

"What about my bike?" he hollered back.

"Chain it to the pole! You can pick it up tomorrow!"

It was about ten miles to Luther's townhouse, a trip he normally would have enjoyed. But with the rain and all the kamikazes zooming the highways—

"Okay! Give me a minute."

He chained the bike to the support column in the entranceway and then dashed down the sidewalk and threw himself into the car.

"Phew! God, what a day," he said, tucking his ponytail under his collar to keep it from dripping on her seats. "I've never seen this much rain."

"I know. I passed an old guy with a boatload of animals a while back." Alana adjusted the car's heater and in seconds the interior was as toasty as the back room of a steam laundry.

"Thanks," he said. "And thanks for the ride."

"Where to?"

Luther gave directions to his place and then fastened his seat belt and crossed his fingers as she charged blindly out into the herky-jerky flow of traffic.

Horns blew, and cars skidded about like billiard balls, but Alana seemed immune to it all. She calmly worked the steering wheel and gear shift as if she were the sole survivor on a world covered with concrete autobahns.

"Uh, did you see that bus?" Luther asked as soon as he got his tongue unstuck from the roof of his mouth.

"I saw it. Why?"

"No reason."

She glanced at his face and laughed. "My driving make you nervous?"

"What gives you that idea?"

"I don't know. Maybe the way you're gripping the door handle."

Luther relaxed his hand.

"So what did you two good old boys talk about after I left?"

"Oh, nothing much. Cal's got a new fish that he—"

"Which is it? He thinks I'm crazy or that I'm making the whole thing up."

"Truth?"

"Truth," she replied.

"He doesn't know what to think. That stunt with the photographs made it a bit difficult for him to take you seriously."

"He wasn't taking me seriously anyway."

"Don't sell old Cal short. He's as sharp as they come. He'll give you the benefit of the doubt—at least until he knows more."

"Crap," Alana snapped, cramming her foot on the brake pedal. "What now?"

The smoldering remains of a Jeep Cherokee and a blood-red Cadillac had brought traffic in the intersection ahead to a standstill. In the middle of all the twisted steel origami, a skinny police officer in a yellow rain slicker was doing his best to keep the rubber-neckers, who were hoping for a little blood or maybe a severed limb to liven up their soggy drive home, moving. After making five yards in five minutes, Alana muttered, "Fuck this!" and cut across the flooded gutters and up onto the sidewalk.

Luther blanched. "Are you nuts?"

"That's what we're trying to find out, isn't it, Lute?"

Ungrateful Dead

The cop's face went blank with disbelief as the Z whizzed past, throwing up a wall of dirty rainwater, which came down on his head. The last Luther saw of him, the cop was yelling and fumbling under his raincoat. Just in case he was going for his gun, Luther scooted down in the seat as far as the seat belt would allow.

"How did you two get to be friends?" Alana asked.

A block later, Luther poked his head up and looked through the rear window. "We attended the American Psychiatric Society meeting down on Key Biscayne a few years back. One of the side trips the Society set up was a scuba trip to Pennycamp Park off Key Largo. We wound up on the same boat, and since neither of us knew any of the others, the dive master buddied us up. After the dive, we got to talking and discovered we both lived in Memphis, we both loved the ocean, and we both had an interest in the occult. To my utter amazement, Cal had even read a couple of my more obscure papers on reincarnation. Not long after I returned home, he gave me a call and we started this little group." Luther watched Alana's expression. "Ghostbusters."

"You're kidding?"

"No. We're just a bunch of academic types who get together once a month to drink tea, share ghost stories, and kick around the latest theories on . . ." He lowered his voice. ". . . the supernatural!"

Alana laughed as expected. "Cal's really into that fish stuff, isn't he?"

"Lord yes, he's nuts about the ocean. Did you get a look at all those aquariums? He's got a pair of Pacific sea snakes, one of the most poisonous reptiles on earth. He named them Beavis and Butthead. I wish I had a tenth of the money he's spent on those things."

"He's married?"

Luther glanced at her face again. "Very. Rachel and Samantha are the only things he cares more about than his fish."

"I've heard that before."

Luther decided Alana was an incredibly complex woman, and he had a feeling she would be ruthless as all hell in going after what she wanted. He felt sorry for her and because of that he didn't trust his instincts.

Take it slow, he silently admonished himself.

"Turn here," he said.

They entered a pocket of identical, two-story, brick townhouses, located in the middle of a field of sycamore and elm trees that effectively screened the subdivision from the busy highway. Each of the buildings had a small, neat front yard, a narrow concrete driveway, and a rough-pine fence around the backyard.

"Kind of small," Alana commented.

"They're actually quite large inside. But you're right about the yards; they are small. I like to keep life simple."

"Life is never simple."

Alana whipped the Z into Luther's driveway and in the process nearly mowed down his mailbox. She set the hand brake, and they sat for a few moments listening to the rapid tick-tock of the wipers, which were trying, without much success, to keep up with the torrential downpour.

"Am I going to see you again?" she asked.

"I don't know if that's a good idea. At least as long as you're seeing Cal."

"Why?" she asked, that crooked half-smile playing at the corner of her mouth. "Jealous?"

"Of course not. But it might muddy the waters."

"I don't think he's going to take me as a patient anyway."

"Oh? Why is that?"

"Can you honestly say he believed anything I told him?"

"I think he believes you believe it."

She snorted and shook her head. "You missed your calling. That's a typical shrink response if I ever heard one."

"Maybe. But you have to admit, it's a pretty wild story."

"You think it's all in my head don't you?"

Luther glanced out the passenger window and thought about her question as he watched the rain wash down his driveway. The wind was whipping the skinny dogwood sapling next door back and forth like a metronome, and sending trash can lids and pieces of asbestos shingles skittering over the ground like tumbleweeds.

"I believe the soul lives on after death. I also believe that in rare instances it can manifest itself to the living. In even rarer cases, I think a soul can inhabit a living host and have an effect on how the person behaves. But possession, at least possession the way you describe it, is as rare as a total eclipse of the sun."

"But it does happen?"

"I've never personally seen one. A priest I know—"

"Yes?"

"Never mind. Why don't we take this one step at a time. Once Cal has exhausted all the medical options—"

"Sometime in the next millennium."

"...then we can look into uh, *other* causes for the phenomena you're experiencing."

She sighed. "I hope to God I'm still around when that happens." She half-turned in the seat to face him. As she did, the slit in her skirt parted, exposing yards of creamy thigh and dark hose. She brushed her hair back from her face, and Luther wondered why she had been so careful to keep her scars covered in front of Cal and yet was so casual about them with him. A sign that she trusted him? he wondered. Or an attempt to manipulate him?

"Luther, I know you probably don't need me piling all this on you right now. But I've never felt so scared or helpless. All my life, Mother controlled me like some kind of puppet. She never let me have a job, never let me play sports. It was always, *'Practice! Practice! Practice! Eat your vegetables! Take your vitamins!'* If she hadn't died when she did, I think I would have killed myself.

"But she did die. And for a while my world was a bright place. Now, once more, it's as gloomy and dark as the world outside this car."

"But possession doesn't just happen, Alana," Luther explained patiently. "There is almost always some trauma involved, a murder or some terrible accident. What happened to your mother? Was she killed? How did she die?"

"She went to Great Britain four times each year. Last summer, while she and Anton were driving to Salisbury, their car went off the road, and she was killed. Anton, the creep, brought her ashes home and presented them to me as if they were the crown jewels."

"This guy Anton, he always traveled with her?"

"From the first day I met him, he was never far from her side."

"Did she ever exhibit any psychic powers?"

Alana laughed bitterly. "You mean other than always knowing when I wasn't practicing the piano? I don't know." She stared out the driver's side window at a black Lab standing like a statue in the middle of the street. The dog stared back at her for several seconds and then turned and loped off. "Mother did a lot of odd things, but I never saw her bend a spoon with her mind or anything like that. I think she was too consumed with her appearance to be much good as a psychic."

"What do you mean?"

"How long have you got? She had all these rules about what you could wear and when: no white shoes before Memorial Day, no fur coats after Easter. Her nails and hair had to be just so. She wouldn't go out in the sun for fear of wrinkles, and she went to sleep every night with about ten pounds of herbal mud on her face. When she hit forty, she became a charter member of the Plastic Surgery of the Month club, and in a period of five years, she had four face lifts, three tummy tucks, two boob lifts, and liposuction."

"Wow!"

"Honestly. The closest I ever saw her come to crying was the day she found the first crow's feet in her bathroom mirror."

"Sounds like neurosis runs in your family."

"Thanks a heap."

"Hey," he said, placing a friendly hand on her arm. "Neurosis is curable. Give Cal a chance."

"So what's it going to take to convince you that what's happening to me is real?"

"Jeez, that's a tough one. Short of your head spinning around and spitting up pea soup, I don't know how you prove you're really not you but someone else. Listen, it's getting late and I've got papers to grade."

"You never answered my original question: am I going to see you again?"

"Alana, I don't know what you want from me."

"Maybe just a friend."

He knew then he was being manipulated, but it didn't matter. "Sure. I'll be your friend."

"Can I call you if anything happens?"

Luther fumbled through his pocket and found a crumpled napkin. "You got a pencil?"

She handed him a pen from the console, and he wrote down his home number.

"Here. Call me if you need me."

"That's a pretty open-ended offer."

He kept his expression neutral. "See you!"

As he bolted from the car, the rain greeted him with a wet slap in the face. Sprinting up the driveway, he let himself in through the side entrance and stood in the kitchen, dripping on the tile floor, until he heard her drive away.

It wasn't until he started shivering that he noticed how cold the house was. Assuming he had forgotten to turn the thermostat up again, he walked around the small, glass-top dining table and paused at the entrance to the living room.

He sniffed.

The air smelled rank, and he wondered if some of the food he'd brought home the day before from his friend Marty's health-food shop could have gone bad. Then he remembered it was all freeze-dried fruits, and he decided to look elsewhere.

Entering the living room, he didn't bother turning on the lamp as he touched his way around the black leather sofa and along the lacquered wood stereo cabinet to the front door.

It was locked.

He glanced at the marble fireplace. A nice fire would go a long way toward cutting the chill. Make a pot of veggie chili, a cup of hot tea, then sit down next to the hearth and grade papers.

And yet he couldn't quite shake the feeling that something wasn't right. He tried to tell himself he was getting all worked up over nothing—he'd done it before. Living alone tended to make people jump every time a floorboard settled and have palpitations when, in the middle of the night, the ice maker dropped a fresh tray of ice in the catch bucket. Hell, you almost had to be a little nuts to live alone anyway. After all, what was he talking about here? A cold house and a bad smell—big deal!

But this time was different. He was almost sure of it.

Tiptoeing up the stairs to the second floor, Luther entered his office, a room he had decorated in teak wood and bottle green, with an old 386 clone and rows of bookcases for his collection of occult esoterica. Nothing appeared out of place and nothing seemed to be missing.

He crept down the narrow hallway to the back bedroom, which he had converted into a weight room with a treadmill, home gym, and nineteen-inch TV to watch while he did his five miles every morning. The carpet was protected by thick rubber mats, but that didn't prevent the floor from creaking when he stepped into the room.

He paused to listen and was amazed when he realized that not only was his heart racing, but he was holding his breath.

"Get a grip."

He took the back stairway down to the kitchen, where he gave his tiny cooking area a quick once-over before stepping into the master bedroom. It was dark, and the air was as cold and damp as a wet grave in winter. He flipped the light switch, but nothing happened.

"Well, damn MLG& W all to hell!"

Memphis Light, Gas, and Water was renowned for its dependable service. If it rained or sleeted or snowed, if the wind blew, if it was too cold or too hot, sometimes if the sun was shining too brightly or the moon was full, you could always depend on the electricity going out. At least that explained why the house was so cold.

He crossed the room to open the vertical blinds, which hung in front of the French doors that opened onto his rear deck, and as he went around the foot of the waterbed, his foot came down in a patch of soggy carpet.

More puzzled than alarmed, he stopped short and stared at his foot. Where could the water have come from? He looked up at his ceiling and then at the blinds. They were swaying ever so slightly. He pulled the chain, opened the blinds and felt the rush of cold wind on his face.

The left door was open about a quarter of an inch, and when he opened it further, he saw that the bottom of the screen door was ripped to shreds.

"Damn it!" he muttered, talking to himself as he often did when confronted with the inexplicable. "What kind of burglar tears up an unlocked screen and then takes the time to pick the lock on a glass door?"

He closed and locked the door, then turned around to survey the bedroom. It was a large room—his favorite. He had special-ordered the pale, marbled-wood suite from a waterbed store in Florida and later added black accent pieces and a matching black comforter. That was why when he saw what had been done to his favorite room, all he could say was, "What the hell?"

Chapter Three

The next day was Saturday, and since it was only a couple of weeks until Christmas and the holiday buying for the store had long since been completed, Alana had the weekend off. Normally so much free time would have induced a major anxiety attack, for as the change, as she now thought of her body's slow metamorphosis, had progressed, she often used work to keep from thinking about it, pushing herself into the wee hours of the morning and then stumbling home and falling into a semicomatose and usually dreamless slumber. When the alarm sounded at six-thirty, she slammed her hand down on the off button, turned over, and stared at the ceiling. Alana always slept nude, and the cool air raised a rash of pale gooseflesh that covered her body like tiny cobblestones. She ran her hand up over the flat plain of her belly to her breasts.

Gary L. Holleman

Thirty-three and single, she thought morosely. *What did I ever do to deserve this?*

Her thoughts turned, as they usually did early in the morning, to Kenny, Morna's father. The only man she had ever loved.

"Man?" she whispered, allowing herself the luxury of a sad smile.

She had been barely sixteen when they fell in love. A year younger than Morna. Ken was seventeen, tall and gangly, with the bluest eyes she had ever seen. How sweet he had been. Dear God, how sweet. She wondered, as she had almost daily for the last seventeen years, where he was, what had happened to him. Was he married? Was he safe? Did he have other children?

Alana's hand went to the scars on her face. The skin felt cold, dead. It was a miracle she could see out of her left eye. It was a miracle she hadn't died. On second thought, scratch that—the girl she had once been was dead.

She squeezed her eyes shut.

"Oh, God."

Her memories were like evil toys that she kept tightly locked away in the darkest, most remote corner of her mind. When she was depressed or tired, she took them out and played with them.

Her mother had been in the kitchen that day overseeing the cook as he prepared a cheese soufflé for the party that evening. It had taken Alana a week to work up the nerve to tell Morgana that she was going to have a baby. She'd had it all planned—she and Kenny would get married right away, but she would continue to live at home until he finished college. Then, they would move to the West Coast, buy a small house, and settle down. Kenny would get a job, and they would send Morgana a card every year at Christmas. She hadn't

Ungrateful Dead

planned on mentioning that last part, but she had been thinking it.

She got as far as the baby, and Morgana had been taking the news relatively well. Until the cook, a huge black man with horrible teeth, made the remark about Mrs. Magnus making a fine grandmother.

Morgana's face had turned deathly white. She reached out, grabbed the first thing she laid her hand on, and hurled it at Alana's head. Unfortunately for her, it was the top half of a double boiler full of scalding hot cheese.

As Alana lay writhing on the kitchen floor, with the cook applying cold towels to her face, Morgana had peered over his shoulder and, in a voice reeking with righteous indignation, said, "The little twerp may change his mind about marriage once he gets a look at that face."

Naturally Kenny never saw her face. Alana always figured Morgana or one of her friends got to him; not that Alana blamed him—they could be very persuasive. But Kenny had never seen Morna and, since that day, Alana had never seen him again.

She sighed, disgusted with herself for indulging in such blatant self-pity.

Rolling out of bed, she padded into the bathroom to pee, brush her teeth and go through her daily routine in front of the full-length mirror on the back of the door. It was a ritual she had come to fear as much as anticipate. Anticipate—for each day without some new change was like a stay of execution—another day in which she could pretend, as Cal and Luther obviously believed, that the whole thing was just a figment of her diseased mind. Fear? How was she going to ever make them understand the fear? If she said she had cancer, they would understand. Or Alzheimer's, or AIDS ...

some nice, neat disease they could put under a microscope and tut-tut over.

Poor Alana, she has XYZ disease. We'll start her on a regimen of bullshit and peach pits, then X-ray her until she glows—that'll fix her up just fine.

Assholes!

Fear was the most debilitating of all diseases. It grew like cancer from watching your body slowly, bit by agonizing bit, change into someone else's, and it spread by waking up with memories that belonged to someone else. Try telling that to Dr. God Almighty Weinberg—he'd slap her in a straight jacket faster than she could say psychosis.

Yes, memories; recollections; events; happenings. Memories like slivers of ground glass in her brain. Only lately she was remembering things that had never happened to her: a dark field full of strange stones; crazy silhouettes dancing around a roaring bonfire; the smell of wood smoke; the taste of bitter wine—Anton, sweating and grunting like a pig over her prostrate body. She could still smell him—still feel him squirming inside her like maggots gnawing their way out of her womb.

She stepped into the shower stall and ran the water until steam rose like volcanic ash, and her flesh turned as red as a lobster. She grabbed the loofah and scrubbed and scrubbed, wanting nothing so much as to scream and keep on screaming.

But she didn't . . . she couldn't. She was afraid she'd never stop once she started. Then Cal, sadly to be sure, would lock her up and throw away the key, and by the time they let her out—if they ever let her out—she wouldn't be Alana Magnus any more.

With some effort, Alana forced her dark thoughts back inside the steel vault of her mind and locked it with her will. She had to stay calm, had to be cool. The more desperate she became, the less likely it was that Luther and Cal would believe her. And she needed them to believe her—needed Luther at least. He was the key. He might not know it yet, but the answer to what was happening to her lay in his world. All she had to do was make him want to find it.

And make him she would!

She didn't have all that much experience with men, but from the time she was a child she had watched her mother manipulate them. How hard could it be? Show them a little cleavage, a little thigh, and they start slobbering like a pack of rabid mongrels.

She had to be careful though. Luther was smart. . . . And kind of—cute, in a hippie-ish sort of way. Not her type at all, really.

Just what is your type?

Turning off the water, she stepped out of the stall and dried off with one of her plush bath sheets. Then she took a deep breath and approached the mirror.

Complete objectivity, that was what was called for. Ignore the big picture and concentrate on the details. Starting with her feet, Alana examined her toes and ankles and then her shins and knees.

Okay. So far so good.

Moving up to her thighs, she noted with dismay that they were fleshier than she remembered. But that was probably from too much work and not enough exercise. Even though Morgana had never allowed her to participate in sports, she had insisted that Alana exercise every day. Calisthenics, ballet, ten-fucking-miles on the Lifecycle! It was amazing the way the things Mother drummed into her head had stuck. And why not? An abused child doesn't know any better than to trust and love her abuser. It's only later—when it's too late—that you recognize the evil that lurks behind the cutting remarks and stone-cold eyes.

Alana's eyes traveled up her trim flanks and over the slightly concave flesh of her belly to her breasts; pale-white and full, round and topped with thick, strawberry-colored nipples.

What a waste!

She squeezed her eyes shut in frustration.

Get off it! Concentrate!

Shoulders, neck, face; she went so far as parting her hair and peering at her scalp, then took a hand mirror and, as best she could without dislocating her shoulder, turned around and went through the whole process again on her backside. When finally satisfied, she put the mirror down and sat on the toilet—hard, her hands and knees shaking like a ninety-year-old woman.

"Thank you, God!" she whispered, the tears coming unbidden. "Thank you for this day."

The nuns would have been so proud.

The house Anton Gadarn rented had been built more than 160 years ago by one of Memphis's most prestigious cotton brokers, an eccentric man who, for his own nefarious reasons, constructed the round, white, two-story mansion out in the boondocks, far from the center of commerce and trade that had made him so rich. What he couldn't have foreseen was, years later, the area was to become the center of East Parkway, an avenue of two-lane, one-way streets separated by a wide, tree-and-brush-choked median strip near Audubon Park and the Zoo. During the fifties and early sixties, the district was the heart of Memphis society, and the mansion, with its massive white columns, arched doorways, dormer windows, and garrets, had been just the sort of oddity that created comment from as far away as New York. Of

Ungrateful Dead

course, since then the mansion had fallen on hard times, as had the entire area. The racial tensions of the sixties had spawned years of "white-flight" to suburbs that spread out from the city's center in ever-widening concentric circles of fear and bigotry. The new tenants of the district were poorer and less able to maintain the rambling estates, and by the time Anton and his followers moved to town, many of the smaller homes had been converted into seedy hotels or crack dens, and the white mansion was little more than a crumbling facade, concealing dark rooms full of dry-rot and termites on acres of cracked fountains and lawns overgrown with weeds and junglelike shrubs.

Anton's assistant, Grover Chang, had rented the mansion from a civil-rights lawyer who, as soon as he had squeezed his first 100K out of the tight-assed, white establishment for their years of systematic abuse of his brothers, had immediately moved his wife, child, and mistress to Germantown—the mistress had to settle for a condo near the Jewish Community Center. Grover was the only member of Anton's entourage who was not of Irish descent. He was a monster of a man with a rather mild, some might say pleasant, face, shoulders as wide as a boxcar, a gymnast's waist, which gave his upper body a somewhat triangular appearance, and hands that looked like sides of cured beef. Originally from San Francisco, Grover had set out to learn the shylocking trade from his Triad cousins, who were enamored of his size and strength and his ability to put on truly awesome displays of maniacal rage at customers who were as little as one week behind on the vig. A misunderstanding with the local police coupled with a minor cash shortage in his collections had forced him to seek employment out of town at the same time Anton and his followers had come through the Bay area looking for a bodyguard/

gofer. It was a match made in—Well, it worked out swell for all concerned, for Anton paid well, although his new employer looked very much like a troll. In all his thirty-three years Anton was the only man Grover had ever been afraid of. In addition, Grover found Anton to be an enigma.

Enigma, that was Grover's new word for the week. His family had only been able to send him to school through fifth grade, a fact which caused him no end of embarrassment. A month ago, he had seen an ad on TV singing the praises of vocabulary tapes, and he had sent off for them. The announcer had promised it would change his life, make him admired and respected. He listened to the tapes every morning, selecting one word each day. It was a twenty-tape set. He figured by the time he finished it would be safe to return to San Fran. Wouldn't his family be proud!

Anyway, Anton was an enigma. He was redheaded, short, and had an aversion to bathing. That was why Grover couldn't understand why most women found him absolutely irresistible. They loved him! The only thing Grover could come up with was that they were overcome with maternal pity for the poor dwarf and mistook his lack of interest in anything other than himself for shyness. After one exceptionally long and boisterous night, Grover had heard two of Anton's consorts whispering together in the back of the van as he drove them home. One asked the other how she stood the little creep. Her friend's answer? Once she got past the raging b.o., she was amazed at the size of his . . . uh, well she didn't say intellect.

Grover followed Anton up the stairs from the cellar and into the parlor, a room sparsely furnished with a hodgepodge of period pieces that the civil-rights lawyer had left behind. Like the rest of the house, the windows were large, taller than the average man, and covered with dusty sheers that were as much cobwebs as lace, and which the years had yellowed to the color of kennel newsprint. The floors were hardwood and creaked like old leather under Grover's feet. Here and there they were covered with threadbare carpet runners that had once displayed some truly magnificent Persian designs.

"What was that cretin thinking?" Anton snapped, his brogue thickening into a high-pitched whine.

Grover shrugged, his answer for most of life's imponderables, and then offered his usual remedy for same: "You want me to break his leg?"

"No, no." Anton replied, his face softening and his green eyes twinkling at the big man's reply. He turned and patted Grover's hand—he couldn't reach his shoulder. "Sure now, Colin meant well and initiative shouldn't be stifled. Only next time, tell me boyo to check first. Now this . . . this what? Teacher? Professor? He probably won't connect it to Alana, but one never knows. Sometimes these academic types can be quite clever, and we wouldn't want him poking his nose where it doesn't belong, now would we?"

Grover looked as if the prospect made him hungry.

"Tell Colin to keep an eye on the good professor for now and to keep his distance as well—no more little visits. He got sloppy last night, and the fact that it was raining is no excuse! Now, where's the cage with the little buggers?"

Grover went into the hall and brought back a wire cage containing half-a-dozen large, white rats.

"Come now, feeding time." Anton chuckled and led his big friend back down into the cellar.

Luther hitched a ride with a neighbor to pick up his bike, then set out for Cal's. The streets were still wet from the previous night's rain and in spite of Luther being bundled up like an Eskimo, the air was uncommonly cold, and he had to pedal hard to keep from freezing. He was in a black mood. Cycling alone usually allowed him to sort out any problems he was having, but even the Tour de France wouldn't have helped him get over the rage he felt at what happened to his bedroom.

He arrived at Cal's New England–style brick house in Collierville a little before nine and let himself in with the key under the potted fern. Cal's sixteen-year-old daughter, Samantha, was stretched out on the white leather couch in the living room, surrounded by a veritable jungle of hanging plants and potted ficus trees, watching the latest reincarnation of *Dance Party*—some guy, who looked like he had bedsprings for hair, was bouncing up and down to a beat that human males became deaf to after the age of twenty-nine. Luther paused.

"What ever happened to the Monkees?" he asked. "I heard they're getting together again."

Sam waved a bored hand in his direction, and he strolled on by into the kitchen.

Rachel, tall, dark, and hours-of-tennis-a-day slim, gave Luther a peck on the cheek as he opened the refrigerator. She was dressed in her usual uniform: a white tennis skirt and sneakers that squeaked on the tile as she moved.

"Where's my OJ?" Luther muttered.

"Never mention that murdering scum's name in my house!" Cal snapped. He was sitting at the table in front of the bay window on the other side of the room, his blond hair sticking up like punji stakes above the top of the morning paper.

"It's behind the milk," Rachel whispered. "Don't mind him. He's in a foul mood. Want some breakfast?"

Looping his arm around her waist, Luther pulled her

Ungrateful Dead

close. "No thanks. I've got a better idea. Dump the bigoted creep and move in with me."

"What'll I do with Sam?"

"She can come too. As long as she agrees to give up rap and go to Juilliard."

Rachel's brown eyes crinkled in pleasure at the idea. "Fat chance. Besides, you only want someone to cook and clean. I do enough of that here."

"Quit groping my wife and get over here," Cal called. "She'll be late for Flushing Meadows."

Rachel twirled out of Luther's embrace, picked up her car keys from the countertop and her tennis bag and racket from the floor next to the back door, grabbed her coat, and then blew her husband a kiss and was gone, leaving behind a spotless kitchen and the aroma of Sung.

Luther poured a glass of orange juice, then went over and sat down at the table across from his friend. It appeared that Cal had just rolled out of bed. He hadn't shaved, and in addition to the punker hairdo, he had on a pair of wrinkled, electric-orange-and-green pajamas covered with tiny reproductions of the Billican, the University of Miami's mascot. He muttered something under his breath and slammed the paper down on the table.

"The whole world's going to hell in a handbasket!"

"Good morning to you, too."

"Look at this! If it isn't drug dealers peddling their shit to schoolkids, it's this!"

The headline read:

BREAK-IN AT ZOO! REPTILE HOUSE VANDALIZED!

Luther took a sip of juice. "So? You know what they say—shit happens."

Reclaiming the paper, Cal gave his friend a dour

glare. "What happened to Mr. Animal Rights? I thought you'd be incensed."

"Not after yesterday."

Cal dropped the paper and leaned across the table. "So tell me, what happened after you left? Did you get laid?"

"Jeez Cal, I hardly know the woman! She was nice enough to give me a lift—"

"I figured that when I saw your bike chained in front of the office."

"What was I supposed to do? Jump her bones in my driveway?"

Cal sat back, disappointment pulling the corners of his mouth down. "I was hoping *somebody* was getting laid. Rachel is so wrapped up in that dumb-ass tennis tournament at the club that she's gone to bed at eight o'clock every night for the last two weeks."

"You ever hear of nooners?"

"Hmph! Obviously you never had a teenage daughter in the house."

"You think it's going to scar Sam's psyche if she hears her mom and dad making love?"

"No, but it might scar mine. So what happened yesterday?"

"Well, when I got home the power was out—"

"There's a news flash for you! Those assholes that run the power company ought to be—"

"You want to hear this?"

Cal held up his hands.

"When I got inside, the back door was open, and the screen was ripped all to hell."

"Somebody broke in?"

"That's the only thing that makes any sense. Only—"

"Only what? What'd they take? Jesus, not the big screen! The bowl games—"

Ungrateful Dead

"They didn't take anything; it's what was left behind!"

"What? Quit milking it. What did they leave?"

"So help me, if you laugh... They must have brought their damned dog with them 'cause it left a big pile of poop right in the middle of my favorite comforter!"

Cal had to clench his teeth to keep from grinning. "What did you do?"

"I cleaned it up and tossed the comforter and sheets in the washer."

"But the big screen is okay?"

Sighing, Luther rolled his eyes to heaven.

"I tell you what I'd have done," Cal said. "I'd have taken my twelve-gauge and shot every frigging dog in the neighborhood."

Just then Marino, Sam's West Highland white terrier, padded over to his bowl in the corner next to the microwave and began lapping up water.

"Every dog?" Luther grinned.

"Well, hell! Marino wouldn't do a thing like that."

" 'Course not. He'd have used the toilet."

Cal waved the remark away and then changed the subject.

"So what did you and Alana talk about on the way home?"

"This and that. Mostly about how you and I met."

Cal sat up. "Oh?"

"What did you think of her story?"

"Oh. I've heard better. But I did find one thing interesting. That guy she mentioned, Gadarn... odd name don't you think?"

"Scandinavian?"

"Close. Irish; Celtic to be more precise."

"How in the world do you know that?"

59

"When I went to school, I did more then burn my draft card and run off to Canada." Luther's face flamed. "Okay, sorry, cheap shot. I did a paper on the Druids for my abnormal psychology class."

"I studied the Druids too, but I don't remember that name."

Cal got up, shuffled across the tile, and entered his den, which was just off the kitchen. He shuffled, because he had on a pair of house slippers shaped like fuzzy orange footballs. He returned with a manila folder.

"I was curious, and since *I* didn't have anything better to do last night, I dug out the research papers I did for my thesis. *Hu Gadarn* was another name for Cernowain, known to the Celts as the Horned God of fertility, or sometimes, the god of the Underworld and Astral Plane."

"Yeah . . . I remember now. Wasn't he usually portrayed as a bull or ram? Something like that?"

"Or a horned serpent. He was supposed to be quite a ladies' man."

"Well, that's interesting as all hell, but apropos of absolutely nothing."

"But I found the Druid connection interesting given their belief in the transmigration of the soul. You *do* remember what that is?"

Luther rubbed his bottom lip with his forefinger. "Hmm, yeah I do. The passing of the soul into another body after death."

"More than that. They had some very strict interpretations of immortality—the soul doesn't die, it just moves on—preferably to a human being, but sometimes to other things. There was a fable in the *Book of Lecan* about a guy who spent three hundred years as a deer, three hundred as a boar, three hundred as a bird, and a like number as a fish; at which point he was caught and eaten by the queen. I remember thinking it must be shitty spending the rest of eternity in the royal latrine."

"Boo! So what's the bottom line? You going to keep seeing her or ship her over to Henry 'Frankenstein?'"

"Henry would have Truman pull your meal ticket if he heard you say that."

"I don't think so. At the last faculty mixer I told old Henry that not only did I know how to put a curse on a guy that would make his balls fall off, I also had the recipe for a love potion that could make Cindy Crawford hot for Don Knotts."

"And he believed you? I guess old Henry isn't as sharp as I thought. Anyway, you spent more time with Alana than I did. What's your take on her?"

"I think she needs help."

"Obviously. But what kind and from whom?"

Luther drained the glass and smacked his lips. "I told her you could help her."

Cal ran his hand through his hair and glanced through the window into the backyard. Here, too, Rachel's careful touch stood out like the shine on a new Rolls Royce. The flower and shrub beds followed the contours of the house with geometric precision. There was a pecan tree that produced paper-shell pecans on-time every summer, a dogwood that blossomed like clockwork in the spring, and a bird bath, now iced over, that the entire Avian Olympic swimming team could have used as a training facility. There was even a dog house, a replica of the big house, set at an angle in the shade of the two-car garage.

Cal turned his attention back to the problem at hand. "I know I could help her. But I always try to remember what Eduardo Ciannelli told his henchman to do to Victor McLaglen in *Gunga Din*: 'Take him and teach him the error of false pride!'"

"You sure that wasn't Cary Grant he was talking about?"

"No, dunce. Cary Grant was the one the thugs had already captured and tortured—Gunda Din's pal. Remember?"

"Gosh, that's right," Luther said. "I should know better than to question you when it comes to old movies." With Cal, a little flattery went a long way. "So does that mean yes you will help her, or no you won't?"

"On one condition—Rachel never finds out about those photographs."

When Luther called with the news, Alana was sitting at the computer in a pair of cutoffs and a black silk blouse, reconciling her checkbook. She listened until he finished, smiling but trying not to let it show in her voice, and then, keeping the saccharine to a minimum, she thanked him and hung up.

"Okay. Now for phase two."

Securing Cal's help had been Luther's idea, and that was fine by her—as far as it went. It would give her a way of keeping both men close, while allowing them to think they were in charge. But finding the real answers to what was happening to her was going to take a lot more than that. If Morgana really was trying to take possession of her—and to even consider she wasn't was to open doors Alana had no intention of looking behind—then Anton was involved up to his lecherous, green eyeballs. That meant he was here—in Memphis. And the trick was going to be finding the little creep without letting him know. Once she located his hideout, then she could figure a way to steer Luther and Cal in his direction—their idea of course. And that's when Luther's knowledge of the occult was going to pull her ass out of the fire—she hoped.

Ungrateful Dead

Now, how to find Anton?

She didn't have a clue.

"Okay. Okay. So who *would* know where he is?"

She glanced at the gold Timex on her wrist. It was 7:20 P.M. which meant that it was dark outside. She closed out the financial program, shut down the computer, and turned off all the lights except the fluorescent bulb over the sink in the kitchen. She then went into her bedroom and turned on all the lights. After brushing her teeth and washing her face, she tiptoed back into the living room, crept up to the front window, and peeked around the sheet. She watched patiently, and fifteen minutes later, just as her eyes were beginning to cross, a match flickered in the window of the house down the street.

Gotcha!

In the kitchen, Alana set the timer on her Mr. Coffee machine for midnight and then filled it with enough strong, New Orleans coffee to dissolve the enamel on her teeth. That done, she slipped back into her bedroom, turned on the TV, set her alarm for 11:45, and lay down on the bed.

Did she know what she was doing?

Hell, no.

Did she have a choice?

As far as she could see . . . same answer.

This was one thing she had to handle herself. Her friend with the smoking problem was always gone when she got up in the morning—maybe, as she sometimes thought, he was like Count Dracula; afraid of the sun. Either way, after all the long nights she'd spent peering at his glowing cigarette, so scared she was shaking as if she had the flu, Alana figured the least the bastard could do was hang around until midnight. After that, unless he turned into a bat and flew away, she'd know where Anton was.

Alana closed her eyes and within minutes she was sound asleep.

A few minutes later, a blast of icy wind buffeted her face and she opened her eyes. It was cold. Breathing hurt and the wind burned her like fire. When she looked down she saw she was standing on the edge of an ice-covered precipice, and in the distance was a city. At first she thought the city was made of glass, like in the fairy tales. It was ice. Far below her, perhaps five hundred feet, a group of men wearing mangy animal skins and carrying whips were driving another group of people across a snow-covered tundra. They looked so small, like ants crawling across a white picnic cloth. Still, she could hear the cracks of the whips... the cries of the driven.

A hand touched her shoulder, and when she turned around a man was standing behind her. His clothes were ripped and torn, his skin red and raw, and he had rags on his feet instead of shoes. And his face... his face was crawling with black worms.

"Help us."

She didn't know where she was but somehow she knew everything around her was old, very old.

The man said again, "Help us."

She stared at him, and then she heard a little girl laugh.

It was well after dark when Luther left Cal's house. They had spent the afternoon arguing over Alana's treatment plan and were still arguing when Rachel came home from her tennis match. She threw together a pot of pasta and fresh clam sauce that any restaurant in Memphis would have been proud to serve, while listening to the men bicker. By the time she set the plates on the table she was ready to scream.

Ungrateful Dead

"Shut up, the both of you!" She glared them into silence. "Now you!" She pointed one perfectly manicured nail at Luther. "You listen to Cal. He didn't get that big office and all those degrees by being a shmuck."

"But Rachel—" Luther interjected.

"Shush!" she snapped. "Is talking listening?" Then she turned to her husband. "And you! What are you grinning at? You should listen to Luther too. He's got a good heart and sometimes that's more important than what comes out of a book. I've got a news flash for you, Mr. Doctor—books are not people!"

Rachel went to the pantry and returned with a bottle of Mondavi Chenin Blanc and handed it to her husband with the corkscrew.

"Here, do something useful." She sat down and then lowered her voice. "You two know you're going to help this woman, so help her! I don't know what all the talk, talk, talk is about."

Later, after the pasta and the frozen yogurt, Cal walked Luther out to his bicycle.

"Sorry about that. I guess the pressure of the tournament is getting to her. It's not like Rachel to snap at people."

Luther snorted. "Like we didn't deserve it? She's right, we were being jerks. And I'm glad you're going to help. Never hurts to have the best on your side."

Cal got all red in the face and handed Luther his helmet. "Here, put on your helmet. Wouldn't want you to crack our sidewalk with that head of yours."

Luther slapped his friend on the back, mounted the bike, and coasted down the driveway. Cal was squatting down, ruffling the fur around Marino's face as Luther pedaled out of sight.

The night was bitterly cold, but the sky was clear, with stars like a million fireflies that seemed to hover right over his head. The streetlights were few and far between, but the way was familiar, the road was wide, and there was little traffic. He had just passed an elementary school, pedaling along a split-rail fence surrounding an open pasture now brown and tinged with frost, when the dog appeared at his rear wheel. It startled Luther so badly that he almost lost control—one minute it was quiet, the next Lord Baskerville's lapdog was baying at his heels.

His adrenal glands responded by dumping about a gallon of epinephrine into his bloodstream. He thumbed the gears down a couple of notches, put his head down, his ass up, and started pumping his legs like mad. As he picked up speed, the hound, a mangy, black cur from what he could see of it, ceased its bellowing and began nipping at the rear tire. Confident that such a large animal couldn't possibly keep up once he got into high gear, Luther nudged the sprocket down another turn and redoubled his efforts. In no time, the wind was whistling past his ears, and the sound his tires made as they flew over the concrete was like a man using one of those electric weed whackers.

Regrettably, the dog had never studied the laws of physics and slowly began to gain on him.

"What the hell did I ever do to you?" Luther panted through gritted teeth.

With visions of Cujo following him all the way back to his house, Luther raised his head and saw the lights of the main highway just past the crest of the hill. At this time of night, the traffic would be bumper-to-bumper, and he was pretty sure none of the drivers would have any qualms about mowing down any cyclist stupid enough to get in the way. For an instant he considered just stopping—after all, most dogs chased cars and bicycles because they were moving targets. But this

Ungrateful Dead

dog didn't act like any dog he'd ever seen, and the idea of having to endure a series of rabies shots held no appeal for him whatsoever.

He looked back over his shoulder. The beast was right there staring up at him with eyes that glowed like embers and growling as if it could already taste him.

He decided to take his chances with the maniacs on the highway and turned his eyes back to the road when a dark-green van shot out of the driveway right in front of him. Luther grabbed both hand brakes and squeezed, but he was going much too fast to avoid a collision. At the last instant, he cut the handlebars hard left and slammed into the side of the van. The last thing he remembered thinking before taking his nap was, *Whoever that dumb bastard in the van is, I hope the fucking dog chews him a new asshole!*

Alana slithered across her backyard on her belly. When she reached the fence that separated the rear of her property from the forest, she raised her head and spat out a mouthful of mud and leaves.

It always looks so damned easy on TV, she thought.

When the alarm went off, she had pulled on a pair of black stretch pants, a black turtleneck sweater, a navy-blue pea coat, and a pair of black, high-top Reeboks—she had even smeared black eyebrow pencil over her cheeks and forehead, though she couldn't remember exactly why the men in war movies always did this. If she hadn't been so damned cold, it might have been funny.

"Move down South, they said. The people are friendly, the climate is ever so much nicer."

She had always hated the winters in New York; ice, snow, more snow, more ice. She hated shoveling snow, hated riding buses, and the subways were always like

Gary L. Holleman

refrigerated cattle cars. But this? If this was the sunny South, she'd take friggin' Montana.

Alana peered through the links in the fence. Without a moon, the trees looked like tar paper cutouts pasted over black canvas. She didn't think Anton would bother stationing anyone behind the house, but she couldn't afford to be wrong. After ten minutes without so much as a branch moving, she scurried over the fence and dropped into the high, brown weeds on the other side. Now that she was moving, Alana was afraid to stop. She dropped into a shallow drainage ditch that ran along the border of her property and followed it around to her left, skirting piles of abandoned building materials and spilled concrete. It was slow going. Trying to creep through tall grass without making any noise was a lot tougher than she had imagined. Her choices were to go fast and probably get caught, or to go slow and maybe catch pneumonia. Knowing Anton—pneumonia was better.

Before crawling out of her garage window, she had stuffed a small flashlight into her pants pocket and thought about using it—just for a second—to get her bearings. But she held off. Twenty minutes later, covered from head to foot with mud, burrs, and dead leaves, Alana crept out of the woods behind the Marlboro Man's last known observation post. If he was doing what he was supposed to be doing—namely watching her house—she'd be okay. If not, it could get sticky.

She tiptoed around an empty swimming pool and entered the garage. As soon as she stepped into the kitchen she smelled cigarette smoke.

Jesus! she thought. *If I had waited a couple more days, he'd have died of lung cancer.*

Now that she was inside, it was time to figure out what to do next. Her plan hadn't been what you might

Ungrateful Dead

call elaborate—get inside, get a look at the guy (to prove to herself that he was real as much as anything else), and find out where he stashed his car so that tomorrow night she could follow him back to Anton—simple!

Yeah . . . right.

It was simple when she was sitting in her nice warm house.

She eased across the kitchen and peeked around the doorway into the dining room. There he was—over in the living room, standing in front of the picture window, sucking on a cigarette. His back was turned so Alana couldn't see his face, but she recognized the raincoat. It was the guy she'd seen at the university.

On the floor at her feet was a hammer and a sack of nails left behind by some workman who had been in a hurry to cash his paycheck. For an instant, she stared at the hammer and thought about what this man and his friends had put her through. It would be so easy—so satisfying—to sneak up behind the bastard and bash his brains in. She could do it! She could! She could almost feel the man's skull crack as the hammer came down.

But what would be the point? He was probably one of Anton's throw-aways and if she killed him she would be back to square one.

What about torturing him?

The idea had appeal. There were plenty of things lying around the house for her to use: drills, saws, even an electric hot-glue gun like the one she used putting up displays. The only drawback was she didn't think she could actually inflict pain on anyone. Kill the bastard, sure! But torture?

She shivered and told herself it was the temperature in the house. No—that was a lie. She was scared, and it pissed her off. She wasn't as hard as her mother. Morgana wouldn't have had a problem torturing the guy. She could do her nails while shoving bamboo shoots under his.

A muted ringing snapped her out of her reverie just as the man pulled a cellular phone from his coat pocket.

"Yeah?... She went to bed a half hour ago.... No. No visitors. Listen boyo, how's about pickin' me up? It's colder 'n me sainted mother's dead arse... No, I tell you she's gone to bed and she ain't never gone out once she gone to bed.... Right as rain!"

He folded the phone, tucked it back into his pocket, and then started a fresh cigarette with the butt of the first.

This could be a real break, Alana thought. If she couldn't follow this guy, at least she might see who picked him up, maybe get the license number. But first she had to find a place where she could see the street without being seen.

Backing away from the door, she retraced her steps through the kitchen and took a right into a murky room off the garage that was stacked high with walnut paneling and littered with power tools and sawdust. The paneling was the same type that had been used in her den, and she figured if the architect had used the same floor plan in this house, then there ought to be a door on the other side of the room that led to a bedroom with a window that offered an oblique view of the driveway.

Sure enough, she saw the door and started across the floor, feeling her way along the wall to keep from bumping into the paneling. Halfway there, she kicked up some of the sawdust scattered about the floor, and before she could stop herself, she sneezed.

It wasn't all that much of a sneeze, but to her, in the confines of the still house, it sounded like Vesuvius erupting. She clapped both hands over her mouth and held her breath.

Ungrateful Dead

For a moment she thought she'd gotten away with it, then she realized that she could no longer hear the man, and her heart began sounding like bongos in her ears.

Wait! she thought. Wait!

Thirty seconds—a minute. Maybe it was okay after all. Maybe she had lucked out.

The tile floor in the kitchen creaked.

Alana ducked down behind the stack of paneling, balancing herself on the tips of her fingers as she mentally kicked herself for not bashing in the guy's head when she had the chance. Now she was trapped, and the best she could hope for was that the guy turned out to be blind or nearsighted.

The floor shook as he stepped into the room, and she was hit by a wave of stale cigarette smoke and b.o., which the guy had evidently tried to hide under about a gallon of Old Spice. A pale circle of light appeared on the wall behind her, slid down to the corner, and then moved diagonally across the floor toward the toe of her sneaker. She got ready to make a dash for the door behind her, but if it was locked—

The unmistakable sound of a heavy engine chugged around the corner and entered the cove. The light paused. A moment later, it winked out, and the man's heavy footsteps retreated toward the living room.

Alana slowly let out through her nose the deep breath she had been holding. After promising to say a least ten Hail Marys the instant she made it back to her bedroom, she bounced to her feet and, as quickly and quietly as possible, slipped through the door behind her, and went to the window.

In the driveway was a dark-colored van, idling with its lights off and white smoke belching from its tailpipe. The man in the raincoat climbed into the passenger seat and turned to close the door. As he did, she caught a glimpse of his face in the weak light from the streetlight at the end of the cove.

It was the man from the university, all right. Same scraggly beard, same pinched face, same tiny, mean eyes and, just as the door slid shut, she caught a glimpse of something else, something totally unexpected and horrifying.

A woman was lying on her side on the floor of the van. Alana only saw her for an instant, which was a blessing, for there was a pillowcase over her head, and she was trussed up hand and foot like a sheep ready for shearing! And then the man slammed the door.

Chapter Four

His head hurt, his body ached, and when Luther opened his eyes, the first thing he saw was a wild-eyed demon with stringy hair and a kabuki dancer's face glaring down at him. He closed his eyes again.

"Damn! Mom always said this was going to happen."

He heard a giggle and when he re-opened his eyes, Sam was standing beside him with a bemused expression on her beautiful, but oh-so-young face.

"Mom! He's awake!"

Rachel hurried into the room. "Don't move. Cal called an ambulance."

Luther raised his head, He was lying on a queen-size bed in a room festooned with girls' underwear and posters of rock stars; the ceiling fan had cutouts of the Beatles' faces taped to the underside of the blades.

"What happened?" he moaned, feeling as if he'd just flunked the tryout as a rodeo clown.

"I don't know. Sam and I were on our way to the store this morning when she spotted what's left of your bike on the side of the road. I pulled over, and she found you lying in the ditch. We thought you were dead until Sam poked you with her shoe and you groaned."

Luther glanced at Samantha. "Thanks. I think."

"Don't mention it. Scared ya, huh?" she said, motioning toward the poster over the bed.

"Alice Cooper?"

"KISS."

"What happened?" Rachel asked.

"Well, it's kind of a funny story."

"I bet."

"I was trying to get away from this monster dog and ran smack into a van."

Samantha laughed.

"Shut up!" Rachel snapped. It was the first time Luther had ever heard her raise her voice to Sam, and Sam's face turned as red as a raw T-Bone steak. "They didn't stop to help you?"

"Guess not," he replied.

"Then you've been there all night?"

"Feels like it." Luther eased his legs over the side of the bed and sat up.

"I told you not to move," Rachel said.

"I'm okay."

Cal appeared in the doorway. "What's he doing sitting up?"

"I told him not to," Rachel replied.

"The ambulance is on the way."

"We have to get his bicycle off the road."

"Get his wallet and make sure he has his insurance cards."

Ungrateful Dead

Luther whispered to Sam, "Thanks."

"Guess the helmet worked, huh?"

He grinned and stood up.

Rachel made a lunge toward him, but Luther held up his hand like a traffic cop and then waited for the black spots to disappear. "I'm okay."

It took a lot of fast talking to convince Rachel he was going to live, and then, when the ambulance arrived, he had to go through the whole thing again with the paramedics. Still, by the time Cal got him buckled into the car, Luther was feeling better, and when they pulled up in front of his house and he saw Alana sitting on the front steps, he was disturbed by how glad he was to see her.

She was wearing a heavy parka over a very pretty, white lace, go-to-meeting dress, and as soon as she saw them she stood up, smiled, and waved. Still, one look at her face and Cal muttered, "She looks like she's about to come apart at the seams."

"Maybe you better come in," said Luther.

As they approached the front stoop, it was plain Alana was holding back the tears by sheer strength of will.

"Where were you?" she demanded.

"I had a little accident on my bike."

She took in the condition of his clothes and the radish-sized, purple lump on his head. "Oh."

His reply seemed to take all the wind out of her sails, so Cal took her arm until Luther unlocked the front door. Once inside, he helped her out of her coat then led her to the couch while Luther turned on the lights and then excused himself to put the kettle on to boil and change clothes. He was back in less than five minutes, with three steaming mugs of strong tea. After placing one cup each in front of Cal and Alana, he took a seat in his recliner. "So, what happened?"

Alana cut her eyes to Cal. "I didn't expect you to be here."

"Would you like me to leave?"

"No. I guess not. But if you stay, you have to promise not to have me locked up."

Cal smiled. "Why would I want to do that?"

She fell back against the cushions and sighed as if her soul were trying to escape through her mouth. "When I tell you . . . what I came to tell Luther, you might change your mind."

Cal made an X over the number on his Miami Dolphins jersey. "Cross my heart, no white coats."

It took Alana twenty minutes, half a box of Kleenex, and three cups of tea to get the story out. When she was finished Luther said, "Gutsy, but dumb. Why didn't you call the cops?"

"And tell them what? I saw some woman tied up in the back of a van?" She gritted her teeth so hard they popped.

"Look, Alana," said Luther. "You admit the light was bad, and from your description you were some distance away. I think the smart thing to do is try to figure out what kind of scam your mother's boyfriend is trying to run on you."

Alana wanted to scream. Instead she got up, held her arms stiff at her sides, and stalked across the room to the glass display cabinet in the corner next to the fireplace. The cabinet was full of the occult artifacts that Luther had collected over the years: a shrunken head; a copy of a thirteenth-century Bohemian demon with the body of a frog and a bulbous, horned head; a yellowed, plastic-encased title page from King James I's book on witchcraft entitled, *Daemonologie. In Forme of a Dialogue*; a full-color miniature Chinese mask from the festival of the Hungry Ghosts; and a tear-shaped drum,

Ungrateful Dead

which had once belonged to a Yurok shaman. On a shelf all to itself was a small, brown book covered in wrinkled human skin set with some kind of odd-looking red gemstone—a copy of *The Grand Grimoire*. On the bottom shelf were three clear plastic envelopes. One contained a dried mandrake root shaped like a human body, the second, a wooden scarab beetle, and the last, a withered bunch of mistletoe.

Alana felt Luther behind her. "Mother never allowed me to bring that stuff into the house."

He followed her gaze. "What? Mandrake?"

"For all I know. No, the mistletoe."

"Interesting. What did she say about it?"

"Oh, nothing. It was just one more thing she wouldn't talk to me about." Alana turned around and met his eyes. "Why can't you two believe me?"

Cal got to his feet. "Excuse me. I think I'll give my wife a buzz before she calls out the Marines." He went into Luther's bedroom and shut the door.

"It isn't that, Alana. Try to see this from our point of view."

"But I came to you because you know about these things!" she whispered. "You're a scientist. You're supposed to have an open mind!"

Luther stared at his feet for a moment. "So you still believe your mother's spirit is trying to take possession of your body and that this guy Gadarn is involved?"

"If you had seen that poor woman, tied up like a sacrificial lamb—" Alana hugged herself and moved in front of the fireplace. "What kind of fiends would do a thing like that?"

"Would you like a fire?" he asked.

"Do you mind? I don't think I'll ever be warm again."

Kneeling, Luther opened the flue, put a match to a

pressed-wood fire log, and watched until the flames spread. Alana noticed an old, weathered spear hanging like the family musket over the mantle. "Have you ever been to a funeral?"

"Several. In all parts of the world."

"Open casket?"

"Some were no casket. Some of the Amazon tribes still eat their dead. Many Africans use bonfires."

"I don't know about that. I'm talking about the way the body . . . the dead person's face looks after it's been embalmed. Like wax, or wood. So smooth and dead it's hard to imagine it ever being alive, ever smiling or speaking. And then your mother takes you up close and makes you look." As Alana spoke, her voice became harsh and the words came faster and faster, as if they were poison and she had to get them out or die. "She says, 'kiss Aunt Betty.' You don't want to, but you're afraid not to, you're afraid to make a scene. So you stand up on your tiptoes and bend over and as you get closer and closer you know! You just know, her eyes are going to open and her mouth is going to open and it's going to be all full of maggots!"

Luther stood and put his hands on her shoulders. It was like trying to steady the world's largest tuning fork.

"And then you kiss her cheek, and it's cold, like a piece of luncheon meat that's been kept in the refrigerator and then set out on a platter."

Her eyes came up—deep, green, feral. In that instant Luther saw that she was close to the edge of madness, and he experienced a mind-numbing, epiphany—she wasn't crazy at all. In spite of his intellect and training telling him she was lying, she believed every single thing she was telling him.

Somehow, she guessed what he was thinking and reached up and touched his cheek.

Ungrateful Dead

He thought, *She's playing me like a bass fiddle.* But it didn't seem to matter.

Cal came out of the bedroom, but when he saw the way Luther and Alana were staring at each other, he did a quick about-face and spent a few minutes perusing the contents of Luther's refrigerator. He came back gnawing on a leftover drumstick.

"This all you got? No beer?"

"Cal, I've decided to help Alana."

Cal took another bite and raised his eyebrows. "Oh? Okay. I've got to go home." He gazed longingly at the big-screen TV. "I was going to stick around and watch the Dolphins, but Rachel is off somewhere doing God only knows what, and Sam's alone."

"Okay."

"Walk me out to the car?"

Once safely behind the wheel and buckled up, Cal lowered the Cadillac's window. "You sure you know what you're doing?"

"Probably not."

"Reinforcing her delusions could be dangerous—to you as well as her."

"I don't think she is delusional."

Cal held the drumstick between his teeth as he put on his sunglasses. He looked like some weird alien insect. "Here. Keep this for your collection." He handed Luther the denuded chicken bone. "I'll make you a deal. You don't diagnose mental problems, and I won't cast any spells. What do you say?"

"Sometimes, Doctor, you just gotta go with your gut. Sure she's messed up, but I think something else is going on here. I think someone really is trying to drive her crazy."

"Short drive, if you ask me."

"Maybe so. But like I said."

Gary L. Holleman

"Just be sure it's your gut you're feeling, and not something three inches to the south."

"Right."

The Cadillac's engine started with a roar of restrained horsepower.

"What are you going to do first?"

Glancing over the roof of the car, Luther saw a black Lab peering at him from behind the holly bush in his neighbor's yard.

People really shouldn't let their pets run free.

"Try to locate this Gadarn character."

"What about your classes?"

"Semester's over in a few days. I can afford to give her a week or so."

Cal grinned. "Luther Spade, P.I."

"If nothing else, spending a little time with her might give me a little insight into her condition."

"Well, since logic obviously isn't going to work, I guess I better go find my wife. Listen, you'll call me if you need me?"

"Absolutely."

Cal drove off, and Luther went back inside.

Rachel left the tennis club by the side entrance and strode across the parking lot, fumbling in her straw handbag for the keys to her Audi. As she inserted the key in the lock, a hand touched her shoulder. She turned and stared at the man who had stepped out of the passenger compartment of the dark-green van parked next to her car. He was short—very short, with wild, carrot-red hair, a ruddy complexion, green eyes, and ears like bat's wings. All in all, he was one of the most repugnant-looking people imaginable.

The man slipped his hand inside her jacket and let it slide over to cup her breast.

Ungrateful Dead

She sucked in her breath. "Are you crazy?"

The man grinned, exposing a set of crooked teeth.

"What if someone sees us," Rachel gasped.

"Never fear, dahlin'. Me chariot awaits." Anton held out his free hand to indicate the open van door and the stained mattress waiting inside; a man with a scraggly beard was leering at her from the driver's seat.

"That's not all that's waiting, either." He cupped his hand over the bulge in his pants and gave it a little jiggle.

Rachel blinked several times rapidly. She wanted to run away, but her mind and her body seemed to be going in opposite directions. *I must be insane*, she thought. *The man's grotesque!* Yet her repugnance was losing the battle with the fire his touch ignited in her loins. She opened her mouth to tell him to get lost, but nothing came out.

"Here you go, lass," he whispered, as he swung Rachel up into his arms. "Oh, for another afternoon of bliss." He tossed her onto the mattress and then climbed inside the van and slammed the door.

When Luther returned, he found that Alana had made a fresh pot of tea and returned to the hearth in front of the fire, sipping from her cup and munching a cookie from the stash of devil's food cookies she found in the coat closet.

"I hope you don't mind?" she asked.

"Not at all."

"This is really a nice place you have."

"Thank you. Let me show you around."

"No need. I looked around while you were saying goodbye to Cal."

"Oh." He didn't know whether to be pleased or perturbed.

He's upset, she thought. *And trying not to show it.*

"I like what you did in the master bath; all black. And your office upstairs, what a striking color combination. What is it, hunter green and oak?"

"Teak. I have this thing about ships—"

"I saw. The models and ship's wheels."

I've got several pairs of black silk Jockeys in my underwear drawer, too! And then he thought, *But she probably already knows that.*

"So, you know all about me," she said.

"Hardly."

"Tell me about you."

Luther's jaw tightened. "Not much to tell. I went to school in North Carolina—"

"Are you from there?"

"No. I graduated—"

He really doesn't like talking about himself, she thought, in amazement. *How refreshing.*

"I moved to Memphis in 1990, and I teach classes in paranormal psychology and comparative religion."

"Whoa, there. What happened to the years in between? Did you join a nunnery or go to prison? What?"

"You want a glass of OJ or something?" he asked.

"No thanks. Tea's fine."

"Be right back."

He went into the kitchen, took several deep swallows directly from the orange juice carton, and then poured the remainder of the juice into a tall mug and returned to the living room. Alana was still sitting on the hearth, gazing at the flames. Standing close behind her, he gazed past her shoulder at the burning log.

"Look, Alana, I appreciate your asking, but I'm kind of a private person. I'm willing to help you 'cause I believe you need help. Why don't we just leave it at that?"

She turned, letting her eyes settle on his face while

Ungrateful Dead

she took another sip of tea. "Oh, so we're being frank? Okay, fine. I know I came to you, but that sure as hell didn't make it easy to bare my soul to you and Cal. I told you two things I never told anybody—personal and very painful things. Is it too much to ask you to answer a few questions so that I know I didn't expose myself to an ax murderer?"

Luther smiled sadly.

He really is kind of cute.

"I guess not," he replied and took a seat near her on the hearth. "It's just—Oh, hell. After I graduated, I went to Canada." Her expression never changed, but the weight of her gaze spoke volumes. "I didn't want to go to Vietnam."

"Okay."

"I mean, I kept getting deferrals, college, then graduate school, and then my doctorate. But the damned war just kept dragging on and on. I guess I got on some bureaucrat's shit list 'cause two days after I got my Master's, I was reclassified, and a week after that I got the notice to take my physical. I guess they were hurting for smart grunts.

"The Canadians were pretty cool about it. The University of Alberta didn't have much use for a bloke with a Master's in Paranormal Psychology, but they gave me a job working with the Inuvialuit up in the western Arctic."

"Working with the what?"

"The who. Intuits . . . Eskimos."

"Oh."

"What they wanted was a cross between a paid Peace Corps volunteer and a social worker. You know, white man have heap big magic called computers and telephones. Me showum you how to get into this century."

He laughed bitterly.

Gary L. Holleman

"I take it things didn't go as planned?"

"Do they ever? They assigned me a 'Familial Group'—'tribe' isn't a PC term any longer—and gave me a Jeep, a map, and a compass and said, 'Go forth and save the noble savage.' I won't bore you with the details, but I got lost, ran out of gas, and would have ended up as a popcicle if the so-called savages hadn't found *me*!

"They took me back to their summer village until I came around. When I woke up I had this." He unbuttoned his shirt and showed Alana a small tattoo of a legless creature with a long, spiral horn jutting from the center of its forehead.

"What in God's name is that supposed to be?"

"A narwhal, it's a kind of horned whale. It was the tribe's totem. Their attitude was, we found you, you belong to us."

Alana laughed and Luther rebuttoned his shirt.

"You can't tell anybody about this," he said. "My students think I'm weird enough as it is."

"So you lived with the Esk—the Inuits for twenty years?"

"Oh no. Only a year. A man can only take so much raw fish and whale blubber."

"You actually lived with them? In their—in their what? Igloos?"

"They mostly live in fixed settlements now, but yes, when they go hunting, they still live in igloos."

"Ugh!"

"It's not that bad. They're good people. When I left, the chief gave me that." Luther nodded toward the harpoon over the fireplace.

"That old spear?"

"Hey, Alana, not everyone can drive a Z. That 'old spear' as you call it was his most prized possession. It

Ungrateful Dead

would be like you giving someone your car."

"I'm sorry," she said.

He chose to believe her.

"Where did you go then?"

"Oh, all sorts of places. I contracted out with the government of Brazil for a year, working with the Amazon tribes. Spent another year teaching in Peru. I distributed food for UNICEF in Haiti and the Sudan. And I spent the last eight years before returning home in England and France, teaching and compiling my book on occult practices."

Alana was quiet for several seconds. "Didn't you leave something out?"

Luther's expression darkened. "I don't know what you mean."

"Where were you when we first met?"

"You know about that?"

"Luther, I know everyone thinks I'm nuts, but I really didn't just pick your name out of a hat. I did some checking around first."

"I didn't know it was common knowledge."

Her tone softened. "It isn't. Unless you know the right people."

"And who might they be?"

"Oh, just some people."

"Come on," he said.

"If you must know, the Dean's wife and I go to the same hairdresser."

Stunned, Luther moaned like he was in cardiac arrest. "You're kidding? Please say you're kidding!"

"It's not that big a deal."

"It is to me. And now... people are talking about me in hair salons. What's next? Oprah, I guess."

"Well, since your secret is out, you might as well tell me about it."

85

Rolling his eyes, Luther muttered, "Shit! I guess you're right. Okay—I'm an addict! There, you happy?"

"I'm not the one making a production out of it."

"I guess you want all the gory details? Was I living in the streets, mugging old ladies to get money for smack?"

Alana remained silent.

"I was in London, working on my book and teaching psychopathology part-time to a bunch of Cambridge doctor wannabes. You've been to England, you know what it's like. It's Disneyland for a parapsychologist. Every castle has a ghost, every bog a fairy. On the weekends I made the rounds of the countryside, looking into the local legends. This one particular weekend in 1988 I was staying at an inn in Devon near Dartmoor, investigating myths of a phantom black dog that the locals called Trash or Skriker. I met . . . someone."

"A girl?"

"Yes, Genny—Genevieve; it means pure. Shows you can't always go by a name."

"But you fell in love with her?"

"Love?" Luther hung his head and considered calling the whole thing off—helping Alana, teaching—everything. "Look, I'm not very good at analyzing feelings."

"Typical."

"They're not scientific, and they're hard as hell to quantify. Maybe it could have turned into love—a very destructive love—but it started out as just good, old-fashioned, American Pie lust."

"Good grief, what did this girl do to you?"

"Nothing I didn't want her to do," he replied hotly. But then he quickly cooled off. "It wasn't any big deal. Genny was a schoolteacher. When she found out what I was there for, she offered to show me the places where the dog had been sighted. Turned out she had been involved with the antiwar movement in Devon. Up until then, I had moved around so much I had kind of missed out on all the—'' His face got red. "Sex and drugs, and since I hate rock and roll—I guess as hippies went, I was a flop. The next thing I knew, a one-week jaunt turned into two and then three. We would go out into the country, picnic, get high, and fool around."

"Sounds idyllic," Alana muttered.

"I guess it sounds pretty dumb now—"

"So what happened to queer this budding *affaire d'amour*?"

"That summer we took a long weekend and drove to the West Kennet burial mound in Wiltshire. The rumor was that the black dog had been showing up there at sunrise each June twenty-second since 1577."

"And?"

"And she disappeared... vanished! The place is a labyrinth of pitch-black caves and passageways. We went in together, got separated, and she never came out. They called out the local militia, combed every inch of the place—*nada*."

"They never found her?"

"Not so far as I ever heard."

"What did you do?"

"Do? Other than feel like shit? There was nothing I could do. The cops, her family, everybody except Prince Charles practically accused me of raping and killing her and burying the body, but they couldn't prove anything. I started taking more and more drugs; coke, when I could afford it, pain pills, grass. Later I was downing anything I could get my hands on. It gave the school a great excuse to dump me."

"And did they?"

"In a New York minute."

"And?"

Gary L. Holleman

"And I came back to the States, sent resumes to everybody I'd ever heard of, begging for a job, and finally managed to convince Tru Connely here at the University to take a chance on me."

Luther stood up and picked up her cup and saucer. "Any more questions?"

"You mad at me?"

"Was he? He didn't think so. "No."

"Still going to help me?"

"Yes."

"Why?"

Why indeed? He looked down into her eyes. Had he missed it before or just not allowed himself to see it? She looked enough like Genny to be her sister.

Cal strolled into the bedroom just as Rachel walked out of the bathroom and began drying her hair. He paused, enjoying the view as she rubbed the towel vigorously back and forth over her head. When she bent over to wrap up her hair he saw the ugly, blue-black bruise that covered her buttocks like a grape stain.

"My God, what happened to you?"

She gasped, spun around and covered her body with the towel. For an instant he saw something he had never seen in her eyes before—fear, and without understanding why, he averted his gaze.

"Oh! You startled me. What?" She looked at the reflection of her backside in the mirror. "Uh, I fell going back for a lob."

He tried to laugh it off. "I thought tennis was a noncontact sport. Come here, I'll make it all better." But when he tried to put his arms around her, she took a step back and kept rubbing herself with the towel.

"So, is Luther all right?" she asked.

Cal's eyes clouded over, but the hurt he felt never

reached his voice. "Yeah. Can't hurt that boy by dropping him on his head. Plus, when we got back to his place that woman was waiting for him."

Rachel pulled the towel down. "The one who thinks her mother is trying to possess her? What did she want?"

"She claims she saw a woman tied up in the back of a van last night."

"Boy, she really is nuts."

"That's what I said. But you know Luther."

"He's not taking her seriously, is he?"

"I don't know. Maybe. I think he thinks the woman's mother is still alive and trying to pull some kind of scam on her—don't ask me why."

"Then he's as crazy as she is. You should tell him to stay clear of her."

Cal looked puzzled. "I thought you said we should help her?"

"Me? I said no such thing. And even if I did, that was before she started spouting off about people being tied up in green vans."

Rachel finished drying off, slipped into her robe, and marched back into the bathroom.

Who said anything about green *vans?* Cal wondered.

Grover Chang waited patiently for his master to finish with the woman. It wasn't his favorite job—waiting. Especially in that house with its cold, drafty hallways. He tried repeating his word of the day. "Rathskeller." It reminded him of the rats that roamed the mansion like hairy brown ghosts. "Rathskeller. From the German." He heard Anton laugh—it wouldn't be long now.

The upper hall was even more decrepit than the rest of the place. Most of the doors wouldn't close properly, and the carpet was so threadbare you could read a newspaper through it. Even the lowest member of the Triad lived better than this.

The woman came out, and he led her down the main front staircase and around to the cellar door.

"This place is a dump," the woman opined.

Grover glanced at the red wig, her long, café au lait legs, and white, vinyl, high-heeled hooker boots, and just smiled.

"This ain't the way I came in, honey," she announced.

"I parked in the underground garage to keep the car out of the rain," Grover explained.

"Underground gay-rage! Well LA-DE-DA! Yo' boss man is some stud muffin." She raked her blood-red nails down Grover's bulging forearm. "You look like you might be pretty good in that depat'ment your own self."

"I'm a eunuch." It was a lie, but Grover was growing tired of the woman's babbling.

"Honey," she said as Grover opened the door to the cellar. "That don't matter none to me. I been with Baptists, Methodists, Cat-licks, and even pulled a chain for a Mormon basketball team once. You religious types don't slow me down a-tall."

Grover flipped the light switch and the sixty-watt bulb at the top of the stairwell cast a cone of anemic yellow light partway down the long flight.

"It sho' is dark down there. Slow down! I can't go setting no track records in these heels." The woman stopped, peered down into the gloomy emptiness of the huge underground room and wrinkled her nose. "It don't smell like no gay-rage. It smell mo' like a goat farm. What you keep down here anyway?"

"Oh, this and that." Grover's voice was melodious, almost hypnotic, with no trace of an accent. In the semi-darkness, he could have passed for James Coburn. "It's

Ungrateful Dead

an interesting place. Let me show you around."

"Time's money, honey. Where de car?"

They started down the steps, the woman's spike heels tapping out a peppy tune on the wood. The air was oppressively hot and dank and did little to dispel the musty stench that clung to the lower levels like a creeping ground fog.

"No, really," Grover said with a friendly grin, "the guy who used to own this place held lavish parties down here. Real orgies, with local bigwigs and dope and the whole nine yards."

"Dey never invite me to none a them org-ies."

"This was a long time ago."

As they approached the floor, the woman began to get a feel for just how vast the place was. "Now don't dat beat all? What's dat over there? A tree? How y'all get that to grow down here?"

In reality, the cellar was a huge, circular vault, with a domed ceiling. Five stone arches spaced evenly around the room led to five unlighted drainage tunnels, each going off in a different direction. The floor, which from where the woman stood looked like bare dirt, was moist and covered with patches of dark toadstools, and as her eyes adjusted, she noticed what appeared to be five massive stone support columns situated between the arches and extending all the way up to the floor above.

But it was the gigantic live oak with its foot-thick branches and strange, dark, waxy leaves that reached up into the darkest recesses of the ceiling that attracted the woman's attention.

"What kind a chicken-shit gay-rage is this? Dirt floor! Hell, my Mama's shack in Tupelo got a better floor 'n this. And why's it so hot in here?"

She stepped down from the last step, and her heels sank about a quarter of an inch into the soft mud. At each step, her foot wobbled and the mud squished, and she looked down in horror at what the gooey stuff was doing to her boots.

"You-all gonna buy me some new boots if'n this stuff don't come off."

"Over here!" Grover called.

Sweat was beginning to run down the woman's face. "Over where?"

"Here!"

She saw him as a lighter patch of darkness standing under the outstretched arms of the oak.

"Right here is where they had all the fun."

The woman stopped, reached down into her right boot, and pulled out a flat box cutter, the kind stock clerks in supermarkets use, and exposed the blade. "Don't you be tryin' nuttin' with me. I don't care how big you be, this here'll cut you down to size."

Grover held up his hands and stepped to the side. "Here!" He tossed a ring of keys to the woman. "The car is down the tunnel behind me. Climb in the back and lock the doors and when you're ready, honk and I'll drive you back to Beale."

It was dark, but she tried to see Grover's face anyway; he appeared to be smiling. She peered around the tree at the arched entranceway to the tunnel and sniffed. A sultry breeze drifted out of the darkness, a breeze carrying the stench of wet putrefaction.

"I don't see no damned car, and it stink in there."

"Jesus Christ! You saw the car when you came here—a black limo . . . remember? It's right there!"

She took a step closer, the hairs on her arms standing up like the fur of a short-haired cat. "What's that smell?"

Sighing, Grover stuck a lighted match to a cigarette.

Ungrateful Dead

"Probably leakage from the sewers. We are underground, you know."

The tiny flame was just enough to screw up the woman's vision. "I'm not going in there. You drive it out here."

"Gimme the damned keys," he snapped. "You can go back upstairs and catch the fucking bus for all I care."

She jumped back out of reach.

It was a long way from Parkway to Beale Street, and at this time of night, in this neighborhood, catching a bus was a dangerous proposition—even for a hooker.

"Okay! Okay. But if you got a dog back there 'n it bites me, you gonna be plenty sorry!"

She ducked under the limbs and stomped around the trunk of the tree, planning to give the big man a very large piece of her mind, but just as she was warming up, her boot came down in an exceptionally soft patch of ground and sank in all the way to the ankle.

"Whoa!" She threw out her arms to keep from toppling over and then glanced down at her foot. "Lookie at this, now!" She tried to pull free, but the mud held on like quicksand. "What is this shit?"

Grover sighed and the grin disappeared. "It's a special fertilizer my boss uses."

She glanced up at the low-hanging limbs—they were loaded down with the largest acorns she had ever seen.

"Sho' look like it's working."

She tried again to pick up her foot, but this time the other one sank into the muck too. Wrinkling her nose at the foul-smelling odor that rose from the stuff, she tried two more times to pull free and then glared at Grover and shook the box cutter at him like a switch.

"You big ape! Get over here and gimme a hand!"

"I'm sorry," he replied. "I can't."

Gary L. Holleman

"What yo' mean you can't?"

"I'm real sorry."

"You gonna be a lot sorrier when I get out—Great jumpin' Jehoshaphat . . . what's that?"

Dozens of black, slug-like things were crawling up her boots. She tried to brush them off with her hand, but they were cold and slimy, and somehow several stuck to her fingers. "Hey—Ow! Hey! Get these things off a me!"

Like tiny, living scalpels, they cut into her fingers, and once the skin was breached, they bored under her flesh like hungry termites, moving up her arms under the skin. The woman waved her hands in the air as if they were on fire and screamed as the creatures slithered up her boots and onto her legs.

Grover turned his head and stared off into the tunnel behind him, while puffing on his cigarette. Each time she screamed, he winced as if it were his flesh and not the woman's the creatures were devouring. He strolled to the arch and flipped the butt into the tunnel, watching the glowing tip spin through the darkness like a comet streaking through the night sky. He lit another and blew a cloud of invisible smoke up toward the ceiling. Behind him, the woman was still screaming, but it sounded a long way off now. He took another puff, and in a matter of minutes, the screaming abruptly stopped. Dropping the cigarette, he strolled back to the tree. An oily-looking puddle had formed over the spot where the woman had stood; as he watched, it was quickly absorbed by the thirsty roots.

On the long climb back up the stairs, Grover thought about San Francisco, about the clean, cool smell of the sea, the bite of honey-covered sourdough bread and dark Chinese beer. It all seemed a long way away.

Chapter Five

Luther arrived at his office bright and early Monday morning and began putting the finishing touches on the final exam he planned to give to his undergrad comparative religion classes. The truth was, he hated giving final exams, preferring to let the kids demonstrate their mastery of the subject—or lack thereof—through classwork, their questions, and the occasional field trip, and he had been putting it off for weeks, hoping for some sign—some inkling—that they had understood one—just one . . . any one, of the concepts he had been trying to pound into their pointy, little heads since September. No such luck. And since he had given up on the old osmotic theory of learning, where the kids sleep with their heads on the textbook, it looked like he was going to have to finish the damned test.

Fifteen minutes later, his door opened and a short,

Gary L. Holleman

black man stepped into the room. After calmly removing a thick cigar from his mouth, he tilted his bald head back and sent a cloud of blue smoke spiraling up toward the ceiling.

"Damn it, Tru!" Luther said. "Put that thing out before someone calls the EPA."

Truman Connely grinned and released a perfectly formed ring of smoke, which hovered, halolike, in the air above his head for a second or two before dissipating. "That any way to talk to your boss, your mentor, not to mention the man who got you this palatial office?"

Prepared from an early age for a career in athletics, Tru had been lured by his intelligence away from the gridiron and into the classroom, where long hours of academic frustration and physical inactivity had manifested themselves in a spreading waistline. Now, in his early sixties, even wearing one of his nine-hundred-dollar, silk-blend suits and size-thirteen wingtips, he looked like a jolly bowling ball. He sauntered up to Luther's desk, his vest pockets bulging with pens and cigars, a copy of the *Commercial Appeal* folded under one arm and a stack of papers under the other. He slammed the papers down on top of Luther's other piles of papers, and Luther's heart sank all the way down into the pit of his stomach.

"Those what I think they are?" Luther moaned.

"TEFs from your adoring students."

TEFs, or Teacher Evaluation Forms, were the forms that the university required all students to fill out near the end of each semester, rating their professors on how well, in the students' opinions, they had conducted their classes. The forms consisted of twenty-five multiple-choice questions, with space on the back for written comments.

"I don't know what you're bitching about," said Tru.

Ungrateful Dead

"You should see some of the others' evaluations."

As head of Luther's department, Tru was required to read all of the evaluations before passing them on.

"Yeah?" Luther muttered. "Well, I know what comes next."

Each semester, the professors with the highest TEF scores were honored at a faculty black-tie at the Peabody Hotel in downtown Memphis.

Tru chuckled. "I gotta admit, this year's crop is the best yet. Some of your co-eds' comments border on the pornographic. I thought about calling a couple of them and suggesting they switch to creative writing." He picked up Luther's key chain from the top of the desk and held the crystal globe on the end up to the light. "What is that in there? A clover?"

"Something like that."

"Where'd you get it?"

"It was a gift from someone in Great Britain. Now quit fooling with it and sit down. I've got something I want to talk to you about."

Truman twirled the trinket between his fingers for a moment and then dropped it on the desk and squeezed his body into the office chair in front of Luther's desk, glaring angrily at the offending piece of furniture for reminding him of his bulk.

"I'm going to get you some new chairs," Tru groused. "A Hindu fakir suffering from anorexia nervosa couldn't get comfortable in this contraption."

"You say that every time you come in here."

"Well, this time I mean it. Now, what do you want?"

"You've got friends at MLG& W and the telephone company?"

"Unlike some people, I've got friends everywhere. Why, you behind on your bills again?"

"No. I'm trying to locate someone who moved here

in . . . oh, say the last three months. Could you ask around for me?"

"Who is it?"

"A guy named Anton Gadarn."

"Gay-darn. How do you spell it?"

Luther told him, and Tru wrote it down in his day planner.

"Who is he?"

"Just a guy I'm trying to find for a friend."

"Cal?"

"No, someone else."

"You don't know anyone else but me."

They went back and forth for five minutes, ribbing each other without mercy, until finally Tru got up to leave.

"Enough! I've got *important* administrative-type stuff to do."

Luther smirked. "Counting the rolls of toilet tissue in the men's room?"

Lighting a fresh cigar, Tru blew the smoke at Luther and reached for his newspaper. "You see the paper? He struck again."

"Who? The Nonconnah Nosher?"

Tru sputtered. "Where did you come up with that name?"

"I overheard it from some my kids."

They were referring to the brutal serial killer responsible for the deaths of seven prostitutes, whose drained, dismembered, and badly decomposed remains had turned up at various locations along Nonconnah Creek over the past two months. The local paper had drawn numerous parallels to Jack the Ripper and Jeffrey Dahmer, and the local women's groups and the Gay and Lesbian Coalition had offered rewards for information.

"Well, if the kids are saying it, it'll be in the papers

Ungrateful Dead

before long. The media has as much taste as Richard Simmons."

"You know," Luther said, watching his friend's expression closely. "The cops are eventually going to call you in to evaluate him."

Tru beamed. "You think so?" Then, just as quickly, a frown appeared. "Aw, they'll probably get one of the big shots: Nathanson from U.C.L.A., or Ketterman from Chicago."

"I don't know," Luther pressed. "You've got a much better reputation locally. What's your take on the guy?"

Squeezing back into the chair, Tru replied, "What makes you think it's a man?"

Luther's eyebrows shot up to his hairline. "You're kidding. Women don't do those kinds of things."

"It's obvious you've never been married. In my experience, when provoked, women can be far more savage than men. What they lack in physical strength, they usually make up for in tenacity and cold-blooded deviousness. Mrs. Bobbitt aside, women rarely explode into fits of rage. When they feel threatened or wronged, they hide their anger behind a passive expression or a pretty face. But inside, they're spinning plots and plans as intricate as their infamous black widow sisters' webs. When the time is right, they strike without compunction or, in many instances, an ounce of regret. To make it worse, because so many of us are genetically and emotionally unprepared to see past their disguises, they often use men as their unwitting accomplices. Mark my words, we're long overdue for just the sort of female monster they're talking about in this newspaper. When she arrives—note I said when, not if—look out!"

Luther was troubled. "For the sake of argument, if the Nosher were a woman, what would her motivation be? Her pathology?"

"That would be a question for our friend Cal. Not a humble, albeit well-read scholar such as myself—"

"Ha!"

"But my guess is, she would suffer from a severe dissociative disorder and has probably become trapped in a delusional world in which she is forced to reenact some horrible trauma from her childhood. Something involving her mother, or an aunt, or perhaps her grandmother."

Luther's blood turned to ice water. "Her mother?"

"That's usually the case when men murder women." Tru glanced at the oversized Pulsar on his wrist. "Anyway, I've got to go."

"Can you put a rush on that address?" Luther asked.

"Sure thing. And I'll let you know when the black tie's scheduled."

Luther stared at the half-completed exam on his desk as he listened to Tru's footsteps become lost in the general scramble in the corridor. The words on the paper, his words—his writing—made as much sense to him as one of Andy Warhol's wall-mounted soup cans. He turned around and looked out the window at the courtyard. It was raining again. It seemed like it was always raining lately, and the kids were running back and forth holding textbooks and papers over their heads. By leaning close to the glass he could see the giant oak at the end of the courtyard. It looked barren and dead, and the opposite wall was dark with accumulated moisture that bled from the porous bricks and mortar like blood. He heard a soft buzzing sound and glanced down at the window ledge where he saw a tiny fly, its wings so damp and new that they wouldn't sustain flight, crawl onto the open petal of his venus flytrap. In agonizingly slow motion, the plant's velvety, red leaf folded up and around the tiny insect, squeezing it loosely in its aromatic death-grip. So enchanted was the fly with its new surroundings that at first it was unaware of what was happening. It was only when the hapless insect noticed its way out was barred by an interlocking web of fine hairs that it saw the trap. It tried to flee, but there was no way out.

Luther turned and tried to concentrate on the exam; he tried to listen to the tapping of the rain on the window panes and ignore the incessant buzzing of the doomed fly. After five minutes, he opened the window and threw the plant as far as he could across the courtyard.

When the alarm sounded at 6 A.M., Alana turned off the buzzer, rolled over, and buried her head under the pillow. Sometime around noon, workers were coming to install new locks on her doors and security bars on her windows, but she had the whole morning to herself. She was sorely tempted to go back to sleep, but all those years with the nuns made such blatant depravity impossible and so, with a huge sigh, she rolled to the edge of the bed and swung her legs over the side. The chilled air brought the usual crop of goose bumps to immediate, screaming attention, and she shivered pleasantly, luxuriating in that soft period of half-sleep as she waited for the cobwebs to clear. She had slept well—for the first time in weeks, and in her mind she downplayed Luther's part in that, choosing to attribute it to not spending half the night staring out the front window. But it was a game. Honesty compelled her to admit there was something about the man that made her feel . . . not safe exactly—she couldn't imagine ever feeling safe. But he was *there*. She'd felt it the first time she had spoken with him. His whole attention had been on her. Not on her face—not on her breasts or her legs or her behind— but on her. It was a refreshing change, for since her graduation from the convent, she couldn't remember ever having a conversation with a man who wasn't talking to her tits to avoid looking at her scars.

The sun was still a promise, and the room was mostly shadows as Alana walked toward the bathroom. On the way, she paused beside her dresser to caress Morna's photograph.

Ten more days!

She continued into the bathroom and stepped into the shower without bothering to turn on the lights. The hot water after the cool air felt good, and the steam hit her system like a good, stiff jolt of caffeine. After shaving her legs and underarms, she applied soap to her body and shampoo to her hair, then rinsed it all off and stepped out, dripping, onto the bath mat and grabbed her towel. At the sink, she dried her hair and then flipped on the lights. As she reached for her hairbrush, she glanced at her reflection in the mirror and stopped short.

There was a mole on her right breast.

It had not been there the night before.

She stared at the black spot until every last drop of water on her body had evaporated. She stared until her arm was numb and her legs quivered. She stared, terrified to take so much as a deep breath, until the tears blurred it away, and then she sat—collapsed really—fortunately the wicker vanity stool was behind her—and shook so hard that her teeth chattered like castanets.

It wasn't there! she thought. *I know it wasn't there! . . . was it?*

Cal normally relished the quiet time between patients. It gave him a chance to feed his fish, catch up on his paperwork, make a few phone calls, or just look out the window and try and purge his head of the inanity he'd had to listen to during the previous forty-five minutes. Not that all of his patients were that bad—Memphis wasn't New York, after all. Mostly just a few neurotics: women who were absolutely sure their children hated them and their husbands were cheating. Kids with emotional problems. A pair of kleptomaniacs (both from very well-to-do families). Sometimes it was hard to keep them all separate in his head. But that was most days. Today Cal was wondering if he was on the way to becoming as nutty as his patients.

The door opened and Rachel came in.

"I'm through with the bills."

"Great," he replied.

When Sam was in school, Rachel worked mornings in the office, sending out statements, paying bills, and even helping Grace with the filing when she got backed up.

"I'm going home now."

Cal nodded, smiling, but Rachel refused to look at him. "Are you feeling okay?"

"Yeah, I'm fine. Just a little tired."

She didn't look fine. She looked like she was about to jump out of her skin.

"You want me to pick up Sam?" he asked.

"I'll do it. See you tonight."

She left, closing the door behind her, and Cal turned around in his chair, staring out the window and tapping on his two front teeth with the eraser on his pencil. He was still sitting like that when the intercom buzzed twenty minutes later.

"Yes, Grace?"

His secretary's syrupy voice came back; "Doctor Weinberg, that Ms. Magnus is here to see you." Grace's voice dropped to a hoarse whisper. "She hasn't got an appointment, but she's awfully upset."

"Who's scheduled next?"

"Patty Anderson."

Gary L. Holleman

Patty Anderson was a teenager whose mother, a local school psychologist, thought the girl had coprolalia because she used the word "fuck" to punctuate all of her sentences.

"Reschedule Patty, give me five minutes, and then send her in."

Straightening his tie, Cal cleared the newspaper from the top of his desk and then ran his fingers through his hair.

Lord, what now?

On schedule, Alana came and sat down in the chair in front of the desk—fell down would have been more accurate. She had on a boy's charcoal gray dress shirt over tight jeans and tennis shoes, and her hair was brushed, but she had on no make-up, and her face was as pale as a porcelain doll.

"You've got to believe me now!"

Cal kept his expression neutral and his voice even. "What has happened?"

She started to unbutton her shirt, but her fingers were shaking so badly she was making a mess of it.

"Wha—what are you doing?"

"You have to see it."

"Wait!" Cal hit the intercom button. "Grace, come in here, please!"

Grace Pruitt had been with Cal for twelve years. She was forty-nine years old, five feet three inches tall and weighted a hundred and ninety pounds—all of it hard-nosed, Southern Baptist, no-nonsense competent. She made twice as much money as any other secretary/assistant in Memphis, and she was worth every penny.

Grace strode into Cal's office like she was on a treadmill, stalked around his desk, and stood at a respectful distance, with her hands clasped together over her rounded abdomen. Her eyes were blue, her hair was gray, and from the look on her face, she might just as well have been waiting for a bus.

"Grace," Cal explained in a reasonable tone of voice, "Ms. Magnus has something under her shirt she wants me to see." When Grace didn't reply, Cal nodded to Alana. "Go ahead."

Alana unbuttoned the shirt and pulled down her bra enough to expose her right breast. Cal leaned forward and did his dead-level best to examine the breast the way he would if it were just an interesting microbe on a laboratory slide. After a moment he sat back in the chair.

"What is it you wanted me to see?"

Alana pointed to a black mole about two centimeters above the large, round areola. Cal leaned forward again, but this time he couldn't keep the confusion out of his voice.

"A mole? What do you want me to say?"

"It wasn't there yesterday," Alana said, rebuttoning the shirt. "You're the doctor. You tell me. Can a mole grow that big overnight?"

"That will be all, Grace," Cal said.

Grace bent down and whispered in his ear. "You sure? She looks disturbed to me."

Rachel often joked that Grace had a crush on him which, in her opinion, went into high gear when it came to Cal's safety. At those times she could be a pit bull.

Cal smiled and assured Grace it was all right and then waited until she returned to her desk.

"I don't know what to say," he began.

"Get the photographs!" Alana snapped. "See for yourself."

Once again, Cal depressed the intercom button and relayed a request for Alana's chart. Then they waited— in silence, while he racked his brain for something safe to talk about.

"You talk to Luther today?"

She shook her head.

That pretty much exhausted his store of small talk so they had to make do with the soft whisper of the aquariums' air pumps and filters until the door opened and Grace stuck her head in.

"I can't find it."

Cal sighed. "I filed it myself. It's under M."

As soon as Grace closed the door, he popped up and went to the aquariums, stopping at each to tap on the glass, just to let his "babies" know he was thinking about them. When Grace came back, her hair was disheveled, and she looked perplexed.

"I can't find it. I looked under M. I looked under L and N. I even looked through all the A's, just in case—no Magnus."

Cal excused himself and followed Grace to the file cabinets. Alana got up and paced first up and down near the windows and then over next to the aquariums. At her approach, the fish and their crustacean sidekicks lined up next to the glass like a mob of spectators at the zoo. After a few seconds, when no food was forthcoming, everything with fins swam up to the tops of the tanks, where they began pushing and shoving against one another, jockeying for a better position near the surface.

They're not all that different from humans, she marveled.

The door flew open, and Cal stormed into the room. His expression looked thunderous. He went to his desk and began rifling through the drawers. When Alana realized what was going on, she got that old familiar sinking sensation in the pit of her stomach.

Finally, he slammed the bottom drawer and sat back in his chair. "The damned file is gone."

Ungrateful Dead

Alana began edging toward the door.

"Where are you going? Didn't you hear me?"

She stopped with her back to the wall near his diplomas.

"What's the matter with you?" he barked. "Say something!"

"You're in it with him," she hissed.

Cal frowned. "In it?" Then realization hit like the house landing on the Witch of the East. "Don't be ridiculous! I'm not in anything with anyone. We've simply misplaced a file."

Alana started heading toward the door again.

"Jesus!" Cal muttered. He took a deep breath and then tried again in a more reasonable tone. "Alana, please . . . the file is missing, but we'll find it. Grace is tearing the cabinets apart as we speak. Please—" He held his palm out toward the chair. "Luther is my best friend. I would never do anything to hurt you."

Alana chewed her bottom lip as she mulled her options.

If he really is in it with Anton, then Luther is in it too. If that's the case, I might as well take a header out the window right now.

Without a word, she went back and eased into the chair. For his part, Cal sat back and did his best to look nonthreatening—no mean feat, considering how furious he was.

"Let's just assume for the moment that the pictures will prove the mole is new. Why don't we consider some alternatives to possession. Like genetics! I was taught that the propensity to form moles can be inherited."

"Did you get a good look at that thing?" Alana asked, her voice dripping incredulity. "It's the size of freaking marble!"

"And you're positive it wasn't there before? Smaller

maybe?" he added quickly. "And you just didn't notice it?"

The fact was, Alana wasn't a hundred percent sure. The way things were going, she wasn't a hundred percent sure she was sitting in Cal's office or that her hair was red. It must have showed.

"Look," he said reasonably. "It's probably been there for a while and with all you're going through you just missed it. But it may have grown a bit, and I suggest you have your family physician take a look at it."

The bitter taste of frustration and fear coated her mouth like cotton. She took a deep breath and said, "Maybe you're right—okay? Maybe! But even if it has been there for a while, that doesn't change the fact that Mother had a mole in the exact same spot on her right breast. Genetics or not, I never heard of that before. Did you?"

"That really isn't my field, but if you don't have a doctor, I can recommend someone—a woman."

The door opened again, and Grace came in with a manila folder in her hand. Cal managed to keep the exasperation out of his voice. "Where was it?"

Her face was blank as she gave him the folder. "It was in the trash can in the ladies' room."

It was Alana's folder. It was empty.

It took every ounce of Cal's patience and experience to calm Alana down. Later, after she was gone, after his last patient of the day, he called Grace into the office.

"When Alana was waiting to see me, was she alone at any time?"

Grace hung her head as if she'd been accused of stealing. "I went to the ladies' room. I was only gone for a minute. I've been on this diet and—"

"Grace, I'm not mad at you. I'm just trying to figure

Ungrateful Dead

out what happened. After you returned, did she go into the restroom? Even for a few minutes?"

"I honestly don't know. I was finishing the filing that Rachel started. You know, she really didn't look well."

"Rachel?" He looked up surprised. "Yes, I know. She hasn't been—Rachel was filing?"

It was Grace's turn to looked surprised. "Well, yes. She usually helps out when I get behind."

"Okay, thanks. Have a good night."

As soon as she left, Cal turned the chair around and leaned back, staring out the window and tapping his front teeth with the eraser on his pencil.

After his last class, Luther got a ride with Truman to a bike shop on Winchester Road. After dickering with the salesperson for twenty-five minutes, he maxed out his credit card to purchase a brand new twenty-one-speed mountain bike with an extra-padded seat to allow for what age had done to his posterior. He also bought a new helmet. Memphis streets were turning into a war zone, and if they had stocked a helmet made of steel and a matching flak jacket, he would have bought them too.

Tru's friends down at public works had found no record of anyone named Gadarn. But rather than come back empty-handed, he presented Luther with a stack of computer printouts of all new residential power and telephone customers for the previous four months. Luther shoved the printouts into his backpack, mounted his new bike, and pedaled home with yet another bank of storm clouds following him like bad karma. Dismounting, he wheeled the bike around the side of the house and let himself into the backyard through the gate. The house, a duplex, was what the real estate moguls liked to call a "zero-lot-line house," which meant that his neighbors on either side could hear his toilet flush, and that the yard was the size of a postage stamp—a fact that during the summer grass-cutting season made him extremely happy.

Though it was small, Luther had filled his backyard with shrubs, hanging baskets, and bird feeders which, when added to the backdrop of tall trees growing just behind the fence created, in his mind at least, his own personal piece of the great Rocky Mountains.

After locking the bike inside the aluminum storage shed attached to the back wall of the house, Luther stepped up on the deck and fumbled in his pocket for his key chain. As he reached the door, he heard a rather unusual noise. It wasn't the wind—it wasn't even especially loud or threatening. It was out of place.

He turned around to see where it was coming from.

At first he didn't see anything out of the ordinary. The squall had turned a rather mild winter afternoon into a cold and damp winter evening. The air was so full of electricity, he could feel the electrons tickling the hairs on his arms, and the clouds were heavy and close full of dark purple streaks and wind that stirred up the dead leaves until they danced and whipped the naked tree limbs back and forth. It was powerful, dark and raw, the kind of brooding tempest that made a person feel small and vulnerable. And yet it was precisely because of all the violent motion surrounding it that the shadow crouching atop the fence caught Luther's eye.

The instant it realized it had been spotted, the dark shape dropped to the ground and began inching along the fence inside the yard, never straying far from the shadows of the overhanging trees. At the corner of the yard it turned toward him, walking—stalking slowly through the wet, brown grass. It was a dog—a large, shaggy-haired black dog, with eyes like bonfires in a prehistoric cave. Closer now, its low growl, the sound that first captured Luther's attention, became a snarl as it bared its impressive set of fangs.

Believing that any sudden movement might precipitate an attack, Luther remained still. Now that he saw it clearly, he was stunned. He had never laid eyes on on the animal before in his life, but he immediately recognized it for what it was.

Christ! The red eyes, that shaggy, black fur!

It was the Skriker! The demon dog of Devon that he had been searching for when Genny disappeared.

But that's crazy! he thought. *It's just a myth! Besides, what would the Skriker be doing all the way over here?*

His chaotic musings cost him precious seconds and very nearly his life. Trapped between the back door and the fence that separated his backyard from his neighbors', Luther had noplace to go.

The beast snarled again—louder—then barked once and wagged its tail.

He couldn't believe his eyes. *The bastard's playing with me!*

A weapon! He needed a weapon or something he could use as a shield. He searched the yard frantically, but there was nothing within reach except his gas grill and a lawnmower. He remembered there was a shovel in the storage shed, but for all the good that did him, it might as well be on Mars. Desperate, he considered his options—that was easy—run or don't run. And from the way the beast was acting, he suspected running was exactly what it was hoping for.

Just then, the woman who lived next door opened her back door to let her cat out. Luther didn't much believe in miracles, but he did believe in gift horses and so, faster than anyone who knew him would have believed possible, he stepped on the lawnmower, clambered up on top of the grill, and vaulted the fence, landing in a heap at his neighbor's feet.

The woman, a middle-aged dental assistant wearing a quilted house dress and curlers, gazed down at him with a smile that said Jeff Bridges had just fallen out of his starship and landed in her lap. She had very nice teeth.

"Why, Dr. Shea!"

That was as far as she got.

The Skriker let out an ear-splitting roar and threw itself against the wooden barrier. Luther bounced to his feet and all but carried the woman back inside her house.

"Excuse me."

He slammed and locked the door, and less than a microsecond later the dog crashed into it hard enough to shatter two of the panes.

"Have you got a gun?" Luther shouted.

The woman stared at him blankly and shook her head.

"Here!" He turned toward the dining table behind him, grabbed the edge of the tablecloth, and gave it a yank—a newspaper and a flowerpot containing a bright-red poinsettia went flying across the linoleum. "Help me shove the table in front of the door."

"What is that thing out there, Dr. Shea?"

"Later! Give me a hand!"

She backed into the corner and shook her head.

"Damn," he muttered.

Made of heavy, dark oak, the table looked like it weighed a ton. He put his shoulder to it and pushed.

It did weigh a ton.

It bucked and its legs shuddered, but he managed to move it—about six inches.

The dog hit the door again, and the door frame began to crack.

"Will you give me a hand?" he panted.

She scooped up her cat, a scrawny, hairless thing that

reminded Luther of a drowned rat, and began stroking its head as if it were Aladdin's lamp.

He pushed again, but the table wasn't going anywhere. "Damn!"

"Dr. Shea? I don't hear anything any more," the woman said.

Luther straightened up. He didn't hear anything either.

He eased up to the door, flipped the light switch, and peered between the lace curtains. His neighbor lived alone and had installed a set of outdoor floodlights that a prison warden would have envied. They filled the tiny backyard with blinding white illumination. But there was no sign of the black dog.

Luther moved the table back to its original location, replaced the cloth, and then helped her clean up the mess. After apologizing profusely and promising to pay for the damaged door, Luther attempted a hasty retreat toward the front door. The woman followed, still clutching the tabby. It was obvious she wasn't buying his story about a runaway Saint Bernard, but she seemed more upset that he wouldn't stay for tea than she was about her back door.

Luther let himself into his place through the front door and made a beeline for the coat closet. A pacifist more by nature than conviction, he had never owned a gun. But he did have a shiny, new, Mark Grace model Louisville Slugger and with it cocked and ready over his shoulder, he carefully searched every inch of his house, going so far as to climb up into the attic and poke each dusty trunk and carton with the end of the bat. Finally, with no small amount of trepidation, he entered his bedroom and turned on the light. The room was a mess. His jeans and plaid shirts were strewn over the chair, the top of the dresser was buried under several pairs of his underwear, and last night's popcorn bowl was sitting upside down in the corner. In other words, it was exactly as he left it.

Breathing a sigh of relief, he briefly considered calling someone. But who? And tell them what? He had no desire to endure the same crap he'd gone through when Genny vanished; the snide remarks, the rolling eyes. Instead, he turned on his back porch light and opened the vertical blinds.

"Son . . . of . . . a . . . bitch."

The hundred-watt bulb in his porch light gave off nowhere near the candlepower of his neighbor's light, but he had no trouble seeing the carnage the creature had wrought. His grill was on its side, and the lawnmower was lying upside down with all four wheels in the air. His bird feeders and birdbaths were shattered, his hanging plants pulled down, and most of his lovingly cultivated bushes and shrubs uprooted. It looked as if a tornado, or the finger of God, had singled him out for individual attention.

Turning out the light, Luther carried the bat up the back stairs to the second floor and went into his office. He pulled his chair over to the bookcases and began running his finger along spines. Obviously, he had missed the connection between Alana's troubles and the dog. He wouldn't make the same mistake twice.

It was personal now.

Chapter Six

Alana spent the next few days creeping around the department store like a slug waiting for the salt to drop; she spent her nights pacing the rooms of her house like a trapped animal, afraid to go out, afraid to turn on a light lest she pass in front of a mirror. Monday and Tuesday nights the watcher was there. Wednesday night she called the cops. They found a lot of cigarette butts, but little else—they promised to send a patrol car around more often. Fat chance.

Fed up, Alana decided to quit playing the prick's little game and let emphysema take its course. She refused to go near the windows, refused to go outside when she didn't absolutely have to, and for almost a day she did a fair job of ignoring the whole thing.

That's when the howling began. Night after night of horrible, gut-wrenching wailing that sounded like a banshee in labor. At first she assumed it was a stray, or one of the neighbors' dogs from the next cove. But the third night, when the baying persisted, she knew she wasn't dealing with a little lost poodle. She called the cops again, and then Animal Control. They all came, and they all went away shaking their heads. She couldn't afford to miss work, and as the week passed and her composure began to crumble, her coworkers began to avoid her more and more. It wasn't just her behavior. Exhaustion had turned her eyes into hard, green marbles and sapped the remaining color from of her already pale complexion. She started wearing the most bizarre outfits: long gloves, which she refused to remove even when working at her desk, and turtleneck sweaters, most of which were either black or navy and only served to emphasize the pallor of her skin. If her job duties had been to work with the public, she probably would have been fired. As it was, on Friday her boss, a rather soft-spoken man from Atlanta, took her aside and asked her as politely as possible if she were doing drugs. Alana started laughing and couldn't stop. She laughed until tears came, which did little to calm the man's fears, and when she was finally able to get herself under control, she apologized and told him that there had been a death in her family.

After the debacle in Cal's office on Monday, she had doggedly refused to call either Luther or Cal, but by Friday she was in such a state that she had to talk to someone. She drove to Luther's house and stood shivering under a cold, gray mist as she leaned on his doorbell.

He opened the door in a pair of cutoffs and a Chicago Cub's sweat-shirt. When he saw who it was, he gave her such a warm, open smile that Alana broke down and started bawling.

Luther gently pulled her inside.

Ungrateful Dead

There was a fire going in the fireplace, Bach on the stereo, and all manner of arcane books and manuscripts scattered over the floor. He led her to the hearth, pressed an oversized cup of steaming hot chocolate into her hands, and she cried even harder, wiping her nose on the sleeve of her fur-lined anorak.

Luther brought her a tissue and took her coat, and as soon as she stopped shivering, he asked, "You feel like talking now?"

She started bawling again.

Luther had never been much of a hugger, but he didn't know how else to shut her up. He held her until she stopped shaking, even though her mascara was ruining his favorite sweatshirt. He figured it was a small price to pay for peace and quiet.

"I—I'm having a bad life," she moaned into his chest.

He chuckled softly. "I figured that much all by myself."

She pushed him away. "Don't you dare be amused at me. You don't have any idea what I've been through." She gave a good honk into the tissue.

"Oh, I don't know. I talked to Cal."

"Well, you still don't know what's happened since Monday."

Luther listened patiently as she filled him in, but stopped her when she tried to show him the mole. Halfway through the story she took a break, and while she was in the bathroom, he made two fresh cups of hot chocolate and took them back to the fire.

After washing her hands, Alana took a moment to poke around. She didn't have much experience with men, but figured you could tell more about one from his bathroom than his living room. The living room was for show; it was the public man. His bath was private.

She ran her fingers over the bristles on his tooth-and hairbrushes, sniffed his colognes, and felt the keen edge of his razor. The razor was so typical of him, she thought, an old-fashioned straight razor with a scrimshaw handle etched with the yellowed likeness of a narwhal.

In his closet, she took down the thick, terrycloth bathrobe she found hanging on a hook inside the door. It was as big as a grizzly-bear rug—the kind of robe you could get lost in. She buried her face in it. It smelled of soap, shampoo, and Obsession, and made her feel strange—warm and sensual, and tingly in places she had avoided thinking about most of her adult life.

Replacing the robe, Alana stared at the stranger in the mirror.

God! You look like hell!

But at least it was still her face—so far. Before long her lips would become thin and cruel, her eyes narrow and hard, and her cheekbones as sharp as ice picks. And her nose . . . Alana didn't even want to think about what would happen to her nose.

No way! she thought. *No way, you bitch! Not as long as I have an ounce of strength left in my body.*

Luther glanced up as Alana came back into the living room. She had washed her face and combed her hair and looked like a new woman—which under the circumstances was a bit disconcerting.

She's one tough cookie, he thought.

She thanked him for the hot chocolate and resumed her story. He listened with a combination of amazement and concern, stopping her only twice to ask questions. At ten o'clock she sat back, exhausted but relieved to have it all out, and then watched his expression as she waited for him to try and explain it all away. Instead, he surprised her.

"I've had a few rather . . . odd experiences myself the last few days."

He reminded her about the attack on his way home from Cal's, and then told her about the visit by the Skriker.

"That's pretty scary all right," she said. "I hate to sound so self-centered, but other than the obvious tie-in between this . . . what did you call it? Striker?"

"Skriker."

"Right, Skriker. Other than a tie between this dog and the howling around my house, what has it got to do with what's happening to me?"

"Actually, Cal made the connection first."

"Connection?"

"Your mom's boyfriend, Gadarn? That was the name of the Druid god of the underworld and fertility, Hu Gadarn—the horned god."

"You're not serious?"

"Stay with me. I haven't worked everything out yet, but nothing I'm going to tell you is any more bizarre than a woman being taken over by her dead mother."

She had to give him that.

Luther threw another log on the fire. "A lot of what I'm about to say you won't hear anywhere else. I got some of it from these manuscripts—" He waved his hand to indicate the books on the floor. "But I got most of it while I was in Great Britain doing research. Here goes.

"No one really knows where the Druids came from. Most of your tabloid historians portray them a tribe of pre-Christian hippies, brainless flower children who worshiped the sun and moon and earth by dancing around bonfires all night in their birthday suits—that may be cutting it a bit fine, but we don't have all night."

"I do," she said softly.

Luther cleared his throat. "Most real historians believe they were Celts, or Germans or Scandinavians who migrated to Wales and Ireland; a few scholars even believe they were the last descendants of Atlantis. But I believe they were the descendants of a much older race—a people who predated them all—the Tuatha de Danaans."

Alana's face went blank.

"Come on, stay with me. I traced the Tuathas back to another tribe, the Japhet." He saw her look and laughed. "I know, I know. Take it easy. This is where it gets good. Now, the Japhet were a race of incredibly powerful magicians, who reportedly derived their phenomenal supernatural powers from Set, the serpent god that many Biblical scholars believe was the serpent in the Garden of Eden. How's that for going back a way?"

Alana tried to remain silent, but she just couldn't help herself. "First dogs and now snakes? What's next? Juggling bears?"

Luther's stern look gradually softened into a wry smile. "All right, I know how this sounds. But you were raised by nuns, right?"

She nodded.

"Then I'll try a name on you that you have to know—Saint Patrick? Guy moves to Ireland, discovers clover, and drives out all the snakes?"

"The Reader's Digest version, but close enough."

"Well, any archeologist worth his salt will tell you that there is no evidence Ireland ever had any snakes—either before or after Saint Pat. No fossil records, no factual written or oral history. Most of them now agree that the climate was always too cold for reptiles, but that's neither here nor there. The point is, for a place that never had any snakes, Ireland is chock full of serpent myths and symbols. Go to any Irish museum and try to find a piece of ancient jewelry that doesn't have either a snake or a winged dragon, which is basically the same thing."

"The point being?"

"Boy," he grinned. "You're a tough sell."

Her face got red. "Sorry."

"S'okay, I don't mind. The point is, when you put all these facts and legends together, you end up with a pretty good explanation for what really happened—it was the Druids, the snake *worshipers* that Saint Patrick drove out of Ireland!"

Alana blinked. "Well that's—interesting."

"I realize this isn't the way you learned it in Catholic school, but remember . . . the nuns look at things from the standpoint of what's good for religion. I dig through ancient texts and occult manuscripts, which I might add were often written by the greatest minds of their time, and try to piece together what the ancients believed. And more importantly, what they could do with those beliefs. It's sort of like an archeologist trying to piece together the past with a few old bones; sometimes I get T. Rex . . . sometimes the Flintstones."

Alana stared at the flames as she tried to decide if she could actually swallow any of what Luther had said. *He* believed it, that much was certain, and whether she wanted to admit it or not, she was beginning to respect his opinion.

"So how do you know this isn't the Flintstones?"

"I don't. I mean I can't say unequivocally, but Alana, I've studied this stuff for a long time. I've been over there, I've seen the ruins, I've read the manuscripts, I've talked to the people. I spent months in the archives at Cambridge and Ulster and Dublin. I may not be Helena Blavatsky, but I'm the best you got. You have to trust me."

She didn't look convinced.

"I'm not saying I have all the answers. But at least I think I can decipher the questions."

She felt a tinge of guilt, which was odd since this was exactly what she had wanted—he was practically begging to help her. Forget that he didn't have a clue what he was going up against. Forget that she had played him like a prize hundred-pound Marlin. Forget that if he were wrong they would both end up as dead as General Grant—or worse. Forget all of that and just remember— this is what she wanted. So what if she felt a little remorse? If she got out of this mess in one piece she'd get over it. Besides, it wasn't like she had a choice.

"Okay," she said with a sigh. "So what does all this have to do with me?"

"First we have to back up a bit. The Druids were heavy into the concept of immortality—not the Christian version you learned, with its angels, harps, and pearly gates. No, this is what scholars refer to as Pythagorean metempsychosis, where at death the soul migrates into a lower life form, an animal or tree or rock."

"I've known a few people who had the personality of a rock," she muttered.

Luther ignored the interruption. "This belief was the way the Arch-Druids—the high priests—kept their followers in line. The Arch-Druids taught that they could *control* where the soul migrated after death—could actually direct it into another body."

The light bulb suddenly went on over Alana's head. "Oh . . . my . . . God!"

"Exactamundo! But that's not the best part. They even claimed to be able to temporally direct a living person's soul into the body of a lower creature."

"Why on earth would they want to do that?"

"If you were a snake worshiper, what better way to

keep tabs on what the peasants were up to? But don't you get it? Guess what creature the priests most often chose? A large, black dog."

"Oh boy!" Alana sputtered. "Now you're really starting to scare me."

"Once I made the connection between the Skriker, Gadarn, and your mother dying near Salisbury—"

"Why is that important?"

"Don't you know what's near Salisbury? Stonehenge."

"That's right!" Alana whispered. "Mother took me there once when I was little. She was absolutely fascinated with the place, kept running from rock to rock, pressing her cheek against them and crooning like they were children. Their touch seemed to somehow, I don't know, energize her."

"That makes a certain sense if you believe, as the Druids did, that configuring stones in certain ways could focus the power of the cosmos."

"I don't get what you mean."

"It's not that radical an idea. Look at the pyramids of Egypt and Mexico. The ancients thought that by arranging stones in certain ways, they could focus power in much the same way a magnifying glass can focus sunlight into a beam hot enough to start a fire."

"But what was this power?" she asked.

"That would depend on the type of stones and the physical arrangement. I've seen papers by mathematicians on the Stonehenge-Avebury Axis that show how these haphazard-looking circles of rock were laid out in precise geometric patterns that aligned perfectly with specific star constellations. Go figure."

Alana shook her head slowly. "I don't know, Luther. This is too weird even for me. Couldn't Morgana have just hired some old voodoo priestess from New Orleans to stick pins in one of my photographs or something?"

"That's not how it works." Luther put a hand on her arm. Her skin was warm from the fire. "I guess comparative religion wasn't very high on the priority list where you went to school?"

"Boy, you got that right. The nuns paid a lot of lip service to tolerance for other religions but they made no bones about it; if you started acting like you believed in any of them, you were going straight to hell." She laughed softly. "So this thing with the migrating souls, how does it work?"

"Beats me," Luther sighed. "According to the myths, their rites were very secret and were usually held in some kind of cave. There were a lot of references to a tree, usually a gigantic oak, but that's probably an idea one of the scholarly types mooched from the Norse Yggdrasil. They dug some kind of pit at the base of the tree and buried the person to be transmigrated in the fetal position—to signify rebirth, we think."

"Buried? Why?"

"Sorry, don't know. That's the problem with dealing with something that happened so long ago. There's a lot of evidence that the Druids had a vast library of manuscripts on human-skin scrolls, but supposedly Saint Patrick and his followers destroyed them."

Alana's eyes filled with tears again. "But why are they picking on *me*? If Mother was one of these Druids, why can't she just migrate to somebody else?"

Luther moved closer to her. "I hate to keep saying I don't know, but—I don't know."

He pursed his lips and scratched the side of his nose. Alana sensed that his mind was wandering and leaned over and kissed him on the cheek.

"What was that for?"

Ungrateful Dead

She quickly arranged her hair over the scars. "For being my friend. For believing in me."

He bounced to his feet, scooped up the empty cups and took them to the kitchen.

Alana smiled, but quickly covered it up. *My gosh. In his own way he's as neurotic as I am.*

She heard the dishes clatter in the sink. A few minutes later he returned with two glasses, one containing a dry, white wine and the other orange juice. He held out the wine glass to her.

"You don't like wine?" She accepted the glass with a smile.

He sat on the floor a few feet from her and crossed his legs Indian fashion. "I don't drink alcohol."

"Yet you keep it in the house. You must have a lot of . . . guests?"

He knew she was flirting but decided to answer the question seriously. "It's a kind of test. It isn't that big a leap from alcohol to drugs. I look at that bottle every day. If I ever take a drink, I'll know it's the first step on the way down the mountain and reach out to my sponsor."

Staring at his face, Alana thought, *He's trying to push me away. Why?* Then she thought, *I guess we're more alike than I thought.* "So where do we go from here?"

He dragged his backpack across the floor. "I have some printouts a friend got for me—names of recent utility subscribers. It's a pretty extensive list, but I thought maybe you could take them home and see if you recognized any names."

"You think Anton's name could be there?"

"I already looked; it's not. But you might recognize one I wouldn't."

"And if I can't find anyone?"

"I guess we go to plan B."

"Then you'll help me?"

Luther casually averted his eyes. He was afraid if he saw the way the fire animated her tired features, or the way she used her tongue to moisten those full lips, he'd do or say something stupid. Instead he shrugged and grinned.

"Sure, I'll help you."

Anton took the stairs down to the cellar one agonizing step at a time. In one hand he held a Burger King sack, the other he used to steady himself with the handrail. When he reached the bottom, he flipped the hidden switch that ignited the more than two dozen, gas-fed torches set in niches around the room. Instead of dispelling the gloom, the flames added a nice medieval ambience that Anton found comforting. As he waddled across the floor, Grover came out of the first tunnel. The giant bodyguard had on a heavy rubber apron, which was splattered with dried blood, his hair was matted with cobwebs, and in the swamp like air of the cellar his mild face was flushed and dripping sweat.

Grover noted the sack in Anton's hand. "She's going to be very happy to see that."

"In a good mood?"

"Hardly." Grover wrinkled his nose. Anton reeked of the cheap cologne he always doused himself with when he was going to see one of his women.

"Oh my. Well, beggars can't very well be choosers, can they now, boyo?"

It had been raining and sleeting steadily all week, and when Anton stepped through the entrance of the tunnel he could hear the sound of rushing water. The creek was high, unnaturally high, so that even from two hundred yards away its rank, slightly sulfuric odor permeated everything. A few yards in, his foot came down on

Ungrateful Dead

something, and he almost turned his ankle. Pausing, he bent over and squinted like a myopic bat. In the muck was a gray, maggot-infested hand lying half-submerged in a pool of oily water.

"Ach! Grover, what am I going to do with you?"

A few yards more and he arrived at the junction where the tunnel intersected the sewer that, after several more serpentine connections, eventually emptied into Nonconnah Creek. Though foul, the air in the tunnels was several degrees cooler, and the ground was mostly sludge—it reminded him of the bogs of his homeland, and he had to tread lightly to keep his footing. Turning the corner, he stepped up onto a concrete walkway and stopped before the barred door of a shallow cell.

"Hello, me love," Anton said, resting his hands gingerly on the rust-streaked bars. "And how are we today?"

The back of the cell was shrouded in darkness, but Anton, though unable to see, could smell the rank, unwashed body of the woman huddled on the floor against the rear wall.

"I brought you a little present." He wedged the sack between the bars and then reached down and began massaging his right knee. "You know, love, I'm going to have to move you closer to the cellar. This little stroll is murder on me bad knee."

"I want to go home."

"I know, lass," Anton replied with a sigh. "It won't be much longer."

"Why are you doing this to me?"

"It's nothing personal. Do you need anything else?"

"I want to go home!"

Anton rolled his eyes. "Tell you what. I'll send me boy Grover back to keep you company. Now here—" He shook the sack. "Come and get it."

The arm that came out of the darkness was almost too thin and white to belong to anything human. It looked more like part of a Halloween costume. The hand grabbed the sack and tried to snatch it back into the shadows, but the paper ripped and the soggy contents spilled into the mud.

"Oh, too bad." Anton snickered. "Better hurry before the rats beat you to it."

Pale, naked, her body covered with sores and filth, the woman scrambled forward on her hands and knees like an animal and began tearing at the sandwich wrappings with her teeth. Her face was hidden behind a mass of stringy blond hair, but Anton could feel her eyes on him and he shook his head sadly. She had really been something.

He retraced his steps down the long tunnel, arriving at the cellar just as Grover hung the rubber apron on a hook near the stairway.

"Ho there, Grover me boy. Don't be puttin' that away just yet. I want you to go back and keep her company."

Grover's face screwed up like he'd just bitten into a lemon. "Aw, boss . . . do I have to?"

Anton walked up to the giant and smiled up into his broad face like a child. "Now if it was you all alone like that—like in the hospital or something—wouldn't you be wantin' a friend to come stay by your side?"

Grover rolled his eyes. "I guess so." He took the apron down and put it back on. "It's just so fucking hot down here."

"I know. Think how she feels." He shifted his gaze to the huge oak tree and pursed his lips as he contemplated the oversized acorns dangling like Christmas ornaments from its limbs. "When she's done, call me. I think we can finish with her tonight."

The big man dropped his eyes.

Ungrateful Dead

"And Grover—" Anton crooked his finger.

Grover bent over.

Anton dug his stubby fingers into the soft flesh of the big man's throat and, with extraordinary strength for someone his size, pulled him down until their noses almost touched. "Get that hand out of there and don't ever let me find body parts lying around like that! Do we understand each other, mate?"

Grover croaked like a frog.

"Good." Anton relaxed his grip, and Grover snapped upright. "Now where's me boy, Danny?"

Grover tried to rub away the marks on his neck. "Upstairs watching TV."

"Tisk, tisk! The boy's mind is going to turn to mush. Why hasn't he left to watch the colleen?"

"Colin called in. She's still over at the hippie's."

Anton paused with one foot on the bottom step. "Our friend the professor tasks me. We really should do something about him."

"Hey," Grover sputtered, "don't blame that on me. Colin's the one let him get away—twice."

Nodding, Anton replied, "Everybody is entitled to a mistake. We're just going to have to do better. Now, I'm off to see what me dark-haired darlin' is up to."

Anton waved and began trudging up the stairs. Half way to the top, he started whistling an off-key version of "Danny Boy."

By Friday evening Cal was ready to find himself an AK-47 and visit the local post office. Over the previous five days, he'd had arguments with four patients, his secretary, his accountant, his wife, and the man who serviced the fish tanks. After fighting traffic all the way home, he had to park in the driveway because the battery in his garage-door opener was dead, and when he went inside the house, he found his daughter lying facedown on the living room couch crying her eyes out. When he asked what was wrong, she replied, "I hate your wife!" When he asked where Rachel was, the girl said, "I don't know, and I don't care." And when he tried to find out what they had been fighting about, all Sam would say was, "You couldn't possibly understand."

Having a verified I.Q. of 161, Cal knew there was a time for reason and a time for Johnny Walker Red. He went into the kitchen, got the bottle down from the cabinet, and poured two fingers into a tall glass. After staring at the liquid for a moment, he added another inch and then downed the whole thing in two gulps. He was contemplating pouring another when the kitchen door opened and Marino trotted in wagging his carrot-shaped tail.

"Thank God!" said Cal. "Someone is actually glad to see me."

He got a Milk Bone from the drawer next to the refrigerator, squatted on his heels, and fed it to the happy terrier.

"Good boy. You want a shot of this?" Cal brandished the empty glass.

The front door slammed, and a moment later Rachel stormed into the kitchen. "Oh! Hi."

Marino ran to greet her wagging his tail.

"Get away from me!" she snapped.

The dog stopped and his tail dropped between his legs.

"Look," Cal said, "I don't know what went on between you and Sam, but don't take it out on the damned dog."

Rachel had been carrying her tennis bag over her shoulder, and she yanked it down and threw it at Marino.

Ungrateful Dead

The bag didn't land anywhere near the dog, but he yelped and ran under the kitchen table.

"Sam's a spoiled little bitch!" Rachel screamed. "And that mutt is nothing but a walking bag of fleas!"

Cal set the glass on the sink and went to his wife. She started to leave, but he laid his hand on her shoulder.

"Jesus, Rach, what's gotten into you?"

It must have been the wrong thing to say, for her body sagged against him, and she started sobbing as if her heart were breaking in two.

"There, there. Nothing is that bad." He eased his hand under her chin and tilted her head up. Her face was pale underneath the tennis tan, and her eyes were glassy. If he hadn't known better, he would have sworn she was on something.

"Oh, Cal!" she blubbered. "I'm so sorry."

"Hey, now," he crooned, "it's no big deal."

"No! You don't know what I've done. You'll never forgive me!"

"Nothing you could do will ever change the way I feel about you."

"But you don't know! I've—"

All at once Marino let out an ear-splitting screech and began running around in a circle.

"What now!" Cal exclaimed.

The dog went round and round so fast he looked like a small white Frisbee, and he kept spinning until he crashed into the table leg and fell over on his side. Cal dropped to his knees and slipped his hands up under the dog's head.

"Come on, Buddy. What's wrong? Come on, boy." The dog was completely limp, but his small chest was rising and falling. "Come on, Marino, open your eyes for old Cal."

The dog's pink tongue popped out, and a moment later he opened his eyes.

"What a good little guy." Cal grinned.

Then Marino bared his teeth and went for Cal's throat.

Chapter Seven

Alana picked up Luther at his house at seven o'clock the next morning to drive him to Cal's. The storm clouds from the previous night had moved off to the east, freeing the sun from its long gray captivity for what seemed like the first time in months. The sky was robin-egg blue, with tiny wisps of clouds that clung to the horizon like campfire smoke, and the air was crisp and just cool enough to make breathing fun.

"You got everything?" Alana asked as she backed out of the driveway.

Luther slapped his backpack. "I hope I'm not wasting our time."

"You don't think he'll believe us?"

Luther shrugged. "If our places were reversed, I wouldn't believe us."

Cal opened the door in his Dolphins bathrobe. His

eyes looked like red olives, his hair was all over the place, and he had a two-inch square piece of gauze on his neck.

"Stand too near your razor?" Luther asked.

Cal yawned. "I don't mean to be impolite but—what do you want?"

"Maybe we should come back later," Alana suggested.

Luther pushed past Cal and walked into the living room. "Ignore him. This is his good mood. You should see him when he's grumpy. He sauntered across the living room and made a beeline for the guest bedroom.

"Don't go in there!" Cal barked.

"I need the jeans I left over here the last time I—" Luther opened the door.

Rachel was curled up in the middle of the bed, snoring like a goat eating glass. Luther glanced at Cal and pulled the door shut.

"Sorry."

They followed Cal into the kitchen, where he stumbled to the counter to turn on the coffeemaker, then went to the cabinet and took down three glasses. After setting them on the kitchen table, he went to the refrigerator and brought back an unopened carton of orange juice, sat down in the chair next to the window, and put his head in his hands.

Luther glanced at Alana and then sat down next to his friend. Alana waited a few seconds and joined them at the table.

Cal raised his head and sighed. "Nobody died. You can relax."

Marino padded into the kitchen with his tail tucked so far up between his legs it looked like it had been amputated. He slunk over to the corner and sat down next to his food bowl.

Ungrateful Dead

"Jesus," Luther whispered. "What happened here?"

"You don't have to whisper," Cal said. "Rachel can sleep through an air raid."

"Okay," Luther said using a more normal tone. "So what happened?"

"I don't suppose telling you to mind your own business would do any good?"

"Of course not."

Cal got up and poured himself a cup of coffee, then returned to the table with the cup and a bag of day-old bagels. "Here, eat."

He sat back down and then told them everything that had happened the previous evening, leaving out a few of the more choice names his wife had called him.

"So enough of my problems," he said. "What brings you two out this time of the morning?"

Luther shook his head. "That's so unlike Rachel—"

"Okay! Enough, already."

Luther pulled a stack of yellowed papers and books from his backpack.

"What's all this?"

"Support."

Like most scientists, Cal resisted new ideas like the plague—especially an idea that didn't come from the accepted texts. However, Luther had come prepared for this. He was patient, spoke slowly, and referred often to his manuscripts and books. At 11:30, Cal got up and poured the last of the coffee into his cup. From his expression, it appeared that Luther's carefully constructed chain of logic was beginning to wear away at his patina of skepticism. He was still far from convinced, but at least he wasn't laughing anymore.

"I don't know," Cal muttered.

"What's it going to take?" Luther sighed. "This

135

thing to land on your head like a water balloon full of sewage?"

Cal shook his head as if trying to rid himself of a pesky mosquito. "A phantom dog—" He glanced at Marino. "Jeez. I just don't know."

Luther threw up his hands. "I give up!"

"I said I'd help a week ago. But it may take a while for me to swallow all this." He saw Alana's expression and added, "Don't get me wrong, Alana. I'm not saying somebody—this guy Gadarn for example—isn't running a game on you. But it's just got to be some kind of scam. He's after something, and when we figure out what it is, we'll know what to do."

"What about the dog that attacked me?" Luther asked.

Cal smiled for the first time in over an hour. "Lute, you're such a dork. Don't you know anything about how these guys operate? Gadarn obviously did some digging into your background and probably found out what happened to you in England. You never heard of a trained dog? The man's just rattling your cage."

Luther sat back in the chair and placed his hands flat on the table. "Man, I wish I had a stack of bills in my wallet as thick as your skull."

"Let it go, Luther," said Alana. "Let's just be thankful for his help."

"I am. I really am. I'm just afraid of what's going to happen if knucklehead here goes off with that attitude. Even if he's right, these people play rough."

"Hmph! I can take care of myself."

"Yeah, right. You can't even protect yourself from a little dog."

Cal frowned, and Marino picked up his ears.

* * *

Ungrateful Dead

Sam spent Saturday afternoon strolling through the Hickory Ridge Mall and listening to her best friend, Malina Marks, babble nonstop about her family's upcoming trip to Boca Raton. Malina talked all the way through The Gap, Goldsmith's, the 5, 7, 9 Shop, and The Limited. When she finally stopped to shove a chocolate chip cookie in her mouth at the food court, Sam muttered, "I hate my mom."

"Your mom? Oh my God! She's so cool. How could you hate her?"

"She used to be; but she's gone totally anal on me."

"Maybe she's going through the change."

"Maybe. She never gives me a break about anything."

Malina grabbed Sam's hand and whispered, "Is that Billy Anderson over there? He's soooo coo—"

"Are you listening to me?" Sam snapped.

"Hoo! What flew up your nose?"

"No, that's not Billy. And I was trying to tell you, Mother treats me like such a *child*!"

"You? My mother still won't buy me a bra. That's anal for you."

Sam cast a critical eye at the smooth front of her friend's gray flannel turtleneck.

Like you need one!

"She's been so bitchy lately," Sam added.

"She's probably feeling her age. How old is she anyway—40?"

"At least. But it has to be more than that! I mean, honestly," Sam lowered her voice to a whisper. "She acts like she needs to get laid!"

A hand came out of nowhere and touched Sam on the arm. She jumped, knocking over her diet soda; luckily, the plastic top remained in place.

"Ho, there darlin'! I didn't mean to give you a start."

Gary L. Holleman

The girls looked at each other and giggled. The stranger was gorgeous! Dark wavy hair, high cheekbones and full lips, and the greenest eyes Sam had ever seen. He spoke with a heavy brogue, and when he smiled, his teeth were dazzling.

"No, it's okay," Sam said.

Malina leaned across the table. "Well, *hello!*"

The man flashed his teeth again. "I was wonderin' if you lasses would mind if I sat with you for a spell?"

He was dressed in a conservative black pinstripe suit and red-and-black club tie. Sam thought he looked okay, but—

"Of course!" said Malina.

The man pulled up a chair and leveled the full force of his charm on Sam. "Me name's Danny. I work for the jewelry store here in the mall and we're having this special promotion see, a giveaway. All you have to do is wear a piece of our jewelry and if anyone asks, tell 'em your friend Danny down at the mall designed it just for you."

"Ooooo," Malina gushed. "Rad."

Danny glanced at Sam's friend. "Sorry, darlin', only one left." He held his right hand out, palm down. "Watch! Magic!"

A gold locket dropped from the man's fist, swinging back and forth on a delicate gold chain. It gleamed like a new twenty-dollar gold piece, but its surface was marred by an odd assortment of foreign letters and designs.

"Oh, wow!" Malina moaned. "Can I see it?"

The smile never left Danny's face, but his voice was a shade less cordial. "I told you dearie, it's for her!"

Malina sat back in her chair and folded her arms.

"What's inside?" Sam asked.

"Not a blessed thing."

Ungrateful Dead

"Then I can put a picture in it?"

"Bless your heart, no. It doesn't open. See—no clasp."

"What good is it then?" said Malina. "A locket that doesn't open?"

"Sure, it's a promotion! If it was a real locket, we wouldn't be giving it away, now would we?"

"I guess that makes sense," Sam said slowly. "Well, thank you anyway, but I'm not allowed to accept gifts from strangers."

"Sam!" Malina groaned.

"You do everything that gorgeous mother of yours tells you to?"

"How do you know my mother is gorgeous?"

"Sure now, and with you for a daughter, what else could she be?"

Sam blushed and Malina giggled.

Walking around behind her chair, Danny said, "Here now, let me put it on you." He draped the necklace around her neck so that the locket rested between her breasts. As he fastened the catch, his fingers lingered on the back of her neck, bringing the short hairs to full, vigorous attention.

"There now," he bent over and whispered in her ear. "Doesn't that look grand?"

Sam wasn't so sure. The man's hot breath on her ear made her feel dizzy.

"We have to be going, Sam!" Malina said peevishly. "All the sale stuff will be gone."

Still bent over her neck, Danny stroked the skin underneath Sam's hair. "Don't you go forgettin' me now," he whispered. "I won't be forgettin' you."

He straightened up and, with a chipper smile and a wave, sauntered across the food court and vanished into the crowd.

Sam watched him go, but didn't return the wave. She looked up and saw Malina standing over her. Her friend's lips were moving, but it took all of her concentration to make out what the girl was saying.

"What's wrong with you? You act like you never spoke to a man before. He wasn't all *that* cute."

Malina went behind Sam's chair. "Can I see it?" She unfastened the necklace's clasp before Sam could respond.

Sam blinked once, twice, and then gazed at the tables around her as if she had never seen them before.

"You're sure acting weird," Malina sniped. "If this old thing makes you goofy, you ought to let me have it."

"What?" Sam squinted at the locket. The harsh fluorescent lights made her head hurt. "Yeah, okay. Keep it."

"You mean it?" Malina squealed. "Oh, you're just the best friend. I really mean it. I'm going to bring you back the best T-shirt from Boca, something with beach boys all over it."

"Yeah, fine. Look Mal, I gotta be going."

"Oh no," her friend whined. "Come on, we still haven't been to Dillard's."

"I don't feel like it," Sam replied. "If you want a ride, come on."

Malina's tone cooled considerably. "Go on, then. I'll call Mama when I'm finished."

Sam felt guilty. "Come on, Mal. I just don't feel well."

"You getting your period?"

A grin tugged at the corners of Sam's mouth. "In spite of what your mom tells your dad, women *do* feel bad for other reasons."

Malina giggled. "Works for her." She began count-

Ungrateful Dead

ing on her fingers. "Fur coat, new Miata, new microwave. Hey, why mess with success?"

Sam hugged her friend, and when they broke, an unaccustomed frown clouded Malina's face. "You do feel sort of warm. Go on. I'll call you tomorrow."

When Sam reached the other side of the food court, she looked back. Malina was flirting with the busboy who had come to clean the table.

"Oh, Mal," Sam sighed and then she headed for the exit.

As soon as the busboy departed with the trays, Malina held up the locket and debated whether or not to put it on. To do so with the turtleneck would be a hassle, so she decided to wait until she got home and tucked it away in the zippered compartment inside her handbag. As she made her way toward the Dillard's wing of the mall, her mind was already busy concocting the story she would tell her friends—how the handsome young Irish guy had picked her out of all the girls in the mall to give the gold locket to.

Rachel crawled out of bed sometime after noon and, after searching the house to make sure Cal was gone, she went into her bathroom and slipped out of her robe in front of the mirror. Her breasts and belly were striped with black-and-blue marks and there were scratches—claw marks would be a better description, on both nipples. She ran to the toilet and threw up.

"God, oh God. What have I done?"

She threw up again and then climbed slowly to her feet and went to the sink and ran a damp washcloth over her face. As she was brushing her teeth, a droplet of blood trickled from her left nostril and fell into the sink. Bemused by the red splotch staining her pristine white porcelain, she peered at it as if it were some kind of test—like a Rorschach test, and she was supposed to find the hidden meaning in the design. Nothing came to mind. Curious, she probed the nostril gently with her finger, expecting to find a small cut or possibly a clot, anything but what she felt.

Something moved!

The telephone in the bedroom rang and Rachel froze.

The phone rang again and again; eight—ten—twenty times. When it finally fell silent, the relief she felt made her knees weak. She took down a bottle of antacid from the medicine cabinet, unscrewed the cap, and downed half of its contents—it didn't help. Her stomach still felt like a clenched fist. She thought about taking a shower, but even that seemed like too much trouble. She glanced at the sink again. What had she been doing?

As she staggered back into the bedroom, the phone started ringing again, and she stood in the center of the floor and clapped her hands over her ears—nothing helped. Each ring reverberated like the bells of Notre Dame inside her head. She kept expecting—praying—that each ring would be the last, but it went on and on.

Finally, Rachel could stand it no more, and she picked up the handset.

"Hello?"

As she listened, all the life drained from her features.

"I told you, no!" she hissed.

Then the voice said the seven words that put an end to her budding rebelliousness: "Do you know where your daughter is?"

Sam stood on her tiptoes at the edge of the parking lot, trying to pick out her Honda's rust-pitted roof from a veritable sea of cars. The lot, packed with after-school cars, was steeped in long shadows that made spotting anything difficult. Sighing, she glanced at her watch. It

Ungrateful Dead

was almost dinnertime and, since she was still slightly muddle-headed from whatever had happened to her in the mall and, as usual, couldn't remember where she had parked, she decided a nice stroll up and down the rows would do her good.

The wind was brutal, which helped clear her head, but it also sliced right through her leather bomber jacket like a knife and made her ears and nose feel like raw meat. Forgetting the fashion police, Sam piled her hair up on top of her head and pulled her sporty red beret down tight around her ears. She was in the middle of the third row of cars when she noticed the dark green van cruising slowly up and down the aisles. Cold as she was, she didn't pay it any mind until it passed up three perfectly good parking spots and turned into her row.

Car thieves, she decided, looking for an easy mark. So she did what most city dwellers do in similar situations: she put her head down and kept right on walking. Besides, it wasn't as if they would be interested in her nine-year-old Honda. In fact, she *wished* they would snatch the rusty piece of junk so she could get a decent car; she just didn't want to get hit in the head for being in the wrong place at the wrong time.

She moved closer to the cars to give the van plenty of room to pass, but when it pulled even with her, it slowed to a crawl, and in spite of knowing better, she glanced up.

The van's passenger window was down, and the driver was grinning at her. One look at the man's green teeth and scraggly beard, and Sam picked up her pace.

She reached the end of the row and there was her faithful old rust-bucket hidden behind a pickup truck with a mud-splattered camper on the back. Breathing a huge sigh of relief, she jumped in, locked both doors, and shoved the key into the ignition. Once the engine turned over, she had to wait for it to warm up, or risk blowing a gasket, and she felt safe enough to scan the lot. When she didn't see the green van, she relaxed.

It was funny, she thought. Now that the van was gone, she couldn't say why it had upset her in the first place. It wasn't as if she had never been leered at before. Maybe it was what she had seen in the man's eyes. They were hungry. She had seen eyes like that in some of the big cats at the zoo.

The needle on the temperature gauge took forever to move, and by the time it did, the windows were fogged, thanks to her heavy breathing, and she had to wait some more for the defroster to do its thing. As soon as the front window was clear, she shifted into reverse and glanced in the side mirror.

The van was right behind her.

Sam laid on the horn, forgetting it hadn't worked in two years. In a panic, she looked wildly around the interior for something to use as a weapon, but her choices came down to a tiny but stylish leather purse or the shopping bag containing her new, cashmere sweater. Her eyes darted back to the side mirror. The van hadn't moved, but the driver was now sitting in the passenger seat, staring at her reflection in the mirror. He had this ... stick in his hand. That's what it looked like, a gnarled, corkscrew-shaped stick! And he was pointing it at her like a gun.

That settles it, she thought. The geek was obviously nuts, and if he got out she was going to pop the clutch and try to pin him against the side of his van. Even if it didn't kill him, it would maybe buy her enough time to get out and run like hell into the mall.

But the man seemed perfectly happy where he was. He waved the stick at her a few more times and then,

Ungrateful Dead

with a confused shake of his head, he climbed back behind the wheel and drove off.

Sam backed out and drove home at warp speed. She didn't care if she got a ticket; she didn't care if she had a wreck. Hell, she'd gladly have thrown herself at the feet of the first cop she saw. At home, she parked on the street, so the rust stains that collected under her car wouldn't stain the driveway, and then ran to the front door. When she walked into the living room, Rachel practically pounced on her; hugging her and crying, laughing and screaming—all at the same time.

"Where have you been?" Rachel demanded.

"Jeez, Mom, chill out. I was shopping with Mal."

"Why didn't you tell me where you were going?"

"Duh! Hello! You were asleep, remember?"

"Don't you dare take that tone with me, young lady!" Rachel screamed.

Sam was sure her mother was going to slap her; instead Rachel wrapped her in her arms and started bawling again.

Postal, Sam thought. *No doubt about it.*

Malina purchased two pairs of hip-hugging jeans and a knit top from the sale rack at Dillard's, and then stopped at the Bath Shoppe to pick up two bottles of her favorite bubble bath. The early-evening rush was in full bloom, and the sudden crush of bodies made it difficult to breathe. She decided to give her dad's credit card a rest and called her mother from the pay phone next to the exit, then went outside to wait at the curb. Her mom was only five minutes away.

Two minutes in the icy air and she was feeling better. After that, the wind lost its charm and she started tapping her foot and glancing at her watch. Figuring that her mother must have stopped at the grocery to pick up something for dinner, Mal was just about to go back inside when a dark green van rolled up and stopped directly in front of her.

Well! she fumed. *The absolute nerve of some people.* Probably from Mississippi, she decided.

Malina was just about to tap on the man's window—it just *had* to be a man, and explain to him he was sitting in a no-parking zone, when the side door slid open, two men jumped out, picked her up, and dragged her into the van. Malina was so amazed that anyone would touch her that she forgot to scream.

The van pulled away from the curb. On the rear bumper was a sticker that read KISS ME I'M IRISH.

Two minutes later, Mrs. Marks drove up and stopped in the no-parking zone. She drummed her fingers on the steering wheel for five minutes and then, with a sigh that could have filled the Hindenburg, she set the hand brake, locked the door, and stormed into the mall to find her thoughtless daughter. Mrs. Marks wasn't worried about her car being towed. Her husband, Mr. Marks, was a well-known Germantown attorney, and no one in their right mind would *dare* tow one of his cars.

It was fortunate that the University of Miami's football team had a bye week that Saturday. Otherwise, there was no way Cal would ever have agreed to go with Luther and Alana to talk to Tru Connely, who, more than likely, was the only man in the entire mid-South who didn't give a hoot who was playing football on any Saturday. They piled into Cal's car and drove to Tru's house, a large, Tudor-style home in a quiet, tree-lined residential neighborhood near the campus. When they started out, the sun was high in a cloudless sky, and the streets were crowded with shoppers anxious to avoid the last-minute Christmas rush. But as they turned onto Tru's block, banks of black clouds were massing over the Mississippi River, and the temperature had dropped at least ten degrees.

Virginia, Tru's wife of twenty-two years, opened the door. She was a very pretty and exceedingly proper lady in her early sixties who walked with a slight stoop from a mild case of osteoporosis. After letting them in, she pointed toward the library.

"Go on back," she said. "But make some noise. Truman hates when people catch him napping."

They found Tru behind his desk, feet up, glass of port at his elbow, eyeglasses perched on the tip of his nose, reading a book on the history of the Ottoman Empire.

"What's this?" Tru asked, peering over the top of the book. "I forget a faculty meeting again?"

Luther introduced Alana, and then Virginia came in and offered everyone tea. Cal accepted for the group, and she went off to the kitchen.

"Move those books out of the way," Tru said, nodding toward the wingback chairs set in a semicircle around his desk.

Alana complimented Tru on the library, a large room with tall windows and dark mahogany bookcases, furnished with aromatic leather chairs and couches. The floor, which was hardwood and highly polished, was softened here and there with area rugs and pedestals topped with hand-carved statues of African gods. The walls were adorned with war shields made of rhinoceros hide, and crossed war clubs hung like coats of arms in an English manor. In the corners, tall, glass display cases showed off the collection of occult artifacts, which Tru had brought back from all over the world.

"You're interested in the supernatural, too?" Alana asked.

"Criminology is his specialty," Luther said. "The occult is his hobby."

Truman shrugged and grinned at Luther. "You travel, you pick up junk. It's one of the things Luther and I have in common."

"And why I have a job," Luther added with a chuckle.

Virginia returned with a tray of tea, four cups, and a plate of homemade sugar cookies. After setting the tray on the coffee table, she asked them to please excuse her, she had to get back to her football game.

"The Tigers are playing Ole Miss," she explained. "Somebody in this house has to root for the home boys."

Alana offered to pour, and once everyone had been served Tru said, "Okay, I can't stand the suspense any longer. Anytime I see you two together—" He inclined his head toward Cal and Luther. "It means trouble for someone."

Cal and Luther glanced at each other to see who would go first. Luther started, explaining how Alana had come seeking his help to locate a lost relative. And how the printouts that Tru had secured for them had helped, but for some reason her relative must have used someone else's name when he arranged for utilities. And was there any way, please, for one of Tru's friends in the financial community to trace any funds transfers originating in Great Britain or Paris in the last four months?

Tru listened politely while sipping his tea. Every now and then he reached over and plucked one of his wife's cookies from the tray and popped it into his mouth. When Luther was done, he brushed the crumbs from his shirt. "Finished?"

Luther nodded.

Ungrateful Dead

Turning to Cal, Tru said, "Where do you fit into this, uh, this quest?"

Cal cut his eye to Luther and then explained that he had come along to lend moral support during Alana's period of emotional crisis.

"Uh huh," said Tru. He then turned his thoughtful brown eyes on Alana, peering at her in silence for several moments. "I can see you're under quite a bit of emotional strain," he said at last. "But as for that story—" He rolled his eyes at Luther. "That is absolutely the sorriest tale I've heard since the dog ate my homework."

Luther pursed his lips thoughtfully. "Which part didn't you believe?"

"Everything after, 'good afternoon.' "

"Okay, you win. I'm sorry we lied to you."

"You're sorry you got caught."

"Will you at least take my word that we need that information? And that we were trying to keep you out of it as much as possible for your own safety?"

Tru licked a cookie crumb from his thumbnail. "Since the young lady came to you, may I assume this has something to do with your area of expertise?"

"You may, Dr. Connely."

"Then may I also assume, from what you just said, that you believe this situation, whatever it may be, could get . . . hairy?"

"As a woolly mammoth."

"That hairy, huh?"

"As a French madam's underarms. As a werewolf on Rogaine. As a—"

"Enough! Enough." Tru laughed aloud. "I get the picture, disgustingly graphic as it was. Just promise me two things. One, it's not illegal—" Cal and Luther crossed their hearts. "And two, that you'll tell me all about it when it's over."

"You got it," Luther promised.

"Okay. I know a couple of people. But I can't do anything until Monday." He saw their expressions. "Better than that I couldn't do for little Billy Clinton from over across the bridge in Hope, Arkansas."

"You'll let me know?"

"The moment I get anything."

"Thanks."

The trio rose and shook hands with Tru. When it was Alana's turn he grasped her hand in both of his and held on. "Luther, you and Cal wait outside in the corridor. I want to speak to the young lady.

"You watch yourself around those two," he told Alana when they were alone. "They get on the trail of something, they just might run over you."

"I will," she promised.

"I don't know how well you know Luther. He's a good man. But he's got something dark bottled up inside and quite frankly, sometimes I worry about him."

"Don't we all have something dark inside, Doctor Connely?"

Anton stopped beside the table his associates had erected in the basement near the base of the huge wooden temple. Grover stopped two paces behind him, folded his arms, and waited. On the other side of the table, Colin O'Dwyer, the man with the beard and bad teeth, and Wardley Morrow, a short, barrel-chested man whose massive arms were covered with tattoos of naked women, also waited. Spread-eagled on the table was a rather flat-chested young girl with long dark hair and muddy-brown eyes. Her hands and feet were bound with thick twine, and a shop towel the men found in the glove

Ungrateful Dead

compartment of the van was shoved in her mouth. When Anton suddenly appeared out of the dark, the girl's eyes went wide, and she began struggling against the ropes.

"Holy Mary! She must get her looks from her father," said Anton. The girl flopped around on the table like a tuna on the deck of a fishing boat. "Sure now, she moves like her Mama. Take the gag out."

Grover stepped to the table and removed the towel.

"Hush now, darlin'," Anton crooned. "I know you got a million questions."

"You're damned right," the girl exploded. "How dare you kidnap me! Do you have any idea who my father is?"

Anton turned to Grover. "Put the gag back."

"You asshole!"

Grover slapped the gag in place and stepped back.

"That's better. Now Samantha, I'm a friend of your mother's."

The girl's eyes bugged out, and she started gnawing at the towel like a rabid beaver.

"Hoo now," Anton said with a chuckle. "Spirited lass, ain't she?"

The two men on the other side of the table laughed lewdly; Grover merely grunted.

"As I was sayin', me and your mum are chums—real good chums." Anton rested his pudgy hand on the girl's belly and rubbed it in a circle. She abruptly stopped struggling and lay as still as a corpse. "The reason I invited you here is that your mum and me have had ourselves a bit of a tiff. I asked her to do something—me being a friend 'n all, and she refused.

"Now what's going to happen is, I'm about to go upstairs and give her another call. This time I think she'll see things my way. If she does, we'll put the blindfold back on, and me boys here will take you back where they got you. If not—well, I was thinkin' about having a go at you, but you're such a skinny little wench, I think I'll just give you as a present to the boys."

The girl's eyes darted to the two men, who grinned and started slapping and punching each other. She shook her head slowly from side to side.

"Now, now. Don't be frettin' yourself. I'm sure your mum will be reasonable."

Anton's monologue was interrupted by the staccato tap of feet galloping down the stairs. "Ah there, if it isn't Danny-o. You remember Danny, don't you Samantha?"

Danny Keats, the fake jewelry salesman, sauntered up to the table with a grin as wide as the Grand Canyon plastered across his handsome face. When he saw the girl, the smile faltered and then died.

"That ain't her!" he barked.

The veneer of good cheer vanished, and Anton practically ripped the gag from the girl's mouth.

"Who the devil are you?"

"That's what I was trying to tell you, you moronic midget. I'm not Sam!"

Anton cracked Malina across the mouth. "Shut the fuck up, you skinny cunt!" He turned on the two men. "You're going to pay for this! Trust me!"

"Boss, wait!" Colin gasped. He grabbed Malina's purse. "Wait!"

While Colin was frantically tearing apart the purse, Wardley started waving the corkscrew-shaped stick in the air like a magic wand. "We used it right, boss. Honest!"

"Here it is!" Colin held up the gold locket.

Anton fixed his icy gaze on Danny Keats.

"I did my part," Danny said calmly. "I gave it to the girl and then split, just like you told me to."

Ungrateful Dead

"I didn't want nobody to see you walkin' out with her, you dunce. I didn't mean you couldn't make sure these two twits snatched the right girl!"

"But Samantha had the Pitag," Danny insisted. "I put it on her my very own self."

Anton looked at Colin.

"Wardley used the gwrack just the way you said." He snatched the stick from his companion and shook it in the air. "It took us right to this one."

Anton sighed. "What a balls-up." He stared at Malina. "So lass, how did you end up with the Pitag?"

"I—I don't know what that is." The false bravado was gone from her voice.

"The necklace, girlie! How did you end up with the necklace?"

"Oh. Sam gave it to me."

"Impossible. Once it's on, she can't take it off."

"Well, I helped her—a little."

"You mean you took it off a her your own self!" Anton tilted his head back and stared up into the dark, his body vibrating like a high tension wire in a strong wind. When he looked down, the jocund mask was back in place. "Well, too bad for you."

"May I go home now—please! I won't say anything to anybody—I promise. And—and my daddy will give you anything you want! Anything!"

Anton's expression was genuinely sad. "Sorry, lass. Daddy doesn't have what I want. Now all the king's horses and all the king's men won't be able to put the little girlie together again." He glanced at Colin and Wardley. "Call me when you're through." He then turned to Danny Keats. "You come with me."

With Danny and Grover in his wake, Anton slowly mounted the stairs. When they reached the landing at the top, Grover paused and looked back. At first his eyes widened and then the blood drained from his face, and he shivered. Eyes down, he turned and walked into the house and closed the door.

"This is really getting depressing," Alana said as the rain began to pound against the windshield. She switched on the wipers and headlights. "Why don't you own a car?"

"What for? They're expensive, they cost a fortune to run, they stink, and more people are killed in them every year than die from heart disease."

"That's only because more people don't ride bikes."

"You ever ride a bike?" he asked. "I mean since you were twelve."

"I've never ridden a bike, period," she replied.

"You're kidding! Never?"

"Mother said I'd break something."

"You want to learn?"

"Why? What's the big deal?"

Luther launched into a twenty-minute soliloquy on the joys of the open road and lactic acid burn. Alana paid little attention to what he said and a lot to how he said it, glancing at his face whenever traffic allowed. She was amazed at the way it lit up, and his hands flew around when he was trying to drive home a point.

What must it be like, she wondered *to feel such passion?*

She was amazed to discover that she liked talking to him and, if the truth be told, liked being with him, too. When he paused for a breath, she asked "How come you never talk about your family?"

It took a moment for Luther to mentally shift gears. "My family? My family was so normal they would bore you to tears."

"Are they still around?"

Ungrateful Dead

"No."

"No brothers? No sisters? Nephews? Nieces? Aunts? Uncles?"

"Nope."

She glanced at his face. His expression was completely neutral.

He's lying, she thought.

"All right, then tell me how you became interested in the supernatural."

"Oh, the usual reasons. I read a lot of science fiction as a kid. Later I moved on to horror. I went to all the scary movies, and Halloween was my favorite holiday."

Alana braked at a stoplight. "I can understand your not wanting to talk to a stranger about your family. But what's the big secret about why you decided to study such an oddball subject? Is it just me? Or do you treat everyone like they're from the CIA?"

She turned and looked at him. Luther was carefully studying the bumper sticker on the truck in front of them. "Light's green."

The truck pulled away, but Alana didn't move. The car behind them honked its horn.

"The light is green."

Alana turned off the engine and switched on the emergency flashers.

The guy behind them pulled around and, as he passed, saluted Alana with his middle finger.

"What's the matter with you?" Luther asked.

"What's the matter with *me*? I may be losing my mind. What's *your* excuse? You might as well know right now, I can be just as bull-headed as anybody. You keep treating me like the dim-witted cousin and we can just sit right here till hell freezes over—which," she added as buckshot-sized sleet began to pepper the windshield, "in this fucking weather, should be in about an hour!"

The street was starting to sound like Wall Street at rush hour: horns blaring, lights flashing, and passing drivers lashing the Z with curses and death-glares. Luther sank down in the seat until his eyes were level with the dashboard.

"Okay, you win. May we go now, please?"

Alana fired up the engine and, with a merry wave to the cars behind her, shot through the intersection.

When they reached his house, Luther started a fire and put the kettle on to boil. Alana slipped off her coat and grabbed a seat by the fire. The humidity was doing weird things to her hair, and her arms were paved with goose bumps. The weather was having its way with her clothing too, the dampness molding her green silk blouse to her body like wet tissue paper. When Luther returned and handed her the cup of tea, his eyes dipped to the cleft between her breasts, and he noticed for the first time how deep the valley was.

He sat down in his recliner, leaned back, and sipped his tea.

"So what's the big mystery?" Alana asked.

The wind moaned around the house, rattling the window panes. The fire popped, and rain and sleet tapped on the front door with their icy fingers.

"No big mystery. I had an older sister, Janice, who was, I guess you could say, something of a free spirit. When she was fifteen she started reading books on witchcraft and demonology. Not long after that, she cut her hair short and wouldn't date. Naturally, my mom and dad thought she had lost her mind. You have to remember, this was the late fifties and early sixties, and back then people weren't quite as open minded as they are today."

Ungrateful Dead

"Really?"

"Relatively speaking. Anyway, Jan was getting so much crap from everyone—our parents, the school, our priest, that she finally ran off to San Francisco and fell in with this cult who spent most of their time getting high and making love—"

"Was she happy?"

Luther looked surprised at the question. "I don't recall Jan ever being happy. She wrote me—several times. But she never said anything about being happy or unhappy just all this strange stuff about the powers of the universe, signs of the zodiac—coffee house crap like that. I guess she was pretty heavy into drugs too—she died of an overdose."

Luther put his cup down, got up and put another log on the fire and then stood there for a moment savoring the warmth. He glanced at Alana to see how she was taking his tale of woe, and she turned and tilted her head so she could see him. Was it his imagination, or were her scars better?

"Do you realize how much time you spend studying me?"

Luther blinked and shook his head. "Sorry."

"No need. Is it just me or everybody?"

He went back to the recliner and sat down. "I guess it's an occupational hazard."

She turned so that her back was to the fire and smoothed her hair down to cover her left cheek. "So, go on. What happened next?"

"I was sixteen when she died, and it hit me pretty hard. I tried to talk to Mom and Dad about it, but they didn't know how to handle it any better than I did, so they just refused to say anything. Matter of fact, they never talked about much of anything after that.

"I became obsessed with finding out what it was that

attracted her to the occult—why a pretty young girl would give up boys and parties and movies for the dark side of nature."

"And did you?"

"Huh? Oh . . . no, not really. I never found any answers, only more questions. As time went on, I began to feel like the answer was there if I only studied harder or translated more manuscripts. After a while I started to believe it was me—that I wasn't smart enough that I was missing something obvious."

"And you felt like you let her down?"

Luther shrugged. "Maybe."

"And then that girl in England disappeared—"

"I don't know. I guess."

Alana went over and knelt beside his chair. "You know, you're as screwed up as I am."

"Thanks a hell of a lot." He reached down and put his hand to her undamaged cheek. Her skin was like finespun silk: cool, with an underlying vitality that made his fingers tingle. Alana felt something, too—his touch disturbed the scab of despair that had formed over her deep, abiding loneliness. She felt drawn to him an almost gravitational pull, like the tide responding to the call of the moon. Something profound was about to happen. Something that might even melt the self-imposed cocoon of isolation that separated them both from the rest of the world.

Slowly, afraid if he moved too quickly she might bolt, he leaned down and brushed his lips across hers. His touch was so slight, Alana closed her eyes and imagined it was a mist falling on a flower petal. She drank in his warmth, inhaled his musk, and tasted the residue of Sweet 'n Low on his lips. He probed her mouth with the tip of his tongue, and she cupped her hand behind his head and held him. Feelings, emotions so alien to

Ungrateful Dead

his heart, so long dead in hers, flickered and then burst into white-hot flame. She kissed him hungrily, almost brutally, and he responded by crushing her lips under his. She pulled him out of the chair and down on top of her, taking his weight, while never for an instant relinquishing possession of his mouth. His hand traveled up over the curve of her hip, past her waist, and over her rib cage. The instant his fingers closed over her breast, she felt something dark slip like an ice-cold knife blade into her mind: *That's it, you slut! Spread those skinny legs! Open that twisted mouth! Fuck him! Fuck him!*

Alana stiffened and turned her head to the side.

"No!" she hissed. And then more forcefully, "No! Don't!"

Breathlessly, he asked, "What's wrong?" But the moment was shattered, and he rolled over onto his side.

She kept her head turned toward the fire so he wouldn't see the terror in her eyes. Morgana was there, and now she was gone—just like that! But where the bitch had been, a cold void remained. Alana had felt something—something wonderful. And now it was dead too.

"Alana?"

"I just can't," she whispered.

He sat up and folded his legs underneath his body. "Did I—did I hurt you?"

"No. It isn't that. I just can't."

He put his hand on her shoulder, but she shrugged it off.

"What's the matter?" she said curtly. "You never had a woman tell you she wasn't in the mood?"

His face turned to stone, and he stared at the fire until the sting of her words subsided. Before he had the chance to say anything really stupid, the telephone in the kitchen rang.

"Excuse me."

He got up and went to the kitchen.

Alana dabbed her eyes on the shoulder of her blouse. She needed to be held so badly and yet she couldn't tell him what was wrong—her mother had been inside her mind! Alana felt dirty. Cold and dirty. And alone.

Luther returned, pulling his coat on.

"I hate to ask you this, but would you mind giving me a lift back to Cal's?"

She scrambled to her feet. "Sure. What's wrong?"

"I don't know. He just said for us to get over there fast."

Chapter Eight

Cal opened the door.

"Thank God!" He grabbed Luther's arm and practically dragged him to the hall outside the master bedroom. Alana followed; when they reached the door Cal paused to gather himself.

"What the devil's going on?" Luther whispered.

"I don't know," Cal replied in the same hushed tone. "When I got home Rachel was moaning about someone kidnapping Samantha."

"Did you call the cops?"

"Sam's in her room!"

Luther glanced at Alana. *Some kind of contagious psychosis?*

"What does Sam say?"

"Nothing. She said something about some bozo in a van at the mall."

Gary L. Holleman

"Then—"

"Don't ask me. Rachel keeps babbling *he* would know, and *he* was going to hurt her baby."

"He? He who?"

"Beats the hell out of me. Listen, Luther," Cal gave Alana an apologetic look, "you ever hear of possession psychosis being contagious?"

Luther nibbled on his bottom lip. "No. But I admit I was just wondering the same thing myself."

"May I go in?" Alana asked.

Cal glanced at Luther.

"Is she violent?"

"No," Cal responded. "She just keeps thrashing and moaning. I'm a doctor, but right now I don't know what to do."

"I don't see how it could hurt," Luther said.

"Me either."

Cal opened the door.

Rachel was lying facedown on the bed with her nightgown bunched up around her hips. Alana hurried over, straightened her clothing, and then gently turned her over. Rachel's face was purple, and her eyes looked as if they were about to pop out of her head.

"Help me!" Alana called. "She can't breathe."

Luther dropped his backpack, and he and Cal ran to opposite sides of the bed.

"What's wrong with her?" Cal whispered.

Alana undid the collar of Rachel's nightgown. Underneath the high Victorian collar, Rachel's neck was swollen to almost twice its normal size.

"Get her mouth open!" Luther said.

Cal put one hand on her forehead and pushed down on her chin with the other, and her lips parted like the jaws of a steel bear trap.

"Check to see if she swallowed her tongue," Luther instructed.

"I am, dammit! You think it's easy to—Good God!"

He leaped back from the bed as if he had been shocked.

"What?" Luther said.

"In—in her mouth—look in her mouth!"

Luther wedged himself between Cal and the bed and tried to force Rachel's mouth open, but she fought him.

"Alana, help me! Hold her down."

Alana jumped in and grabbed the woman's arms and used her body to keep Rachel's head from turning. Luther pushed down with all of his strength.

"Damn—she's strong." He leaned down and peered into her mouth. "Cal, get a light."

"Way ahead of you." Cal aimed the flashlight beam down his wife's throat.

"Good grief!"

"What are those things?" asked Alana.

"I don't—You know, I read about—" Luther released his hold on Rachel and ran to fetch his backpack.

At this point Rachel's eyes were blood-red and starting to roll back in her head.

"Luther?"

Luther emptied the pack on the floor and pawed through the contents until he found a small, leather-bound book, which he then began flipping through until he found what he was looking for—a paragraph highlighted in yellow marker.

Rachel's eyes closed.

"Luther, for crissake!"

"Here it is."

"Here what is?"

Luther skimmed down the page, his lips moving silently. "Oh, shit."

"What?"

He began sifting through his papers and vials and notebooks. "I need—Here!"

He bounced to his feet and returned to his place beside the bed. He had two glass vials in his hand; one contained several shriveled, brown leaves; the other, a clear liquid. He unscrewed the top on the first vial, removed one of the leaves, and forced it between Rachel's lips.

"What's that?" asked Cal.

Luther focused on Rachel's face and didn't reply. For several seconds nothing happened, and then her eyes flew open and her body convulsed; once . . . twice.

"Help me get her up," Luther said, and the three of them pushed and pulled her into a sitting position.

Eyes bulging, face as purple and swollen, as a three-day-dead corpse. Rachel grabbed the front of Cal's shirt in both hands and yanked as if she were trying to rip it off of him. Luther and Alana took her arms, but their combined strength couldn't break her grip. Her eyes became frantic and her mouth opened and then she vomited about a gallon of chunky, black liquid all over the champagne-colored carpet. She sucked in a lungfull of air and then threw up again, more watery, black fluid and more long slender chunks of . . . something.

Rachel coughed and began gulping oxygen like a fish stranded by a retreating tide. Cal wrapped her in his arms and rocked her gently back and forth.

"There, you're okay now."

Luther pulled one of Cal's pencils from his friend's pocket, squatted down and used the point to examine the lumps.

"Luther, that's gross," Alana said.

"More than you think."

Cal lowered Rachel back on the pillow and unbuttoned her gown.

Ungrateful Dead

"My God, Luther, look at this."

Her chest was crisscrossed with dark bruises and red, puffy scratches.

Luther examined the marks. "What happened to her?"

"Those marks look old to me. A day or two at least."

Rachel was out cold, but Cal kept his finger on her pulse until both it and her color returned to normal.

"I better call 911," he said.

"I wouldn't," said Luther.

Puzzled, Cal inquired, "Why not?"

"I don't think we should let her out of our sight."

"Why not?" Cal repeated.

"Look at this."

Cal kneeled down next to Luther. "Is that what I saw?"

Nodding, Luther poked at one of the lumps with the pencil.

"Jesus, it looks like a little snake. What is it?"

"I don't know, some kind of worm—a parasite."

Alana looked like *she* was going to be sick. "Oh my God."

"Hardly."

"Are they dead?" Almost a dozen of the creatures were lying still on the carpet.

"I think so."

"What was that you gave Rachel?"

"Mistletoe."

"How did you know . . . ?"

"I wasn't sure. It was something I came across in one of the manuscripts."

"About worms?"

"Leeches. Stories—myths really, about creatures called 'the Children of Set', a kind of leech that invades a person's body, attaches itself to the internal organs, and feeds off the blood of the host."

"A myth?" Cal returned to the bed and smoothed a lock of hair back out of his wife's eyes. "You gave my wife a piece of dried-up leaf based on a myth? How did you know these things were the same leeches you read about? Wasn't that book written a long time ago?"

"True. But it described the hosts as becoming irrational, violent, and having unusual strength."

Cal glanced at Luther's backpack. "You always carry mistletoe around with you?"

Grinning, Luther shook his head. "Only at Christmas. No, actually I was reading up on it because of its reputation among the ancients as an 'All-heal'—a kind of ancient aspirin. I though I might try it on Alana."

"Thanks a lot," Alana said wryly. "Headaches aren't my problem."

"What was in that other vial?" Cal asked.

"Uh, nicotine."

"You were going to give that to Rachel?" Cal sputtered. "That stuff's poison."

"Yeah, well that's why I said 'shit'. However, it is also a potent, natural insecticide that has been used to control annelids."

"And I suppose you were going to try that on Alana too?"

"Not really. I use it to make a patch to help me stop smoking."

Cal shook his head in disbelief. "Well, listen, buddy, the next time you feel like playing a hunch, do me a favor—go to Vegas."

"Sorry," Luther added. "The way Rachel was going, I didn't think we had a choice."

Cal rested his chin on the part in his wife's hair. "I guess not. I suppose I owe you one."

Ungrateful Dead

Luther emptied the dried mistletoe into an ashtray on the night table and then scraped one of the worms into the empty vial. "Here."

"Get that thing away from her. I don't know how those things got into her, but I never want to see it again."

"I think we ought to have it analyzed. There could be side effects."

"Such as?"

"Eggs."

Cal's eyes squeezed shut. "Oh, man. It just gets better and better."

"The main thing is, we should know if they released any type of toxin or hallucinogens into her system."

"You're kidding, right?"

"Not at all. Many creatures, ground toads for one, sweat powerful hallucinogenic compounds through their skin."

Cal's eyebrows peaked in surprise. "You think that's why she's been acting so strangely lately?"

"Could be."

The idea seemed to comfort Cal, and Luther decided not to tell him what else the book said about the "mythical" Children of Set.

The phone on the night table rang, and all three of them jumped. After five rings, the answering machine kicked in.

"Rachel? It's Kay Marks. If you're there, pick up."

"Damn!" Cal muttered as he picked up the phone.

Luther turned and gave Alana a sheepish grin.

She smiled. "Don't worry. I know you meant well. And it seems to have worked out okay."

They both watched Rachel sleep for a few seconds.

"Yeah, maybe." He held the vial up to the lamp, holding it between his forefinger and thumb and tilting

167

it back and forth from top to bottom. The slug, or leech, or whatever the disgusting thing was, was beginning to liquify. What remained slipped back and forth like viscous motor oil, coating the glass with a thick layer of slime. Luther didn't believe in premonitions, which, considering his choice of profession, he had always secretly considered odd, but he had a "feeling", a strong feeling, that he was holding the key to the whole mess right in his hand. He just didn't know what it fit.

Cal hung up the phone.

"What's up?" Luther asked.

Instead of answering, Cal made for the door.

"Cal?"

"I'm going to check on Sam."

"Why?"

"Malina Marks, the girl Sam was with at the mall—she's disappeared."

Malina knew all she had to do was keep her eyes closed and lie on that cold, hard, table, and pretty soon she would wake up. The things those men had done to her—it was all a dream. A horrible, horrible bad dream. It had to be. Because if it wasn't, then she'd keep her eyes closed anyway and wait to die.

Yet she wanted to live—she wanted to see what would happen to *them* when her father found out. She tried to imagine what he would do; what he could possibly do that would be half as bad.

A rough thumb forced her eyelid up, and the sudden light made her moan.

"She's awake!"

It was the fat one—the smelly one that grunted like a pig—the one they called Ward.

"Open your eyes, little sister."

Ungrateful Dead

The dwarf with the merry smile and dead eyes was back.

"Open up!"

A hand stroked her naked thigh, and Mal's right eye popped open like one of those hard-faced, Tiny Tears Dolls—her left eye was so swollen it couldn't open.

The man's smirking face filled her entire field of vision. His head was surrounded by a halo of diffused torchlight which, combined with the cheerful smile, made him look almost angelic—what a laugh! He had changed out of his leisure suit into a long white robe and a flat white head covering that resembled the things the nurses wore in those old war movies. In the center of the cowl, right above his eyes, was a likeness of a serpent with bright red eyes, and around his neck was a circular, onyx medallion inscribed with the likeness of a golden oak tree.

"You're a mess," Anton said pleasantly. "I guess me boys were a wee bit rough."

Mal heard muffled laughter behind him and closed her eye again.

Anton pinched her cheek hard enough to bring tears. "Come on, girlie! No nodding, I need you awake. Here now, let me tell you what's about to happen." He grinned engagingly again. "I promise you're going to find this fascinating."

Danny and Colin stepped out of the shadows and raised her into a sitting position. Mal wished they hadn't. Any movement beyond simple breathing sent waves of white-hot agony shooting all over her body. As the spasms passed, she opened her eye and looked down at her body. She was nauseated by the sight of the what those animals had done to her.

"Perk up, my dear. We have company."

The cellar was full of people—why hadn't she heard

them? They were holding torches and wearing the same goofy-looking white robes the dwarf had on. She had always been self-conscious about her body, especially her small breasts, and she wished they had at least allowed *her* a robe.

She couldn't see their faces, for they clung to the shadows like vampires with skin cancer, but when she cared to listen, she could hear their heavy breathing and sense their sick anticipation.

"You see these magnificent columns?" Anton held a real torch up to one of the massive stone pillars. "You probably think they're made of concrete, but they're not. No siree. All save one are lodestones the late owner of this poor house brought over to this country by boat, all the way from Erin." He glanced at Malina. "What do you say to that?"

"Ro...ro..." She swallowed with difficulty. "Rocks?" Her lips were so mangled that intelligible speech was almost beyond her.

"Oh, much more than rocks. Much, much more!" He caressed the clammy stone as if it were a woman's flank. "Do you know what a cromlech is, darlin'?"

Mal wanted to shake her head, but was afraid she'd throw up; instead she grunted.

"No? The textbook definition is an ancient monument made of stones around a mound or altar—you have heard of Stonehenge, I take it?"

Had she? She couldn't remember. But since the dwarf was really playing to his groupies, she saved her energy and remained mute.

"What strange myths surrounded that sacred site. Moon worship, sun worship, sky worship, star worship!" His laughter sounded like a little boy giggling at his first lewd joke. "Historians! Archeologists!—Buffoons!"

Ungrateful Dead

Anton made a slow circle of the room, parting his followers as he slipped in and out of the torchlight like a ghost. He touched each of the megaliths in turn, drawing strength from them as most people would from food.

"They looked everywhere but in the right place. They looked up!" He raised his free arm toward the ceiling. "They should have looked down." The arm dropped toward the floor. "Down to the earth, the great engine of creation . . . of power! The earth—" His voice rose like that of a Baptist minister delivering the punchline to his Sunday fire-and-brimstone sermon. "—the realm of Set!"

At the mention of the ancient god's name, the crowd dropped to their knees.

"These great stones, which once rested deep in the soil of my homeland, are part of the Great Serpent's backbone, which stretches through mountains and oceans all around the world. They are like batteries—gigantic batteries to be sure, but instead of electricity, they store the essence—the power that binds the universe."

Mal sighed. She'd been right; the guy was as nutty as a fruitcake. Which only made her situation more desperate.

Anton stopped in front of the largest monolith, a greenish-black slab of porous rock as wide as a school bus. "And this is the *Fâl* stone—the stone discovered by Conn Cetchathach, the greatest king of all Ireland. And how do we use such power?"

When Anton was sure his audience was properly impressed, he strolled over and pointed to the oak tree.

"The Dair, or, for the benefit of our guest"—he motioned with his hand toward Mal—"the oak. The temple of Set, from which we derive our name, Dairaoi—dwellers in oaks; that which the cursed Saxon Christians bastardized into the nonword Druid. The *Fâl* stone provides the power, but the Dair is our strength, our church and our salvation, for its roots run deep into the earth—*Deep!* All the way to the very core of Set's domain."

"Please!" Mal muttered.

Anton smiled at the battered girl. "Ah, ye of little faith." He grinned at his followers. "Shall we show our young friend here the error of her ways?"

The cowls circling the gloomy cellar nodded solemnly.

"Dig!"

Colin and Wardley came forward with shovels, removed their robes, and began digging near the base of the tree. Anton motioned to one of the robed people and pointed at one of the oversized acorns, hanging about three feet above his head. The man stretched and, with some effort, plucked the woody fruit and handed it to his master.

Anton went to Mal's side, showed the acorn to her and then set his shoulders and twisted off the cap. The cellar filled with an eerie, high-pitched keening that made the fillings in Mal's teeth pulsate, and the crowd cram their fingers into their ears; even Danny and Colin stopped digging and covered their ears. Anton just smiled.

"Make it stop!" Mal cried.

And finally, the unearthly cry did stop. However, Mal's ears continued to ring for almost half a minute.

"The clans call what you just heard the wail of the banshee. And with good reason. For this is the fruit of death and death always follows that sound."

He held the acorn down so that Mal could see inside. The bottom half of the cuplike fruit was brimming with partially congealed blood.

"Ugh!" the girl said. "That's disgusting!"

Ungrateful Dead

"You think so? Look again—LOOK!"

Something long and sleek and black poked its slimy head up out of the blood. It kept coming and coming like a worm squirming out of an apple, coiling its wet, glistening body around Anton's wrist. It didn't appear to have a mouth, or ears, or eyes, and yet somehow it knew where Mal was, for it raised its blunt head and pointed it directly at her.

Anton stroked the creature with his finger. "I think he likes you."

"Wha' is it?"

"This is the Lord Set."

One of Mal's eyebrows went up, the other went down. "Tha' ting? It looks like a worm!"

"In a way he is, a very special kind of worm. But do not let his appearance fool you. This is but one of many parts of his glorious body." Anton glanced at his men. They had scooped out a hole about three feet wide by three feet long by one foot deep and piled the excavated muck beside the table. "That's good."

The men hopped out of the hole and put their robes back on—everything their fingers touched was stained red.

Mal tilted her head enough to see down into the hole. She wished she hadn't.

Blood and mud were seeping into the pit from all sides; blood and dozens of those . . . things! At the bottom, half buried in the icky goo, was the nude, partially decomposed body of a woman. Her skin was white—not pale—white. As if every drop of blood had been extracted from her with tiny needles. The creatures were all over her and in places had removed huge chunks of flesh. In those places, the denuded bone stood out grayish white against the slick, black bodies.

Anton followed her gaze into the pit. "That's were you come in, dearie."

Mal swallowed and tasted bile. "I don't get it."

His smile was sad. "Sure, 'tis not your fault. The stones take the place of the sun, they provide the power, but the Dair must have nutrients—food. Fertilizer, like. Otherwise, it would wither up and die. Since we came here we have been using some of the local, ah . . . ladies who ply their trade on the streets. But now that you're here— Well, you know what they say—waste not, want not!"

Mal didn't have a clue what the little creep was babbling about. Nor did she understand why all of a sudden the rest of the creepoids were shuffling out of the shadows and crowding around the tree, their eyes shining like hellish stars. What she did understand was that the fat pig and his friends were coming toward her, and she saw her death in their eyes. Nothing was going to save her—not pleading, not mercy, for there was no mercy in those eyes.

When they tied her hands and feet she didn't fight. When they lifted her up, she made no protest. When they carried her to the hole she closed her eye so she couldn't see the pack of white robes circling the hole like sharks hot on a trail of fresh blood. They lowered her in, but left her head above ground and began shoveling the mud in on top of her. The stuff was cold and slimy. The remains underneath her bare buttocks were slick and spongy, and she began to shiver, wondering as she did if her murderers were cold under their robes. But she supposed it didn't matter much now.

Something slithered across her thigh.

When the mud was up to her neck they stopped shoveling, and the white robes crowded around the pit, their eyes hungry, their lips dry. Mal put them out of her mind

Ungrateful Dead

and thought about the big sale the mall was having next weekend. She'd always wanted a fur coat. Not PC, Sam would say, but Mal would have worn it anyway.

She felt a tickle as something inched across her belly.

Odd, she thought. She had expected them to be cold, but they weren't. They were warm. They made her fingers tingle and caused spots to appear before her eyes.

Thirty minutes later, the last to leave, Anton walked over to the switch by the stairs and gave it a turn. One by one the torches winked out. Then, in the renewed silence and stygian darkness, he dragged himself slowly up the stairs.

Alana didn't know where she was or how she got there, but she didn't like it. It smelled like a sewer and all around was a darkness so vast and all-encompassing that a match flame would have appeared as bright as the sun. She couldn't move. She could feel her arms and legs, but they were dead weight, as if they were encased in cold, wet cement. Frantic, she opened her mouth to call for help. But something soft and slimy oozed past her lips and slid down her throat. It reminded her of eating raw oysters—she hated raw oysters, they made her want to—Another of the things crawled into her mouth ... and then another! She was going to be sick.

"Alana!"

Alana's head snapped up, and she gazed blankly around the room. The fog cleared from her head, and she saw Luther, standing in front of her with his arms full of books.

"I'm sorry. I didn't mean to startle you."

"That's okay. I guess I dozed off."

Cal raised his head from the bed where he had been napping beside Rachel—she was still unconscious, but her appearance had much improved.

After Mrs. Marks called, Cal went to check on Samantha. The girl was fine and hadn't had any idea where Malina was. They grilled her about the mall and what happened to her in the parking lot, and she told them about the men in the green van. After that, Cal told her to stay in the house and returned to the bedroom and climbed into bed next to his wife. Luther had borrowed Alana's car and drove back to his house to see if he could find a record of the worms in any of his other reference materials. Before leaving, he asked Alana if she wanted to go with him, but she decided to stay in case Cal needed help with Rachel. She must have nodded off. And then there was the dream.

The door opened and Sam stuck her head in. "Is Mom okay?"

Cal nodded and gently disentangled himself. "What time is it?"

"A little after ten," Luther replied.

"Sam, how 'bout scrambling some eggs for everybody?" asked Cal.

"Mom, too?"

"No. Best we let her sleep."

The girl nodded and headed for the kitchen.

Cal yawned and stretched; his sweatshirt crept up over his hairy belly.

"You need to go on a diet," Luther said.

"Yeah? Well, not all of us have the time to eat tofu and go tooling around on a bicycle like some kind of friggin' schoolkid."

"Maybe a rich doctor will buy me a Z like Alana's. That thing really moves."

Cal asked, "What did you find out?"

"Let's go into the kitchen. I need room to put this stuff down."

They trooped into the kitchen where Samantha was

Ungrateful Dead

already hunched over the stove, slowly running a whisk around a skillet full of semicongealed eggs.

"Bagels or toast?" she asked.

"Bagels," Cal replied.

Luther piled his books on the end of the table in the breakfast nook.

"You got enough books?" Cal muttered.

"I'm glad I didn't have to bring all this on the bike."

"What is all that?"

"I brought everything I had on Irish myths and Druids."

"So what did you find out?" Alana asked.

"All sorts of interesting stuff." He grinned and Alana got the feeling he was enjoying himself too much.

What's the matter with him? she thought angrily.

"Okay, you remember Sam mentioning a stick the guy in the van was pointing at her?"

"He was waving it," Sam corrected him. "And it was funny looking, like a bedspring."

"Whatever. Druid priests sometimes used sticks called—" Luther ran his finger down the lines of text in one of his books. "Gwrack sticks, or Hag's sticks, grew on some special kind of tree and were a cross between magic wands and a directional finder." He pointed to a drawing of a locket in the book. "Sam, come take a look at this."

The girl moved the skillet over to a cool burner and hurried to the table. "Oh, wow!" she said when she saw the picture. "That's just like the necklace that guy Danny gave me."

"And you gave to Mal?"

Sam looked at him, and her eyes filled with tears. "I didn't give it to her, she took it."

Cal grabbed her hand. "Honey, it's not your fault."

Pulling free, Sam went back to the stove and began beating the eggs with the whisk.

Luther lowered his voice. "The locket is what's known as a Pitag, which is a Gaelic word meaning witch, or, as it's used in this case, a witch's charm. It was reputedly used to keep tabs on someone from a distance. The priest would put the pitag on the spellee and, should the need arise, he used the gwrack to track them down."

"So these assholes were trying to use this thing to—"

"Track Sam. But instead they got—"

"Malina." Cal looked like he was about to explode. "That's it, we're calling the cops."

"Okay, fine. Just what are you going to tell them?"

"About the men in the van. About Gadarn."

Luther nodded. "I guess that makes sense. But then what? We don't have a license number on the van. We don't know the make. Sam didn't mention anything about a midget, so we can't even swear Gadarn's involved. We don't have a location for him or even know if Gadarn's his real name. And what do we say when they ask how we know all this? Do we tell them about Alana? About her mother?"

Tilting back his head, Cal clenched his teeth until the veins in his neck stood out like cables. "I hate it when you go logical on me."

"I know. It's so unlike me."

"So what do we do, then? Keep quiet? When I think of what those creeps could be doing to Malina—" He lowered his voice to a whisper. "It could have been Sam!"

"I know. My suggestion? Go to a pay phone and make an anonymous call; tell them about the van at the mall. Tell them the color, tell them Gadarn's name, and then hang up."

Ungrateful Dead

Cal obviously didn't like it, but he agreed. "First, what else have you got?"

"You asked about mistletoe. Mistletoe was sacred to the Druids. It grows on oak trees, which were the most sacred of all plants, and thus came to be imbued with all sorts of magical powers."

Frustration and fear were making Cal truculent. "I can't believe you actually buy any of this crap."

"Look Cal, I've seen some pretty bizarre things in my travels. I once saw a Hungan—that's a witch doctor to you civilized folk—reanimate a man that I knew for a fact had died of AIDS the week before."

"You're kidding."

"I wish. Scared the tee-total crap out of me. And the worst part was, he did it just because I pissed him off."

"That part I can believe."

"I made fun of his Mojo—"

"His shtick?"

"Whatever. Anyway, I let on to some of his clients that I thought this voodoo business was a lot of hogwash, and the next thing I knew, this dead guy, his name was Francois by the way, shows up at the door of my hut, skin like scaly milk, eyes bugging out, smell—" Luther glanced at Alana. "Well, let's just say he didn't smell very good."

"A dead guy? Knocked on your door?"

Luther nodded and crossed his heart.

"Sheesh!"

"But we're getting away from the point," Luther said. "If I'm right about the Druid involvement, and it looks like that necklace the guy gave Sam was an honest-to-gosh Pitag, then there just might be something we can do for Rachel."

At this, Cal focused the entire weight of his attention on his friend. Luther turned to the top book, which turned out to be the scrapbook of his travels around the world. Taped to the open page was an envelope. He pulled it loose, opened it, and extracted a withered, but still green, three-leaf plant.

"What is that?" asked Alana. "A clover?"

"Close. It's actually *Medicago lupulina*—the black nonesuch."

"Which is?" Cal asked.

"While I was over in Ireland, I learned that this little fellow, rather than the more common clover, is the true shamrock, or *shamrog*, and was, in fact, what Saint Patrick used to explain the Mystery of the Trinity. They use it in everything over there: designs for pottery and clothing, charms, jewelry. It's what's embedded in the crystal of that key chain of mine."

"Well, that's all very interesting," Cal muttered. "But so what?"

Undeterred, Luther forged on. "Strangely enough, Ireland isn't the only place the shamrock is held in high regard. It is found in the wand of Hermes—the Greek messenger of the gods—on the head of Osiris, and in Mexico."

"I didn't know that either, but again, so what?"

"Well, for one thing, Osiris was the Egyptian god who went through an annual ritual of death and resurrection, which personified what the Egyptians saw as the self-renewing vitality and fertility of nature—resurrection, if you will. For another—let me read you a passage from this book: *Irish Druids and Old Irish Religious*, by James Bonwick.

> *Chosen leaf*
> *Of Bard and Chief,*
> *Old Erin's native Shamrock!*
> *Says Valour, 'See*

Ungrateful Dead

> *They spring for me,*
> *Those leafy gems of morning!'*
> *Says Love, 'No, no,*
> *For me they grow,*
> *My fragrant path adorning!'*
> *But Wit perceives*
> *The triple leaves,*
> *And cries,—'O do not sever*
> *A type that blends*
> *Three godlike friends,*
> *Love, Valour, Wit, for ever!'*
> *O! The Shamrock, the green, immortal Shamrock!*

"Jesus, Lute! Will you get to the point!"

"Okay. The point is, there's a recipe here for a tea made from shamrock's which is supposed to counteract the aftereffects of our old friends the Children of Set."

Cal blinked and chewed on his bottom lip. "Those things aren't poisonous or anything, are they?"

"Not as far as I can tell."

"Then you can try it first."

As soon as they finished the eggs, Samantha boiled a pot of water, into which Luther dropped three of the leaves and then poured about three ounces of the brew into two cups.

"Bottoms up," he said. He downed the tea in one swallow, made a face, and started coughing.

"What's the matter?" asked Cal.

"Bitter! Yuck!"

For the next ten minutes, Cal watched Luther like a hawk. At the end of that time he asked, "How do you feel?"

"Silly," Luther replied. "Quit staring at me like I'm gonna sprout horns."

"Wouldn't surprise me." Cal sighed. "I guess we might as well give it a try."

"Should I reheat it, Daddy?" Sam inquired.

"No. I don't want to scald your mom if we spill any trying to get it down."

Back in the bedroom, Cal took the cup from Luther. "You sure you feel all right?"

Luther nodded.

"Tell me again why we aren't taking her to the ER."

"You tell them your wife was attacked by black worms, and then they get a look at those bruises all over her—you'll be lucky if they don't lock you up for spousal abuse."

"That's not funny."

"It wasn't meant to be."

Sam was over by the dresser, listening to the discussion. "Go on, Daddy. Uncle Luther knows what he's doing."

"Yeah, right." Cal leaned over and tilted the cup to Rachel's lips.

For almost two minutes, nothing happened. Then, still in her sleep, she made a face like she'd just swallowed a mouthful of vinegar.

"I know how she feels," Luther whispered.

She stretched and in a moment opened her eyes. When she saw them standing around the bed, she blushed.

"Why is everyone staring at me?" Her voice was hoarse. "Cal, what's going on?"

Cal took her hand. "How do you feel?"

"Like I have the worst sore throat of my life."

Sam sat down on the bed next to her father. "Mom, I was so scared."

Rachel glanced at Luther. "You want to tell me what's going on?"

"You don't remember anything that happened tonight?"

"It's all kind of—fuzzy. The telephone was ringing. I remember I didn't want to answer it." She glanced at Cal. "Why do you suppose that was? Was it you calling? Did something happen?"

Cal smiled and shook his head.

"I remember being worried about Sam." She looked at her daughter. Fat tears were rolling down the girl's cheeks. "What's the matter? What's happened?"

Sam glanced at Cal.

"Later," he said.

"No! Now."

"Malina's disappeared," the girl said, and all her hard-fought restraint crumbled as she collapsed into Rachel's arms.

"Malina?" Rachel stroked her daughter's hair and looked from Cal to Luther. "What happened to Malina?"

"We don't know," Cal replied.

"How long was I asleep?"

Cal told Rachel everything he knew about what had happened to her, and then Luther showed her the vial with just enough of the worm left to tell what it was. Rachel paled.

"I never saw that thing before in my life!"

Cal glanced at Luther. Luther had the distinct feeling she wasn't telling the truth; from his friend's expression, he was pretty sure Cal did too.

"What about this?" Cal loosened the top of her gown enough to expose the bruised tops of her breasts. Rachel's eyes were haunted.

"I—I don't know. I must have fallen . . . or something."

Luther tapped Cal on the shoulder and motioned for him to follow him out into the hall.

As soon as the men stepped out of the room, Alana glanced at Sam. "I need to talk to your mom alone for a minute. You mind?"

Sam nodded and went to her room.

Alana sat on the bed. "You want to talk about it?"

Rachel's eyes bounced all over the room. "I don't know what you mean."

"Just tell me one thing—was it Anton?"

Rachel still refused to look at Alana, but her body began to shake.

"Rachel, I know what he's like. He never tried anything with me; Mother would have cut his balls off, but I saw the way he acted around other women. I never knew about—" She cut her eyes to the glass vial on the night table. "I don't know what that does to you. But I know how I would feel if I found out—"

"Found out what?" Rachel hissed. "That you were a whore? That you betrayed your husband, your family? That you did things with—" Rachel squeezed her eyes shut as if the darkness could make it all go away—it didn't. "You did things in front of those two—"

Alana took Rachel's hand. "Shush! Don't do this to yourself—he isn't worth it. Listen to me." She shook Rachel until she opened her eyes. "That thing Luther got out of you, I think we're going to find it . . . I don't know, changed you—made you do things you wouldn't have normally done."

Rachel glanced at the vial. "I knew something was wrong. I felt so . . . so angry all the time. I hated everyone, Sam, Cal, Luther—you. Especially you. I took your file from the office and gave it to him. He asked me to, but I probably would have done it anyway."

Ungrateful Dead

"It's okay. Can you tell me, did he ever take you to his house?"

Shaking her head, Rachel replied, "No. We . . . he always—" She clenched her jaw and faced Alana. "We always did it in the back of his van." She swallowed with some difficulty and then seemed to relax a little. "Afterward, he usually grilled me about Luther and Cal and you. What were you saying? What were Luther and Cal planning? How much did they know about him?"

"What did you tell him?"

"Not much. I didn't know very much. I told him about Luther and Cal, their backgrounds—stuff like that."

Alana knew Anton. She knew how damaging the least bit of personal information could be—the man was a genius at twisting things. But she patted Rachel's hand and said, "It's okay. The important thing is you're all right now."

"Am I?" Rachel whispered bitterly. "Am I really? What about Cal? What am I going to tell him?"

Alana didn't want Cal or Luther distracted. "My advice? Nothing."

"But I've never kept anything from him. I don't know if I could."

All at once, Alana didn't feel so good. "If you want to keep him . . . try. Men don't take things like this very well."

"I don't know." Rachel looked lost. "Maybe you're right."

"Rachel, could I use your bathroom?"

"Sure. It's right in there."

Alana glanced around. "Maybe—the guest bath?"

Rachel gave her directions, and Alana hurried out into the hall, passing Luther and Cal, who were locked in the middle of a heated discussion. They paused until Alana

185

was out of earshot and then continued where they left off.

Cal wanted to wait until Rachel was stronger to fill her in on everything, but Luther said they should lay it all out right away. Secretly, he wanted to press Rachel about what had really happened to her, but he was worried about what she might say and how it would affect Cal. Instead, he told his friend that they should find out what they could ASAP, for he had a creepy feeling that time was running against them.

"So help me," Cal hissed. "If she relapses—"

Luther laid a hand on his friend's wide shoulders. "I love Rachel almost as much as you do. But this thing is getting out of hand. We're going to have to stick together if we're all going to get out of this mess in one piece."

"Okay. I'm going to run down to the 7-Eleven at the corner and call the police. When I get back, we'll see what we can find out." Cal looked around. "Where did Alana go?"

The guest bathroom, like the rest of Rachel's house, was cool, modern, full of shiny brass fixtures and the tart smell of disinfectant. Alana closed and locked the door, and then went to the sink and threw some cold water on her face. Out of habit, she checked her reflection in the mirror, searching her face for lines or splotches—any change at all.

None were apparent, but that didn't mean she liked what she saw.

God, how could you do that to Rachel? How could you do it to any of these people?

Luther's getting involved—that had been the plan from the start. But Cal? And now Rachel? Seeing Rachel like that! Lying to her! Telling her to lie to Cal!

Ungrateful Dead

But what about her? What about Alana? Didn't she have the right to protect herself? The *right* to use them in order to survive? It had seemed like such a good idea at the time.

She gazed at the tired face in the glass. The overhead lights weren't kind.

"Mother would have been so proud."

So put an end to it!

Her stomach was killing her.

Why not put an end to it? she thought. What else did she need Luther for? After talking to Rachel, she knew she wasn't crazy and that her suspicions about who was behind it were correct. She should be able find the little creep on her own—eventually. And when she did—

Her hand dropped down to her purse at her feet, squeezing the hard outline of the .380 automatic. After what he'd done to her, shooting Anton would pose no real problem at all—she could worry about getting away from the cops later. Luther! That was the real problem. She had done such a good job of tangling him in her web of lies that even if she just vanished she was afraid he would come after her. She needed a way to cool his jets before she split.

You'll miss him.

"Christ!" she muttered. "Where did that come from?"

But it was true. It appeared that while she had been charming her way into his life, he, with his dumb smile and boyish naiveté had gotten under her skin too.

"Fuck it!"

All at once the bathroom felt incredibly cold. She looked up at the mirror, but everything appeared normal. She rubbed her eyes, and as she did, it was as if an icy hand reached into her head and sank its sharp nails into her brain.

"Hello, daughter!"

Chapter Nine

Truman Connely had just finished signing a letter he had written to a friend in New York when he heard the floorboards creak in the hall outside his study. The only light in the room came from a green-glass shaded banker's lamp on the desk, and when he looked up all he saw was shadows.

"Virginia?"

Tru's eyes darted to the assagai fighting spear on the wall, but it was all the way on the other side of the room.

A man stepped into the light.

He was big and dark, but he crossed the floor very quickly and quietly for a man his size. Stopping opposite the desk, he peered down at Tru with the coldest pair of eyes the old scholar had ever seen. But Truman was too old and too tired to be frightened. He just sighed.

"I don't keep any money in the house."

"You had visitors this afternoon."

The man's voice carried no discernable accent.

"And if I did?"

"I understand they were looking for someone. I want to help you find him."

"Alana?"

Luther rapped gently on the bathroom door. When he received no reply, he knocked harder.

"Try the knob," Cal suggested.

He did, and the door opened.

"She's not here, but the bathroom's a mess."

They searched the house and the garage, and when they couldn't find her, Luther went to the front door.

"Her car's gone."

"Where could she have gone?" Cal muttered.

"I don't like it. Alana wouldn't have just gone off on her own. She was too frightened."

Cal shook his head. "You sure we're talking about the same person? I don't think that woman's afraid of anything."

"You don't know her."

"And you do?"

The tavern was full of multicolored mood lighting and the smell of fried cheese—the days when the local gin mill was dim and heavy with cigarette smoke had gone the way of the Hula Hoop. The place was dark wood, booths with checkered tablecloths and flowers, and a dartboard that had yet to feel the prick of a single dart. The bar was made of heavy mahogany. It didn't have a brass rail, but was surrounded by a picket fence of tall, padded stools, every one occupied by a male member of the legal or medical professions, or a sleek woman wearing "fuck-me" pumps in hot pursuit of same.

Since most of the action was at the bar, Alana slipped into an unoccupied booth in the back near the restrooms. When the waitress came over, she ordered a beer, any brand as long as it was cold. The woman pointedly avoided looking at Alana's scars and went to get the order. A guy showed up before the beer.

"Hi! The name's Kevin Carter—not to be confused," he added with a self-deprecating chuckle, "with Kevin Costner."

Alana gave him a long, cool up-and-down. Fat, sweaty, he waited patiently beside the table in his pinstripes and wing tips.

"And what, pray tell, is a Kevin Carter?" she asked, keeping the ruined side of her face in the shadows.

He flashed a set of caps that had put some lucky dentist in a new Lexus. "Well, right now I'm a paralegal at Brock, Klein, and Blum, but I'm in my last year of law school at U of M."

A fat baby in a Brooks Brothers suit, she thought. "Have a seat."

Confidence soaring, he slid into the booth opposite Alana; his bottom squeaked on the polished wood. "What's your name?"

"Betty Ford."

"What are you drinking, Betty?"

The waitress showed up with a Bud Lite in a frosty bottle. Kevin looked up at her as if he had just had a flash of divine inspiration. "Vodka tonic, lime twist in a cold glass."

The woman set the beer down in front of Alana, rolled her eyes, and then trudged back to the bar.

Kevin talked about himself for fifteen minutes, pausing only to pay the waitress and down the vodka, and then he glanced around the room as if all of the well-dressed yuppies had just beamed down from space.

Ungrateful Dead

"Look at all of *them,* will you? Once, you could come in here after work, have a few drinks, play a little darts, just kick back—you know?"

Alana scanned the crowd. Suits without faces; twisted, lipstick-smeared mouths wrapped in silk-blend, Jones New York cocoons. She leveled her gaze on Kevin, who was still talking a mile a minute, his hands fluttering in the air like chubby little butterflies, but his face was nothing but stark-white skull.

She drained the last few drops of beer and set the bottle down hard on the table. "You got a place or are you still living with mommy?"

He looked like she had slapped him. "Why—I—that is, of course I have an apartment. Germantown Trace, the nicest ones in Germantown. It has a lake, and a weight room, and spa, and—"

"Can the commercial." She slid out of the booth and wove her way through the maze of tables. In the parking lot she waited for him to catch up. "Where's your car?"

He was panting from running to keep up and had just caught a glimpse of her scars. "Well, I—"

"Is that too hard a question?"

She could feel his hot eyes on her body.

"I'm right here, the red Caprice."

She walked to the Z. "I'll follow you."

"Oh wow, Betty! A Z! I always wanted a Z. Has it got a turbo?"

"It's got an engine that, assuming I don't change my mind, will get me to your place sometime tonight—I hope."

She followed him east on Poplar to where the streetlights stopped, and the trees closed in. He turned into a complex of two-story, fieldstone and pine buildings, drove around a tennis court, and parked in front of a

Gary L. Holleman

bungalow-style cottage in the back. He unlocked the door and waited for her reaction.

"Swell," she muttered when she walked up behind him.

The apartment looked like what you got when Marlin Perkins went shopping in the Sharper Image catalog. The pit group was white "leather," and the coffee table was glass. The walls were covered with fake lion and zebra skins and spears, and in the corners, faux-African tribal drums surrounded stereo speakers the size of small skyscrapers.

"Come on in. Want to watch some TV? It's a sixty inch and has surround sound."

Alana shook her head.

"How 'bout something to drink?" He began making the rounds, turning off or dimming the lights.

Alana shook her head again.

"I know!" he said. He scurried over to one of the tribal drums, removed the top, and took out a plastic bag half-full of white powder. "How 'bout a little blow?" He tried for a wicked grin. "Put you in the mood."

It would take an elephant tranquilizer to put her in *that* kind of mood.

"No thanks. You go ahead."

"Well, maybe just a little." He scooped up a few grains of the powder, took a quick snort, closed his eyes, and sighed. "I don't do it all the time, you understand." Alana shrugged. "I just do it now and then to relax." He rubbed two fingers over his gums and then grinned. "I know." He snapped the same two fingers. "How 'bout some pizza? I got a great frozen pizza. Just take a minute."

Instead of answering, Alana shrugged out of her coat, tossed it on the couch, and then pulled the tail of her blouse out of her skirt and began undoing the buttons.

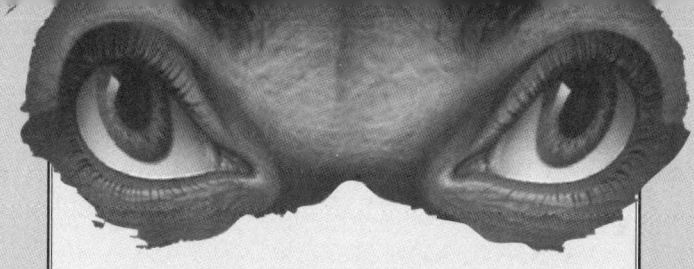

Experience the Ultimate in Fear Every Other Month... From Leisure Books!

As a member of the Leisure Horror Book Club, you'll enjoy the best new horror by the best writers in the genre, writers who know how to chill your blood. Upcoming book club releases include First-Time-in-Paperback novels by such acclaimed authors as:

*Douglas Clegg   Ed Gorman
Elizabeth Massie
J.N. Williamson   Charles Wilson
Bill Pronzini
Robert J. Randisi   Tom Piccirilli
Barry Hoffman*

**SAVE BETWEEN $2.48 AND $4.48
EACH TIME YOU BUY.
THAT'S A SAVINGS OF UP TO NEARLY 40%!**

Every other month Leisure Horror Book Club brings you two terrifying titles from Leisure Books, America's leading publisher of horror fiction.
**EACH PACKAGE SAVES YOU MONEY.
And you'll never miss a new title.**

Here's how it works:

Each package will carry a FREE 10-DAY EXAMINATION privilege. At the end of that time, if you decide to keep your books, simply pay the low invoice price of $7.50, no shipping or handling charges added.
HOME DELIVERY IS ALWAYS FREE!
There's no minimum number of books to buy, and you may cancel at any time.

AND AS A CHARTER MEMBER, YOUR FIRST TWO-BOOK SHIPMENT IS TOTALLY FREE! IT'S A BARGAIN YOU CAN'T BEAT!

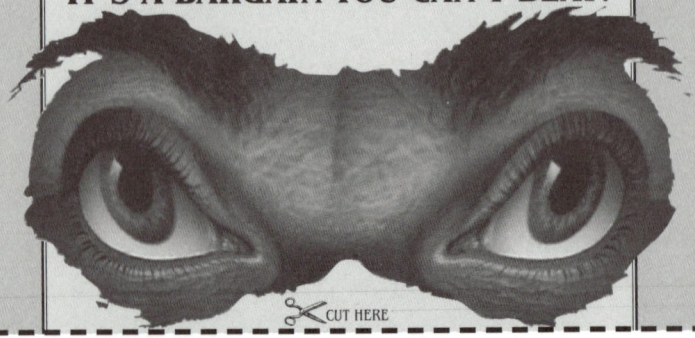

✂ CUT HERE

Mail to: Leisure Horror Book Club, P.O. Box 6613, Edison, NJ 08818-6613

YES! I want to subscribe to the Leisure Horror Book Club. Please send my 2 FREE BOOKS. Then, every other month I'll receive the two newest Leisure Horror Selections to preview FREE for 10 days. If I decide to keep them, I will pay the Special Members Only discounted price of just $3.75 each, a total of $7.50. This saves me between $2.48 and $4.48 off the bookstore price. There are no shipping, handling or other charges. There is no minimum number of books I must buy and I may cancel the program at any time. In any case, the 2 FREE BOOKS are mine to keep—at a value of between $9.98 and $11.98. Offer valid only in the USA.

NAME:_____

ADDRESS:_____

CITY:_____ STATE:_____

ZIP:_____ PHONE:_____

LEISURE BOOKS, A Division of Dorchester Publishing Co., Inc.

Ungrateful Dead

When she was done, she let the blouse hang so that the soft fabric framed the cups of her lacy black bra.

Kevin's entire fantasy life flashed in front of his eyes. He muttered something unintelligible, ripped off his jacket, almost fell trying to get out of his trousers, and yanked his undershirt over his head. Then, still in his blue-and-red Chicago Cubs boxers, he began pawing through his wallet. "Don't worry, I have protection."

"Lucky me."

Alana took his hand and led him into the bedroom.

As was the rest of the apartment, the master bedroom was a monument to tacky. The trampoline-sized waterbed and black silk sheets weren't that bad. The red lava lamp on the night table, next to a year's supply of Rogaine, she could have let slide. But the gilt-framed photograph of the cast of *Baywatch* hanging over the bed was enough to make even Roseanne gag.

With an embarrassed smile, Kevin excused himself, swept the Rogaine into the night table drawer, and darted into the bathroom. A few minutes later the toilet flushed, and he sashayed back into the room surrounded by a red silk robe and a cloud of English Leather. He punched one of the buttons on the stereo remote, and the soothing sounds of Kenny G filtered out of the hidden speakers. Finally, with a flourish, he held up a bottle of Guava body lotion.

"Massage?"

Hugh Hefner would have died of shame.

Alana grabbed the front of the robe and pulled him over to the lamp on the chest of drawers. Sweeping back her hair, she angled her face to the light. "Like what you see?"

He cringed, but managed a weak smile. "S-sure. You—you're a very . . . attractive woman."

She laughed, then released the robe, put a hand on his

Gary L. Holleman

chest, and shoved. Kevin stumbled backward, his arms windmilling, hit the padded edge of the waterbed, and fell flat on his back.

"Just lie back and enjoy the show." She turned up the volume on the stereo. "This bother the neighbors?"

He shook his head. "The guy on the right works nights, and the people on the other side are members of a country-and-western band."

She gave the knob another twist, then slipped the blouse off her shoulders and let it slide to the carpet—Kevin was all but drooling. She threw back her head, closed her eyes, and let her body sway with the music as she used her fingers to walk the hem of her skirt up past her knees.

Kevin slipped his hand inside the waistband of the shorts.

Alana wagged her finger. "Naughty, naughty! Don't start without me."

With the skirt bunched around her waist, she did a slow pirouette, inviting his eyes to stroke and probe every inch of her voluptuous body. Next, she unzipped and stepped out of the skirt, slipped her arms through the bra straps and let them hang—by some miracle, the flimsy lace barrier didn't crumple under the weight of her breasts. Bending all the way over, she rolled down her stockings, her back and flanks glistening now from a fine layer of sweat, and her eyes, when she looked up at him, made promises that Kevin wasn't sure he was going to be able to keep. Inside his shorts, the hand was frantic and just as his eyes began to roll back, she stopped.

"Wh—what's the matter?"

Hands on hips, she stomped around the room. "This is boring. Wait a minute! I saw a ball of twine in the living room. Don't go away."

Ungrateful Dead

She vanished into the next room for what seemed to Kevin like hours, and when she returned she was carrying a ball of shipping twine and a feather duster in one hand and the Swiss butcher knife from his kitchen in the other.

Eyeing the knife, he asked, "Wh—what are you going to do with that?"

She gazed at the reflection of her eyes in the shiny blade. "Don't be such a baby," she scolded. "We're gonna have some fun."

"What kind of fun?"

Using the knife, Alana cut four three-foot sections of string and then went to the side of the bed. "Scoot up."

"I don't know—I don't like to be hurt."

Leaning over, she ran the feather duster up one chubby thigh, across the bulge in his shorts, and down the other thigh. His mouth formed a ragged "O" and his hips shot off the bed.

"Oooo!"

"Did that hurt?"

He shook his head.

"Then come on. It's so much better this way."

She tied his wrists and ankles to the bedposts and then unhooked her bra and stepped out of her panties.

"Slow down," he whined. "You're going too fast."

Something dark moved behind her eyes. "Sorry, lover. I haven't got all night."

She slipped the blade of the butcher knife under the waistband of his shorts and ripped; his erection went down like the Hindenburg.

"Hey! Those are my special Mark Grace edition shorts."

"Be patient." She put down the knife. "It'll be worth it. Now," she picked up the duster, "close your eyes."

Frowning, he did as she asked. "Okay. But do you have any idea how much those cost?"

The instant he closed his eyes, her whole demeanor changed. The provocative smile vanished and her eyes became hard, the pupils slitted and reptilian. She dropped the duster and picked up the butcher knife, and then leaned down next to his ear. "Ready or not," she whispered, "here I come!"

Positioning the blade directly over Kevin's thyroid, she made a lightening-quick, in-and-out jab with just the point. It made an negligible hole, there was virtually no blood, but his vocal cords were neatly and completely severed. Kevin made no noise, but his eyes and mouth flew open, and his body tried to levitate off the bed.

Alana kissed his cheek. "See, aren't we having fun?"

Two hours later, Alana stood in the apartment's space-age shower, lathering her hair with Guava all-over body shampoo and whistling "Sympathy for the Devil," while around her feet, water the color and consistency of tomato soup spiraled down the drain. When done, she stepped out, dried off with one of Kevin's oversized bath towels, and then put her clothes back on and stood in front of the mirror.

"Helloooo there. I see you. Do you see me?"

She giggled and tilted her head to the side and brushed back her hair. Yes, the scarring was clearly better. She ran her fingers through her damp locks. They were longer and thicker too. Things were really looking up.

She tiptoed through the blood-splattered bedroom to the living room, where she used the remainder of the twine to bind up a brown paper–wrapped shoe box. She wrote Luther's name across the top of the package with a felt-tipped pen.

"There!"

Ungrateful Dead

Looking around one last time, she smiled, picked up the phone, and dialed Cal's number.

Luther hung up the phone.

"Where is she?" Cal asked.

"Some apartment in Germantown."

"What the hell is she doing there?"

"I don't know." Luther stared at the unfamiliar address he had scrawled on the back of one of Cal's envelopes. "Her car broke down."

"So what do we do now?"

Luther listened to the house. It was cold and still, and he could feel something waiting in the silence. "I don't like the way things are going."

"No kidding."

"I think we should all pack some things and go to Tru's for a few days."

Cal glanced around the room. "I can't just pick up and leave. I have patients, Sam has school."

Luther lowered his voice. "It might not be safe here."

Crossing to the bed, Cal sat down next to Rachel. "What do you think?"

Her eyes were bleak and frightened. "It would be nice to see Virginia," she whispered.

Cal's shoulders slumped. "Okay, then, let's do it."

Luther stood in the corner with his hands in his pockets while Rachel and Sam packed bags, and Cal telephoned Grace to tell her he had to go out of town unexpectedly and to reschedule his patients for next week. Samantha walked through the living room with two suitcases and placed them in the foyer next to the front door. She turned on the porch light and started to unlock the door.

"Wait!" Luther said. Hustling over, he peered through the peephole.

Gary L. Holleman

"Uncle Luther," Sam whispered, "can I talk to you a minute?"

"Sure."

"That guy at the mall, do you think he's out there?"

"I don't know."

"Do you think they're holding Mal for ransom? Her dad's rich."

"I'm sorry, honey, I don't know that either. I guess I'm not a very good uncle, huh?"

She put her arm around his neck and hugged him. It was so unlike Sam, Luther let her.

"No. You're wonderful." Then she lowered her voice to a whisper. "Don't let those people hurt Mom and Dad."

"I'll do my best," he whispered in return. "Remember, your dad's pretty good at taking care of things."

"Not when it comes to Mom. If anything happened to her, I don't know what he'd do."

"Honey, nothing's going to happen to any of you."

"Promise?"

He had no business promising anything, and no way to back it up, but looking into her eyes was like looking into the sad, trusting eyes of a puppy. "I promise."

Cal steered Rachel around the corner and pointed her toward the door.

"How are we going to do this?" Cal asked, frowning as he looked at all the suitcases. "It looks like we're heading for the Gobi Desert."

"Why don't you load everything into your car and take Sam and Rachel and head over to Tru's?"

"And you can take the Audi and go get Alana? Okay, here are the keys."

"Thanks." Luther put his eye to the peephole and got a fish-eye view of the long, winding, dimly lit walkway, flanked by a forest of thick shrubs and trees. "Oh, boy."

Ungrateful Dead

"What's it like out there?" Cal whispered in his ear.

"Quiet. I wish you'd taken it easy with the landscaping."

Cal suggested Luther wait with Sam and Rachel while he ferried the luggage out to the car. By loading himself down, he made it in one trip, slipping in and out of the shadows as he maneuvered between the trees. Luther lost sight of him for a moment when he reached the driveway, but then he heard the Cadillac's trunk slam and a second later Cal reappeared, trotting back up the walk with an ex-linebacker's rolling gait.

"No problemo. It's as quiet as siesta time at Aunt Esther's. Come on."

The night was clear and cold with the pale light from a three-quarter moon filtering down through the naked tree limbs. Halfway to the driveway, Samantha abruptly stopped.

"We forgot Marino!"

"I'll get him," Luther said.

Cal tossed him the house key. "Probably on Sam's bed."

Luther sprinted back to the house and let himself into the foyer.

"Marino!"

Behind him, the Cadillac's big V-8 came to life, but the house was quiet. He crossed the living room and entered Sam's room. "Marino!" He whistled. "Here boy!"

Man! he thought to himself. The only thing scarier than his empty little house was an empty big house. He felt like there were a dozen pairs of eyes watching his every move.

"Marino!"

The little terrier poked his whiskered snout through the dust ruffle on the bottom of Sam's bed.

"There you are, you scamp. Come here."

The dog crept across the floor on his belly with his tail down between his legs. Luther scooped him up in one arm and scratched his ears. "You were on the bed before I came in, weren't you?"

Marino pleaded the fifth.

Sam's aluminum softball bat was standing in the corner next to the door. "What say we borrow this?"

The dog looked up, his liquid brown eyes trying to read the expression on Luther's face.

"You know how to use one of these things, don't you? Just point and pull the trigger."

The terrier grinned in reply.

On the way out, Luther locked the door and paused to take a quick look around.

It was almost midnight, and Cal's neighbors, mostly professionals of one sort or another, had long since gone to bed. The weatherman had been predicting snow for several days, but there was no hint of moisture in the air, only that wicked wind that sucked every last ounce of warmth from his body and left his hands and face red and raw. With Marino under his arm and the bat slung over his shoulder, he trotted down the walk toward the waiting Cadillac. He was about ten feet from the car when Marino started to whine.

"What's the matter, old fellow?"

The pup was trembling like a leaf.

"What's wrong?" Cal called.

"I don't know. He's—"

The terrier started scratching at Luther's arm until, to save his jacket, Luther put him down. Marino hit the ground running and made a beeline for the car.

"Well, that's gratitude for you."

"Luther—"

"Wha—"

Ungrateful Dead

The Skriker was crouching behind the elm tree that grew next to the sidewalk. At Luther's approach, it eased back into the shadows, but as it moved, Luther caught a glimpse of the beast's hellish red eyes. He swung the bat down from his shoulder.

"Where did it go?" Cal shouted.

Without bothering to reply, Luther walked slowly toward the car, his body tense, his eyes straining against the gloom. Every time a leaf moved, he stopped; when a tree limb rubbed against its gnarled neighbor, it was like a cold knife in his gut.

"Come on, come on," he whispered.

A single blood-red eye appeared from around the base of the tree.

Luther froze. "What the hell are you waiting for?" he muttered angrily.

His eyes were slowly adjusting to the sparse moonlight.

There was something—a silhouette, a pool of dirty oil, standing out like a dark stain against the dead-brown grass. It appeared to be just lying there, not moving, and Luther was baffled by the animal's behavior. He racked his brain trying to recall everything he'd ever read about the creatures, and when that provided no clue, he thought about the way it had acted in his backyard. That triggered something, and a nagging suspicion wormed its way into his mind.

"You're trying to keep me away from the car."

"What did you say?" Cal hissed.

"It's trying to keep us here!"

Cal threw up his hands in exasperation. "It's a dog for crissake!"

"Someone is coming, and I don't think we want to be here when they arrive."

As Luther moved toward the driveway, the dog raised

201

its head and growled. He stopped, and the dog settled back.

"What's he waiting for?" Rachel whispered.

"Well," replied Cal, "knowing Lute, he's probably waiting for the dog catcher to show up, so I guess it's up to us." He glanced at Sam. "Help your mother into the car and stay there."

Cal tiptoed toward the tree with his arms outstretched. As soon as he set foot on the sidewalk, the dog sprang to its feet, spun around faster than the eye could follow, and bared its fangs.

"Stay back!" Luther barked.

Cal held his hands out in surrender. "You'll get no argument from me, but what are you going to do?"

"How fast can you run?"

"Damned fast when I have to. Why?"

"Run for the Caddy."

"What?"

"Go on! Run!"

Cal running was a bit like a bear lumbering uphill, but it distracted the black dog just long enough for Luther to raise the bat over his head, lunge forward, and bring it down across the creature's back. The Skriker let out a horrifying screech and shot straight up into the air. Luther ran.

Rachel and Sam were in the Caddy's backseat with their faces pressed against the window. Cal leaned across the front seat and waved Luther on with one hand while holding the passenger door open with the other. Luther saw the tension in their faces as they watched him. They were so close. He figured he needed another five seconds—five seconds and he'd be safe inside the car. He glanced over his shoulder.

The Skriker was streaking across the lawn like a black cruise missile. Luther didn't have five seconds—he

Ungrateful Dead

didn't even have two, so he did the only thing that made sense—he skidded to a stop, turned, and assumed the classic Reggie Jackson batting stance; bat cocked, left elbow out, eyes fixed on the charging animal. It seemed to grow as it came at him, its inky-black fur laid flat by the wind, its eyes blazing like molten balls of Greek Fire, its mouth open. Luther could almost feel the ground shake, but he told himself he was ready—ready to fungo the black bastard into the left centerfield stands.

At the last instant, as he stepped forward and swung the bat at the beast's massive head, the dog launched itself into the air, and the aluminum stick sailed harmlessly under its legs. The force of Luther's swing spun him completely around, and he ended up on his knees in the leaves.

He closed his eyes.

The explosion was so loud that Luther opened his eyes.

In midleap, the dog seemed to slam into an invisible wall. It let out a high-pitched yelp and flew backward, slamming into the ground hard, rolling over twice, and then lying still.

Lights came on all around the street.

Luther got up and staggered to the car. Cal was leaning on the passenger door holding a nickel-plated automatic at his side.

"You have a gun?" Luther panted.

"You noticed."

"A gun? I can't believe it. What about Sam? What if she got hold of it?"

"I keep it in the car."

"Why didn't you tell me?"

"What, and have to listen to one of your left-wing sermons? Give me a break."

"But you're a doctor for crissake."

"And lucky for you, a damned good shot. Or did you forget about Cujo?"

Luther blinked. "Oh! Right."

They approached the dog the way any sane person would a wounded lion—Luther with the bat ready, and Cal holding the gun out in front of him with both hands.

Luther lowered the bat and let out a low whistle. "Wow."

The dog was lying on its side, leaking blood from an inch-wide hole in its throat. As they stood over it, the beast growled once, its chest rose and fell two more times, and then it didn't move any more.

"Come on," Cal said. "Let's go before the cops get here." Luther didn't move. "What's the matter?"

Shaking his head, Luther replied, "It's just a dog. A big dog, but just a dog."

"What did you expect?"

"I don't know. After all this, I guess I half expected it to turn into a man or at the very least a bat."

The dog's eyes were open, staring sightlessly at the night sky.

"It wasn't a werewolf or a vampire," Cal said. "Maybe it wasn't even this demon dog of yours. Maybe it was just a mutt with a bad attitude."

Luther shook his head. "No. You didn't see its eyes. Maybe it was never human, but a human was controlling it."

"You realize how that sounds?"

Luther sighed. "Yeah. But do me a favor before you call for the white coats—take a look at that worm thing in the glass vial one more time."

Chapter Ten

It was ten after one in the morning when Luther pulled up behind Cal and shut off the Audi's engine. Tru's house was dark, and the street was so quiet he could hear the mournful wail of the train whistle all the way over on Southern. He stepped out of the car and into a puddle; gritty water filled his shoe.

"Not your night," he muttered.

He helped ferry the suitcases up to the porch, then kept an eye on the street while Cal smoothed the wrinkles out of his clothes and pushed the doorbell. The porch light came on almost immediately, and the door opened, and Tru stepped out. He was wearing a blue silk robe and reading glasses, and he had a thick, leather-bound book tucked under his arm.

"How nice," he said. "Company."

Looping his arm around Rachel's waist, Tru led them

down the hallway to his study. A reading lamp on the desk provided the light and there was a tray with a pot of tea and four cups on the typewriter stand.

"You expecting someone?" Cal inquired.

Tru pointed Sam to the couch in the corner, then helped Rachel into the wingback chair across from the desk and smiled and patted her hand. "You okay?"

She nodded her thanks and returned a wan smile.

He walked around the desk and began pouring tea. "I have been calling your houses for the last hour. I had a visitor tonight and after he left I figured you all might be by."

"Visitor?" Luther said, remembering their run-in with the black dog.

"Largest Asian gentleman I ever saw. Said his name was Grover, but he wouldn't tell me his last name." Luther glanced at Cal and shrugged. "Said he worked for a man named Anton Gadarn—I see from your expressions you know the name."

Rachel dropped her chin on her chest and started sobbing. Tru hurried around the desk with a cup of tea, but Sam got to her mother first and took it from him.

"I'll do it," she said.

Tru glared at Luther. "Why didn't you tell me about this man? You didn't think I could help, or you didn't trust me?"

Luther shook his head. "You know better than that. But listen, I don't have time to go into it right now. Alana's stuck somewhere out in Germantown, and I have to go get her." He nodded toward Cal. "Cal can fill you in. Our immediate problem—we had intended to ask if we could hang out here for a few days. But that was before we found out Gadarn and his cronies know about you. Now—"

"I think you'll be safe here," Tru broke in. "And it

might interest you to know I know where Gadarn is. Besides," he glanced pointedly at Rachel. "She looks about done in."

Luther nodded. "Okay, thanks. I'll be back as soon as I can."

When Tru returned from locking the front door, he put his hand on Cal's shoulder and said, "What say we get the ladies to bed, and then you and I can have a good long talk."

Luther found the Z parked right where Alana said it would be, but she wasn't in it. A piece of notebook paper under the windshield wiper informed him she was inside. He assumed she meant the bungalow the car was parked in front of, so he climbed the steps and knocked on the door. Since it was the middle of the night, he arranged his face with a sheepish smile and prepared a sincere mea culpa, in case he had assumed incorrectly. The smile died when the door opened.

"My God!" he gasped. "What happened to you?"

Alana's hair was a mess and her clothing looked like she had been in a wind tunnel. She grabbed his jacket, pulled him inside, then closed and locked the door.

"Thank you for coming." Her voice sounded strange, almost as if the act of forming words was taking everything she had.

Luther gave the room a quick once-over. It was a weird-looking place—the set of *Star Trek Voyager* came to mind—and the air smelled funny, but there were no obvious signs of trouble. "What's happened? Why did you run off like that? Whose place is this?"

With each question, her face became a little more pale, her lips a little more drawn. Taking a deep breath, Luther slowed down and softened his tone. "Alana, talk to me."

Her hands looked more like claws and her fingernails had almost disappeared into the armrests. "She—I was in the bathroom at Cal's..."

"Yes. You were in the bathroom. Go on."

"It happened so fast, I wasn't expecting it. I was—you know, going to the bathroom? And all of a sudden she was all over me, squeezing me back inside my own mind."

Luther tried to make sense of her babbling, but something in the room kept distracting him. It was that smell. Hot, metallic, and rancid, it reminded him of something—something... Then he remembered; the copper refinery near Cornwall.

Strange incense, he thought.

"Okay, so you're telling me your mother took over your mind, is that it?"

"It was horrible. I've picked up a few of her memories before, nothing concrete—flashes, but this—She made me leave Cal's, get in my car, and drive to this bar here in Germantown."

"Why?"

"I didn't know then. It was like I could see pictures in my mind, but I couldn't read her thoughts. When I tried, it was like slamming up against a heavy black wall."

"Could she read your thoughts?" *If she can, we're in trouble.*

"I—I don't think so."

Luther walked over and put a hand on her shoulder. Her body was as taut as a guitar string. "Take it easy. You want some water?"

She nodded.

On his way to the kitchen, Luther passed a door that he presumed led to the master bedroom. He stopped, sniffed, and then continued past a dining alcove full of

Ungrateful Dead

plastic plants and heavy glass and chrome furniture, and on into the kitchen where he went to the sink and filled a glass half-full of water. On the way back to the living room, he paused at the bedroom door, as he considered checking to see if there were any aspirin in the bathroom medicine cabinet.

He reached for the doorknob.

"I wouldn't go in there if I were you," Alana called out.

"Oh?"

"It smells like something died in there."

"I noticed."

He walked over and handed her the glass. "I thought you might want an aspirin."

She shook her head. "Thanks."

Luther sat down on the sofa and watched as she downed the water and set the glass on the floor. "Okay?" She nodded. "So go on. You went to a bar—"

"*I* didn't go to the bar! *She* went to the bar! I was just along for the ride."

He couldn't help it; he rolled his eyes. "Right. So you're at the bar—"

"You said your friend Truman was going to help us. Have you spoken to him yet? What did you two come up with?"

"Later. What happened at this bar?"

Her face clouded over. "I don't know why you're being so mean to me. You don't know what I've been through tonight."

You don't know what I've been through tonight either, he thought angrily, but he let it pass. "You're right. But I haven't had a chance to talk to Tru yet. I dropped Cal and the girls off at his house and came straight over here."

"Oh." For some reason she seemed disturbed by his

answer and he noticed she didn't ask why Cal and his family had gone to the Connely's in the middle of the night.

"Look, if it makes you feel any better, Tru told me he knows where Gadarn is."

That got her attention. She grabbed his arm. "How did he find out?"

Nonplussed, he stared at her. "Are you going to tell me what happened tonight or not?"

"First, I insist you answer my question."

"You insist?" Luther shook off her hand, picked up the glass, and stalked into the kitchen before he said something he would regret.

"Luther!"

He poured himself a drink of water and stared at his reflection in the window over the sink. "Women!"

He tried reminding himself that she'd had a tough night and did his best to put on a happy face. It wasn't easy. Nothing was easy. Relationships weren't easy— Who was he fooling? Relationships were the pits. That whole "men are from Mars–women are from Venus" thing missed the mark by light years. Men and women weren't from different planets, they were from different solar systems.

He rinsed out the glass, opened the dishwasher, and pulled out the top rack. The only item in it was a large butcher knife, which was covered with something that looked like chunky barbecue sauce. He placed the glass upside down beside the knife and closed the door.

That whole left brain–right brain thing was a crock too. Who cares what side of the brain you balance your checkbook with? Genetics made men explorers and hunter-gatherers, able to go for weeks without contact with the tribe. Women were social animals. They went to beauty salons and spilled their guts about the most

Ungrateful Dead

intimate details of their sex lives to the first stranger in curlers they came across.

"Are you going to hide in there all night?" Alana yelled.

"No. No, I'll be right there."

The problem was, the game was rigged in their favor. He was tired of being alone. Tired of feeling guilty about Genny and Janice. Tired of living like some kind of emotional Howard Hughes. He was just tired. There were times watching Cal and Rachel when he'd envied Cal. Looking at Sam, he saw all the kids he'd always wanted—teaching was a poor substitute for fatherhood. Maybe it was time to take a chance.

"Luther!"

This time as he passed the bedroom door he noticed a faint, reddish-brown smear about the size and shape of a shoe on the otherwise immaculate gray shag. He stopped short, puzzled, staring at the stain, and then slowly raised his eyes to the door. He got the oddest sinking feeling in his stomach.

"I'm sorry I was such a bitch," Alana said. "Come here and sit down. I have something I want to give you."

"Alana, who lives here?"

"Oh, a friend of mine. Come—look!"

She was staring at him, so Luther smiled and did as she asked.

"See this?" She had a package in her lap about the size of a shoe box. "I got you a present. To get it, all you have to do is tell me who told Truman where Anton is."

His eyes went from the package to her face and back to the package. His name was on it; scrawled across the top in a bold, heavily slanted hand. The feeling that something was wrong was so strong that for an instant he thought his heart had stopped beating.

"Hey... Luther." Her voice was like honey. "Lighten up. Look, I know what you need."

She placed the package on the table, then got up and went to the funky-looking drum in the corner and removed the top. Reaching inside, she pulled out a plastic bag containing about two ounces of white powder. Luther was pretty sure the powder wasn't baking soda. She came back, sat down, and placed the bag on the coffee table in front of him.

"Go on. Take a hit—you'll feel better."

The horrible part was; she was right. Cocaine always made him feel better—infinitely better. At least for a few hours. But those few hours—

Opening the bag, Alana held it up to her nose. "Ummm. That smell. That tingle. Nothing like it—remember?"

Luther ran his tongue over his lips. "I—I don't think—"

"What's to think about? Take a hit, kick back, we talk a little, and maybe, who knows, we go into the bedroom and have some fun. That doesn't sound so bad, does it? A little fun?"

Luther tore his eye from the plastic bag and forced them to focus on Alana. Her expression was contemptuous, her eyes huge and deep, swirling like pools of muddy water where beneath the surface something waited and watched. He should get up right now and leave, let her find her own way home—he should. He really should.

His eyes darted to the space-age telephone on the table next to the couch. Maybe he should call his sponsor— What the hell was that guy's name?

He looked back at Alana. She was grinning. Grinning

and licking her lips, swinging the bag back and forth in one hand while fooling with the buttons on her blouse with the other. The buttons began to fall—One . . . two . . . three . . . The blouse parted. Oh man! Her nipples looked like a couple of thumbs about to poke their way through the flimsy lace bra.

"What's wrong?" she purred. "You want it—you know you want it. It's what every man wants, a nice uncomplicated piece of ass."

A wave of molten heat spread through his groin so that he had to close his mouth to keep from drooling.

That wasn't true anymore, he tried to tell himself. He wanted a complicated piece of ass . . . No, what he meant was . . . That sure was a lot of creamy white flesh contained in one tiny, black bra. An awful lot. And that mole . . . That mole? That big, black mole!

The passion infecting his blood like a raging fever instantly turned into a cold creeping terror that spread through his system like ice water.

"Okay, enough!" he hissed. "Either tell me what's going on, or I'm outta here."

"Okay fine." Alana shot up out of the chair, stomped over to the drum and made a show of returning the bag to its hiding place. Then, without a hint or word of warning, she grabbed one of the fighting spears from the wall-mounted display and spun around.

"You don't want to fuck!" Gripping the handle of the spear with both hands, she dropped into a crouch. "You know what they say about a woman scorned."

Incredulity made Luther hesitate—Alana didn't. She charged across the room and made a swipe at his head with the broad blade of the spear. Scrambling over the back of the couch, he managed, by the width of a cat's whisker, to avoid being beheaded. He didn't waste breath asking what the hell she was doing? Or, why she was doing it. The answer was written all over her face. She wanted him dead—right then, right there!

"You move pretty good for a college professor." She slowly stalked him around the couch, her eyes blazing with demonic fury.

Luther circled in the same direction to keep the sofa between them. "*University* professor."

Her laugh had little humor in it. "Touché. Now let's see if that puny academic brain of yours can figure a way to get you out of here with your liver intact."

She feinted left, made another swipe at his head, then chased him around the pit group and through the dining room—he lost her for a second in the rubber jungle, but she cornered him again behind the rolling island in the kitchen.

"Damn it," he gasped. "Don't they put back doors in these places anymore?"

"You might try the bedroom," she suggested with a grin.

He grabbed an aluminum pot to use as a shield and yanked a knife from the knife holder. Unfortunately, it was a paring knife.

"Shit!"

She laughed again.

He threw the knife in the general direction of her head and took his lucky key chain from his pocket.

"What do you think you're going to do with that?"

He gripped the keys between his fingers so that they pointed out like the spikes on a chain-mail gauntlet.

She laughed all the more. "Temper, temper. Anyone would think you're not having fun."

"Try this for fun, bitch!"

He leaned into the heavy island, and one of its hard, plastic wheels rolled over her foot.

"Ow! Shit, you bastard!"

Ungrateful Dead

Once the island was in motion, he kept pushing, and she kept backing up until he had her pinned in the corner between the stove and the butcher block counter. The impact knocked the wind out of her and would have taken the fight out of any normal woman, but Alana went berserk, spitting and shouting curses while hacking at his head like a deranged lumberjack. If it wasn't for the pot, which Luther used like a tennis racket to fend her off, he would have been in serious trouble. As it was, the island wasn't going to hold her forever, and he had just about run out of ideas.

"What's the matter, *Professor?* Getting tired?"

Was he ever! Anybody else and he would have used his reach advantage and his trusty cooking utensil to brain her, but he didn't have the heart—after all, it obviously wasn't really Alana. But he didn't have time to debate her, either—she was a hell of a lot stronger than she should be, and his arms were beginning to feel like rubber bands. So, when her face started getting red from trying to escape her jury-rigged prison, he had a brainstorm.

Bracing the island with his leg, he transferred the pot to the hand holding the keys, reached over to the sink, and turned on the cold-water faucet.

"Thirsty?" she panted.

"No." Switching hands, he held the pot under the faucet and filled it to the rim. "But I thought you might be." He threw the water in her face.

Alana's head snapped back and crashed into the vent hood over the stove. Her eyes crossed and her legs buckled and, if not for the island, she would have collapsed.

Luther quickly refilled the pot and doused her again—this time she dropped the spear and threw up her hands.

"Stop it! What are you doing? Trying to drown me?"

He refilled the pot again and waited.

Alana groped behind her until she found a dish towel and used it to wipe her face. She stared at Luther for several seconds, then shifted her gaze to the pot.

"You can put that down. I'm okay."

"Alana?"

She nodded. "Yeah."

His eyes narrowed. "How do I know it's really you?"

She touched the scarred side of her face. "With a face like this, who else could it be?"

"You know what I mean," he replied, but he let the pot rest on top of the island.

"Yeah." She hung her head. "Oh, God, Lute. Oh, God."

He rolled the island aside and went to her. Lifting her chin, he said, "Look at me."

Her eyes were bleak, but there was no sign of the rage and madness he had seen in them a few moments before. "What the devil's going on?"

She started to cry. "You have to see it."

"See what?"

She took his hand and led him to the bedroom door. "It's horrible." And then she opened the door.

She was right.

He pulled the door closed. "We better call someone."

"And tell them what? I did it, but it wasn't really me? Tell them they should go arrest a dead woman? They'll lock me up, and that's just what Mother wants."

Confused, Luther ran his fingers through his hair. "What are we going to do?"

"Do you have to look at me like that? It *wasn't* me!"

Luther planted Alana on the couch in the living room. "Stay here."

"Yes, master."

Ungrateful Dead

He found a pair of rubber gloves under the sink in the kitchen, then went around the apartment with a bottle of disinfectant and a roll of paper towels, wiping down everything either of them might have touched. When he got to the bedroom, he took one look, and almost said to hell with it—ten people couldn't put a dent in that mess; it looked like a slaughterhouse. Tiptoeing around pools of crusted blood, he made his way to the bed. He had seen his share of horrible things, but nothing to compare to this. The man had been skinned, eviscerated, and filleted like a tuna. The only things she hadn't cut to pieces were his eyes, which were staring up at the ceiling as if waiting for God to intercede. Of course, they had no choice but to stare, for the eyelids were gone.

Luther pulled the bedspread up to cover the body and then started in the bathroom and worked his way back through the kitchen and dining room to the living room, where he found Alana curled up in a ball on the couch, asleep. Her body was twitching, her eyelids fluttering as she grappled with shadowy monsters in her dreams. He put his hand out to wake her and then paused, wondering who would be in charge when she woke. He saw the package with his name on it sitting where she had left it on the coffee table. It wasn't likely Morgana had brought him an early Christmas present—at least, not one he would want, and the last thing he wanted to do was open it. But then he couldn't just leave it behind either.

He picked it up. Whatever was inside moved heavily from side to side when he shook it—not a good sign. Tiptoeing into the kitchen, he went to the sink and removed the outer wrapping and then the top. Inside was a note with his name on it and a lot of tissue paper. He unfolded the note:

Gary L. Holleman

Luther,
A little something to help you and my daughter put the **Heart** *back in Christmas!*

Luther removed the tissue paper—it was stiff with dried blood. He glanced inside the box, then replaced the note and closed the lid and shuddered uncontrollably for almost a minute. All the years he'd studied the occult; years of witchcraft, voodoo, mysticism, and devil worship. The years in the jungles and swamps and arid plains. All those years, and it was only now, staring into that shoe box, that he understood the true meaning of evil.

He couldn't turn Alana over to the police. There was just no way she could cut out a man's heart. Having seen more than one psychopath, he was positive she didn't fit the profile—and no one could convince him she was that good an actress.

He took the shoe box into the bedroom and placed it under the bedspread next to the body. He couldn't imagine what the police were going to think when they found it, but then, looking at the room, they might not think about it at all.

On the way out he caught a glimpse of his reflection in the mirror.

"Jesus!" he muttered. He looked a fright. If the police pulled him over, they'd think he had been bathing in blood—even his hair was stiff with it.

He deposited the stained towels in the washing machine and turned both it and the dishwasher on, removed the gloves and flushed them down the toilet, and returned to the living room and shook Alana awake.

"Come on, we have to go. It's almost four."

Turning over, she stretched and opened her eyes. One eye was sea-green, the other was a dull shade of brown,

Ungrateful Dead

and the scars now looked no worse than cheap make-up badly applied.

"You're a mess," she said.

"I know."

"What happens now?"

"Is your car really broken?"

Her face reddened. "No."

"Then follow me back to Tru's."

"What about—No cops?"

"No cops."

"I need to go by my place to pick up a few things."

"Not wise. You can probably borrow what you need from Virginia . . . Tru's wife."

Alana stared at him pointedly. "There are some things one woman doesn't borrow from another."

"What? Oh! Okay, but we gotta make it fast; just in and out."

On the way out, Luther paused to wipe down the doorknobs with his handkerchief and then they stood in the umbra of the balcony upstairs and scanned the parking lot.

He'd half expected to see cops in riot gear and S.W.A.T. team members in black Ninja suits running around. But it was as quiet as any apartment complex should be with two hours to go until sunrise, and there was nothing to see but lightless windows and empty cars and stars glaring down at him like a billion reproachful eyes.

For once, Luther was glad to be driving a car. He stuck close to the Z's bumper all the way to Alana's house and walked close behind her up the dark sidewalk and waited, casting nervous glances in every direction as she fumbled with her house keys. When she finally managed to get the door open and stepped inside, she stopped so fast that Luther bumped into her.

Gary L. Holleman

"Shush!" she hissed. "Someone's been in the house."

"Damn!" he whispered back. "I knew it."

"What should we do?"

"Well, considering what I'm covered in, I don't think calling the cops is too keen an idea." He stepped around her. "You got anything we can use as a weapon?"

"Knives, in the kitchen."

Remembering the shoe box, he shook his head. "Anything else?"

"No."

He tiptoed halfway into the living room and stopped.

"What are you doing?" Alana was right behind him.

"Trying to listen!" he hissed.

"Well, you don't have to bite my head off," she whispered in return.

They listened to the sounds of the house settling, the wind rattling the gutters, and their hearts pounding, and after about five minutes Luther whispered, "How do you know someone was here?"

"Look down."

A trail of muddy footprints led from the front door into the hall.

"Maybe I should go first," she said, drily.

Biting his tongue, Luther followed the tracks into the hallway and stopped in front of the closed door to Alana's bedroom.

"I never shut that door," she whispered.

"Great." He put his ear to the wood.

"Anything?"

He didn't reply for several seconds. "Did you leave a radio on?"

"No. I'm sure I didn't."

He led her back into the living room. "This is the strangest burglar I've ever heard of. He leaves a trail of footprints a blind man could follow—don't say it! He traps himself in a back bedroom and turns on the radio. If I didn't know better, I'd say we had Goldilocks in there."

Alana's eyes opened wide. "Oh, my God!"

She rushed down the hall and threw open the bedroom door. "Morna!"

Alana's daughter sat up and rubbed her eyes. "Hi, Mama."

The girl was stunning—about five-five, with Alana's shiny auburn hair and emerald-green eyes. Her cheekbones were high and pronounced and her lips full and her skin looked like pale milk that had been sprinkled with just a touch of cinnamon.

"What are you doing here?" Alana demanded. "You aren't supposed to be home until next Wednesday."

The girl smoothed her plaid skirt down over her knees and gave her mother a sheepish grin. "Well, uh—" She noticed the blood on Luther's clothes. "Oh Mama, is your friend hurt? What happened?"

"Never mind that. Answer me."

But the girl smiled at Luther; it lit up her whole face. "Hello there. Who are you?"

It was like looking at a younger, undamaged version of Alana, and Luther felt his spirits lift. *Careful!* he admonished himself. *This one's a heartbreaker.*

Before he could say a word, Alana inclined her head in his direction and snapped, "That's Luther. Now tell me why you're here."

Morna rolled off the bed and took Alana's hand. "Aren't you glad to see me?"

The tension drained from Alana's body; she smiled and put a hand to the girl's cheek. "Of course I'm glad to see you. It's just—it's kind of a bad time."

Gary L. Holleman

Morna's smile widened. "Mom! Your face! It looks—"

Alana dropped her hand and sighed. "I know. But we don't have time to go into it now. We're going to visit some friends, so I want you to pack enough things for a few days."

The girl pointed to the suitcases in the corner. "I haven't *un*packed yet."

Alana smiled tiredly. "I should have known."

While her daughter was in her own room changing, Alana showered, changed, and then began throwing clothes into a suitcase. Luther stood in the corner and tried to stay out of the way.

"What are you going to tell her?" he asked.

"Nothing."

"But—"

The look she gave him could have frozen air. "She's *my* daughter! I decide what she's told."

Far be it from him to come between a woman and her cub—Luther shrugged.

She slammed a pair of jeans down on top of the pile, then folded the suitcase closed and beat on the clasps with her fists.

"Here, let me do that." Luther pressed down on the top with his knee and snapped the clasps home. He placed the suitcase on the floor next to the girl's and when he turned around Alana was right there.

"Let her stay a child," she whispered. "Just a while longer, please."

He put his hands on her hips and pulled her close. "It isn't up to me."

His touch felt so good and yet the tears were there—waiting. "I know."

"She's you, fifteen years ago."

Smiling grimly, Alana replied, "It was a bit more than

Ungrateful Dead

fifteen years, and I was never as pretty as she is."

He tried to brush her hair back, but she shied away. He smiled and tried again and this time she let him.

"How can you stand to look at me?"

She spoke so softly he could barely hear her, and he cocked his head to the side. The scars weren't nearly as bad as never being certain who he was talking to. He felt like the man who was dating identical twins—he never knew which one was going to show up. To make matters worse, because of his feelings, he wasn't sure he could trust his instincts. "I don't know—maybe looks aren't that important to me."

She chuckled. "No kidding."

"Maybe I like tough redheads."

"Me? Tough? That shows how much—"

He stopped her with his lips, but won the argument with his arms, pulling her so tightly against him that she gasped for breath. He kissed her throat, her chin, the tip of her nose, the lobe of her good ear.

And Alana couldn't get enough. She was like a beautiful but flawed flower that had been withering away in the desert of self-denial. Each of his caresses was sunshine, each kiss like soft rain, and her response was terrifying.

"Whoa, there," he said with a chuckle. "Let me get my breath."

She pulled back. "I'm sorry, I—"

He put a finger to her lips. "Don't even think it. I want you as much as—"

Morna cleared her throat from the doorway. "Sorry to interrupt, but you said we were in a hurry."

Alana grinned at Luther and stepped out of his arms. "It's okay, honey."

When Luther picked up the bags and carried them out to the car, Morna turned to her mother, stuck up her thumb, and whispered, "Way to go, Ma."

They arrived at Truman's just as the first rays of dawn turned the tops of the elm trees at the end of the street to gold. Luther got out first and looked around. A dark van was coming up the street, and he almost panicked until he saw the driver toss a newspaper into the driveway.

Shitty job, he thought.

He walked to the driver's side of the car and rapped on the window. "Wait here," he said, when Alana lowered the glass. "I'll see if anyone's awake."

He waited until the van drove past and then hurried up the walk.

Morna, who had been pushing the buttons on the radio trying to find a station more to her liking, touched Alana on the arm. "Hey Mom, look at the bumper sticker on that van."

It read, KISS ME I'M IRISH.

Chapter Eleven

After a long, hot shower, Luther donned the jeans and flannel shirt he had borrowed from Tru and went downstairs to the kitchen. Virginia was standing at the counter in her housedress, buttering a whole-wheat bagel. She smiled at him when he walked in.

"You look a little better."

The others were sitting around the table. Tru peered at him over the top of his glasses, while Cal, who'd had his nose buried in one of Tru's reference books, looked up and nodded. Several other dusty volumes were stacked in the middle of the table. Morna was sitting next to Alana, who was sitting opposite Rachel and Sam. The two mothers were busy eating and avoiding each other's eyes, while the girls, who were old enough and smart enough to feel the uncertainty in the air, were picking at their food.

Luther took the chair next to Cal. "What a happy little group."

Tru fixed him with a very cool gaze. "I can't speak for everyone else, but I'm not."

Alana turned to Morna. "Go up to your room and try to get some rest."

"You too," Rachel said to Sam.

"I'm not tired," Morna replied.

"Me neither," Sam added.

Cal put a finger in the book to mark his place. "Samantha Ann!"

Sam rolled her eyes at Morna.

"Go on," Alana said.

In a huff, Sam pushed her chair back and stomped out the door, but Morna carefully folded her napkin, made eye contact with everyone around the table and said, "Excuse me." She got to her feet, thanked Virginia for the breakfast, and followed Sam upstairs.

Cal looked at Alana and shook his head. "What nice manners. It's all we can do to keep Sam from wiping her chin on the tablecloth."

"She's not that bad," Rachel said softly.

Once the coast was clear, Tru pinned Luther with a steely gaze. "What in God's name happened?"

Luther sighed. "It's kind of hard to explain."

"Cal filled me in on what went on before, but I don't understand why the devil you didn't come to me with this."

Virginia set a plate with a bagel and a glass of orange juice in front of Luther. He nodded his appreciation. "I don't know what you're so uptight about. When Alana came to me with her story, I didn't believe it. Who would?" He glanced at Alana and smiled sheepishly. "Sorry."

"That's not exactly a news flash," she replied curtly.

Ungrateful Dead

"Anyway," Luther continued, "once I realized what we were up against I didn't want to put you and Virginia in danger."

"But you had no qualms about bringing Cal and Rachel into it."

"That's not fair, Tru," Cal said. "Luther brought Alana to me as a patient. Under the circumstances, I don't see what else he could have done."

"Maybe." Tru pulled a cigar from the pocket of his robe and glanced at the ladies. "You mind?" Rachel and Alana shook their heads and Virginia just snorted. He stuck a match to the end of the cigar and leaned back in the chair. "So what did you do? Fall in a vat of pig's blood?"

"No," Luther replied. "I'm sorry to say it wasn't pig's blood."

With Alana's okay, he filled them in on what happened at the apartment. When he got to the part about the bedroom, even the staid and normally imperturbable Virginia Connely appeared shaken. Tru asked Alana, "What was it like? Can you describe your feelings?"

She wasn't keen on the idea, but she gave it a try. "I remember I was ... upset." She glanced at Rachel. "Seeing Rachel—Seeing what was happening to her family—I was angry and tired and disgusted. Then she was in my head. I had no warning—nothing."

"She?"

"Mother. She said something like: 'Hello daughter'. And then I fell down this long, black tunnel into the world's most terrifying virtual reality game. Except in this game, she had all the controls. I moved, but I couldn't control it, and I could feel this huge ... thing all around me, trying to force its way into my head."

"Like in a dream?" Tru broke in.

"No. Believe me, it was no dream. I could see everything I was doing in perfect detail—she made sure of that. And there wasn't a damned thing I could do to stop it—I couldn't even close my eyes!"

"How do you know it was your mother?" Luther asked. "You recognized her voice?"

"No, it wasn't like that. It . . . wasn't verbal. I could feel her. Pressing, probing. Ugh! It was like a million tiny maggots trying to gnaw their way into my brain."

"Did she communicate anything else?" asked Tru.

"No. Not really. But she was gloating. I know she was. I could almost see her clapping her hands in glee."

"And this man—Carter? Did she know him or his family? Had they done something to her?"

Alana's voice was flat. "Do something to her? Nobody *does* anything to Mother. You remember his eyes," she asked Luther.

"I'll never forget them."

"She didn't touch his eyes so he could watch what she was doing." Tru exchanged a look with Cal. "She wanted to send me a message—he was it."

"And Luther?" Cal asked. "Why did she try to kill him?"

She turned and looked at Luther. "Because he was there."

Tru pursed his lips. "I don't think so. I don't think she really wanted to kill him. I think she just wanted to frighten him."

"Did a damned fine job," Luther said.

Everyone except Alana chuckled.

Then Rachel asked, "But what about the shoe box? Why in God's name cut out a man's heart? Why wrap it up like some kind of demented Christmas present and leave it for Luther?"

"It wasn't just for Luther," said Cal. "It was for all of us."

Ungrateful Dead

Tru nodded. "I agree. She wanted to show us what we were up against—show us how powerful she is. She tried to scare Luther off with the spear and us off with the heart. She wants Alana isolated, alone."

"Well, it didn't work," Luther muttered darkly.

Cal ran a finger along the side of his nose, a gesture Luther had seen him do when he was puzzled.

"What's eating you?" asked Luther.

"Well... since you asked. I don't understand why she let you off so easy."

"Easy!" Luther sputtered. "She tried to turn me into shish kebab."

"But she didn't."

"You sound disappointed."

Cal grinned. "I'm not. It's just—in my experience, women like that, even if they aren't actually trying to kill you, they'd still want to hurt you—leave you a nice little scar to remember them by. And yet there isn't a mark on you. Why not?"

"I don't know. Maybe it was my culinary combat skills, the way I wielded that pot—you should have seen me. I was awesome."

"No doubt." Tru looked at Alana. "You have any ideas?"

She nibbled her bottom lip. "Well—not really. When she overpowered me in the bathroom I tried to break free, but it was no use. Then the trip to the bar—in that apartment... it was like watching a horror movie. The worse it got, the more helpless I felt. Then, when Luther arrived, I fought her with everything I had."

"How do you mean?" Tru inquired.

"I don't know how to say it. I pushed out with my mind, trying to break through. I remember thinking if I could just get a couple of words out—warn him. But it was like I was entombed in a wall of Jell-O. I knew the instant she decided to kill him but then, when they were fighting in the kitchen, all at once her grip on me weakened."

"That must have been when I hit her with the water," Luther opined.

"No. Right before that actually. It was just for an instant, but I pushed out with everything I had."

"And she—she what?" asked Cal. "Vanished?"

"I guess. When the water hit me in the face, there was this explosion of light inside my head, and the next instant I was dizzy and dripping wet. I felt around for a towel and wiped my face, and when I opened my eyes she was gone."

Tru and Cal exchanged glances again.

"What do you think?" Tru said.

Cal shook his head. "I don't think it was the water."

"Then what?"

"Something else. Something we don't know about yet." He turned to Luther. "Was there anything else in that kitchen, something you threw at her? Something she might have shied away from? An amulet or charm?"

"Not that I'm aware of. Maybe she's allergic to cooking stoves; a lot of women I know are."

"Boo," Virginia said.

"My guess," Cal interjected, "and it's just a guess, is that Alana's mother took over in a moment of emotional and physical distress. From what Alana told me at the office, most of the changes occur when she's asleep. If we want to prevent this from happening again, we're going to have to keep her calm and relaxed, but awake."

"Is that possible?" Rachel asked. "I mean, look at her—she's exhausted."

"We're going to have to try. I have something in my

travel bag I can give her, but we're all going to have to pitch in."

Virginia raised her hand. "I'll keep the coffee on."

"Won't the caffeine make her more anxious?" asked Rachel.

"Some. I admit, it's going to be touch and go." Cal smiled at Alana. "You up for this?"

She returned a halfhearted smile. "Anything is better than—you know."

Rachel got up and walked around to Alana's chair. "Why don't we go upstairs? Maybe take a cool shower?"

Alana glanced at Cal.

He nodded. "Couldn't hurt."

She gave Luther a long look and then followed Rachel upstairs.

"Now," Tru said to Luther. "What about this phantom dog?"

Luther's eyebrows arched across his forehead. "The Skriker? Why do you want to know about that?"

"Humor me."

Luther summarized the legends surrounding the creature and then went on to explain how he thought it tied in to the Druids and to Alana. Tru puffed on his cigar and listened without comment until Luther was finished.

"Clear, concise—very academic. Unfortunately, about as far off base as one can get."

"What?"

"Don't get your knickers in a twist." Tru nodded to Cal. "Show him."

Cal slid the book he had been reading across to Luther.

"What is this?"

"A book on Celtic Mythology."

"I have dozens of books on Celtic Mythology."

"Not like this one."

The book consisted of about a thousand yellowed pages half-bound in cracked black leather and a brownish substance that looked and felt like human skin. Luther thumbed down to the bookmark, where the first thing he saw was a freehand drawing of a shaggy black dog, done in plant dyes that were so old and faded it looked like a comic book image someone had inadvertently sent through the wash.

"What language is this?" Luther asked referring to the scratchy hand writing.

"Cymric. It's a Gaulish dialect used by Brythonic Celts."

"I've heard of it, but it's so obscure I never saw any reason to study it."

"Ah," Tru said sagely, "there's a lot to be said for historical linguistics."

Luther glanced at Cal, rolled his eyes, and mouthed, "boring."

"In 1610 a cleric named Glastonbury was sent to the mountain Abbey atop Cruachan Aickle in West Connaught. There, mixed in with hundreds of manuscripts and bark scrolls the church confiscated from the local pagans, he found a stack of stone tablets. Since it was what he was trained for, Glastonbury began translating the tablets which, it turned out, were dated between 857 and 850 BC. He found that they contained, among other things, an eyewitness account of a druidical rite in which a man's soul was passed from his body to that of a large black dog."

Luther took a closer look at the drawing. The creature's eyes were more cranberry than red, but that was probably because of the book's age. "What about this drawing? And why haven't I heard about this book before?"

Ungrateful Dead

"Well, our friend Glastonbury wasn't exactly Homer. And as for the picture—who can say? Maybe it was something he saw. Maybe it was something he heard about."

"Looks pretty real to me." Luther scanned down the page to another drawing. "What's this? Another oak tree?"

Tru turned the book around and ran his finger along the inscription. "The Temple of Nathair."

"Nathair? Hey!" Cal said. "Wasn't that the Gaulish name for our old friend Set, the serpent god?"

Luther turned the book back around. "Yeah. Saint Pat's old nemesis. But this tree—I don't recall seeing one quite like it in any of the other texts. The leaves look . . . wrong."

"With good reason. It isn't in any of the other texts. As a matter of fact, old Brother Glastonbury was excommunicated just for drawing it in this book."

"You're kidding," Cal chuckled. "Why?"

"For providing the answer to the one question the Irish Church never wanted asked."

"Which was?"

"When Saint Patrick drove the snakes out of Ireland—or as we know now, the snake worshipers—where did they go?"

Cal and Luther looked at each other in surprise.

"I never thought of that," Cal said with a sheepish grin.

"Neither did I," Luther admitted, and then he pointed at the book. "It's in here?"

"According to Glastonbury, the tablets were written by a Druid neophyte named Clwyn, a scribe who had been lured into the cult by one of the local vamps shortly before the big showdown between Saint Pat and an Arch-Druid named Milcho. Clwyn claimed that in the big battle, Saint Patrick and his followers killed more than twelve thousand druids and forced the survivors to flee."

"How did he manage that?"

"Doesn't say."

"Where did they go?" Luther asked. "England?"

"*Underground* in England."

Cal was confused. "You mean they ditched their robes and stuff, but kept meeting in secret?"

"Well, yes and no. They did hold their meetings in secret, but they went *under ground*! They literally dug huge pits or found deep caves and constructed entire complexes with temples and kitchens—whole villages, all underground."

"I'll be damned," Luther whispered. "So that's what the old texts meant when they said the snakes slithered off into the bowels of the earth."

"But that doesn't make any sense," Cal opined, shaking his head. "People don't just climb into a hole in the ground. They still have to eat. Till the fields. Trade. Don't they?"

"That's right," Luther added. "Besides, once they were safe in England, why go underground?"

"Maybe they had no choice." Tru turned the page and pointed to a notation in faded ink on the bottom of the page.

"What's it say?"

"It's from the Book of Revelation, chapter 20. Then I saw an angel come down from heaven, holding in his hand the key to the abyss and a heavy chain. He seized the dragon, the ancient serpent, which is the Devil or Satan, and tied it up for a thousand years and threw it into the abyss . . . , 'abyss' is underlined, . . . which he locked over it and sealed, so that it could no longer lead the nations astray until the thousand years are completed.

Ungrateful Dead

After this, it is to be released for a short time.''

Tru looked up and stared at each of his friends in turn. Cal opened his mouth, closed it, then opened it again.

''You're not saying—''

''Of course he isn't!'' Luther snapped, but then he turned to Tru. ''Are you?''

''I'm not saying anything. Here... listen to this: 'And God, through Saint Patrick, bound the ancient serpent up in chains—in parentheses here it says a giant tree—for his transgression in the Garden, and cast him and his minions down into the darkness.' Sound familiar?''

''Vaguely,'' Luther replied.

''It should.'' Tru opened another of his esoteric manuscripts. ''This is from *The Serpent's Egg*, by Joshua Kantrell.

''For Nathair's dominion had become the dark, dank places in the earth; the realm of the worm, of decay, of the slimy crawling things that shunned the light of day. As the Tuatha, [the Druids], spread like a black plague through the uninhabited countryside, they dredged deep, lightless pits beneath barren fields and forests into which they planted the terrible acorns that carried his seed. Drawing power from massive monoliths dragged into their lairs and formed into circles, and nourished by captured and tortured human souls, his bark-covered temples sprouted up almost overnight, sending their gnarled roots deep into the blood-engorged muck and spreading wide their thick, leafy arms under which unspeakable rites of human sacrifice were performed for his pleasure.''

''Well, that certainly sounds grim,'' Cal muttered. ''But what does it mean?''

"It's just that thing the Druids had about trees," said Luther.

"No," Tru disagreed. "It's more than that. It's the way they channeled souls—man to dog, dead to living. And it lends credence to what Cal was saying earlier. Listen . . .

> "The dark power of the malignant Tree broke down the barriers between man and animal, man and man, allowing his disciples to enter and control the four-legged beasts of the field, and to usurp the bodies of their kin. For it was only through the blood of a feeble kinsman could the black soul take permanent root in its new home, where it lay for years festering like a pox until it was forced to move anew."

"A feeble kinsman, huh?" Luther said.

"Feeble—" Tru nodded. "You know. Weak, sick—mentally unbalanced."

"Physical states in which one's grip on reality would be somewhat tenuous," Cal pointed out needlessly.

Tru pulled another book from the stack and flipped to the back. "What about this? You ever see this before?"

Luther looked at a more recent drawing depicting a shamrock contained inside a small, round crystal.

"Oh sure. They're called Serpent's Eggs. All the shops in Ireland sell them; the tourists are crazy about them. Here—" Luther fished his key ring out of his pocket and tossed it to Tru.

Catching it in one hand, Tru held the crystal at the end of the chain to the light from the chandelier. "Odd looking shamrock," he said, noting the brown and shriveled plant inside.

Ungrateful Dead

"Why did you ask about that?" inquired Cal. "What's it say in the book?"

"Nothing," Tru replied. "But this drawing is on almost every page."

"They have all kinds of stories and legends about it over there," Luther stated, as Tru returned his keys. "It can ward off evil, it's a good-luck charm. It can capture the heart of the one you love. Depends on how gullible the shopkeeper thinks the tourist is."

"How gullible were you?" Cal glanced at his friend and chuckled.

"Me? Don't be goofy. It was a gift—from Genny."

"Oh." Cal averted his eyes.

"So, what now?" Luther said, to change the subject. "We know where Gadarn's hiding out; what do we do? We can't just call the cops."

Truman nodded in agreement. "They wouldn't believe us anyhow. I guess if I pushed it, they might send someone to his house and ask him a lot of dumb questions."

"And tip him off that we were on to him," Cal muttered.

"We need a plan," Tru said, pounding his fist on the table.

"A battle plan!" Cal added.

"An attack plan!" Tru responded with a grin.

"Whoa there, Stonewall," Luther moaned. "You and Patton slow down a minute. We can't just go charging into this maniac's mansion. Suppose by some miracle we get in without being killed? What are we going to do then? Say, please, Mr. Gadarn, you and Alana's dead mother quit trying to take over her body? How many people has he got working for him? What other *things* are we going to be up against? What we need is information. Once we have that, we can hit the books and perhaps find something to help us go at him. Otherwise, we may just be putting all of our necks in a noose."

Cal and Tru looked disappointed, but they agreed.

"What was the name of the guy that came here?" Luther asked.

"Grover."

"You say he just showed up and told you about Gadarn—why?"

Tru shrugged. "Got me. At first I thought one of my students put him up to it—you know how their devious little minds work. But then . . . Well, you have to see the man. He's huge. He looks like a side-by-side refrigerator on two legs, but his face is strangely . . . I don't know. Pleasant."

"Pleasant?" Cal said drily.

"He's a mountain of a man, hands and knuckles so scarred and etched by violence that just looking at them made my soul hurt. But his face belongs on a monk. And when he told me about the things he had seen since he joined Gadarn in San Francisco, his voice broke and his eyes . . . He didn't say he was scared, but I think he is and, what can I say—I believe him."

But Cal wasn't convinced. "If he's so scared, why come see you at all? Why chance angering his boss?"

Tru stubbed out his cigar in his coffee cup and then took his time lighting another. "Okay, you've got me. I don't know the answer to that. If you must know, I didn't ask him, because the whole time he was here—which couldn't have been more then ten minutes—I hardly opened my mouth. He was awfully big. But a couple of things were obvious to me. One, he was more afraid than I was. I think he senses Gadarn is worried about something, and I think *he* thinks it's you two. And two, he wants out, for whatever reason. And I think for him it's either us or go it on his own."

Ungrateful Dead

"So you trust him?" asked Cal.

"Trust him?" Tru snorted. "No way. I wouldn't trust him as far as I could throw him. But I do believe what he told me."

"Could it be a trap?" Luther asked.

"Why go to all the trouble? From what you told me, and from what Grover said, they could have taken you at any time."

Luther rolled his eyes at Cal. "Boy, that makes me feel a lot better."

Cal smiled grimly. "Maybe we should set up a meeting with this guy."

Virginia Connely had given Alana and Rachel the bedrooms on the second story at the east end of the house—the side that faced the backyard with its huge old sycamore tree that her grandkids loved to climb when they came to visit. After settling in, the women left Sam and Morna in the rear bedroom with orders to get some sleep, while they went across the hall to the other bedroom and held a long, whispered conversation about Anton Gadarn and the horrifying effect he had had on both of their lives.

The girls showered, then Sam put on a long T-shirt and Morna dressed in the floor-length flannel nightgown she had packed, and they climbed into bed. They tried to obey their mothers' wishes and go right to sleep but, though exhausted, they were keyed up and spent a few minutes whispering together before nodding off. Even in their sleep, they felt the reflexive need for human contact and lay with their shoulders and thighs touching; one girl with hair the color of new pennies, the other with locks as dark as night. One snored softly, her head turned from the strips of gray first light that filtered in through the blinds; the other moaned, her pale face rotating slowly from side to side as her nightmares took her again and again to the mall, to Malina, to the handsome young man with the dazzling dead eyes. They slept the day away, and just as the sun set, a shadow moved like a jagged finger across the blinds. A tiny gap no bigger than the width of a man's finger formed between the window sash and the sill, and an instant later, something long and black and slick-looking slithered across the sill and dropped to the carpet behind the night table. A moment later, the window closed.

Chapter Twelve

The ice skating rink at the Mall of Memphis was not the first place most people would think of when selecting a site for a clandestine meeting. Located just inside the main entrance of the huge, two-story edifice, it was generally crowded with surly teenagers and screaming children windmilling across the ice like runaway pinwheels on skates. And, deservedly or not, its reputation for petty crime and violence often resulted in nights where there were more armed private security officers than shoppers. Which was exactly why Truman picked it.

Tru and Luther sat at a table in the food court next to the rail overlooking the oval arena, sipping diet sodas and trying not to jump out of their skins every time some child squealed.

Luther glanced at his watch. "You sure he's coming?"

Tru nodded toward the escalator.

Gary L. Holleman

The mobile stairway brought this "person" into sight a few inches at a time. As his enormity became apparent, Luther did his best to keep a straight face, and by the time Grover reached the second level and started walking toward them, Luther was pretty sure they'd made a horrible mistake.

As the giant man wove carefully through the maze of white, toadstool-like tables, all conversation stopped and heads turned. Yet if he noticed he gave no sign. He pulled up a chair across from Luther and sat down with his legs stretched out in the aisle.

"Afternoon, gentlemen." His voice was soft, well modulated, and without accent. He noticed the look that passed between Luther and Tru. "Sorry I'm late. I had some trouble getting away from my employer."

Tru placed a hand on his friend's arm. "Thank you for coming, Mr. Grover."

Grover nodded. "It wasn't exactly what you'd call a snap. Anton and his pals got something big brewing, and they're as nervous as fleas." He glanced at Luther. "So you're the guy who knows all about spooks and shit like that? Anton don't like you much. Matter of fact, he'd just as soon see both of you on a slab."

Grover had a linebacker build and eyes as expressive as puddles of stagnant mud. His teeth, exposed when he greeted Luther, were white enough, but crooked. But Truman was right; he had a strangely genial face, and Luther pledged not to let the man's appearance sway him—one way or the other.

"I'm crushed. Can we skip the chitchat and get on with it?"

The big man smiled. "A tough guy, huh? Good! You're gonna need to be. What you've stuck your nose in ain't—isn't nothing like grading term papers."

Ungrateful Dead

Tru cleared his throat. "Mr. Grover, we're all a bit on edge. Maybe if you could tell us exactly what we *are* up against?"

"Grover... just Grover." Grover glanced over his shoulder and carefully scanned the crowd. The main aisles were thinly packed with children and families, lots of smiling faces. It made him want to scream. He forced his attention back to the table and the two men sitting across from him. "Okay. I don't know much about this stuff. All I know is I don't want nothing more to do with it. I don't want nothing to do with Anton and even less to do with those three clowns he's got working for him."

"You said something about a tree?" Tru said.

Grover nodded. "God awfulest thing you ever saw. We moved into that old house over on the Parkway. We ain't—we hadn't been there two days, and I go down to the basement and there's Anton standing underneath this great big mother of a tree. I mean, Christ, it's gargantuan!" "Gargantuan" was Grover's word of the day. "It has these twisted and gnarled roots that look almost like fingers, and dark, dried-out-looking bark, thick limbs that go all the way up to the ceiling plus down till they nearly touch the ground. And leaves—dark, thick, puffy-looking leaves. And old—man, that thing looks like it's been growing down there in the dark forever, but it couldn't have. I mean, I had just lugged about ten dozen boxes down there the day before, and it wasn't there!"

Grover's eyes clouded over as if he suddenly realized that his darkest nightmares had somehow followed him out into the daylight.

"The prostitutes?" Tru prodded.

"Huh? Oh, yeah." Grover cut his eyes to Luther. "Like I was tellin' the Doc here, Anton is a real ladies' man. I never seen anything like it. The guy's no bigger than a kid and is as ugly as a fence post, but the women can't seem to say no to him. Still . . . with all that, he has this thing about whores—brings them in by the dozens. First he takes 'em upstairs and does his thing with them and then he has me take them down into the basement and—Jesus!" Grover reached over without asking and took a sip from Tru's straw. "Sorry."

"That's all right. Keep it."

"The basement . . ." said Luther.

"He feeds 'em to the tree."

"What?"

Grover's eyes swept the crowd again. "Keep your voice down!" He pushed the straw up and down through the plastic top several times. To Luther, the noise it made was as bad as chalk scraping over a blackboard. "I tied 'em up, dug a hole underneath the tree, and put 'em in it."

"You buried them alive?"

Grover snorted. "They was alive when I put them in, but they was well on the way to being dead before I covered 'em up."

"Will you quit talking in riddles and just say it!" Luther snapped.

"I am saying it, man!" Grover hissed back. "You ain't listening! This ain't—shit!" Frustration at his diction made the muscles in the big man's jaw quiver. "This isn't any regular tree! It's got these big . . . I don't know . . . things growing on it."

"Acorns?" Tru shot a glance at Luther.

"Yeah, whatever. Couple of days after I first saw it, two of 'em fell on the ground and popped open. They was all full of thick, red gunk and these slimy black worms. Soon as they popped, the gunk soaked into the

Ungrateful Dead

ground, and the worms burrowed right in after it like they was bees and that stuff was honey."

"These . . . worms," said Tru, "what did they look like?"

"Worms! Black, about an inch long—at least at first. Slimy, shiny; they leave trails in the dirt like snails when you douse 'em with salt.

"Anton was standing there with me when it happened and he turns and says," Grover made his voice high and squeaky, " 'You should feel privileged.'

" 'What are them things?' I said.

"He says, 'Nothing to concern yourself about. They are a very old and very rare life form.' Then he says, 'Just don't let one get on your skin.'

"Like I would let one of them things near me. So that's fine, I'm thinking. Everything's cool. We set up shop in the old house, and I make sure if there's anything needs taking down to the cellar, Colin or Danny or Wardley done it. Then, one night, Anton tells me to go out and bring back one of his girls—he means one of the whores he's been banging regular since we got to town. I asked, 'Which one?', and he says, 'It makes no difference to me.' So I go down to Beale, pick up this nigger in the blond wig." Grover glanced at Tru. "No offense."

"I prefer African-American."

"Yeah well I bring her back and make myself a sandwich while she's upstairs flogging Anton's donkey. Anton comes down about an hour later, all sweaty and with this big, shit-eating grin on his face. I know he likes to brag, so I says, 'So how'd it go?' or something like that. And he says, 'She'll be bowlegged for a week, Grover me bucko!' So I go to get my coat to take her back like I always do and he says, 'Hold on. You won't be needin' that.' And I says, 'She staying the night?'

And he laughs—real nasty-like, and says, 'Oh, the colleen will be stayin' a lot longer than the night.'

"Now me, I don't know no better. I think okay, so Anton's talked the whore into joining our merry little band of brain surgeons, but no—he says, 'When she comes down, bring her down to the basement.' Then he trots off down the stairs. Man... when he said that, I got this real bad feeling."

Picking up the cup, Grover took a long pull on the straw. After a couple of swallows, the soda ran out, and the residue rattled in the bottom.

"Want another?" Tru asked.

Grover gave him a smile that would have made a nun blush and nodded. "That'd be nice."

As soon as Tru left the table, Grover glanced over the rail at the gaggle of kids wobbling across the ice. "You ever notice how the word discotheque sounds like disconnect?"

"What?"

Grover turned his steely gaze on Luther. "You don't like me much."

Luther shrugged and hoped it didn't look like a shudder. "I guess I don't really know you."

Grover laughed—it was a surprisingly pleasant sound. "Bullshit! But that don't matter. Thing is, I can help you."

"And in return—"

The big man's stare didn't waver. "Maybe—maybe you can do something for me."

"Like help you get out of this with your skin?"

"I look like I need help like that?"

Against all his survival instincts, Luther nodded. "Yeah. With this, I think you do."

Something moved behind the big man's eyes, and Luther got ready to duck. But Grover fooled him and smiled and it appeared genuine. "Badass professor. As old Anton would say—" His voiced raised back into that irritating falsetto, "Saints preserve us."

Tru returned with a tray of diet sodas, and the smile disappeared from Grover's face so fast Luther wondered if it had been a mirage.

"Thanks," Grover said.

"You're welcome," Tru replied. "Now—"

Grover sighed and peered over the railing at the ice skaters. "He made me tie her up, then told me to dig a hole 'neath the tree." His voice was flat, no inflection, no emotion, like a man reciting a boring story he had told many times before. "I didn't know what he was up to, and the whore sure as hell didn't know—she kept screaming at him that she didn't do bondage and that this was going to cost him big time. When I pushed the shovel into the ground, I remember thinking how mushy it was and how that ought to make the digging easier. A little later I noticed that this reddish gunk was seeping in from the sides—boy, did it ever stink! And then, those worm things started popping out of the dirt around the sides and dropping into the hole.

"Let me tell you, when she saw them things she let out a yell like to busted my eardrums. Anton, he just stared down into the hole with this funny smile on his face. 'Grover,' he says, 'gag the lady please.' Like he was asking me to get her coat. So I stuff an old sock in her mouth and wrap packing tape around her head. Then he says, 'Now, put her in the hole.'

"I looked at them things squirming around down there, and then I looked at Anton. 'Put her in the hole?' I says. Now I guess I knew all along what he was planning on doing; at least, I knew he didn't tell me to dig that friggin' hole 'cause I needed the exercise. But—I mean, put a woman in with those things! 'That's correct,' he comes back. 'Put her in the hole.'

"Okay, I think. No sweat off me. So I picked her up and put her real gentle-like down in the hole.

" 'Now, shovel the dirt back in,' he says, like he's talking to a child.

"Fine, I think, cause she's looking up at me with these real scared eyes. Anyway, I start scraping the muck back into the hole as fast as I can. Only trouble is, I put her in sittin' up, and because of all the roots and stuff the hole was only deep as her shoulders so her head's sticking out, and all of a sudden them things must'a started gnawing at her or something 'cause she lets out this God-awful scream, and her face goes all white. I mean, this ni—this African American whore's face went white, man!"

The memory didn't do much for Grover's face either.

"I had to close my eyes to keep from barfing all over everything."

"And that made you want out?" Luther asked.

Grover drummed his fingers on the table, as if trying to decide just how far he was willing to go. "That, and what they did to that little girl."

Luther leaned across the table, his voice as tight as a wire. "What little girl?"

"The little Jew girl that Danny and the others grabbed by mistake." He saw Luther's expression and knew he'd struck a nerve. "I mean, I seen—the Triads in San Fran know some pretty nasty tricks, but I never—I mean, that little girl's face—It was like her head was a balloon and somethin' went and let the air out real slow like. 'Fore it was over she looked like a raisin." Grover took another long pull on the straw. "That's when I knew I had to get out. Roughing up some dude behind on the vig's one thing. Turnin' schoolgirls into worm food—that's a whole 'nuther ball game."

Ungrateful Dead

Stricken, Luther leaned back in his chair.

"So just leave," Tru suggested.

Grover chuckled. "Right."

"Why not just leave? There must be someplace you can go, people who will take care of you . . . family."

"It ain't that." He looked from Luther to Tru and back. "It's not that. You two know about this weird spook crap, huh?"

Tru shrugged. "Some."

"It's funny. People, mostly you round-eyes, look at me and see this big-ass chink come strolling down your streets, and you start pullin' your kids into the house. Maybe some others see this ugly freak and they call the cops, even when I ain't done nothing wrong. Now I ain't saying I never I done my share of mischief, but Danny and Colin and Ward . . . they look like a bunch of Irish choirboys, but underneath all that grinning and back-slapping and 'boyo' this and that crap, they're real hard core. When I first joined up, Danny and the others was already with Anton—had been for a time, from what they said. And I guess they thought I was the same as them—like the stuff they did was no different from what everybody does. We'd get together for a few beers, and they'd get to talking about Anton and the 'good old days.' At first I thought they was just jerking my chain—showin' off, you know—impress the new guy. But I was wrong. That little man . . . he's evil. He goes down in that cellar and spends half the night talkin' to that tree. Then he goes out and runs whores into the house, porks 'em, and then shoots 'em down to the cellar like they was cattle at a slaughterhouse. He has this pack of rich fruitcakes shows up once a week or so, and they hold all kind'a weird ceremonies down there, bowin' and scraping to that tree. You ever hear of anything like that?"

Luther nodded. "We suspect Anton is the high priest and sorcerer of a very ancient religious order. These Druids, as he and his followers are called, worship various elemental gods—oak trees in particular."

"But we believe the tree you describe," Tru added, "is far more ancient and, as you pointed out, evil. It is known as the Temple of Nathair, or in more recent times, the Temple of Set."

"That's a name I heard before," Grover muttered.

"Centuries ago, Druids constructed temples in vast underground pits and caves or, as in this case, deep cellars. If we are right, and this is the mythical Temple of Nathair, and this man Gadarn is the high priest, then you have every right to be afraid of him."

Grover laughed so hard he had to grab the cup and take another drink. "Anton? You think I'm afraid of that little twerp?"

Luther and Tru glanced at each other.

"You're not?" Luther asked.

"Hell no! Well, maybe a little. But if it was just him I would have been out a here weeks ago—it's that thing lives in the tree. There ain't no place I can go to get away from that!"

"What is it?" Tru asked.

"I don't know. He talks to it like it was a woman—calls it Morgana.

"You sure that's the name?" Luther barked.

"Morgana? Sure, that's right—Morgana. Danny says it's the ghost of some broad he fell in with. Hell, according to Danny boy, before she found him, Anton was nothing but a carny geek, working with some other old broad in Dublin runnin' one of those crystal ball scams. His name ain't even Gadarn. It's Gilhoolie, or Gilbride—something like that."

"What else did he say about her?"

Ungrateful Dead

"Nothing. Even Danny and the boys is scared of this broad."

"They ever talk about why they're doing what they're doing?"

Grover shook his big head. "Nope. I get the feeling they don't know what Anton's up to their own selves."

"Then why do they work for him?" Truman asked.

"Money, same as me. Could be he taps those assholes that come to his freak show, but Anton seems to have a bottomless bank account."

"Money? That's it?"

With a shrug, Grover glanced back down at the kids. Their laughter and energy seemed to fascinate the big man. "I guess they kind of get a kick outta the things he can do. They're power freaks—fear junkies. They get off on making people hurt, and believe me—that thing in the tree is a wizard at making people hurt."

"What about Alana?" Luther pressed. "Why are they hassling her? What are they after?"

"Beats me. All I know is Anton told the boys to push her, but not hurt her. He told Ward if she so much as broke a nail, he'd nail *him* to the tree—" Grover shuddered. "Man, I don't think he was kidding. Can you think of a worse way to go?"

Luther looked frustrated, but Tru smiled in spite of himself. "Grover, I hope you don't mind me saying so, but I have a hard time seeing you as the type of man who would be afraid of a ghost in a tree."

"Well, I guess that's 'cause you ain't seen what this thing can do. Listen up—one day Anton shows up with this big black Lab...ugliest mutt you ever saw. He calls us all down to the cellar, and once we're down there, he lights all them torches, then tells Danny to lay down on this table he set up under the tree. Danny gets comfy, then Anton strolls right up to the tree, leans over, and whispers something we can't hear. A minute later, the worms start doin' the hula up outta the ground, and Anton prances around in a circle, chanting a lot of gibberish don't make no sense. Next thing I know, the dog starts spinnin' around like a top, and when it stops, Anton goes over, pats it on the head, and starts talking to it like it was Danny. And the mutt—it sits there like it's watchin' TV, listens to his every word, and then trots up the stairs and disappears.

" 'Okay,' I says to Anton, 'that's a cool trick, but what now?' He tells us to bring down chairs from upstairs and wait. So we do, and then we all sit there in that hot, smelly hole in the ground, starin' at Danny lying on the table, like we was at an Irish wake—'cept we ain't got no beer or anything to eat.

"An hour goes by . . . then two. My ass is gettin' stiff, and I'm about to expire from the heat." "Expire" was one of Grover's words the previous week. "Just when I'm about to say something, Danny starts twitching like he's got ants crawlin' up his ass, and Anton scoots over to the table, leans over, and whispers in Danny's ear, 'What do you see?'

"The Mick's eyelids flutter—you know, the way people's do when they're dreaming? And he whispers back, 'She's walking across the parking lot to her car.' Anton says, 'Is anyone with her?' and Danny replies, 'No. She's alone.' So Anton tells him to follow her back to her house and wait till Colin shows up. Then he turns to Colin and tells him to go to the Magnus broad's house and keep an eye on her til morning."

Grover finished off the soda and put the cup down on the table, all the time watching the skaters gliding across the ice below the balcony.

"We pretty much knew all that," Luther said.

"Point is," Grover turned and peered directly at Luther. "I don't intend to spend the rest a my life shittin' my pants every time I see a stray mongrel. I ain't gonna ever get a decent night's sleep until that tree is cut up and burned, and the dwarf is dead, his head cut off, his body cut into a hundred pieces, burned, and the ashes scattered over the ocean!"

Tru cleared his throat. "Well, I don't know if we can guarantee that. But if you help us, I can promise you Mr. Gadarn will end up behind bars and the tree—well, we'll want to study it of course."

Grover rose to his feet, towering over them like Godzilla as he shifted his eyes from Luther to Truman and then back to Luther. "I can see I ain't making myself clear. I'll get you two into the basement. You take care of the tree . . . I'll take care of Anton. As for studyin' the thing—" He chuckled. "When you see it, you might just change your minds." He handed Tru a piece of paper. "Here's the address. You know where that is?"

Tru looked at the number written on the paper and nodded.

"Then get ready to do what you do fast and get back to me." He placed a hand on the beeper on his belt. "You know how to reach me. And gentlemen . . . watch your backs. Remember, no place—*no* place is safe."

"One more thing," said Luther. "The girl . . . where is she now?"

The giant man shivered like a man standing naked in a freezing wind. "Still down there, man. Down in that stinking mud."

On the way back to Tru's house, they stopped at a drugstore to pick up some shampoo and a few other things that Luther needed. As he returned to the car, he spotted a small brown-and-black beagle relieving itself on a telephone pole on the corner. He stopped so quickly that he almost fell off the curb.

After finishing its business, the dog sniffed the pole and then trotted off down the street in the opposite direction, and Luther chuckled at his own foolishness and climbed into the car.

"I'm beginning to understand how our friend Grover feels," he said to Truman.

"No kidding."

"Listen, you see any reason to mention what happened to the Marks girl?"

Tru thought it over. "What about Cal?"

"I'll tell him, but Alana and Rachel—"

"Yeah, and Virginia. I don't know how she'd take hearing that."

Back at the house, they herded everyone except the girls into Tru's study, where Tru began filling them in on their meeting with Grover. Luther was standing with his back to the sliding doors, listening with no small amount of admiration to Truman explain how he, with only his intellect and a token amount of help from Luther, browbeat information out of this eight-foot Triad hitman. As Tru was winding down, Luther thought he heard a noise on the stairs, and he opened the door a crack and peered into the hallway. He didn't see anything, so he stepped out into the hall and checked the stairs. They were empty.

Shaking his head, he slipped back into the study just as Tru was reaching the end of his epic. The news that they now knew Anton Gadarn's whereabouts didn't appear to lift anyone's spirits.

"What do we do now?" Alana asked.

"I'm not going near that man," Rachel said with such vehemence that everyone else was silent for several seconds.

Ungrateful Dead

Truman smiled hesitantly. "I have a friend down at the hall of records. Maybe a blueprint of the mansion would be helpful."

"Good idea," Cal said. "Meanwhile, Lute and I will see what we can dig up on the Temple of Nathair—pardon the pun. There's got to be something in the texts on how to combat the thing."

"What about us?" Alana asked, holding out her hand to include Rachel and Virginia.

"Cal?" Luther said.

Cal smiled and put a hand on Alana's arm. "It is imperative that you stay calm. Try to clear your mind, meditate maybe read a book." He turned his gaze on Rachel and Virginia. "I need you two to keep Alana awake as much as possible. We don't know enough about the mechanism of the change she's going through, but it looks like she's most vulnerable when she's asleep. I suggest Virginia stay with her first, so Rachel can get some rest, and then switch in about—" He glanced at his watch. "Five hours."

Virginia nodded and took Truman aside. "Try to remember you're not eighteen anymore." She grabbed the front of his shirt and pulled his head down so she could kiss his cheek. "And put on something warm. It's snowing, and if you catch cold you'll miss the caroling next week."

Rachel hung by the doorway until Virginia was finished, then glanced at Cal. She looked for a moment as if she wanted to say something to him, but turned without speaking and followed Virginia upstairs.

Cal watched his wife go with a blank expression that did little to disguise his growing concern. Her condition seemed to be deteriorating, and he felt helpless to do anything about it. He thought he understood how traumatized she must feel after what happened, but until she opened up to him there was little he could do.

Alana waited until the other women were out of sight and then said, "You're going to need me on this. None of you has any idea what Anton looks like, and even less of an idea what he's capable of."

Luther grinned. "I promise, I won't let any redheaded midgets sneak up on me."

"That's exactly what I mean! You keep thinking of him as some kind of bad joke and all three of you are going to wind up dead . . . or worse."

Luther patted her shoulder. "You could be right, and that's even more reason for you to stay here. You can hardly stand. What happens if we run into trouble? I can't watch out for you and myself at the same time."

She let her head drop to his chest. "That's not fair."

"I know."

"Why won't you let me help? I feel so . . . useless. I'm not an invalid you know."

"You're not useless. You're the reason we're doing this. If anything happens to you, it's all for nothing. Now please—let's go up and check on the girls, and then Cal and I have to run over to the U of M library."

Alana grudgingly allowed him to lead her up the stairs and down the hall to the guest bedrooms. The door was ajar, and Alana stepped through just as Morna was climbing back into bed.

"Oh. You're awake."

The girl glanced at Sam's outline under the covers, put a finger to her lips, then walked out into the hall. "I had to use the bathroom," she said, eyeing Luther's heavy topcoat. "Where are you going?"

"I've got to go to the library."

The girl yawned. "What's going on, Mother? What happened to your face? Why are we here? I haven't even unpacked yet."

Alana hugged the girl and stroked the side of her face. "I know. Go take a shower and we'll talk later. I have a lot to tell you."

"Has this got something to do with Grandmother?"

Alana held Morna at arm's length. "Why would you ask that?"

"I don't know. When you get weird it always has something to do with Grandmother."

Overwhelmed with guilt, Alana crushed Morna to her. None of this was her fault, Alana thought miserably. Her daughter had had the cosmic bad luck to be born into the wrong family. "The sins of the mothers," she whispered.

"What?"

She kissed the part in the girl's hair. "Never mind. Go on, get cleaned up and then we'll sit down and have a talk. There are things I should have told you a long, long time ago."

Morna nodded to Luther. "Dr. Shea."

"Luther."

And then the girl returned to the bedroom.

"This has to end," Alana said.

"It will," Luther replied.

"It's her or me, now."

"You mean him or you, don't you?"

Alana snorted. "No. This time she dies and stays dead."

Twilight always reminded Anton of his years with the New Castle Carnival. It was the time of day when the rubes, fresh from their ten-hour drudge in the mills and mines, came to the midway hoping to escape the lethal sameness of their boring lives. Pug or Tommy or John, their rough clothing stained with oil and grease, came dragging their homely wives and snot-nosed brats or, in the case of the younger louts, their skinny, half-witted girlfriends, to gawk at the bright lights and funny people who worked at the carnival. And the stupid sluts always, *always,* came to Madam Zodiac to have their fortunes told.

Is Johnny faithful to me?
Will it be a boy or girl?
Will my Tom ever pop the question?

Always the same. Same questions, same moronic giggling, same look of amusement and disdain when they saw Madam Zodiac's funny little red-headed assistant.

As those memories, along with the gray sunlight oozing through the crack in the dusty drapes, began to fade, Anton sent the others away, changed into his ceremonial robes, and went down into the cellar. He didn't light the torches, preferring instead to let his stubby legs feel their way across the floor. Besides, it wasn't totally dark; the tree gave off a subtle green bioluminescence that he found added to the air of wonder that surrounded it.

As usual, the cellar felt like a greenhouse, and Anton undid the robe's sash and let it hang. Through the tunnels he heard the wet hiss of the rainwater-swollen creek, and he went to the wall beneath the steps and pulled the lever that released the steel, water-and sound-proof doors. Now it was quiet; he needed quiet to commune with his god.

"Good evening, my dear."

The tree's massive limbs creaked as if something dark and heavy had come to rest upon them.

"And how are you this—I know, I know. The time passes slowly. But it won't be much longer. And then we shall be together forever."

Danny and Colin had started decorating for the upcoming festivities, and Anton dragged one of the chairs over near the base of the tree, arranged the legs as best he could around the thick roots, and sat down and gazed at the weathered bark the way another man might look upon a shapely woman's calf. When he spoke, the wistfulness in his voice was almost heartbreaking.

"I do so miss talkin' to you face to face, hearin' the sound of your voice. Lass, you were the only one was ever nice to me. I mean me—the real me. The others—all I ever was to them was a dirty little joke for them to whisper about over tea. Their own private little roller coaster ride to their jollies!"

Reaching out, Anton ran his hand over the trunk.

"It was never like that with us. Soul mates, that's what we be lass . . . soul mates. A couple a more days, and your soul will be reunited with its rightful body, and then—all the things you promised, immortality! My new body!" Anton chuckled. "That Shea fellow, the one that's been givin' us such fits . . . he's tall and straight, a bit long in the tooth, but I wouldn't mind movin' in there. Serve him right!"

The leaves, which in normal light would have appeared unnaturally thick and so green that they were almost black, rustled angrily.

"What?" Anton leaned forward, his thick brow wrinkled in concentration. "Somebody's been talkin' outta school? Who? I don't understand. What?"

He looked down at his feet and saw a single black leech squirm up out of the soggy ground and inch toward his foot. He reached down so the creature could climb up on his finger and then brought it up to his nose. In a blink, the leech slithered onto his lip and disappeared up his right nostril. Anton made a noise like a cat trying to hack up a hairball, then threw his head back and closed his eyes.

Chapter Thirteen

It was December 20, the eve of the winter solstice, and the weather was doing its part to live up to the season. A freak blast of Arctic air swept down from the Dakotas, bringing a mixture of snow and freezing rain that sent the temperatures plunging into single digits. Memphis was in every sense a Southern city. Which meant that as soon as the first snow-flake hit the streets, a kind of chemical reaction took place: Every car in motion tended to remain in motion until it collided, violently, with its neighbor. In other words, the streets were a disaster.

After sitting stalled in traffic for two hours with groups of Christmas shoppers who were full of just about everything except holiday cheer, Truman and Luther let themselves into the foyer and stomped the snow off on the mat. Marino came out first, wagging his tail

Ungrateful Dead

a mile a minute, followed closely by Virginia, Cal, and Rachel.

"Welcome back," Rachel said.

"What's it like outside?" asked Virginia.

"Like?" Luther muttered. "It's like Disney World on Ice. Dopey and Grumpy missed us by an inch as we drove over the railroad tracks on Southern, and Goofy ran a red light and almost totaled Tru's car." He glanced around. "Where's Alana?"

"Upstairs in her room reading," Cal replied. "Sam's with her."

Luther took off his parka and hung it up with the other coats on a hook next to the front door and then jogged up the stairs. When he reached Alana's bedroom, he opened the door a crack and peeked in. Sam was sitting in a chair across from the foot of the bed, and Alana was lying on top of the bed with a book opened face down on her chest—both were sound asleep.

"Damn!"

Throwing open the door, he charged across to the bed. The door banged into the wall, and Sam sat up like she had been goosed.

"Uncle Luther! What—what happened?"

He wanted to scream, but was able to control the urge. "Sam, do me a favor, run down and get your dad."

One look at his face was enough to send the girl rushing out of the room.

Luther stood over Alana and ran his fingers through his hair. What now? he wondered.

Cal came pounding up the stairs with Truman puffing at his heels.

"What's up? Sam's downstairs bawling like I just took away her charge card."

Luther gently brushed the hair back from Alana's face. "Take a look."

"Christ!" Cal hissed.

The last of the old scars had vanished, leaving the left side of her face as smooth as an alabaster bust.

"I'm sorry."

Luther glanced over his shoulder. Sam was hovering in the hall just outside the door.

"I didn't mean to go to sleep. It was so warm in here—"

Luther gave her a tired smile. "It's not your fault."

"What do we do?" Cal whispered. "Wake her?"

"I'm almost afraid to."

"She won't sleep forever," Tru pointed out.

"Okay." Luther put his hand on Alana's shoulder and shook her. When she didn't wake, he shook her again—harder. This time she opened her eyes; they were both dark brown.

They stared at each other for several seconds before she spoke. "You're back?"

He nodded. "How do you feel?"

"I don't know—strange." She saw Cal hovering at Luther's shoulder. "Is something wrong?"

"You fell asleep."

She sat up and looked around the room. "I did? I guess I did."

She swung her legs over the side of the bed and then put a hand to her forehead. "Phew!"

"What is it?" Luther squatted on his heels so he could watch her face.

"Dizzy."

He put a hand on her shoulder, and she looked him in the eye.

"I'm okay. Just a little dizzy."

He searched her eyes looking for—he wasn't sure

Ungrateful Dead

what, a glimmer of recognition, fear—hate. She gave him a lopsided grin.

"It's me."

"Maybe," he replied. "She fooled me before."

Alana held out her hands for Tru and Luther to help her up. "I don't know what the big deal is. I fell asleep. I'm sorry."

Luther held on to her hand. "Come, I'll show you."

He led her to the dresser and positioned her in front of the mirror on the wall. She gazed at it in awe, as if it were the glass rather than the reflection within that held her eyes in thrall. Then, ever so slowly, she raised a hand to her left cheek and, as if driven by some hypnotic compulsion, inched closer to the mirror.

"My God," she whispered. "I never thought—" She pinched the pink flesh of her cheek. "I mean, I was just a child when—" Then Alana noticed the color of her eyes. "My eyes! What happened to my eyes?"

"You tell us."

"Easy, Lute," Cal said. "Alana, tell us what you're feeling right now."

Where to begin! she thought. Her mind was a tangle of contradictory emotions, the foremost of which was terror—she wasn't stupid, she knew what these changes meant. Morgana wasn't clawing at her mind at the moment, but she had been there—and not long before, sneaking through her unconscious like a thief. The residue of her foul presence hovered like the foul stench of a decaying corpse. She haunted Alana's dreams, whispering! Stealing her memories one by one and replacing them with ones of her own. No wonder it was becoming harder and harder for Alana to tell fantasy from reality.

But her face! Her face was real—wasn't it? She had been to doctors, dozens of them! They all said the same thing, *Sorry, the scars are too old and too deep. We can try grafts, but*—They'd never had the guts to say it out loud, but even if the grafts took, her face would always look like ruts in a mud road.

To see her face this way . . . the way she had always dreamed! Why couldn't they understand?

"Alana?" Luther squeezed her hand.

"I don't know what I can say. It's me. I know it's me, but—I can't prove it." She pulled her hair back from the left side of her face and reached out and touched the mirror. "This . . . it terrifies me! And yet, it's so incredibly wonderful!"

Luther had to admit, she did look pretty good. He still had doubts, but the emotion in her voice sounded real.

"Seeing myself this way, it . . . it almost makes everything I've gone through worthwhile."

Luther cut his eyes to Sam listening at the door and brought his mouth close to Alana's ear. "That's exactly what she wants you to think. I don't mean to rain on your parade, but knowing your mother, do you think she did this for *you*?"

Alana dropped her eyes and turned around. "No, I guess not."

"Mother? What's wrong?" Morna had joined Sam at the door. When she saw Alana's face, her eyes widened in shock. "Oh . . . I—I don't—Mom, what's going on?"

"Look," Alana said to Luther, "either you believe I'm me or you don't, I don't care. Right now, I think it's time I had a talk with my daughter."

"Okay, but make it quick. Tru and I have a lot to tell you, and then we're all going to have to sit down and decide what to do." She started to walk away, but he held on to her hand. "Remember—no matter what happens—I liked you the way you were when we first met."

"Yeah?" The old sardonic smile didn't work as well on her "new" face. "But I bet you like me better now."

Ungrateful Dead

Gently but firmly she pulled her hand free of Luther's grasp and went to Morna. "Come on, kiddo, we need to talk."

"Use my study," said Tru. "I'll make sure no one disturbs you."

Downstairs, Alana shut the double doors and watched her daughter stroll around the study, gazing with wonder at all the strange and beautiful artifacts. She paused at almost every display case and statue, turning her head this way and that as she examined with obvious delight whatever object caught her fancy; she looked but never touched.

Alana sat down in the chair next to the fireplace. "Rachel is right, you are a very well-behaved young lady."

Morna seemed surprised at the praise. "The Sisters don't leave one much choice."

"How well I know. Some of those same nuns taught me."

"I know."

That pretty much exhausted Alana's store of the small talk, and Morna went back to inspecting Truman's mini-museum.

"Mother, it has been my experience that when an adult studies one thing quietly for such a long time, they usually have bad news." Morna came over and took the chair across from Alana. She crossed her ankles and folded her hands in her lap.

"Perceptive *and* well behaved. The nuns really did a good job."

"If by perceptive you mean I'm no longer a child, you're right. I'm well read, well traveled, I've had my period now for several years, and I've been dating for almost a year—no one steady," she added hastily. "The Sisters made sure of that."

Alana tried to hide her smile. The last thing she

265

wanted was to appear patronizing. "Oh? So there's no one special?"

"No one. There was this one boy, Todd Henstridge. He was at Saint Michael's across the lake—but his father transferred him to a military academy."

"And what made Todd different?"

"Oh, any number of things. He was the captain of the soccer team. He rowed second in his class. And he's very intelligent."

"I'm sure he is. But is that all? He's intelligent and a good athlete?"

"Well . . ." Morna nibbled at her bottom lip with her incredibly white teeth. "He is nice looking."

"Nice?"

"Kind of tall, slim, but muscular." Her face flushed. "I mean, if you care for that sort of thing."

"Naturally."

"He has brown hair, which he keeps a bit too long—I think that's one of the reasons his father made him transfer; he thought the Brothers were too lenient about that sort of thing. And he has blue eyes and a very nice smile. He reads incessantly and writes poetry and these lovely short—" Morna caught they way Alana was looking at her and dropped her eyes into her lap.

"That's all right honey, don't stop."

The girl raised her eyes. "It doesn't upset you? I mean—"

"Why would it upset me to hear about your young man?"

"I don't know—I always felt sort of selfish."

"Why?"

"Because—because, you know, your face—you didn't have anyone."

Alana refused to go to pieces. She was afraid if she did, Morna might close up again. "But sweetheart, I

Ungrateful Dead

want you to have boyfriends, I want you to be happy."

"Then"—Morna's voice cracked—"why did you send me away?"

The question was like a slap in the face, but it reminded Alana of why she was there. She got up, pulled her chair around so she could sit at eye level and hold the girl's hands. "I never wanted to send you away. Every time you left it was like tearing my heart out with my bare hands."

"Then why?"

"I wanted to protect you."

"From what?"

Alana held onto her daughter's hands as if they were a lifeline. "If things go well the next few days, I promise you'll never have to go away again. But first, I guess I better explain about what's going on . . . that's the bad thing I have to tell you. You remember when you were a little girl, and I'd tuck you in at night and brush your hair?"

Morna nodded. "Yes."

"And you remember, every time, before I turned out the light, you made me check under your bed to see if there were any monsters?"

"Yes, but—"

"And I always told you there were no such things as monsters? I lied."

Luther and his merry band of Druid fighters, as they called themselves when Alana wasn't around, were sitting at Virginia's kitchen table having tea, coffee, or a Coke and discussing the mess they found themselves in, when the telephone on the wall rang. Truman got up and answered it. He listened for a few minutes, then said good-bye and returned to the table. He nodded to Cal and Luther.

"That was our friend Grover. It's like we thought, the ceremony is being held for the solstice tomorrow night. He said the fruitcakes, as he calls them, will start arriving about nine and Gadarn will be upstairs getting decked out between seven-thirty and eight-thirty. He said he'd send the other three off on some errand or other to get them out of the house and then be ready to let us in."

"That's a great plan," Cal muttered. "Now all we have to do is come up with some way to get past Gadarn and his army of crazies and destroy this mythological tree."

"I don't understand," Sam said. "What's so important about tomorrow night?"

"Like Luther was saying, honey, this cult believes all the power in the universe is controlled by the alignment of certain celestial bodies, and that by holding their rites when these bodies are arranged just so, they can tap into this power. The winter solstice, which in our hemisphere is the shortest day of the year, is one of these times when the planets and stars are aligned."

"But that doesn't make any sense. What has the time of year got to do with some old tree?"

"Sam, honey," Rachel said softly, "don't ask so many—"

"No," Cal said. "That's all right. Sam's in this, too, and she has a right to know what we're doing."

"I don't *want* her to know about any of this!" Rachel insisted.

"We've never kept anything from her, and I don't intend to start now. Besides, after what happened to Malina, I think she needs to know."

"We don't know what happened to Malina!" Rachel snapped.

Luther looked sick. "Uh . . . yeah, we do."

Ungrateful Dead

Everyone stopped talking and stared at Luther.

"You know where Mal is?" Sam asked.

Luther looked to Cal for support.

"Uncle Luther, she's my best friend."

Cal finally spoke up. "We'll talk about it later, Sam."

"She's dead, isn't she?" Rachel said in a stunned whisper.

Luther shook his head defiantly. "I'm sorry, that's as much as I'm going to say right now."

Before Sam could jump in with anything else, Alana and Morna returned to the kitchen. Morna's face was pale, and it was obvious both mother and daughter had been crying.

"May we come in?" Alana asked.

Cal went to Sam and placed his hands on her shoulders. "Sure, Alana, but I think maybe Sam and Morna should excuse us for a while."

For an instant it appeared that Sam was going to argue, but Cal gave her shoulder a squeeze and, with a sigh of resignation, she finally agreed. Once the girls were safely up in Sam's room, Luther decided it was time to lay everything out just the way Grover had told it to them—including what had happened to Malina. And, feeling it was important to drive home exactly what kind of fiends they were facing, he spared none of the details. When he finished, he could tell from their expressions that he had succeeded.

Without a word, Truman got up and went into his study. Likewise, Virginia got up and put a pot of extra-strong coffee on the stove to brew. The rest of them sat around the table, staring at each other. Ten minutes later, Tru came back with his arms full of books and slammed them down in the middle of the table.

"One way or the other," he said, "before the sun

comes up in the morning, we're going to have a way to put a stop to all this.''

Sam came out of the bathroom and sat down on the edge of the big, four-poster bed in front of the window. She bounced a couple of times on the mattress. It was a nice, big room with high ceilings and hardwood floors and big lamps with frilly white shades. The bed was nice and big too, and even had a homemade patchwork quilt on top and big fluffy goose-feather pillows. It was the kind of bed made for sleeping in on cold winter mornings when the wind howled and the window panes rang with the tap-tap-tap of rain and sleet.

Morna was sitting on a mahogany vanity stool in front of a matching dressing table, brushing her hair with the brush she had found on the table.

"What's it like, living with nuns?" Sam asked.

"The pits."

"Everybody thinks you're so cool."

"Cool? Me? Who said that?"

"Oh, Dad and Mom . . . Uncle Luther. They think you're so polite."

Sam said it like politeness was a social disease.

"You try living day and night with a bunch of old women carrying rulers. You'd be polite too. It isn't like I want to be—it's more like a trained response, like a dog coming when you whistle."

Sam giggled. "You have very pretty hair."

"Thank you. I always wanted to cut it short like yours, but the Sisters wouldn't allow it." Morna glanced at her plaid dress and carefully eyed Sam's clothes as she ran the brush again and again through her silken strands. "I like your jeans."

"These things? I ran out so fast I didn't have time to get anything nice. You brought jeans, didn't you?"

"I don't have any jeans."

"You're kidding!" The concept was so alien that for a moment Sam was struck dumb.

"No."

"Cutoffs?"

"Them either."

"Wow. What were you in, a prison?"

Morna grinned. "It wasn't that bad. Mom would have bought them for me if I'd asked, but the Mother Superior has very definite ideas about how young ladies should dress and blue jeans don't fit in anywhere."

"So I guess you didn't date much, huh?"

"Not much. There was this one boy, but he transferred to a military academy last quarter."

"That's tough. Were you two, you know . . . close?"

Hot blood spread like a rash up the back of Morna's neck. "Oh! No, we were just friends."

Morna put the brush down and checked her eyes in the mirror. They were still red and puffy from the talk she'd had with Alana. Sighing, she turned around to face Sam. "I look like death."

"No you don't. You could use some make-up, but—let me guess, you don't use make-up either?"

They laughed at the same time, and the room seemed a little warmer.

Sliding off the bed, Sam got her duffel bag from the chair next to the door. After rifling through it for a few seconds, she came out with a stylishly faded and holey pair of jeans.

"Here. I think we're about the same size—try 'em."

Morna blinked back surprise. "But, I don't have anything with me except school blouses."

"No problemo." Sam went back into the bag and came out with a man's long-sleeved white dress shirt still in the cellophane bag. "Wear this. It's one of my dad's, it'll drive him bat shit."

Morna grinned. "I couldn't."

"Aw, go on. He won't mind. I always break them in for him."

Morna began skinning out of her school uniform.

"This thing that's happening to your mom," Sam said. "You understand it?"

Down to her bra and panties, Morna paused with one leg in the jeans. "Not really. I mean, Mother would never lie to me, but what she told me—it sounds so fantastic, you know?"

"Yeah." Sam dug her comb out of her purse and stood in front of the dresser, combing her hair. "These people, these ... druids. They kidnaped my friend Malina. I think ..." There were tears in Sam's voice. "I think they killed her."

"That's what Mom said. Why?"

Sam put away the comb and dried her eyes on her shoulder. "I don't know. It doesn't make any sense. What do you think they're going to do?"

After removing the shirt from the wrapper, Morna carefully removed the pins. "Who?"

"Uncle Luther and Mr. Connely."

"Why ask me?"

"I figured your mom might have said something."

Morna slipped on the shirt and began doing up the buttons. "You know adults, they wouldn't tells us the sun was up if they didn't want us to go to school."

"Yeah." Sam chuckled, but her expression was dead serious. "Well, I intend to do something."

Morna took the belt off her dress and slipped it through the loops in the jeans. "What do you mean?"

"Do something. Do something! Mal was my best friend. I'm not going to just sit around here with my thumb up my butt..." Morna's eyes widened. "... while Mom and Dad and Uncle Luther talk it to death."

"But what can you do?"

Sam went over to Morna, pulled out the shirttail she had just tucked in, and tied it in a knot in front. "There. I don't know what I can do yet. But I want you to help me—okay?"

"Gee Sam, I—"

"It's no big deal. Just keep an eye open, see what they're planning, and let me know. Can you do that?"

"Well—"

"Look, Morna," Sam said earnestly, "your mom's the one in the most danger. How are you going to feel if something happens to her and you find out you could have helped stop it?"

Morna's pretty face closed up like a fist. "Oh, God! I can't let that happen."

"Then just keep your eyes peeled and leave the rest to me."

Chapter Fourteen

Other than the cellar, the darkest and gloomiest part of the mansion was the attic, a long, rambling room filled with old boxes, battered steamship trunks, and crates. The floor consisted of a few rough wooden planks laid side by side over dirty-yellow fiberglass insulation, and the roof was high and peaked, with enough cobwebs between the rafters to provide parachutes for an entire airborne division. It smelled of dust and age, and was so cold that it could have been used as a storage warehouse for meat.

Grover found himself up in the attic rummaging through one filthy crate after another because Anton, the dunce, couldn't find his spare ceremonial robe. After starting in the back corner, he had methodically worked his way all the way up to the steamship trunks at the front, sneezing his head off from the dust, and wondering how the damned attic could be so cold when the cellar was so friggin' hot.

Danny appeared at the top of the stairs. "Yo! Anton wants you in the cellar."

"Shit!" The steamship trunk lid slipped out of Grover's hands and slammed with a bang that shook the floorboards. "Shit! Shit! Shit! Why do you have to creep around like that all the time?"

Danny grinned. "A wee bit jumpy, are we?"

"What does he want now? Ain't it enough I'm up in this freezing dust bowl, plowin' through all this shit lookin' for his costume?"

"Hey, don't go killing the messenger, boyo. I'm just doin' what I'm told, same as everybody else 'round here. 'Cept . . . I wouldn't be letting him hear me call it a costume."

"Yeah, yeah."

Grover stomped past Danny and lumbered down three flights of stairs to the kitchen. He paused at the sink to draw a glass of water, ignoring the column of reddish, sulfur-smelling liquid that spewed from the tap as he fought to keep his hand from shaking.

Man, he mused, he'd be glad when tomorrow night was over and done. Once he got past that, he'd just help himself to old Anton's cash stash and then off he'd go to San Fran, see the hills, the streetcars, hear the skree of the gulls, and smell the clean, salty air of the bay. No more of this creepy shit. No more buryin' little girls in bloody mud. No more assholes in funny robes. No more of that fucking tree!

Grover downed the water in two gulps, made a face, placed the glass in the sink, and then took another second to peer out the window. The backyard looked like the fucking Antarctic, and as he watched, the shadows of twilight closed like skeletal fingers over the frozen underbrush. He suddenly felt cold, colder than he ever remembered feeling in his life. His mother, when she was high, which was most of the time, used to tell him to be home before dark because the shadows of twilight were the fingers of death and would reach out and steal his soul. He had never known if it was the opium or just her idea of a fairy tale, either way, he finally understood what she meant. He had never given much thought to souls—his or anyone else's. But lately it was all he could think about. The night after he'd put that little girl in the ground; the night he'd gotten drunk for the first time in two years and made the mistake of eavesdropping on one of the periodic lectures Anton gave Danny and the boys—that was the very night Anton had chosen to wax poetic on the subject of human souls, which, according to Professor Anton, were nothing more than tiny, inconsequential bundles of energy masquerading as thoughts, ideas, and memories. And like all energy, Anton had said with a chuckle, souls could neither be created nor destroyed, but they could be altered in form.

"Altered in form," Grover muttered. "Jesus!"

The images that phrase brought to mind had kept him awake for three nights in a row and now, during the day, every sudden noise made him jump, and he broke out in a cold sweat if Anton so much as looked at him. But that was okay . . . he only had to keep it together for one more day. One more day. Besides, the little creep was too involved with the preparations for his big party to pay any attention to him. Yeah, that was it, he was too busy.

Grover opened the door and clomped down the cellar stairs. The place was lit up like a Carnival midway: torches going full blast, portable floodlights trained on the tree. Anton had even made Colin and Wardley string Christmas lights over the tunnel arches, handrail, and table. Grover thought the place looked like a Southern Baptist tent revival.

"Ah, Grover me boy, there you are."

Anton was standing by himself, gazing up at the crop of giant acorns hanging like dark apples from the heavily laden branches of the tree.

"You wanted me?"

"Yes indeed. What do you think of the decorations? Grand, aren't they?"

"Peachy."

Anton chuckled. "Peachy—yes, very apropos; fruit—tree. Yes, I get it."

Grover hadn't meant anything by saying peachy except . . . peachy. But then, Grover had never known a man who enjoyed the sound of his own voice as much as Anton.

"We've never talked much, you and I, you being somewhat of a quiet and retiring sort of fellow. I guess you've wondered what all this is about." He held out his chubby little hand to indicate the tree.

Having seen Anton buoyant and bragging after sex, angry or drunk most of the rest of the time, an affable Anton made Grover nervous. He glanced around to see if Danny or one of the others was lurking in the shadows, but they were alone. He blotted his sweaty forehead on his shirt sleeve. "Not really. Only thing I wondered is why it's so friggin' hot down here all the time."

"Well now, see, you come to the right person. I can tell you that. At least, I can tell you what happens. I can't tell you the how or why.

"As the Temple sinks its roots deeper and deeper into the ground, it starts to gobble up heat and moisture. The more it feeds, the faster it grows, and the more heat it pulls in."

"Don't make no sense," Grover said. "Why heat?

Where does it come from? And where does it go?"

"Boyo, all plants need some heat. You ever see a flower growin' in the snow?"

"Well—"

"Where does it come from? The very air around us. The air in the cellar, then around the house, then the block, and then finally around the city." Anton stretched out his arms and made claws of his hands. "If it keeps on growin', it keeps pullin' in more and more heat until nothing else grows, and everything for miles around is one glorious sheet of ice."

"That's nuts." Grover opined.

"Is it? Is it really? You looked outside lately?"

Grover wiped his forehead again. "But where does it all go? If that thing uses that much heat, it has to go somewhere."

"Down." Anton pointed at the ground. "Through the roots, into the ground."

"The ground?" Grover echoed dully, staring at the mud as if he had never seen it before. "That don't make no sense either. What's the ground have to do with it?"

Anton shrugged. "Aye, that's the question, ain't it, me boy? Maybe the little wormies need it. Maybe it goes deeper . . . much, much deeper, if you get me meaning."

Grover's shirt was plastered to his body like a wet sheet. "Then what?"

"Then—I don't know! Then again, did you ever think, boyo—the world was once all ice, from pole to pole, as far as the eye could see. Aye, and a grand sight it was too, I hear. Mankind was different. No fancy electronic gizmos, no flyin' machines. They looked up to different gods. They knew then who was in charge, who the boss was. Not much love thy neighbor in a frozen cave—everybody's too busy knockin' each other out o' the way to get close to the fire." He chuckled. "Then the world changed—got warmer. People got spoiled. Men started listening to the women they lived with, stopped fighting, started diggin' in the dirt like bloody dogs." Anton stared at the tree. "Time comes around again . . . who knows?"

Grover stole a glance at the dwarf. He was crazy as a loon and that made him even more dangerous. Grover considered what might happen if he just grabbed the little creep by the neck and twisted his head around.

"Big man like you, you probably think I'm a bit funny to look at. No, no, my friend that's perfectly understandable. Most people would agree. That's why when I met her and she was able to see past this ridiculous exterior to the real person inside . . . well, I started to say she captured my soul, but truth be told, I gave it to her of me own free will."

"Her?" Grover grunted.

"Come on! Don't be playing the dunce. You must have picked up on at least a wee bit of what's been goin' on. The colleen's Mother."

"Uh, she's in the tree?"

Anton turned around and grinned. "Not exactly *in* the tree, just kind of stayin' there—temporary like."

"I don't get it. How can she—"

"I don't have time to explain the workings of the universe to you! Her soul, her being, all life is energy. When she died, this energy—the thing that made Morgana special—became part of the living sap in the tree. She will stay like that, indefinitely, as long as the tree lives or until the time is right for her transfiguration."

"You put her in there?"

"Me?" Anton laughed out loud. "Good gracious, no. I could never have preserved her soul like that. She did that her own self. I just did what she told me."

"I . . . I don't get it." Grover felt something was terribly wrong, but figured it never hurt to keep Anton talking. "I thought you were some kind of magician or something."

Pursing his lips, Anton rolled his eyes up to the ceiling. "Yes, 'tis true I know how to do a few things—minor little tricks. But Morgana—ah, now that woman knows things! She was a pretty little thing, but old. If I told you how old she really was, you would call me a liar right to me face."

"Then how—"

"How did she end up inside that tree?"

Grover nodded.

"Well, as is wont to happen, things did not go quite as planned. You see, Morgana was in England preparing for her next transfiguration. Anton saw the confusion on Grover's face and frowned. "Okay, okay, without makin' it too fucking complicated—Morgana was born in a village on a tiny island in Donegal Bay, which, if you hadn't already guessed, is off the coast of Ireland. When she was nine, a famine swept the island, and by the following winter, all the food was gone and the people of her village were starting to look at each other in, shall we say, an entirely new light." Anton chuckled again. "Just then or, as the bards so love to say, just in the nick of time, this group of people washed up on the beach near the village. Bloody, half-drowned, they looked like a pack o' rats that jumped a sinkin' ship which, as it turns out, wasn't too far off. For you see this here group was the survivors of a rather famous religious dispute, which had taken place on the mainland. Needless to say, they lost.

"They asked the village chief for sanctuary, claiming their enemies would be looking for them, but the headman told the newcomers to take a look around—the village was down to boiling sandals to make soup! They

Ungrateful Dead

had no food, little clean water, and no place at all to put them up.

The leader of the newcomers put his arm around the headman, took him aside, and told him to give him two children—any two children, to offer up to his god, and he promised that the village would never go hungry again. Things being what they were, the headman took one look at his fields and then at his people—it was a good bet they were all going to be dead by spring anyway, and he said, 'Which two do you want?'

"Well, don't you know, even as a girl, half-starved and covered with filth, Morgana was a looker. The newcomer's new leader, name of Matha MacUmoir, pointed her out and another girl and then he led them and his people off into the forest and set about digging this huge pit. Naturally, the villagers didn't know what to make of this, but within a month, men in robes just like mine started showin' up with baskets of corn and potatoes. And in the meanwhile, old Matha took such a shine to Morgana that he brought her into the sect and even began teaching her their secret rites. When the temple was ready, he let her—all five-and-a-half foot of her—officiate at the sacrifice of the other village girl to Set."

"Set?"

"Uh, that's not important. What is important is what she learned. Secrets! Deep, dark secrets—the keys to the kingdom. A power so vast that it virtually destroyed death forever."

Now Grover was totally confused. "But, I thought—she's dead, isn't she? I mean, the ghost—"

Shaking his head, Anton glanced at the tree. "No, far from it. Sleeping, some of the time, but far from dead."

"So how did she wind up as a tree?"

"She *ain't* a tree!" Anton slowly counted to ten. "Look, it was like this—We had a little accident drivin'

281

through England—the roads over there! Ach! You wouldn't believe. Anyway, she went through the windscreen and got all cut up. I went all to pieces, but she was real calm like; even with blood pourin' out'a her like rain out of a boot, she says to me: 'Anton me love, I'm hurt bad so listen careful and do exactly as I say. We're close to a real special place. Now what you have to do is dip your hands in my blood.' You can bet I wasn't too keen on that, but she says, 'Do it! Now go there, find your way down inside, and do exactly what I tell you to.'

"So she tells me what to do and off I go by me self, up and down through them moors. And boyo, let me tell you, it was cold and foggy and raining, and getting dark ... but I found it—a big old cave. And just where she said it would be, too. I go in and guess what? I find a circle of stones just like these" Anton pointed to the huge granite megaliths. "And a tree just like this one." He gestured toward the oak. "Only smaller and looking kind of droopy and sad.

"So I do like Morgana said; I drop to my knees and start rubbin' my bloody hands over the roots, which were sticking partway up outta the ground. And you know what? Within a minute or two, them roots start sucking up her blood like they was sponges, and then dozens of black worms start wiggling up outta the ground. That's right, the very same worms! So I scoops a bunch of them up in my hands and go tearin' back to the car, only when I get there, Morgana is lying there in the mud all still and white. She ain't breathing, her eyes is open, starin', and when I check, I can't find no heartbeat."

Anton sighed dramatically and hung his head.

"I tell you, me friend, it near broke me heart seein' her like that. The woman was everything to me! And

Ungrateful Dead

now here she was lying like a busted doll in the rain. I almost gave up and walked away. Almost! But then a funny thing happened. The worms! I forgot all about them! Here they go wiggling and squirming about to beat the band, and I remembered what she told me to do—it didn't make no sense at the time, but what did I have to lose, right?

"I sat down in the mud, lifted her head up in my lap, and then held the hand with the worms up to her face. Man, I may not have known what I was doing, but those little rascals sure did. They slithered up her chin, across her cheek and homed right in on her mouth and nose like little guided missiles. I admit, when those things went sliding up her nose, I thought I was going to be sick, but when Morgana started shaking and twitching I was soooo relieved I started to hug her. But she—she—" All at once Anton wasn't smiling anymore and his voice had become strained and cold, as if the sudden memory had infected his vocal cords with a killing frost. "She opened her eyes. At first—at first I thought they had turned black. But I looked closer and saw . . . they were full of worms, twisting and—"

Anton's eyes flicked over to Grover's face and he forced the smile back in place.

"Of course, later I realized that it was the worms that brought her back to me; they can do so many wonderful things, but that was later. Right then all I wanted to do was get her back to the tree.

"I buried her between the roots, like she told me to, and as I was walking out, the stones in the circle began to hum. It got louder and louder and finally I had to run out with me hands over me ears. I kept going and came back three days later and dug her up. After the funeral, I went back to the cave and there, hanging on one of them limbs, was a single black acorn. I did as she told me and picked it, but when I did, the tree, it just sort of ... crumbled. It was so weird. One minute it was a tree, the next ... dirt. Kind of like human beings, huh?''

Squatting down, Anton scooped up a handful of the mud from around the roots and let it ooze between his fingers. Grover watched the little man with the same wary intensity he would a poisonous snake. Anton wasn't crazy—Grover knew that, but why Anton had told him that cock-and-bullshit story, he couldn't guess. Whatever the reason, it wasn't good.

"Right about now you're probably asking yourself, 'Why is this crazy-assed dwarf tellin' me all this shit?' " Anton stayed where he was and spoke without turning around. "I think you should know more about Morgana, you being me righthand man and all. She's not at all like other women. She was given the secret of immortality by a god and has lived the lives of countless mortal women, using their frail bodies one after another and then discarding them like suits of old clothing."

Anton continued absentmindedly scooping handfuls of spongy earth with one hand and slapping them down in a pile. "Aha!" he muttered and then stood and turned around. "Look here. Isn't he pretty?"

In the palm of Anton's hand was a fat, black worm. He walked toward Grover with his hand out, as if offering to share some rare treasure he'd found. Grover took a step back.

"No, here ... look at it."

Grover had seen all he cared to of what the slimy things could do, and he wanted nothing to do with this one. He took a quick step backward, and when Anton kept coming toward him, another.

Anton stopped and stared at the giant for several seconds and then sighed. "I had hoped we could do this the easy way."

Ungrateful Dead

"What?" Grover snapped. "What the hell's going on?"

"That's what I was tryin' to explain to you, boyo! You can't keep no secrets from *her*!"

"What are you talking about?"

Anton stroked the worm with his finger. "Ach, hear that now? Go on with him, he doesn't know."

Grover started backing slowly toward the stairs. "No, really, Anton—you know me."

"Aye, I thought I did. But then you went and started tellin' tales to that spook professor and his pals."

"You're crazy." Grover backed into the bottom step and put out a hand to grab the rail. That's when the dogs growled.

Grover stopped dead and very slowly turned his head.

There were two of them, a black Lab and a huge black-and-brown Rottweiler, sitting calmly on the stairs with their tongues lolling like they were posing for a picture.

"Hey man, there's no need for this."

"I agree." Anton's tone was completely reasonable. He took another step toward Grover, but the big man shook his head. Anton sighed. "It's either this," he held up the hand with the worm, "or them." He nodded toward the dogs sitting like spectators in the bleachers.

Grover's mouth felt like he'd been eating sandpaper. He glanced at the black slug squirming in Anton's hand and then at the hounds, and he licked his lips.

"Why are you doing this? Why are you feeding people to that fucking tree? It's evil . . . *evil*!"

Rolling his eyes, Anton snapped, "Why do you have to turn this into a soap opera? Besides, I checked you out before I took you on. You got no room to cast stones, boyo."

"Maybe." Grover frantically searched for a way out.

"Maybe you're right. Maybe I done a few things, screwed a few people, even broke a few legs." The entrance to the tunnel was directly across the room. It was a good twenty yards there and then another fifty or so to the creek, but if he made it that far, he just might lose the mutts in the water. "But I never done nobody didn't have it coming. I never hurt a kid, and I never touched a woman til I worked for you."

"How noble."

Grover inched away from the stairs. "Well then tell me, Mr. Wizard, what's in it for you? What do you get out of all this? Money? Women? Drugs? What?"

Anton stared at the slug twisting and coiling in his palm. "You see my little friend here? See how it moves? How it glistens? That's slime. It protects its body and lets it move about easier... but it also leaves a trail everywhere it goes. It's not its fault, that's just the way it is." He held his palm up to Grover again. "Look at you. If you could only see your expression. Is this tiny creature so repulsive? Why? Because of the way it looks? That look on your face is the same one I've seen on people's faces all my life. Morgana is going to change all that. Once I help her through her transfiguration, we will have a child together—a male child. It will be strong and straight and *tall*! And then, when he's old enough—The body must be mature, you see, else the transfiguration might not meld. When he's old enough, Morgana will do for me what I did for her."

"And the boy?" Grover asked. "What happens to him when you take over his body?"

"Ah, well you see, there's that old saying..." Anton cocked his head in the direction of the tree. "The devil to pay."

"You would give your own son to that thing?"

Anton closed his hand and squeezed until black gel

dripped from his fist. "A damn site better 'n me Da did for me! You think being packed off to a carny 'cause your old man don't want no fucking freak for a son is any kinder 'n that?"

Anton looked at his hand and wiped it on his robe. It left a black tarlike smear on the lapel.

"So she promised you immortality? The oldest con in the book. You sold out cheap!" Grover edged away from the stairs a little more. He figured if he took it slow and kept the little geek talking he had a chance.

"You think so?" Anton spat on the ground. "You overgrown moron, I would have sold me very soul for six months as a normal man! Trade immortality for a kid that isn't even born yet? No problem."

Grover was about twenty feet from the stairs. Another ten and he had a real shot at the tunnel.

"There's just one thing I don't understand."

"Oh," Anton sneered. "One thing? Pray do tell."

"This thing that lives in the tree—"

"She's not a thing. She is an incredibly beautiful woman."

"Whatever. You said she needs you to help her through this—"

"Transfiguration. Yes. So?"

"So the guy you mentioned before—MacUmoir; the big muckety-muck who shared all these big secrets with this incredibly beautiful woman—where's he? How come he's not around? Where are all the other bozos who helped her through this whatchamacallit all these other times? You ever ask yourself that?"

As the implications of Grover's question slowly sank in, the cold, sardonic grin Anton wore like a mask evaporated like a snowball in the Sahara, and for the first time in Grover's recollection, the malignant little man was speechless.

Gary L. Holleman

Grover snuck a peek at the dogs. They seemed to be engrossed in the little creep's growing angst, so while they were distracted, Grover made his move; running, stumbling, yet, all in all, moving deceptively fast for a big man.

Unfortunately, the dogs spotted him and, approaching from behind at a dead run, turned his calves into bloody hamburger with their razor-sharp fangs—and Grover went down like he had been chopped off at the knees.

Anton laughed. "Ward, Colin! You know what to do."

Unwilling to give Anton the satisfaction of hearing him scream, the big man remained mute as the dogs took his heels in their mouths and dragged him across the mushy ground to the tree. As soon as he realized where they were taking him, the image of Malina Marks flashed in front of his eyes, and his courage faltered.

"Come on, Anton. Not that!"

Ignoring the agony in his legs, Grover used his fingernails and every ounce of his considerable strength to try and anchor himself to the earth. It was no use. The beasts bore down with their murderous jaws and, with his fingernails leaving furrows in the earth like tiny plows, dragged him a few agonizing inches at a time over to the tree.

When the animals released him, Grover turned over and pushed himself into a sitting position with his back resting against the trunk. He glanced at his legs without any trace of emotion, but did grab both thighs just above the knees and squeezed, to try to slow the flow of blood.

The old sly grin back in place, Anton strolled over and gazed down with mock concern at the blood pouring from Grover's mutilated legs. "Tsk, tsk. Quite a mess you are, Grover me boy."

Ungrateful Dead

"Can the fake concern! I don't suppose it would do any good to ask for help?"

Anton grinned all the more. "Oh, help's on the way, boyo—just not the kind you expect."

The worms swarmed out of the ground like spring grass growing at time-lapse speeds. Before Grover could react they were on his feet and legs and crawling up inside his clothes. His felt the sting of hundreds of tiny mouths as the creatures fastened themselves to his belly, chest, and back and he tried to beat them off by slapping at his body, but that only made the worms dig deeper into his flesh. Finally, when he could stand it no more, he screamed and screamed.

"GET THEM OFF! GET THEM OFF MEEE!"

Grover had almost no legs from the knees down, and yet he tried to stand up—and he almost succeeded. When he fell back, he tried to claw his way up the trunk, but the creatures were all over his arms and hands, and each time he tried to grip something, one or more of their pulpy bodies squished between his fingers like rotten tomatoes, coating his hands with layers of gelatinous slime that made holding onto anything impossible.

Grover slid down the trunk, rolled over on his back in the mud, and lay still. His strength, the one thing he had always been able to depend on, was gone, and the best he could do was stare mutely while the leeches gradually enveloped his body. Soon, every inch of exposed skin was covered, and the remaining creatures forced open his lips and slithered inside his mouth.

The pain was indescribable. His skin began to shrivel and crack. In a matter of minutes, his cheeks hollowed and his eyes sagged back into his skull—he looked like a corpse—but he was still breathing.

Danny Keats walked up behind Anton.

"He dead?"

Gary L. Holleman

Anton shook his head. "No, 'tis not his lucky day. The little beasties know just how much milk to take without killin' the cow." He waddled over to the toolbox resting on the ground under the table and took out a hammer and a sack of nails. "Now, Danny me boy . . . stand him up."

It was almost 2:30 in the afternoon when Truman returned from the hall of records carrying five large round, cardboard tubes. Virginia brushed the snow from his shoulders and helped him out of his coat.

"Where is everyone?" he asked.

"Where else?" she replied with a good-natured smile. "The kitchen. That Luther can pack away more food than a troop of starving boy scouts."

Tru hung his scarf on the hook by the door. "Long as food's all he's packing away."

Virginia's expression turned serious. "You're worried about him?"

Sighing, Tru hooked his leather cap over the scarf and turned to face his wife. "You know his history."

"Yes, but he's been straight for a long time."

"True. But I'm worried anyway. You see the way he looks at this girl—"

"Alana?"

Tru nodded. "Luther's still carrying a lot of baggage left over from that other girl, the one that disappeared. He's managed pretty well so far by building a wall around himself and staying on a strict routine—all that bicycle riding and tofu is just a way of protecting himself. If we get out of this mess but anything happens to her—"

"Then I guess we'll just have to make sure nothing happens to her. You know, in your own way you're as bad as Luther."

Ungrateful Dead

"Me? What are you talking about, woman?"

"Pessimists! You're all, every last one of you, pessimists. Gloom and doom—doom and gloom, that's all men ever see coming. If women looked at the world that way, we would have stopped having children and mankind would have died out years ago. Luther's a good boy. He feels too much, is his problem. You go on in there and figure a way out of this mess—I know you can do it. And don't let Cal run things. He's an intelligent man, but so are you." She handed him the cardboard tubes. "Play nice."

Tru pushed his way through the swinging door into the kitchen. Luther and Cal, who were spooning down the last few bites of Virginia's key lime pie, looked up. Cal had yellow pie filling on his shirt collar.

Tru dumped the tubes on the table and went over to the stove to pour himself a cup of coffee.

"You get the blueprints?" Cal asked.

"Copies. I had to go to three different departments. I tell you, it's a wonder the city of Memphis can find its behind with both hands." He opened the first tube and unrolled a long sheet of thermal copy paper. "This here is the most current set of plans, the ones done up for the last renovation. It's easy to read, but—" He pushed the paper aside and took out another roll. "This one is from 1823—"

"You can hardly read it," Cal muttered, tracing his finger along the faded lines.

"Yeah, well, that's because it's a copy of the original set of plans, and the only reason we have it is because the house is on the National Registry of Historical Sites."

"Weird-looking thing," Luther commented.

"It's round," Tru replied unnecessarily.

"We can see that," Cal chuckled.

"Funny thing . . . there was this old guy worked down in the basement at the Hall, looked like he'd been there since de Soto landed on the beach in Florida. He was telling me about the history of the house."

"History?" Luther broke in. "Let me guess, George Washington slept there."

"Robert E. Lee is more like it," Cal opined.

"U. S. Grant," Luther came back.

"Naw. If it was Grant, nobody around here would tell anybody—"

Tru cleared his throat. "You two want to hear this or not?"

Luther and Cal gave each other a look and grinned.

"Go on, Professor," said Luther.

"The original owner of the house was a man named Patrick Grendel, an Irishman reputed to have had a lot of money and a very bad temper. When the old guy in records said the name, I thought it sounded familiar, so I looked him up at the main library. Seems Grendel owned a fleet of ships and, before the Civil War, ran slaves into New Orleans. After the war he made a bundle bringing down supplies for the Union troops. Rumor was, he got the contracts by claiming he had been a member of the Underground Railroad before the war and had helped dozens of escaped slaves make their way up North. To prove it, he invited a group of Union officers to his house, took them down into the basement and showed them these special tunnels he had built that he claimed were used to smuggle slaves in and out. And they bought it, at least at first. Then, according to the clippings I found in the Appeal archives, about eight months after the end of the war, a young black woman showed up at the Federals' barracks, claiming that before the war, she and her brother had run away from a plantation down near Mound Bayou in Mississippi. On their

Ungrateful Dead

way to Boston, they hid out in a barn on the outskirts of Memphis. The girl said she had been out stealing food and when she returned she saw a group of men in white robes shove her brother into the back of a covered wagon. She followed them to this big, round, white mansion where the men took her brother out of the wagon and dragged him inside. She waited and waited and just after sunup a bunch of white men in suits came out, but her brother never did. She said she waited three days, circled the house twenty times, but he never came out.

"Naturally the soldiers had a good laugh and told her the man she had accused was a hero and then chased her away. But she didn't stay away. She found a reporter down from one of the northern papers and told him the story."

"Must of been Bob Woodward's great grandfather," Cal whispered to Luther.

"Anyway!" Truman said sharply. "When he went to the Army with the story, they told him it was probably klansmen and they'd look into it when they got a chance. But the girl insisted this had happened before the war, and she raised such a stink that, to shut her up, they sent a squad of soldiers to Grendel's house. As luck would have it, the captain in charge was one of the officers who had been on the tour of the place, and he remembered the basement. Grendel wasn't home, but while his man was showing the soldiers through the place, this officer decided it would be a good idea to show the girl the tunnels in the basement so she could see for herself what a hero Grendel was.

"Now this was where the story gets kind of . . . fuzzy. The Memphis paper only had a small article about Grendel's disappearance, with a side note about some bodies found in his basement. But stuck in the archives was a plastic pouch, with the article written by that New York reporter that said Negro slaves and freemen—that's how they referred to freed slaves back then—freemen had been disappearing for several years before the war and that though most had been assumed to have made it safely up North, several mutilated bodies had turned up over the years in, of all places... Nonconnah Creek! Sound familiar?"

Luther and Cal exchanged dour looks.

"The dead hookers," Cal said.

"Oh no," muttered Luther. "I don't even want to think where that trail leads. Let's just stick to the problem at hand."

"The point is... the soldiers dug up the mutilated bodies of ten black men in that cellar, and look here—" Tru pointed to several large, oblong structures situated equidistant around the basement.

"What are those things?" asked Cal.

"The answer to that took more digging. I had to go back to the article written when the house was first built—as you can imagine, the design caused something of a stir back then, and it was covered quite extensively by the society columnists. Anyway, I found a quote that the reporter attributed to Grendel himself. Listen—" 'I missed me homeland so much I brought over some of the finest Irish stone I could find to form me house's foundation.'"

Luther and Cal peered at the faded blueprint copy.

"Stones," Luther hissed. "Look at these dimensions! They're... they're—"

"Immense," Cal supplied.

"Say, as large as the megaliths of Stonehenge?"

"No," Cal said, running his finger along the tiny, precise numbers printed underneath the rectangular renderings. "Larger."

"Incredible," Luther said. "Then the basement must

be huge. I wonder why our friend Grover didn't mention it was so big."

"Ask him," Cal replied. "But he did say the tree was big. Perhaps we should have figured it out for ourselves."

"He won't call before we go in tomorrow night," Tru said. "He's too paranoid; who can blame him? But as I remember, he did say the thing was a monster, that it filled half the cellar. How are we going to attack something that size?"

"Well," Luther spoke up. "Cal and I were working on that while you were gone, and we think we've come up with just the thing."

Cal turned to the largest of the books on the table, a thick tome with a slick, black, leather cover that was completely blank.

"Hey," Truman exclaimed, "that's one of mine."

"I know. You've got the best occult library this side of Duke," Luther chuckled. "Have you read this thing?"

Nibbling at his bottom lip, Tru eyed the heavily slanted handwriting warily. "Uh—it looks sort of familiar."

"You old fraud," Cal snorted. "Lute found this down behind a stack of dusty psychology journals, one of which contained an article by old Sigmund himself."

"I know you love to collect old books, but you really ought to read one of them now and again," Luther said with a grin.

"I do read them," Tru replied huffily. "At least, I've read most of them. Even *I* can't read everything. Now quit jerking my chain and show me what you found."

Luther opened the book to the sheet of notebook paper he had left as a bookmark. "Did you know this book has no title and no indication who the author was?"

Gary L. Holleman

Tru flipped to the first page of the book and then back. "You know, I do remember this book. I purchased it in a little curio shop in the Mission District of San Francisco. The proprietress was a stunningly beautiful woman; West Indian I think, with dreadlocks that looked like bedsprings. Paula something—"

Luther winked at Cal and grinned.

"Oh, go on with you both," Tru said, catching the wink. "The reason I remember her is that she had a reputation as some sort of super fortune-teller, and I was doing that paper on phony spiritualists."

"Oh, yeah," said Cal. "The one that old geezer from Palm Beach sued you over."

"Madam Edna? That's the one."

"So this woman who sold you the book, she pissed at you too?" Luther asked.

Truman snorted like the question was beneath him, but he looked decidedly uncomfortable.

"No, come on—what's the story?"

"Well . . . She wasn't exactly like the others I wrote about in the paper."

"We know," said Cal. "This one wasn't eighty years old."

"Quiet, Cal," Luther grinned.

"That's all right," Tru replied with dignity. "He can't help it. No, there were several things that made this woman different. First of all, she took no money for helping her clients. She made her living selling occult artifacts, art, and potions."

"I suppose the *spirits* never told her customers to buy any of her potions?" Cal muttered.

"Stop it," Luther hissed.

Tru continued as if he had not been interrupted. "And she was very open about what she did. She invited me into the back of her shop, showed me her stock, her deck

Ungrateful Dead

of Tarot cards. All the others, as soon as I told them who I was and what I was doing, they closed up faster than a bushel of New England clams."

"Sounds like the most dangerous kind of con artist," Cal opined. "The honest, heartfelt, really care about your wellbeing kind."

Truman shook his head. "No. It's hard to explain." He looked at each of his friend's faces. "You know I don't believe in fortunetelling and things like that."

"I do," Luther said.

"You get paid to," Cal came back.

"And what do you call what you do? Science? Ha!"

"Children," Tru said with a sigh.

"Sorry," Luther said.

"Anyway, she had this book." Tru placed his hand on the blank leather cover.

"What did it set you back?" asked Cal.

"She gave it to me, insisted I take it actually. She said one day my . . . life would depend on it."

Everyone was quiet for a few moments and then Luther said, "She just may turn out to be right." He turned the book around. "What we found is a formula for a—what did you call it, Cal?"

"Druid Herbicide."

"Yeah, well. Listen to these ingredients: bark from the ash tree—for the World Tree, Yggdrasil Mistletoe—for the winter solstice. Yew bark—for All Hallows. White Clover—vernal equinox. Vervain for the summer solstice, and red apples representing the autumnal equinox. We're supposed to boil it all down and apply the liquid to the Temple of Set's roots."

"And that will do—what?" Truman asked.

"Kill it, make it shrivel up, I don't know. It's the only thing in the book that comes anywhere close."

"Let me see that." Tru scanned the page. "This is Latin."

"Naturally."

"This doesn't say anything about the Temple of Set! This is a potion for some kind of poisonous vine found in the Blackwater Moors."

"Yeah well, it's a plant, and it's from Ireland," Cal pointed out.

"Read a little further," Luther said. "The vine was called the Serpent Vine because it grew out of the deep caves found in and around the moors and often trapped and killed animals and small children."

"I never heard of any vine like that."

"Then I guess the potion worked," Cal said, brightly.

Tru rolled his eyes. "We have to do better than this."

"Alana doesn't have time for us to do better than this," Luther replied. "Gadarn's little get-together is tomorrow night. If we don't stop him before then, as far as she's concerned, it's too late."

"But where on earth are we going to get this stuff?"

"That's the easy part," Luther replied. "The guy who owns the health food store where I buy all that food you two make so much fun of . . . he's a witch."

Alana's world had become a never-ending, sleepless nightmare. The drugs Cal gave her kept her awake, but they also robbed her of nearly all sensation, so that most of the time she felt as if she were walking around the bottom of the ocean in one of those old-fashioned diving suits. Everything looked washed out—dull. No texture, no life. And if anyone spoke to her, it sounded to her like she had cotton jammed in her ears. Most of the time, the best she could manage was to sit in the chair next to the bed and stare at the flower vase on the night table and hope she wasn't drooling on herself.

Ungrateful Dead

The bedroom door opened and just as quickly closed. Alana's head rolled back against the chair. She tried to focus on who had just come in, but the shades were drawn, and the lights had been left low so she could relax—how the hell was she supposed to relax when she was so damned tired?

A shadow moved slowly along the wall, until it was across from her on the other side of the room. Alana tried to say something, tried to ask who it was, but her tongue felt as thick and dry as a lizard sitting on a rock in the desert sun. She tried to swallow, but that didn't go so well either. Finally she tried to clear her throat.

"Alana?"

She blinked and gripped the arms of the chair.

"Alana, can you hear me?"

It didn't really sound like her mother's voice. It was soft, soothing; a whisper almost like the fluttering wings of a great dark bird—but there *was* something vaguely familiar about it. Something she had heard before—

Why are you fighting me? This can end only one way. Even now you can feel yourself beginning to slip away. Don't resist! Just let go. Let the darkness absorb you. It is so nice and cool; no pain, no more fear—just a little pop when your soul tears loose. There . . . it's so easy. See, you can no longer feel your toes. Or your legs. Isn't it nice? That silky, creeping coldness? It's in your belly now, churning, bubbling, spreading like that cold serving of vichyssoise that you had that winter's day for lunch. Not much longer now. Your nipples are hardening in anticipation of the ecstacy, waiting, longing, for oblivion's icy caress.

Everything the voice said was coming to pass, and yet Alana was torn. So many times over the years she had contemplated ending her life. Times when her life was spinning out of control, years of pain and doubt and loneliness. In her fantasies, she had always seen Morgana standing over her coffin—crying. She'd be sorry then! And death—death would be a little girl's revenge. It would be like going to sleep, only she would be able to hide and watch to see how much everyone missed her. It would be a warm place, a safe place.

But that was before! Before she found out her mother was incapable of tears. Before she discovered that death was no escape and that, far from being warm and safe, death was cold. And that was before Luther. Death was not coming as a friend. It was coming, as the poets said, like a thief in the night to rip her soul from her body and cast her out into a darkness that waited for her like a ravenous beast. She had to fight! She had to—

The door opened, and the ceiling light came on, and it was all Alana could do to keep her heart from exploding. She struggled to turn her head.

"Hey," Luther said with a smile. "How you feeling?"

He started across the room but stopped short.

"Hey, Sam. What are you doing here?"

The girl dropped her eyes and shrugged. "Just keeping an eye on Ms. Magnus, making sure she's all right."

"That was very nice of you." He went over to Alana's chair and squatted down on his heels. She was shivering so hard her teeth were clacking.

"Sam, bring a blanket over from the bed, please."

The girl did as he asked, and he wrapped it tightly around Alana's shoulders.

"Co-co-cold-d-d-d," Alana stuttered. "So cold."

He rubbed her shoulders briskly. "It's this freakish weather. Nobody ever remembers anything like it."

"She . . . someone was here," Alana whispered.

Luther peered at her face. "Your mother?"

"No—yes—I don't know. Maybe I was dreaming."

Ungrateful Dead

The color was slowly returning to her face, so Luther stopped rubbing her shoulders and moved to her hands.

"You're like ice." He massaged each finger in turn. "You better not have been dreaming. If you were, Cal is going to be very upset."

"I'm sorry."

"Not your fault. He just needs to adjust the dosage. I'll go get him."

She held on to his hands. "Don't go!"

"We have to go out for a little while," he said. "We found something in one of Tru's books that we think just might do the trick, but we have to get the components."

Her hands tightened around his. "No! Please don't leave me alone!"

The firmness of her grip took him by surprise. "Okay. Don't worry. Sam's here."

Alana cut her eyes to the girl. "No," she murmured. "Not her. Send Rachel."

Luther frowned, but nodded. "Right you are. We'll be back in a couple of hours." He gave her hands one last squeeze and then rose and went to the door. On the way he motioned for Sam to follow. In the hall, he closed the door, then smiled.

"Ask your mom to come up and stay with Alana, will you?"

"I'll do it," Sam said with a shy tilt of her head.

He hesitated. "No—better your mom." He started down the stairs, but paused on the top step. Something was bothering him, but he didn't know how to say it without hurting the girl's feelings, so he tried to make a joke out of it. "Why did you come up, anyway? Hanging out with the old folks driving you nuts?"

Sam started drawing designs in the hall carpet with the toe of her moccasin, a sign that, in Luther's experience, meant she was either embarrassed or hesitant to talk about something.

"Come on . . . what is it?"

"I wanted to talk to Ms. Magnus."

"What about?"

"Oh . . . nothing."

"Sam, this is like pulling teeth."

"Uh, how well do you know Morna?"

"Morna?" If she had asked him how many aliens were in a flying saucer, it would have made more sense. "I just met her. Why?"

"Oh, it's probably nothing—"

"But?"

"Well, I just thought she was acting kind of weird. But then, I don't know her all that well."

"Weird? Weird how?"

"You know—talking to herself. Staring at herself in the mirror."

That got Luther's attention. His had often read that mirrors could act as psychic speakerphones between the netherworld and mankind. But that was the last thing he wanted Sam to know.

"Well, I wouldn't worry Alana about it. You know Morna has been away at school. It's probably just one of those little habits a girl picks up, living so far from her family." It sounded lame even to him, but Sam nodded as if it made perfect sense and trotted off down the stairs.

Great! he thought. One more thing to worry about.

The health food store where Luther bought his groceries was sandwiched between a hardware store and a toy shop on one of the busiest streets in Germantown. It was snowing heavily when they turned off the main highway, and the parking lot was packed with minivans and sta-

Ungrateful Dead

tion wagons. Cal not only had to cruise for a parking spot, he had to dodge roaming packs of snowsuit-clad children who were busy making snowballs and trying to turn each other into ice sculptures with high-powered water guns.

"Where are all these brats' mothers?" Cal muttered.

Luther nodded his head toward the ultramodern stone building at the far side of the parking lot. "Victoria's Secret. Probably stocking up on winter jammies."

They made a circle past a video arcade which, in spite of it being near the dinner hour, was packed with teenagers dressed like refugees from a Salvation Army clothing outlet.

"Well, thank God Sam doesn't hang out in places like this."

"Oh, like she's never been to a video arcade? Get real. I suppose she's never been kissed either?"

"What!" Cal turned his head to glower at Luther and almost turned a little boy with a water gun into roadkill.

"Watch where you're going."

The front of the health food store was painted pale, earth tone yellow and had huge windows, punctuated with hanging asparagus ferns in the center of each pane. Inside were brightly colored booths lined up against both walls, and about a half-dozen small, round tables in the center of the floor—all done in soothing earth tones. On the back wall were rows of chrome and glass shelves, full of bottles containing vitamins and minerals, pills and potions, and all manner of vile-smelling concoctions guaranteed to add zest to your lovelife and hours to your time in the bathroom. In front of the shelves was a long, glass-top counter with stacks of bright green plastic serving trays on one end and a computer cash register on the other—each serving tray had a huge, daisy appliqué in the center.

"This is a health food store?" Cal asked. "It looks like Little Mary Sunshine's playhouse."

Luther ignored his friend's crabbing and made his way to the counter. As they approached, a stoop-shouldered woman with a shock of snow-white hair pulled back into a bun came out of the back and stood at the register.

"Hey," Cal whispered. "This place wouldn't be made out of gingerbread by any chance?"

"Relax."

"I mean, you said she was a witch, but—"

"That isn't the witch," Luther muttered out the side of his mouth. "That's the witch's mother."

He walked up to the counter and smiled. "Hello, Beth."

"Hello, Dr. Shea."

"Is Marty around?"

"He's in the back unloading a new shipment. Shall I have him come out?"

"Beth, this is my friend Cal Weinberg. We'll go back, if it's okay."

"Certainly. You know the way."

They went through the doorway, turned left, and followed a dimly lit and very narrow corridor to a small storeroom at the back of the shop. The room was mostly floor-to-ceiling shelves with a knock-together wooden table in the center of the floor. At the back of the table was a metal stand supporting a glass distillation apparatus, and toward the front of the table was a microscope, a dissecting tray, and a small Bunsen burner. Sitting with one eye glued to the microscope lens was a painfully thin man with short, coal-black hair, a high forehead, and, when he looked up, the bluest blue eyes

Ungrateful Dead

Cal had ever seen. His age was hard to determine—somewhere between twenty-five and thirty-five, but when he spoke, his accent was pure south Bronx.

"Yo, Prof," Marty called out with a grin. "Long time no see."

"Hey, Marty—I want you to meet a friend of mine."

He introduced Cal and then got down to business.

"Marty, I have a list of things I need."

The man watched Luther with a bemused expression. "I gather this isn't your usual alfalfa and sprouts?"

Luther handed over the list he had prepared. "No. This is a little different."

Halfway down the list, Marty's smile began to falter, and by the end he let out a low whistle. "I'll say it's different. What the devil are you planning on doing? Defoliating a rain forest?"

Luther tried to play coy. "What do you mean? Nothing on that list is dangerous."

"By themselves, no, but mixed the way you have here? What's doing?"

"Better you don't know."

Marty gave Luther a thoughtful look and then walked over to the shelves and began scanning the labels on the bottles. "Not for nothing, but once this stuff is mixed, it can be pretty dangerous if it isn't handled properly."

"We know."

"Uh . . . dangerous how?" Cal asked. "It's not going to blow up or anything?" He laughed as if to say he was only kidding.

Marty glanced at Cal. "You're the shrink, right?" Cal nodded. "Lute talks about you all the time."

"Good things, I hope?"

"You're not the one going to be mixing this stuff?"

Luther laughed, and Cal got red in the face.

305

"Just kidding, Doc," the man said. "Lute tells me you know quite a bit about the occult."

Cal shrugged. "More than some, less than others."

Marty winked at Luther. "Typical shrink answer. Lute, you know how you get into shrink school? Ya have to prove you can go a whole year without saying the words yes and no." Luther chuckled and Marty turned to Cal. "No, Doc, it won't blow up—at least not the way you mean. The occult laws of physics are different. By themselves," he held up a tall, stoppered bottle containing four lacy, green leaves, "these little babies are as harmless as soup stock. But like any chemical reaction, you have to know what you're doing. You mess up mixing chemicals and you lose a finger or an eye. You mess up with this stuff, and it'll suck your soul down into a darkness so deep that a black hole will look like Liberty Bowl Stadium in comparison."

The man's knowing attitude was starting to get under Cal's skin. "So, Luther tells me you're supposed to be some kind of witch. I thought the term for a man was warlock?"

"Cal!"

Marty pulled down several bottles from the shelves and took them to the table. "No, Lute, that's okay." He glanced up and gave Cal a lopsided smile. "Witch, warlock—it's all the same. Women have always been closer to nature. I guess it has to do with birth and the cycle of the moon, but while men were still out bashing in each other's heads with rocks, women were out gathering the plants and herbs to patch them up. I've studied healing and the occult most of my life and that, to some people, makes me a warlock—I prefer witch, it's a sign of respect. You're a doctor—which to some people makes you a quack."

Ungrateful Dead

The blood rushed into Cal's face again, but he held his tongue.

"Dr. Weinberg, you went to medical school for—what? Four years? Then another five or six of internship and residency? You passed a battery of tests drawn up by a bunch of other doctors, so they gave you a piece of paper, which you hung on a wall in your office, so people would feel safe to come to you and let you crawl around inside their heads?"

"Uh, Marty," Luther said softly. "That's a bit harsh."

Cal said, "Let him finish."

Marty went back to the shelves for more bottles and tins.

"Don't get me wrong. I hope you and I can be friends. But you have to understand—I take what I do very seriously. You invested nine or ten years getting where you are. I've been studying plants and herbs most of my life, and *I* apprenticed in places where the nearest bathrooms were measured in degrees of longitude. Between delivering babies in mud huts using hot water and string, and curing whole tribes of Dengue Fever using a broth I made by condensing mosses, I figure I paid my dues. It's hard enough when newspapers and Hollywood make out people like me to have fangs and run around sacrificing babies under a full moon, without freaking medical Nazis looking down their collective noses at me."

He put the new load of bottles down on the table beside the others and began taking glass pipettes, graduated cylinders, and measuring cups from the drawers.

"Marty—" Cal said earnestly. "May I call you Marty?"

Marty stopped what he was doing and visibly relaxed. "Okay, sure."

"I'm sorry if I insulted you."

He took a deep breath, rolled his head around on his neck, and grinned. "I guess I'm a tad sensitive."

"No, I was rude."

"No, no, it was all my—"

"You're both nuts," Luther muttered.

Marty shrugged and turned serious again. "Maybe. But not crazy enough to let you two mix this stuff yourselves. What's it for?"

"A kind of bush."

Marty snorted. "Some bush. You know, this is going to make about twenty gallons."

"Yeah."

"Come on."

"It's a tree, actually. A very big tree."

Marty scanned the list again. "Yew bark . . . okay . . . okay . . . white clover! I get most of this—it's obviously a very virulent necromantic toxicant, but the vervain? If it were arrowroot, I could understand. But vervain? It's almost as if—" Marty's eyes almost popped out of his head. "Good lord! It's the Temple of Set!"

Luther snatched the list from Marty's hand. The witch made a quick grab for it, but missed by inches.

"It's really here?" he hissed. "It's never been reported in this hemisphere before—hell, it hasn't been reported anywhere in—jeez, I don't know, twelve or thirteen hundred years. Oh, wow! Where is it? Can I see it?"

"Cool your jets!" Luther tucked the list back into his pocket. "I can't go into everything, but we're in a real mess here, and we need your help."

Luther's tone, coupled with a very stern expression, slowly brought Marty back down to earth.

"Oh, I guess there might be some rather extreme people involved, huh? But still, this is fantastic. You know, I should have known something was up."

"Why do you say that?" Cal asked.

"Well, tomorrow is the winter solstice and this weather—Have you ever known it to be this cold or snow this much? The rest of the country is unseasonably warm—everyone thinks it's the Greenhouse Effect. And yet here in Memphis it's like the frigging ice age."

Luther shook his head. "I never thought about it."

"Well, you better start. There are powerful forces at work here. And unless I miss my guess, you two are about to go up against one of the most powerful. In fact, the way I remember it, wasn't the Temple supposed to be some kind of heat sump?"

"You know?" Cal picked up the pencil Marty had lying beside the Bunsen burner and started tapping his two front teeth. "I do remember something about that. This one guy, Knudson? Arronson? Some guy from Sweden, anyway, postulated that the severe winter weather patterns over the British Isles today were formed hundreds of years ago by something he called 'heat black holes' located throughout England and Scotland."

"Shit!" Luther muttered.

"Well said." Cal turned to Marty. "He's a full professor, you know."

"How were you planning on applying the toxicant?" asked Marty.

"I don't know," Luther replied. "I thought we'd go in and dump the stuff on the roots."

"And Set's followers? What do you propose to do about them? As I recall, they were reputed to be a rather fanatical bunch."

"We have, uh, someone on the inside."

"Well, that's good. However, unless you find a safe

way to transport this stuff and apply it, you could be dead before you get wherever it is you're going. It's going to be very volatile. No metal of any kind, no cellulose or any organic-based compound can come in contact with it. And please, whatever you do, do not stand anywhere near the tree when you pour it on. Everything I've ever read about this Temple thing leads me to believe it will not go quietly. There is liable to be a very violent reaction when this stuff hits the roots, so don't stand too close! Got it?"

"Hmmm." Luther glanced at Cal. "Any ideas?"

"A pump sprayer," Cal replied. "One of those yard things they use for insecticide and junk."

"Good idea."

Cal beamed. "That's why they pay me the big bucks."

Marty snorted derisively as he slipped a white filter mask over his nose and mouth. "I'm going to start mixing now. There's a hardware store next door. You two go buy your sprayers. I'll be done in about thirty minutes."

Grover didn't know how long he had been hanging there—hours—days—centuries. Time no longer had any meaning. Pain! That had meaning.

It was funny, he thought, how staring death in the face altered a man's focus. The things he had wanted to do in his life, the places he planned to go, the family he'd always wanted to start—when he found the right girl, naturally. The house he'd wanted to build—he'd never actually lived in a real house, with a backyard and a swing. All the things he kept putting off because he had all the time in the world. All the time in the world.

How clear it all was now, the way he had wasted his life. The things he had thought important, the things that stole his hours and minutes—he'd never seen it! Right under his nose, and he'd never even seen it! Like cheap beer on a hot night, he had just pissed his life away.

Was this remorse? he wondered. This thing . . . this emotion that he was feeling? He had never felt it before, had always thought it, like all those other emotions people were always ragging about—love, fear, compassion—was a crock. Was it remorse? It could be. He'd heard being near death made people view their lives in a whole new light. Maybe that's what this was all about? Maybe this was his chance to repent? Naw, he was too stupid to change now. Too stubborn. Besides, what kind of God would forgive all the shit he had done? One with a short memory.

Grover chuckled soundlessly as blood bubbled out of his mouth.

He had always heard God had a plan. Well, if He did, it was on a need-to-know basis and obviously, old Grover didn't need to know. Was it remorse? he wondered. Or was it that hoard of hungry worms having lunch inside his skull?

They had been still for a while now. Maybe sleeping, if creatures like that slept. At first, right when they had come out of the ground and started boring into his skull, he had thought the pain was going to drive him mad. Maybe it had. It would drive anybody mad—hearing them crunching and gnawing like a hundred tiny little dentist's drills grinding their way into his brain. Then, just before he passed out, they had stopped. At that point he figured he was going to die, either from blood loss from his mangled legs or maybe of shock from the nails Danny had driven through his hands and feet. But no, he wasn't going to be that lucky. Maybe the same viscous substance that gave the leeches life and mobility also acted as a coagulant and balm. If so, the downside was it also heightened his senses so that he could feel each time one of the little suckers so much as farted. He could feel one of them even now nibbling on his optic nerve. Every time it twitched, it was like a hot nail being driven into his eye.

And they were clever—so very clever—and devious. Each time they started moving they'd take him right up to the edge of unconsciousness and then back off—and wait. Wait for him to regain a bit of his strength, or maybe just wait for him to start thinking it was over, that they'd had their fill of his brain and would just go away. But he was on to their tricks now. They wouldn't fool him again. They wouldn't go away until he told them about Luther Shea and his friends. But he'd beat them. He wouldn't tell. No matter what, he wouldn't tell. For the sad fact was, Grover's only hope of getting out of the cellar alive was that wimpy professor and his pals. How was that for a God with a fucking sense of humor?

Cal and Luther returned to the health food store loaded down with plastic bags from the toy shop next door.

"I thought you were going to the hardware store," Marty commented.

"We did," Luther replied. "The only sprayers they had were either stainless steel or aluminum."

"Oh."

"But we passed a bunch of kids on the way in," Cal added. "And they gave us an idea."

He reached into one of the bags and removed a large, orange-and-yellow plastic gizmo that looked remarkably like a Star Wars laser rifle.

"What the devil is that?" Marty asked.

"Super Squirter! The howitzer of water guns. See here—it has an oversized reservoir, and you pump it up like this." He worked the slide under the barrel back and forth about twenty times. "Now watch." Like a kid at Christmas, Luther's friend, the psychiatrist, aimed the gun's long plastic barrel at the corner of the room thirty feet away and let fly.

"Hey!"

"Not to worry, it's only water."

Marty looked at Luther and rolled his eyes toward heaven. "Saints preserve us from grown-up little boys. You two are going to take on what from all reports is one of the primeval forces of the universe with what? Water guns?"

Luther grinned and shrugged. "Well, they fit your criteria. They're made of nonorganic materials and will deliver the mixture from a pretty good distance."

"And they're neat!" Cal added. "Look how tight that stream is." He moved the gun up and down and the water responded by wetting a narrow strip of the corner shelf. "We're gonna annihilate 'em!"

"Will you stop it!" Marty snapped. "Some of my stock doesn't react well to water."

"Oh—sorry."

"And we brought these to carry the stuff home," Luther added, holding up two ten-gallon plastic gasoline cans.

Mollified, Marty replaced his mask and put on a pair of heavy rubber work gloves. "Okay. But I still think I should go along."

"No need. Honest," Luther replied. He would have given anything to have Marty's help, but didn't want to put anyone else in harm's way.

"Then remember, soak the roots good and get the hell out. If you don't . . . hell's likely to get you!"

It was dark by the time Cal and Luther reached the end of Truman's street. The streetlights were on, but dimmed by a million fat snowflakes swirling down out of the pitch-black sky like autumn leaves. A biting wind swept the nearly deserted byway, turning asphalt to ice and parked cars into igloos, and spawning tiny white tornadoes, which spun like Tasmanian Devils for a few moments then vanished, only to spring up again a few yards away. It was an cerily beautiful landscape; stark, serene, a scene from a time when troglodytes were still working their way up to the top of the food chain. On any street in Alaska, or possibly even the Siberian steppes, it would have been idyllic. In Memphis, after what Marty told them, it was grotesque.

Cal pulled the car up as close to the house as possible, so as to avoid exposing themselves to both the freezing wind and anyone or anything that might be lurking in the dark. They each grabbed a ten-gallon gas can and a plastic bag and ran bent over like old men. The instant they reached the door, it opened, and Tru came out to meet them in his shirtsleeves.

"Morna's gone."

Chapter Fifteen

Luther stood at the window in Tru's study and watched as the low-hanging clouds slowly turned from indigo to steel gray. It was still overcast, still snowing, and still cold, but at least morning had arrived—for that he was grateful.

It had been a bad night. Bad for Luther. Bad for Cal and Tru and their families. Horrible for Alana. The screen had been removed from the window outside Morna's room and there were footprints in the snow on the roof. The girl's abduction was very nearly the straw that broke Alana's grip on reality. She became hysterical, screaming, and crying, and thrashing about like a mad woman. Then, later, as the night dragged on and her meager reserves of adrenaline gave out, she became despondent, her mind fading in and out like an AM radio signal on a stormy night. Several times Luther was certain they were going to lose her completely, and yet each of those times Cal, with judicial applications of pills and patience, coaxed her back from the abyss.

But Morna—unless they found the girl soon—

What Luther couldn't figure out was how the bastards got the window unlocked. Truman swore he checked it—several times—and both the screen and the window had been locked.

Virginia shuffled into the study in her fuzzy house slippers. "Coffee's ready. Come on before it gets cold."

Luther poured himself a cup of steaming coffee and sat at the table. He took it as a good sign that, in spite of everything, his mind admonished him to watch his caffeine intake. A few moments later Rachel came in, her hair wild and her eyes ringed like a raccoon. Luther tried not to stare, but it was the first time he had ever seen her when she wasn't perfect. She pulled out a chair next to him and sat down.

"Good morning," he said.

"What's good about it?"

Virginia set a cup of coffee in front of Rachel and then mumbled something about kicking Tru out of bed and shuffled off.

Rachel looked so miserable that Luther just had to ask, "You okay?"

She was quiet so long he didn't think she was going to answer. Then, she looked up and the tears just seemed to spring from her eyes. It was Luther's worst nightmare—a woman crying and he didn't have a clue what to do.

"Uh, jeez, Rachel . . . what's wrong?"

She was sobbing and choking, and she couldn't seem to speak or stop her nose from dripping. Springing to his feet, he practically ran to the sink and came back with a napkin.

Ungrateful Dead

"Here."

She gave her nose a healthy honk and wiped her eyes, but wouldn't look at him.

"Uh, should I go get Cal?"

She shook her head. "No. Please.—I wanted—" She glanced over her shoulder to make sure they were alone. "Can I talk to you?"

That sounded like a very loaded question, but Luther said what a friend is supposed to say. "Sure."

She scooted the chair closer and lowered her voice. "Luther, have you ever done anything so awful, so horrible, so despicable that you didn't think you could live with it?"

"Wow." He fell back against the kitchen chair and glanced at the snow piled up like spilled sugar on the windowsill as he tried to come up with a reply that didn't sound patronizing or flip.

"And don't you dare make a joke," she hissed under her breath. "Or so help me I'll kill you."

"No, really. I—I'm trying to think how to answer that."

And he was, truly. But he was bone tired, and his mind was as blank as an eggshell, and the last thing he wanted was to do or say anything that would add to Rachel's anguish.

"You know I have a problem with drugs?"

She nodded.

"When I was doing them, I did some pretty awful things."

"Like what?" He gave her a look so she reached out and rested her hand on his arm. "It's not morbid curiosity. I need to tell you something. Something so painful and personal that—that when I tell you what I want to tell you, I'll know you'll never tell anyone—ever!"

"Rachel, I would never betray your trust."

"I believe you mean that, but I have to be sure. You have to tell me something you've never told anyone. Something just as important to you as this . . . thing is to me."

She was serious and obviously frightened, and she was watching him like a hawk. One lie, one evasion, and he would probably lose her friendship forever. He was stunned by how much the prospect distressed him.

"Once, when I was in England—this was a long time ago, you understand?" Rachel nodded. "One night I got held up at school and missed my connection."

"Connection?"

"The guy I bought drugs from."

"Oh."

"It had been a particularly grueling day. My thesis advisor was ragging on me for not getting my outline in on time, and the kids in the class I was student-teaching were acting like animals. I felt like shit, and when I was late and the guy wasn't there, I went nuts."

"Why didn't you just go to someone else?"

Luther grinned sadly. "You see, the guy worked in a pharmacy, skimming pills from old folks' prescriptions, shorting them a few here and there and selling them to me. I told myself as long as I was buying the stuff from him instead of from some scummy street pusher, I wasn't really an addict. I know, but hey—the lies a junkie tells himself would fill an encyclopedia."

"I didn't say anything."

"You didn't have to. Anyway, I was feeling rather poorly and on the way back to my flat I—well, I passed this homeless guy sleeping underneath the stairs three buildings down from my flat. I don't know what made me stop—it wasn't the best neighborhood, and there were homeless people around there all the time. Looking back, I guess I must have caught a glimpse of his face

Ungrateful Dead

and thought I recognized him or something. Anyway, the next thing I know, I stepped off the sidewalk and started down the steps. I called out something like, 'You okay, man?' Something like that, and when he didn't move I went a little closer, telling myself the whole time I just wanted to make sure he was all right, patting myself on the back—it was the kind of thing one human being should do for another, right?

"Then I saw his face. It was this guy I had seen hanging around, hitting on the local pushers. And, boy, was he out of it—higher 'n a box kite in March. You had to be a junkie to know the look—chalk-white face, mouth open, body twitching like a cat on a high-tension wire, sweat dripping from every pore. Soon as I saw him I knew what I was going to do. I got down on my knees and started going through his pockets. He was covered with dried vomit, piss, dirt, and sweat—I was so strung out I didn't care. He had to have something on him and I meant to have it.

"I turned out the pockets of his jacket and went through his wallet—he had four pence and a faded photograph of a horse. A pack of cigarettes, a syringe with a bent needle, and a card from a blood bank in Soho telling him when he could sell blood again in his pockets. He also had a tin containing a Dilaudid tablet he was saving for an eye-opener."

"You have quite a memory," Rachel said softly.

"Yeah. His name was Jack Mulrey."

"That's the horrible thing you did? Rob an unconscious man?"

"Robbed him? Yeah, I robbed him. And when he woke up and found me holding his precious tin, I beat his head in and left him lying in a pool of blood."

Rachel's hand went to her throat. "Oh my God, Luther. Did he—"

"Die? I don't know. I don't think so. I locked myself in my room for two days, afraid to go to class, afraid to buy food, even. When I came out, the talk on the street was a bunch of kids mugged a junkie and that he had been taken to the hospital. I checked the obituaries for days after that, but there was no mention of a Jack Mulrey."

"Oh Luther, it's so hard to believe. You're so . . . so gentle."

"I never told anyone that. A lot of times over the years I almost managed to convince myself it was all a bad dream. But the blood, you see. The blood was there. On my hands . . . on the concrete. Do you know what blood looks like at night? It's black, like oil. I never raised my hand to anyone after that."

"Like you said—wow."

Luther watched Rachel's expression, trying without any success to fathom what was driving the pain he saw in her eyes.

"So," he said kindly, "is that important enough?"

Swallowing a sip of cooling coffee, she peered at him for a moment and then replaced the cup in its saucer. "Yes. If that story is true."

His eyebrows went up in amazement. "Jesus! You think I'd make up something like that?"

She dropped her eyes. "No. I guess not. Please forgive me. This thing is driving me crazy. I don't trust anyone anymore—especially myself."

"Come on. Nothing can be that bad."

"I only wish that were true." One more glance at the door and Rachel began. She told him how Anton approached her at the tennis club. How she had found him to be an exceptionally ugly individual and yet strangely captivating—a real gentleman. He'd bought her a drink,

Ungrateful Dead

made her laugh, and then offered to escort her to her car.

"He must have slipped something into my drink, because the next thing I remember is waking up on this smelly mattress in the back of his van." Rachel covered her eyes with her hand. "God, Luther," she hissed. "I was stark naked and these men—there were two of them, they were leering at me like—And the worst part was, I didn't care."

She started crying anew, and Luther ran to the sink and brought back the whole roll of paper towels. He took his time to give her a chance to collect herself, but when he returned she still refused to meet his gaze.

"Thanks," she said as she accepted the towels.

"Look, you were drugged. No one is going to blame you."

"But I kept seeing him!" She brought her fist down on the table with enough force to jar the coffee dregs from Luther's cup. "It was like I couldn't stop! Like I was addicted to him. UGH!" Rachel shivered and blew her nose on a soggy towel. "Each time—each time he made me do . . . the vilest things."

Luther squeezed her hand. "You don't have to do this. I think when we get a chance to analyze that thing that came out of your nose, we're going to find it secretes some kind of hallucinogenic, or perhaps even aphrodisiacal substance. No one—certainly not me, is going to point any fingers at you."

"He said—he said if I told anyone he'd tell Cal."

Luther gave her hand another squeeze. "As far as I'm concerned, we never had this conversation."

"He can't know," she whispered. "He can't! I know the way he acts. Everyone thinks Cal is this big jock, but inside he's a big, bumbling, puppy dog. This would kill him."

Gary L. Holleman

"Don't worry, it'll work out."

"But you're going after him. What if—"

"Rach, if things go as planned, Gadarn will be too busy to worry about you or Cal or anything."

"And if they don't go as planned?"

Luther shrugged. "Then I don't think it's going to matter."

"Am I doing the right thing, keeping it from him?"

"You're probably asking the wrong person. Most people would say no—be honest with him. But you see, this is exactly the kind of thing most men say they would want to know, until they do know, and then they wish they didn't. Does that make any sense?" Rachel nodded. "The PC answer has always been that love is built on honesty and trust, and I guess that's true as far as it goes. But I think real love—lasting love, is also built on compromise, hard work, and sacrifice. Believe me, if you do decide not to tell him, you'll find out all about hard work and sacrifice. Keeping something like this inside is going to be like wearing fifty pounds of body armor the rest of your life. It'll weigh on you, make you start to doubt yourself, and him. But if you love him enough, you'll fight it. And you'll win. I know you will."

Rachel wiped her nose once more and then put the roll away. "How did you get to be so smart?"

"Me? Ha! Living on the outside looking in, it's easy to see other people's mistakes. Even easier to give advice. Living, making it work—those are hard."

The kitchen door swung open, and Truman shuffled in wearing a fuzzy, royal-blue bathrobe with the crest of the Intercontinental Hotel-Paris on the pocket.

"There you are," he muttered. "Cal's looking for you."

"Me?" asked Rachel, quickly trying to rub the red from of her eyes with her sleeve.

Ungrateful Dead

"No. The mad professor there."

Luther climbed out of the chair and stretched. "You okay?"

Nodding, Rachel whispered, "Thanks."

"What are you thanking him for?" Truman muttered. "I'm the one got stuck making breakfast this morning."

Rachel popped up out of the chair. "I'll help. Where are the eggs?"

Luther loped up the stairs and eased into Alana's room. Cal was sitting in a chair beside the bed, whispering to her in a soft monotonous voice.

"What's up?"

Cal glanced up. His eyes were red-rimmed, and his face sagged like it was made out of soft candle wax. "She was so out of it I had to put her into a shallow hypnotic trance. I was afraid to give her a sedative, and it was the best I could think of to calm her down."

"Can she hear us?"

"Not really. She responds to voice commands, but the rest of the time she's drifting between consciousness and unconsciousness."

"You want me to watch her for a while?"

"No. I wanted you to hear this."

Luther took up a position behind his friend's chair and gazed down at the woman who, until a few days ago, had been as horribly scarred as anyone he had ever seen. She was pale, her sweat-drenched hair framed her face like a fox-fur hood, but her skin was as smooth and unblemished as raw silk. And yet it was that very perfection that was so terrifying. Facial skin just did not heal itself. Ears did not reform or eyebrows regrow. And lips, especially lips which once resembled a pair of burned and twisted rubber bands, just did not ever, ever, all by themselves, turn into perfect little red cupid's bows.

"Quit gaping at her and get a chair," Cal whispered.

"It's scary."

"What? Her face? You want to hear something really scary, sit down!"

After pulling a wicker vanity stool over, Luther sat down and leaned forward with his elbows on his knees. "What?"

"Listen." Cal lowered his voice to a murmur. "Alana . . . Alana honey—"

"Who is it?"

It was the voice of a little girl.

"It's Cal, honey. Luther's here with me."

"Luther?"

The way she said it came out sounding like "Oother."

"Tell us what you see."

"Don't want to."

"Come on, honey."

"It's dark. It smells funny. I don't like it here."

"Tell me what you saw before."

"Crawly things, black things. All around me . . . in me . . . part of me. And people—lots of people. I can't see them, but they're in here with me."

"Here? Where is here?"

"I don't know. A bad place . . . cold, bad, bad people."

"Who are they?" Cal pushed.

"People. Strangers. They're touching me—pulling at me."

Alana's face contorted, and her voice showed the first signs of panic.

"Easy now," Cal said soothingly. "They can't hurt you. Let yourself float—"

Alana's breathing slowed.

"Honey, look around. Listen. Can you hear anyone?"

Underneath the lids, her eyes were bouncing back and

Ungrateful Dead

forth like marbles rolling around under a blanket. REM sleep, Luther wondered, or was her semi-conscious mind somehow linked to her mother's nightmarish world? What was it like? Soulless creatures roaming a cold, lightless void, filled with a voracious hatred and envy of anything living? What would such beings do to a helpless soul? Devour it? Try to cling to it? Or snuff it out like a match dropped into a sea of never-ending night? It made him shudder.

"Cal, maybe this isn't such a good idea."

"Shush! Alana, tell us what you feel."

"They won't let me go—I can't move. I'm scared. I don't like it here."

"Cal—"

"Shhh! Alana, honey, try to focus. Isn't it just one person holding you? Just one?"

"I—I don't know. I feel fingers—lots of fingers, pulling at me. And . . . lips . . . cold, wet lips, kissing and biting—OW! It hurts!"

"Cal, stop it right now."

"Okay, okay. Alana, listen to the sound of my—"

"Something's coming! I can—Mommy? Mommy, is that you?"

"Goddamn it, Cal, wake her up!"

"Alana! Listen to me!"

"NOOOooo, Mommy, don't! Mommy, please DON'T!"

Luther reached for her with the intention of shaking her awake, but Cal blocked his hands and shoved his friend none too gently back into the chair.

"You crazy? Do that and the shock could kill her!" Cal immediately returned his attention to his patient. "Alana, listen to me. You are not a little girl anymore—you are stronger than she is. Fight her! She has no more power over you. Fight her! The only weapon she has is fear, and she has used it against you all of your life. You must stand up to her—NOW!"

Alana's head began whipping back and forth on the pillow; her sweat flew like drops of rain, staining the sheets and pillowcase.

Cal grabbed Luther's arm. "Speak to her! I'm losing her."

"Alana, don't give in to that bitch—fight!"

She either couldn't hear or couldn't break free from whatever horror had captured her mind. The cords in the sides of her neck were as tight as mooring cables, and her hands clutched desperately at the sheets as she fought to hang on to some little piece of reality, but she was obviously losing.

"Can't you help her?" Luther hissed.

"No, but you can. Give her something—something to hang on to. Something to hope for! Be her anchor!"

Her anchor? Luther thought wildy. *What the hell's that supposed to mean?* "What should I do?"

"Jesus Christ! You're a man—she's a woman . . . she needs you!"

Luther snared one of Alana's hands and held on so tightly her knuckles turned white. Leaning forward, he whispered in her ear. "Alana! Alana, please wake up. I don't know what I'd do if anything—if you—Alana, listen to me . . . only me. Concentrate on my voice. I know she's trying to keep me out, but you can hear me—I know you can. We have a connection, you and I, a bond. And it's much stronger and deeper than anything she could ever have with you, because we chose this bond together. You came to me, remember? You came because you needed help, but you stayed because you trust me. Trust me now. Turn away from her, from the darkness—she *is* the darkness. You are the light. That's why she has always tried to keep you close to her—not because she loved you, but to control you—possess you. Remember those times she made you exercise, but never let you play with other kids? Remember how she watched everything you ate—things that were good for the body, but not for the soul? Remember the hours at the piano? Even then, she was preparing you, breaking your spirit while breaking in your body like you were a new pair of shoes. You never had a chance before, but you have one now. You have something you never had before—someone who . . . loves you. That's right, goddamn it, I love you. Don't quit on me now. We're close. We're so damned close. If you feel anything for me, anything at all, then—''

Alana opened her eyes.

"Thank Go—"

Luther's prayer of gratitude lodged in his throat—her eyes were ice cold and as red as burning embers lying in the bottom of a coal bucket. They locked on his face, and her mouth twisted into a caustic grin.

"How touching." She pushed herself up on her elbows and gazed around the room. "What a dump. This is the best you could do?"

Luther moved his chair back and stood up, but Cal remained where he was, studying Alana the way an entomologist might study a new and potentially lethal insect.

"Morgana Magnus, I presume."

The woman's dead eyes moved in slow motion from Luther to Cal. "Ah! The witch doctor. Morgana Magnus? Yes. And Morgana Traxler and Morgana Shane and Morgana Crowe and on and on all the way back to Morgana Milucradh, who some of my less enthusiastic followers once called the Hag of the Waters for turning that moron, King Fionn, into an old man."

"So you expect us to believe you're—what? A thousand years old? Two thousand?"

"I don't expect you to believe anything. In fact, I expect your disbelief to be the death of you all."

"Then what are you doing here?" asked Luther. "Since you obviously don't fear us or need anything from us."

Luther watched closely as her head ratcheted back to him.

Odd, he thought. *The last time Morgana took over she seemed to be in complete control.*

"Of course I don't need anything from you. I'm just tired of you two hovering around my daughter like vultures. You," Morgana said, nodding to Luther, "I know what you want." She sneered at Luther. "You've been sniffing around the little bitch like a mongrel in heat since the day she strutted into your office. But you—" She tilted her head at an odd angle toward Cal. "What's in this for you? She has no money, at least none she knows about. So why do you keep poking your nose where it doesn't belong?"

"It's a concept you could never understand. It's called caring. It's what we do, we poor mortals who have to struggle along with only our normal allotted span of life. We care for each other. Protect, support, and help each other. Sometimes, with just a helping hand, companionship, or just being together, we can push back the darkness—push you back. Even if for just a little while."

Alana made a sound in her throat that Luther finally realized was the creature's version of a laugh.

"What a pretty speech. Mankind marching along arm-in-arm, one for all, all for one. So tell me, *Doctor*, why didn't you give as much consideration and support to your wife?"

Ungrateful Dead

It was Cal's turn to sputter. "What the hell are you talking about?"

Luther put his hand on his friend's arm. "Uh, Cal, why don't you wait—"

Cal shrugged him off. "You don't know the first thing about my wife."

"Me? No, that's true. But Anton? Ah, now that's another story all together."

"Gadarn?" Cal gave Luther an incredulous look. "Is that supposed to be funny? Rachel wouldn't know him if she bumped into him on the street."

"Oh, she knows him all right." Alana's lips twisted into a cruel parody of a smile. "In the Biblical sense, at least."

Cal looked as if he were about to explode. "You—you rotten, lying bitch!"

"Sticks and stones—"

Luther wrestled Cal from the chair and physically steered him out the door. Meanwhile, Cal was looking back over his shoulder, sputtering and spitting.

"Ask her!" Morgana shouted. "Better yet, ask your hippie friend there. Why else do you think he's trying so hard to get you out of here?"

Luther shoved Cal out into the hall. "Wait here."

"What's she talking about, Luther?"

"I don't have time for this right now. I can't leave Alana alone."

"She's not alone. That fucking bitch is with her."

"Think about what you're saying."

"I know what I'm saying, goddamn it! I'm saying—" Cal ran his fingers through his sandy hair. "My God, what *am* I saying?"

"Just wait here!" Luther hissed. "Don't do anything, and for God's sake, don't go off half cocked."

Cal grabbed his friend's arm. "Just tell me one

thing—do you know what she's talking about?"

"I—I don't have time to go into it. Just wait."

With that, Luther closed the door and rested his back against it.

"Men!" Morgana chuckled. "Can't live with them, can't cut their livers out with rusty knife."

"Funny."

Alana—at least her body—collapsed back against the pillow. She looked wasted, limp, as if the very act of breathing was taking everything she had. He wanted to go to her, to touch her and reassure her, and he had to concentrate on the woman's eyes to remind himself who he was really dealing with. Red within red—no pupils, no irises. He had never seen anything like them.

He approached the bed cautiously.

"So," Morgana said with a tired sigh, "what shall we talk about now?"

He studied her for almost a minute without responding. It appeared to him that Alana wasn't the only one who was exhausted. Morgana seemed to be having trouble maintaining control over the body she had hijacked. The question was: why bother?

What is she doing, he mused. *Why is she here? Why now? Morgana had to know we were around, that we would know. So why?*

"You're not still mad at me for that little prank I played on you in that buffoon's apartment?" Morgana asked.

"Prank? You call cutting out a man's heart and wrapping it up like a bloody Christmas present a prank?"

"You make too much of it."

Her voice seemed to be growing stronger. He had to get her out of Alana before she got too comfortable.

"Why are you here, Morgana? Why now?"

"Does a mother need a reason to visit her daughter?

Ungrateful Dead

How else am I to find out the kind of riffraff she's hanging out with?"

"Cut the crap. Alana's starting to give you trouble, isn't she?"

"You don't know what you're talking about."

"Oh no? Funny, the instant I told her I loved her, you showed up. Could it be that the little girl you bullied when you were alive is starting to fight back? What if she found someone to give her emotional support? What do you suppose would happen to your plans then?"

Morgana shook her fists at the ceiling. "Great Set, don't make me laugh! You expect me or anyone to believe you *love* her?" The way she said the word love made it sound dirty. "Look at her! She has all the backbone of a bowl of oatmeal. HA! Until I took care of it, her face *looked* like a bowl of oatmeal."

Luther figured she was trying to provoke him, and he came damned close to giving her what she wanted. Instead, he tried to bluff it out. Sitting in Cal's chair, he scooted it up next to the bed and then set his face with his most relaxed and charming smile. "It won't work. I'm on to you."

But it seemed, for a dead woman, Morgana was a pretty fair poker player too. "Okay. Come on then, come closer. Look me right in the eye, and tell me you find this quivering mass of emotions appealing. Tell me you can't live without her."

Luther tried, but he had two problems. One, peering into her eyes made him dizzy to the point of nausea. And two, he wasn't one-hundred-percent sure how he felt about Alana. Sure he liked her—a lot. But love? He could lie, but that might be playing right into the bitch's hands. And yet, he was in too far to back off, so he decided to keep going and, to paraphrase Miss Scarlett, worry about the consequences tomorrow.

"Yes, I love her. Deeply, emotionally, passionately. But I guess those words are meaningless to you."

"You're lying," she sneered.

He leaned closer; the hatred and malevolence in her eyes almost made him sick. "Am I? Are you sure? Are you willing to bet your . . . life?"

The glow in Morgana's eyes dulled to a rich burgundy. Going strictly on instinct now, Luther took this as a sign of doubt and decided to push it as far as he could. He took a deep breath.

"Let me show you just how wrong you are."

He pinned her arms to the bed, leaned down, and pressed his lips to hers.

Morgana's response was immediate and violent.

She tried to scratch his eyes out with her fingernails. Failing that, she bucked and twisted and fought so that it took every last ounce of his strength and skill and weight to control her. But he held on, crushing her lips, bruising his own, and all the while watching, and waiting, but mostly praying, until the red slowly began to fade from her eyes. At last her body relaxed and, a bit at a time, he loosened his grip on her wrists and pulled back. In a few moments her eyes return to normal.

"You okay?" he whispered.

"No." She put her arm around his neck. "More."

Luther couldn't believe his ears. "You're kidding?"

Her arm was as light as a strand of spaghetti, but she didn't need a lot of strength to pull his mouth back down to hers. This time, her lips were soft and warm and eager, and in a moment her other arm came up to join the first. Luther opened one eye—she was staring at him.

"You're cheating," she mumbled around his mouth.

Her eyes were tired, but human, full of little flecks of light that sparkled like stars.

What the hell, he thought.

Ungrateful Dead

He closed his eye and let himself go, feeling her heat, the cushiony firmness of her breasts, and the pleasant tingle her fingers left behind as they trailed through his hair. Too soon, he broke away, holding himself over her on stiff arms as he studied her expression.

"What was that all about?"

She sighed. "I was in that dark place. Alone, lost. And then I heard this voice—your voice. You said we had a bond. You said, turn away from the darkness. I tried, honest I did. But she—it was like being all tangled up in this huge black blanket. I couldn't see, couldn't move, I could hardly breathe.

"That's when I heard you say not to give up and that you . . . you loved me. And it was like the blanket loosened—just a little, and I could breathe again. I knew you were near, and I knew you were fighting her, and I tried to fight too. I pushed and kicked and—oh Luther, there just aren't any words for what it was like. I thought I was doing good, that I might be able to break free, but then all at once the darkness came down on me like a giant fist and I knew it was all over. I could feel my soul slipping away, sucked down by an icy wind into a bottomless pit. And I couldn't even hear myself scream."

"Jesus," Luther muttered.

"I don't think He could have helped, but again, you did. 'I love her deeply, emotionally, and passionately!' Those were your words. And they reverberated in the darkness as clear as a bell. The next thing I knew you were kissing me."

"I, well, I—"

She caressed his cheek. "Don't panic. I know you didn't mean it. But you said it to help me."

"And it did?"

Alana shrugged. "Possibly. More likely it was the

333

kiss. When she was alive, Mother indulged in every type of sexual perversion imaginable, but true human affection always repelled her."

"Oh."

He pushed himself up and started to slide off the bed, but she took his face in her hands.

"Where do you think you're going? I'm not through with you yet."

"But—I thought—"

"Just because you aren't madly in love with me, that doesn't mean I'm not crazy about you."

Luther's face got all red, and Alana laughed for the first time in what seemed like weeks.

"Okay," she chuckled. "Maybe it's not love. How about good old-fashioned lust?"

He checked her eyes again.

"Don't look at me that way."

"Well, you have to admit it's a bit strange. Your daughter's disappeared, and a minute ago you were doing a header into the abyss and now—"

"And now I'm alive. Don't you see? I was that close to oblivion !" She held her fingers an inch apart. "That close! It was an enlightening experience!

"Mother never loved me, but I realize now, it wasn't my fault. Her plan from the day I was born was to make my life so miserable that when the time came for her to take my body, I would give up without a fight. A damned fine job she did too. I doubt if there was ever a week my whole life that I didn't consider suicide at least once. That's why Mother was always able to do the things she did to me, because I was never really alive. I was the zombie valet, the lump of walking flesh keeping the new body in shape until she was ready to move in. So perhaps what you said did make a difference after all. A person has to be real, has to be alive for someone to love her. Perhaps Mother reasoned that if I believed you actually cared for me, I might start believing I was alive, and then her power over me would be gone.

"As for Morna... I'm absolutely terrified for her. But I know now that's exactly what Mother wants, so I have to control the terror, use it. The more I dwell on it, the crazier I get and the easier it will be for her to control me. When I can think rationally about it, I know she won't hurt her."

"Why not? I mean, if anything happened to Morna—not that it will, but if it should, wouldn't that—might that not push you over the edge for good?"

"Of course, it would. Morna is my whole world. But I'm beginning to understand Mother and one thing I know—she always covers her bases. If what Cal said before is right—and I believe now that it is—then the last thing she would do is hurt Morna."

"I don't get it—why?"

"Because if anything happened to Morna because of me, I would probably kill myself. Mother knows that. And then what would she do? No, Morna is her backup plan."

"Backup?"

"That's right. Cal said for the transformation to take place it has to be a *blood* relative."

"Oh, man."

"Morgana wouldn't dare hurt her—physically, at least. But what she could do to her mind..." Alana shuddered, but quickly got herself under control. "But you and Cal won't let that happen."

"We won't?"

"No. This thing you two have cooked up, it's going to work and both Morna and I are going to be rid of Mother forever. It's the only way. It *must* work!"

"Well." Luther cleared his throat. "I think it's a pretty good plan."

"But in the meantime, my first official act as a newly living person is going to be to take a lover. Interviews to begin immediately."

She tried to pull him to her, but he resisted.

"Uh, Alana—"

Her eyes suddenly went wide, and she released him so quickly he almost fell backward off the bed. "I—I'm so sorry. I didn't think. You're afraid my face will go back—"

He put a finger to her lips. "Shush! Don't even think it. It's not that at all—honest. It's just that Cal has a problem, and he needs me right now more than you do."

"Cal?"

"Something your mother said."

"Oh. Then it isn't—"

He brushed the back of his hand down her cheek. "No, it isn't."

"Then hurry back. I have a lot of living to catch up on."

"Maybe you should rest?"

"After."

He delivered a quick kiss to her forehead, then went to the door. "I'll send Virginia in to stay with you."

"Thanks."

He stepped into the hall, but Cal was nowhere to be seen, and he followed the aroma of cigar smoke, first to Tru's study, and then down into the basement.

Virginia and Tru were busy filling the plastic water rifles with the mixture from the health food store, while Rachel and Cal were standing at opposite ends of the room pouring the remaining liquid into balloons. One look at Rachel and he didn't have to ask if Cal had heeded his advice.

Ungrateful Dead

"Ooo-iee!" Virginia exclaimed. "This stuff smells worse than a Mississippi cesspool in August. What's in it?" She had on yellow rubber dishwashing gloves that went all the way up to her elbows, and Tru was wearing an apron with the message: "Don't ask me, I'm Polish!" in block letters across the front.

"You don't want to know," Luther replied. "The good news is, I've come to take you away from all this."

" 'Bout time."

"You mind going up and keeping an eye on Alana? I need to have a word with Cal."

"What about me?" Tru asked.

"You keep pouring."

"Oh, sure, I get all the fun."

Rachel walked over to the table and touched Tru on the arm. "I'll help you."

Luther tapped Cal on the shoulder. "Cup of coffee?"

Cal peeked at his wife. "Sounds good."

Up in the kitchen, Luther poured two cups of Virginia's strongest coffee and then dug through the pantry until he found Tru's stash of Twinkies. Cal glanced at the treats and nodded his thanks, but it wasn't hard to see his mind was light years away.

"Bad night," Luther said as he sat down.

"Don't start!"

"Right. Far be it from me to tell you what a shmuck you are."

Cal ripped into the Twinkie's wrapper with his teeth. "Some goddamned friend you are. You knew, and you didn't think to tell me?"

"Exactly how much did you allow Rachel to say before you made an ass of yourself?"

"Enough. Besides, why do you always take her side? How do you know it was my fault?"

"I know you."

"Okay, Mister 'I'll Be a Bachelor til I Die,' what would you have done? Cut a deck of Tarot cards?"

Luther gave him a lopsided grin. "No. I'd have probably done the same thing you did. Only I don't have a sensitive and suave friend I can depend on to help get me out of the mess I put myself in."

"What makes you think I want out?"

"You're dumb as a post, but you're not that dumb."

"Thanks. That's a compliment?"

"Look, you saw that thing that came out of her. You know the way she was acting. That wasn't Rachel."

Cal shoved a whole Twinkie into his mouth and followed it with a slug of steaming coffee. He glared at Luther and chewed in silence for several seconds. Swallowing, he sat back in the chair.

"I know it wasn't Rachel."

"Then what is it? Pride? Ego?"

"You don't leave a man much."

"I'd say you pretty much had it all. I'm just trying to keep you from throwing it away."

Cal put the cup down and balled his fists until his arms quivered. "You can't understand! Every time I think of that—that animal, I just go—"

"Cal, did you ever see a porno flick?"

Cal gaped at him like he had lost his mind. "What?"

"Porno flick? Skin flick? You ever see one?"

"I think all those drugs you did must have fried your brain."

"Just answer the question."

"Once or twice, in college."

"The women in those movies . . . did it bother you to see them do those things?"

The conversation was obviously not to Cal's liking. "What is this? A trick question? I say yes, then why

Ungrateful Dead

was I watching it? I say no, I'm a misogynistic bastard who gets off seeing women humiliated?"

"Why does everything have to be a debate? Just answer the damn question."

"It's not the same! It's not the same at all!"

Luther grabbed Cal's arm to get his attention and to keep him from shoving the second Twinkie into his mouth. "The woman who slept with that man was no more Rachel than those women in the movies. She was a stranger. Not your wife—not Sam's mother—a total stranger."

They locked eyes and Luther could see the pain and doubt in his friend's.

"But—"

"No buts, Cal."

"No, dammit, it's not that simple. She remembers! She knows—"

"Knows what? Horror? Humiliation? How do you know what she remembers? Maybe nothing. Maybe things she prays she'll forget. Will it make you any happier to drag her through all of it again?"

"But don't I even have the right—"

"To punish her? To make her as miserable as this whole thing has made you? Maybe you do. But if you're smart, you'll go back down in that basement, take Rachel aside, and tell her you love her—no matter what, you love her. And that your lives start right now."

Luther's words were as hard for Cal to swallow as the Twinkies, but he mulled them over for almost two minutes. Luther knew the exact instant his friend decided to take his advice—Cal's shoulders slumped, but he smiled and nodded.

"You should be the shrink."

"Wait til you get my bill."

"Listen, I had a thought—"

"Hard to believe."

"No, really, what about the dogs? Grover is going to take care of Gadarn's flunkies, but what if there are dogs?"

Scrunching up his face, Luther said, "What's your idea?"

"Tru has a dart gun, and I have some pretty powerful tranks in my bag. What do you think?"

"Good idea. What's Tru doing with a dart gun?"

"Who the hell knows. Probably uses it to round up faculty members for his parties."

"Speaking of drugs, you got any speed in that little bag of yours?"

Cal eyed Luther oddly.

"It's not for me. It's for Alana. We can't take a chance on her zoning out. It's imperative she stay awake the next twenty-four hours. After that, it'll all be over."

"Or?"

"Or not."

Cal climbed slowly to his feet, grabbing his back and stretching as he did so. "Yeah. I've got some stuff that could make a dead paraplegic do the funky chicken. What are you going to do now?"

"Well, uh—after you medicate Alana, I thought I'd spend a little time with her."

"A little time?" Cal's eyebrows wiggled up and down like Groucho Marx's.

"Don't be crass."

"Oh, it's okay to discuss the most intimate details of my sex life, but not yours?"

"Who said anything about sex?"

"Right. You two are going to discuss the first five chapters of the Bible."

* * *

Ungrateful Dead

Because of the weather, the cars began arriving earlier than expected; the first showed up at sundown. No Chevys or Fords, not a single pickup truck, but Mercedes and Lincolns, and quite a few limousines driven by large men in dark suits and caps. They parked haphazardly on the frozen ground around the silent fountain, rolling carelessly over stunted rose bushes that had been planted back before the Civil War by slaves, some of whom lay rotting in the mud in the basement of the mansion. Most of the visitors were dressed in expensive casual clothes—designer jeans, L. L. Bean bush jackets that had never been anywhere near the bush, but they all wore old shoes or scuffed sneakers on their feet.

Danny Keats met each new arrival at the door, ushering them into the large banquet hall where a table with rich foods, French delicacies, and fine wines had been set up. Few of the guests noticed Grover's absence, and those who did were clever enough not to ask questions. Everyone did, however, ask where Anton was to be found, and Danny, ever smooth and handsome in his turtleneck sweater and black jeans, promised that his master would put in an appearance soon. Not surprisingly, no one inquired about Colin O'Dwyer or Wardley Morrow, both of whom were also missing but who most of the guests considered unsophisticated boors.

At about 8 P.M., just when things were starting to swing, Anton appeared at the top of the main stairway with a gorgeous young stranger at his side. Soft auburn hair, sea-green eyes, and skin so fair that it was no wonder several of the guests whispered to one another that she was a ghost.

All conversation ceased.

The girl was awfully young, several of the woman whispered.

Maybe too young—even for Anton, who, as most of

the women in the crowd already knew, had an insatiable appetite for young flesh.

He led the girl down the rickety stairway and sashayed through the crowd like Moses treading the slippery path through the Red Sea. He nodded benignly to familiar faces on the left and right, but did not stop to introduce his companion, though several people tried to strike up a conversation. He opened the door to the basement and, with a wave to the staring throng, disappeared down the stairs.

Halfway down, Morna noticed a strange glow emanating from the darkness. She stopped and then saw the dark outline of the massive tree, its limbs outspread like the feathers of a giant peacock.

"What's that?" she asked.

" 'Tis nothing to be a feared of a'tall. Come now, let me show you around."

Placing his small, yet incredibly powerful, hands on the girl's frail shoulders, he propelled her deeper and deeper into gloom.

"What's that smell?" she asked in a small, tight voice.

"That's nothing but the drain tunnels that empty into the creek. Nothing to worry your little head about."

At the bottom of the stairway, Anton flipped the switch, and the torches ignited with a series of muted pops.

"Oh my God!" Morna gasped as the full extent of the tree and the shadowy dungeon sprang into view. Then she noticed something else; there was a man nailed to the tree. At least it looked like a man. But it was dressed in tattered clothing, so she decided it must be some kind of weird scarecrow.

"Is that—that's not a man, is it?"

Anton glanced at his formed henchman and chuckled.

"No, my dear. That is an object lesson in loyalty."

"What?"

"Of course it isn't real. It's what you might call a party decoration."

It didn't look like a party decoration to Morna—not even a Halloween decoration, much less a Christmas ornament. But then, she had spent most of her life with nuns so what did she know?

"Come on now, here we go."

They crossed the slippery floor to the table at the base of the tree. In honor of the occasion, the table was covered with a black silk sheet, with a plump, black silk pillow set on top. Two sets of wool-lined, leather restraints had been bolted to the four corners of the table. In front of the table were thirty-six folding chairs arranged in six neat rows, and in the branches of the tree someone had added a nice holiday touch—two dozen strands of Christmas tree lights which, when Anton stooped and plugged them in, began to twinkle like multicolored fireflies.

"There, now," Anton beamed. "Ain't that a pretty sight?"

Morna didn't know what to make of the odd little man. The top of his head barely came to her chin, he had bad skin, horrible teeth and breath, and the worst case of dandruff she had ever seen. And yet, in the short time she had been in his presence she had felt that same hot, fluttery knot in the pit of her stomach that she used to get around Todd. It made her feel afraid and unsure and somehow . . . dirty. And if those things weren't bad enough, most of the time she didn't have a clue what he was talking about.

"Yes, it's very nice, Mr. Anton. When can I go home?"

"Now, now. I told you, we're gonna have a party here

Gary L. Holleman

tonight and your mum is to be the guest of honor."

"And—and your...friends took me as a...trick you're playing on Mother?"

Sighing, Anton gave the girl a slow up and down look. She was a tasty little morsel. A bit slow witted, a bit small in the chest for his taste, still... "That's right, dearie. You'll see. When she gets here we're all gonna have a big laugh. Now come on. I want you to do something for me." He reached into his pocket and pulled out a green-and-black capsule. "Be a good girl and take this."

Morna was well aware there were a lot of things going on out in the "real" world that she was unfamiliar with, but pills weren't one of those things—the sisters had made sure of that. Morna's entire class had once volunteered for a month at the free clinic in Bern, so they could witness firsthand the joys of narcotic addiction. Street people, prostitutes, addicts of every race, nationality, and creed...they all had bedpans, and they all had to be emptied. Uh-uh, no way.

"No, thank you."

Anton presented a smile that didn't go anywhere near his eyes. "It wasn't a request. Come on. It's just something to let you sleep until the party gets rolling."

Looking around the dank basement, she said, "You want me to sleep here?"

He patted the table. "Soft as down. Hop up, give it a try."

One look at the leather restraints, and she made a break for the stairs. Anton was quicker than he looked, and as she passed he caught her by the arm and spun her around.

"Not so fa—"

She hit him square in his very prominent nose with her fist. The nose splattered like a rotten squash, showering them both with spots of blood and mucus, and Anton let go of her arm to cradle his nose with both hands.

"You goddamned little bitch!"

Morna took off again, but her feet hit a patch of super-slippery mud, and she ended up on her backside, staring up into the face of the scarecrow on the tree.

Grover opened his eyes. "Way to go, girlie." He grinned. At some point in his ordeal his teeth had shattered like glass beads and several long, black worms slithered through the wide gaps. "Now get up and kick him in the balls."

Morna passed out.

The first time around, they went at it like a pair of starving sumo wrestlers trying to read a Braille menu. There was a lot of grunting and twisting and saying, "Oops, sorry!" But they stuck with it, and when the deed was finally done, they rolled apart and stared at opposite sides of the room. When the silence became painful, Luther said, "Well, I think that went . . . well."

Alana peeked over her shoulder. "You do?"

He looked over his shoulder. "Yes. You don't?"

She rolled partway back. "Of course. It's just—"

He rolled partway back as well. "Just what?"

"I just thought I was a little . . . stiff."

"Stiff?"

"You know, rigid—unresponsive?"

"Not at all. I thought I was a little—clumsy?"

"Not at all—"

They looked at each other for another moment and then laughed.

"They lied," Luther whispered. "It's not at all like riding a bicycle."

"No, nothing like riding a bicycle," she agreed.

"Maybe arm wrestling."

She laughed. "Jousting in rusty chain mail!"

"Rusty, boy, that says it all."

The silence returned, but this time it was comfortable. Alana pulled the covers up and turned onto her side facing him, reaching out to caress the hair on his chest.

"It really wasn't that bad—for a first time."

"I know," he replied. "It's been a while."

"For me, too."

"Maybe it isn't very manly to admit, but—"

"What?"

"It was like I was sixteen again—it was scary."

Alana laughed in delight. "No! Really?"

"I mean, back then, looking at all that naked female flesh was intimidating. Now, not that you aren't beautiful, you are—"

Alana's hand tried to sneak up to her cheek, but he caught it, kissed each finger one at a time, and then continued.

"This was somehow more scary. I knew all the things that could go wrong. I kept telling myself, 'Do this, don't do that. Be gentle.' Worst of all . . . kiss of death—be suave!"

She giggled again and fluttered her eyelashes. "My hero!"

He pulled her to him, and she rearranged the sheet so she could relish the hard, lean heat of his body.

"You think maybe we could try it again?" he whispered.

Grinning, she whispered back, "You think you're up to it?"

He sputtered in mock indignation. "Young lady, I may not be eighteen anymore, but I'm certainly not ready for the retirement home."

Amazed and secretly pleased at her own audacity,

Ungrateful Dead

Alana threw back the sheet and allowed his eyes free reign. "Then go for it."

One hand—that was all he allowed himself, one hand on the curve of her left thigh. He moved it slowly up to her hip.

At his touch, her skin pebbled and bathed his sensitive fingertips with her heat.

He rubbed the tips together, feeling the tingle, and then brought them up to his nose, inhaling the musky aroma of her pheromones and silky secretions. He replaced the hand and continued up over the swell of her hip, past her waist, exploring the soft rise and fall of each individual rib, all the while reveling in the feel of the fine, white hairs that covered her torso like an almost invisible coat of down. When his fingers stopped inches short of her breast she gasped, grabbed his hand, and forced it hard against her.

"Don't tease!" she panted. "It's not nice."

The nipple was as hard as a marble under his palm. "I'm not teasing." He grinned. "I'm savoring."

"Well savor a little faster."

"My mother always said patience was a virtue."

"My mother always said virtue was for fools."

"Hmmm." He pursed his lips. "I think I like your mother's saying better."

She attacked his mouth with her lips and tongue, but he quickly counterattacked with his own tongue and drew little circles around the nipple with his index finger. She tried to pull him on top of her, but he resisted.

"What are you doing?" she gasped.

"It's called foreplay. I read about it in *Cosmo*."

Her voice was rough. "To hell with *Cosmo*! I want to fuck, not read about it."

He laughed. "You mean you don't want a man to be sensitive to your needs?"

Gary L. Holleman

"Be sensitive tomorrow—if we have a tomorrow. Tonight, I want to do all the things I've always read about—the things the nuns promised us we'd go to hell for even thinking about. I want to try them all. I want to get out of this bed sore and be stiff for a week. Now, quit talking and go to work!"

Luther stared at her with a bemused half-smile on his face. She was starting to sound like the "old" Alana again, the spitfire who had showed up at his office and shoved a gun in his face and made him believe the unbelievable—he liked it.

Luther flipped her over onto her stomach—not roughly, but none too gently either, and brushed her hair aside, resting his lips next to her right ear.

"Oooo, feeling feisty are we?" He forced her legs apart and wedged his body between them. "Well, me old Mum had another saying: 'No good feast begins without the hors d'oeuvre.'"

He started with the short hairs at the base of her neck and then blazed a slow trail of kisses down her shoulders and back. Halfway to her behind he switched to his tongue, teasing and licking and occasionally nipping at a scar or dimple with very careful teeth. She tasted wonderful! Warm honey and cinnamon, seasoned with just the right amount of passion-induced perspiration. It was an intoxicating mix, one that ignited a fire in his brain, which quickly spread through his blood to other, less cerebral parts of his body.

He picked up the pace, licking, kissing, kissing, licking, down the small of her back and over the mounds of her buttocks. Once there, he paused and raised his head.

On his trek down the back country of her body, Alana had alternately clawed the mattress and moaned, while gritting her teeth in ecstacy. When he paused, her head popped up, and she cast a baleful eye at him. Her hair draped at an angle across one eye, a look he found very erotic.

"You are on very dangerous ground," she growled playfully.

"I just wanted to give you fair warning."

His head went lower and Alana had to bury her face in the pillow to muffle her shrieks of joy.

"There!" Anton grunted as he fastened the last buckle around Morna's ankle. "Neat as a pin."

"You are an animal, you know that?" Grover coughed until it sounded like his lungs were tearing loose.

Anton glanced up at what was left of the once-powerful bodyguard. Grover's face looked like a skull, and his skin was the color and consistency of papier-mâché. "You still with us, boyo? Aye, you are one tough McGilla." That said, Anton turned his attention back to Morna.

She really was something—when she was quiet. A face and body that belonged to a Helen—aye, she could launch a ship or three. There was a bit of Morgana in the girl's face too—around the nose and mouth—especially the mouth. A younger, softer version to be sure, but it was there. He reached out and probed her lips with his finger—they were soft, pliant. His eyes walked down the sweep of her neck to the pale flesh exposed by the "V" in her blouse. Her skin looked soft, young and warm and fresh, bursting with vitality. He could almost feel the blood pulsing through the tiny blue veins that ran just beneath the surface, could almost hear the rhythmic beating of her heart, could see the rise and fall of her breasts as the breath of life rushed in and out.

All at once his mouth was as dry as a desert—the old

anticipatory dryness that made his fingers sweat and his heart gallop. He glanced around to make certain Danny or one of the other cretins wasn't snooping around, and then he bent over and undid the top button of her blouse. She had freckles across her chest. He undid the next button and discovered that she was wearing one of those lacy, skin-colored bras that hooked in the front. His fingers were shaking so badly he had to flex them a couple of times to get control. He took hold of the clasp and—

"She said to stop it!"

Anton's heart leapt up into his throat and lodged there like a lump of cold pudding. "What?"

"She said you better stop," Grover rasped.

Danny's toolbox was still on the ground at the base of the tree. Anton grabbed a screwdriver from the top shelf and plunged it up to the handle in the soft, meaty part of Grover's thigh. Grover hardly blinked.

"What the blazes are you yammerin' about?" Anton shouted. "Who says I better stop?"

"Morgana."

The dwarf's jaw dropped. "Now I know you've gone 'round the bend."

"Really?" With great effort, Grover raised his head. "I think I'm a bit closer to her than you at the moment." He open his mouth, and a foul mix of leeches and black vomitus spewed out.

Anton leaped back to the table and began refastening the buttons on Morna's blouse.

"Good thinking," Grover said. "She says, you touch the girl and you'll be sorry."

In his haste, Anton's stubby fingers kept slipping off the stubborn buttons. "You're daft! She speaks only to me."

"Maybe you were so busy you didn't hear her. She

Ungrateful Dead

says she has plans for the girl, and she doesn't want her molested."

There! One more button to go. "Shut up! One more word, and I won't wait for the worms to finish with you."

Grover laughed—it wasn't a pretty sound. "Do it. You'd be doing me a favor. Far as that goes—go ahead, mess with the girl. See what happens."

Just as Anton pushed the last button home, Morna opened her eyes. For the first few seconds she was confused, turning her head left, then right, and then her memory must have kicked in, for her eyes locked on Anton, and she stared at him in total, abject terror.

"Don't go all bonzo on me, girlie," Anton said with a smile.

She screamed and kept on screaming.

Anton tried to cover her mouth with his small hands and when that proved ineffective, he covered his ears.

"Shut up! Shut up! *Shut the fuck up!*"

Morna wasn't in a cooperative mood. She paused, took a deep breath, and opened her mouth again, and Anton slapped her across the face hard enough to bring tears—that didn't even slow her down. For a girl her size, Morna had incredibly powerful lungs.

"All right, you little bitch!" he hissed. "You want something to scream about?"

He grabbed the shovel from under the table and began scraping at soft mud like a deranged sheepdog looking for a lost bone. He didn't have to go far, only a few inches, and then he threw the shovel down, grabbed Morna by the hair, and twisted her head around.

"Take a good look. Pretty, ain't she? One more sound, girlie, and that's what you'll look like."

Morna fell silent, but didn't close her mouth. It remained a ragged hole in the middle of her face. She couldn't close her eyes either, though at that moment she wanted to more than anything else in the world. The way Anton was gripping her hair, all she could do was stare at the mutilated body lying partially exposed in the shallow hole.

It was female; that much was plain. But what she had been like before—old or young, pretty or not, it was no longer possible to tell. Her eyes were empty sockets, her face was gray and riddled with oozing lesions, and her mud-slicked hair had come out in clumps, leaving a wrinkled scalp with patches of startlingly white bone showing through.

"My God," Morna gasped. "What did you do to her?"

Releasing her hair, Anton picked up the shovel and scooped up a glob of mud. "Me little friends here have an awful big appetite."

The mud was alive with leeches, their thin, glistening bodies intertwined as they twisted and fought to extract every last molecule of blood from the moist dirt.

"What are those things?" she asked.

"Well, some say they be worms, others leeches, 'cause a the way they take to blood. Me—" He cupped his hand under his nose and snorted. A leech about three inches long slithered out of his left nostril and plopped into his palm. "I says they're the stuff of life everlastin'." He held the creature between his forefinger and thumb and dangled it over Morna's face. "Now dearie, it's either this,"—he jiggled the leech—"or this,"—he opened his other hand and showed her the capsule. "What's it gonna be?"

It wasn't a difficult choice. Morna opened her mouth.

Anton dropped the capsule in, and then held his hand over her nose and mouth until she swallowed. Giving the girl one last murderous glare, he placed the leech on

Ungrateful Dead

his chin where the creature paused for a heartbeat, and then scurried up over his lips and vanished up his nose.

Anton shivered once, sighed, and then said, "Do try to keep quiet. Me shindig is startin' and I can't be having me guests disturbed."

That said, he waddled over and flipped the switch on the wall, plunging the basement into twilight. Sighing, Anton mounted the stairs, huffing and puffing at each step like an asthmatic plow horse. Morna waited until she heard the door at the top of the stairs open and then close, then she whispered: "Mister? Mister, can you hear me?"

The basement was dark and as hot and muggy as a swamp, but because of the strange radiance given off by the tree, after a while she could pick out a few things—shadows of things really. And it was quiet. She could hear a few things: the soft moan of the wind in the drainage tunnels. Another sound—a hissing sound, which could have been rushing water, and every now and then a solitary drop of condensation hit the ground like a gob of spit.

"Mister?"

The man had looked pretty bad. Maybe he was dead, she thought.

The pill she'd swallowed was beginning to make her feel woozy, and she wondered if she had imagined him. Maybe all of this—that horrible little man, the worms, the big dirty house—all of it, was just the revenge of that slice of pepperoni pizza she'd had for lunch. *Yeah,* she thought, *it's all a nightmare. I'm not really on this rack they call a table. My wrists and ankles aren't really bound and I'm not really sweating like a pig!*

"Damn!" she muttered.

"No kidding."

Though little above a whisper, the voice seemed to

come from everywhere at once. In a moment, the man groaned and started coughing. When he stopped, she said, "Can those worm things get up on this table?"

"I don't know. If they want to, I guess."

"That doesn't make me feel much better."

"Sorry."

He coughed nonstop for almost a minute.

"Do you know why they brought me here?" she asked when he stopped.

"I have a pretty good idea."

"Well—"

"You don't really want to know."

She was quiet for about thirty seconds, but the silence was scarier than anything the stranger might say. "Do you know my mother? Her name's Alana Magnus."

"We've never been what you might call formally introduced, but yeah, I've seen her a few times."

"When I was waking up, I heard you say that she didn't want that man to do something . . . was it Mother you were referring to?"

"No, your grandmother."

"Nanny's dead."

"Yeah, I know. And she doesn't like it."

"Mother told me some really far-out things. I . . . I don't know if I understood or believed all of it."

"Word of advice—believe it."

"Then . . . Nanny was talking to you?"

Grover sucked in his breath and groaned like he was passing a kidney stone.

"You okay?"

"The little buggers are getting a bit rambunctious. Nanny? You mean your Grandma?"

Morna nodded, then realized he probably couldn't see her and replied out loud. "Yes."

"No. I was just pulling the little twerp's chain about

that. She doesn't talk to anyone but him, and all things being the same, I'm just as happy. I never met the woman, but I don't think I missed much—no offense."

"I only saw her once myself. She and Mom didn't get along."

"Point for your mother."

"But I don't understand—I don't understand any of it."

"I know. There's a lot I don't understand about it myself."

"Mother said—when I was a little girl . . ." Morna's eyelids began to feel like lead weights. "She used to tell me there were no such things as monsters. Now—now she says—" She yawned, and her voice got very faint. "She says she lied."

Grover raised his head. So far, the worms had left his eyes alone, and he had been down in the semi-darkness long enough so that he could see relatively well. He could make out the girl's face, just not all of her features. She looked like a good enough kid; pretty and probably bright. As he was studying her, he saw the glint go out of her eyes and figured she had finally succumbed to whatever it was Anton had given her.

"Yeah, kid, there are monsters. But sleep, and pray your nightmares turn out to be worse than what's waiting for you when you wake up."

It was almost 5 P.M. when Luther and Alana joined the others in Truman's study. Virginia had started a fire in the oversized fireplace, and the warm, woodsy smell of burning hickory filled the room. The windows were frosted with condensation and snow, and the flickering lights from the huge Christmas tree in the living room threw intermittent shadows across the floor—a sad reminder of what they should have been celebrating. From their friends' expressions, Luther gathered that they had walked into the middle of a heated discussion.

"What's up?" he asked.

"We've been kicking around the notion of calling in the police. Rachel thinks we ought to," Tru replied.

Rachel jumped in. "I've thought that from the start. Why do we have to do this alone? They have men and guns and—I don't know, S.W.A.T. teams. Shouldn't we let them go in and rescue Morna?"

Luther glanced at Alana who, still in the grip of an amphetamine high, was pacing back and forth in front of the fire like a caged tiger.

"I keep pointing out that we can't go to the police," said Tru. "We have no proof that Gadarn has Alana's daughter, and they aren't likely to just take our word for it. At best, they would maybe knock on his door and ask a few questions, and I think that would probably put Morna at even greater risk."

"I don't think it matters one hoot what we think," Virginia said. "What do you think, Alana?"

Alana stopped pacing, but wrapped her arms around herself, as if she were trying to keep her body from flying off in a dozen different directions. "Don't take this the wrong way—you people have been wonderful to us. You've put yourselves in danger to help us and I'm grateful—"

"But?" Cal said.

"But I still don't think any of you has grasped what we're dealing with here."

"Don't bet on it," Rachel muttered.

Alana nodded to acknowledge her mistake. "Rachel aside, the rest of you act like Anton is some kind of Mafia Don and all we have to do is round him and his gang up and throw them in the hoosgow."

"That's not exactly fair, honey," Luther said.

Ungrateful Dead

"Okay, maybe not. But the police can't help us. Lawyers can't help us, and judges can't help us. This isn't about law. It isn't even about right and wrong—those are abstracts. This is about the power of evil, and what one person will do to get that power and keep it." Alana glanced at Rachel. "You faced it. You felt it. Am I wrong?"

Rachel dropped her eyes. "No," she mumbled. "You're not wrong."

Alana's outburst dropped a chill over the room. Luther cleared his throat and glanced around the circle of somber faces.

"Okay, well, now that that's settled, it's time Tru, Cal, and I packed up and hit the road." Luther looked at Truman. "What time are we supposed to meet Grover?"

"Hold on a minute," Alana snapped. "I hope you don't think you're leaving me behind?"

"Or me!" Virginia and Rachel said almost in unison.

The men exchanged troubled glances. In truth, they had never considered anything else.

"Well—" Truman began.

"Don't you 'well' me, Truman Connely," Virginia said.

"And don't you two make those cow eyes at each other," Rachel snapped at Luther and Cal.

"That bastard has my daughter!" Alana was trembling. "Nobody and no power on this planet is going to keep me from going to get her."

After twenty minutes of debate, the men were able to convince Virginia and Rachel to stay home to watch after Samantha, but nothing they or anyone else could say was going to dissuade Alana from going. With the scheduled rendezvous with Grover only an hour away, they carried the water guns, dart gun, and balloons out to Tru's car. Then, once everything was safely in the trunk, Luther paused to look around.

On the surface, everything appeared normal. The street, which could have been a template for a Currier & Ives Christmas card, was all snow-laden roofs, houses bedecked with holly wreaths and strings of blinking lights, and fir trees, their green shoulders bowed under heavy shawls of snow. But at the curbs, lined up like the skeletal remains of a giant dinosaur, were huge mounds of snow, which just a few hours previously had been automobiles and trucks. The yards on both sides of the street were populated with shadowy snowpeople, rolled and shaped by neighborhood children unperturbed by the unnatural depth and duration of the falling snow, and the wind was a living presence, howling as it stalked the deserted streets like a hungry beast.

"What do you think?" Cal whispered.

"Why are you whispering?"

"It's kind of... creepy. Don't you think?"

"I don't know. Except for the wind, everything looks quiet." Cal tried to imitate Vincent Price's low, maniacal laugh. "Too quiet."

"Will you cut it out?" Tru muttered.

"Vincent Price," Tru said. "In *The Raven*."

"Sounded more like Gracie Allen."

"Where's Alana?" Luther asked.

"Here she comes." Cal nodded toward the porch.

"Then let's get out of here before Cal starts doing Mel Brooks."

They piled into the car, backed out of the driveway, and made their way slowly and carefully down the icy street. A few moments later, an engine started and one of the snow mounds began to move. By the time it reached the end of the block, the snow had fallen away, and the green van turned on its headlights.

Chapter Sixteen

"Oh my God!" Rachel exclaimed.

"What is it?" Virginia was at her side in an instant.

Rachel had been standing at the window, watching the men drive away, when she saw the green van pull out behind them.

"That van! I know that van. It's Anton's men!"

Virginia peered through the glass. "You sure?"

"Believe me—I'll never forget it. They're following Cal and Tru. We have to call the police. They're walking into a trap."

"We can't do that!"

Rachel and Virginia turned. Samantha was standing in the doorway.

"Didn't you hear what I said?" Rachel hissed. "Your father and the others are walking into a trap!"

"And didn't you hear Daddy? If we go to the cops, those men might kill Morna."

Rachel looked to Virginia. "What do we do?"

"I'll tell you what we're going to do," Sam said. "You and I are going to get in Daddy's car and go warn them."

"How? We don't even know where they're going."

"I do," the girl replied smugly. "I heard them talking and wrote it down."

Confused and frightened, Rachel looked to Virginia to tell her what to do.

"I don't know what to tell you," the older woman said. "But we sure as shooting have to do *something*."

"I know exactly where they're going," Sam insisted. "I have a girlfriend who lives about a block from there, and I know a shortcut—we can head them off and warn them."

"I—I don't know."

"Mother!"

"But what if we miss them? What if they—those men—What if they get us?"

"Mrs. Connely can give us an hour, and if we're not back she can call the police. If everything goes all right, we should be back long before then."

"Maybe I should come too?" Virginia suggested.

"No!" Sam said, a bit too loudly. "No. Mother could be right. If they get us, you have to be here to make the call."

Virginia glanced at Rachel. "You decide."

Rachel chewed her bottom lip. "Maybe Sam's right."

"Yes, Mom. Now come on, let's get our coats before we lose any more time."

It was like driving through Siberia. Every street and highway was packed with snow and littered with ice-

Ungrateful Dead

covered cars, many of which had spun out and crashed into something. Drifts stood higher than the mailboxes, and the weight of snow and ice had dropped tree limbs onto power lines, plunging whole sections of the city into freezing darkness. The going was slow and torturous, and the only thing that seemed to be making any progress was the digital clock on Tru's dashboard.

"It's like the frigging ice age," Luther muttered. "Can't we go any faster?"

Tru maneuvered around a glaciated Volvo whose front bumper had lost an argument with a telephone pole.

"If you want to wind up like that," Tru replied, jerking his head toward the Volvo.

"Can't we at least turn the heat up?" Cal inquired. "I'm freezing to death back here."

Tru shoved the heat switch all the way to the right and set the blower on high.

"Where is everybody?" asked Alana. "It's like we're the only people left on the face of the planet."

"Unlike us," Tru said, "they're probably smart enough to stay home in front of a nice, warm fire and drink hot chocolate."

"You didn't have to come," Cal retorted.

"What? I'm supposed to let you three go off by yourselves? You wouldn't last ten minutes."

"I'll have you know I have made an extensive study of the occult."

"Yes, I'm sure the Internet is very enlightening."

"Internet? You hear that, Luther?"

Luther was looking over his shoulder, trying to see through the fogged rear window. "I think there's a car back there."

Truman glanced in the rearview mirror. "Could be. We can't possibly be the only fools out tonight."

"I don't know. They've been back there for a while. See?"

Tru caught flash of headlight beams, but they were quickly swallowed up by the snow.

"They're way back there. It's probably a cop wondering what we're doing out on a night like this."

"Yeah." Luther felt himself relax. "That's probably who it is—a cop. I hope he doesn't stop us. We're running behind as it is."

"I hope he does," Cal opined. "Maybe we can talk him into going with us."

Tru nudged Alana with his elbow. "Oh, yeah. I can just see it now. 'Hey there Officer, I'm Dr. Weinberg. My friends and I are on our way to rescue a young girl from a pack of murderous Druids and an ancient temple that looks like a giant tree. Want to come along?'"

"I don't know why we talk to him," Cal said.

Tru looked at Alana and grinned.

Shaking her head, she just stared out the window at a world gone mad, muttering to herself, as if all this male posturing did not deserve comment. A few minutes later, they turned off Poplar and onto the Parkway, and the way became really tricky.

"What the hell happened here?" Cal exclaimed. "It looks like a demolition derby."

Gale-force gusts had felled tree limbs, which covered the road like tank traps and toppled heavy concrete light posts onto the roofs of cars, crushing them like aluminum cans. A pickup truck had skidded into a fire hydrant, and the resulting geyser had flipped it onto its side, and the water had frozen into a solid block of cascading ice. The wind, which rocked the car and whistled around the windows, was blowing so hard that the snow was falling up.

"This is fantastic," Alana whispered, as Tru wove

between tree debris and ice sculptures. "I've never seen anything like it. It must be twenty below out there."

"What the hell happened to the Greenhouse Effect?" Cal wondered aloud.

"This can't be natural," said Luther. "It's like the gates of the netherworld are beginning to open."

"Oh, that's encouraging," Tru said. "What the dickens are we doing here anyway? We're college professors." Cal cleared his throat. "Oh, right...and a shrink."

"It's my fault," Alana said in a small, miserable voice.

Luther strained to see as the snow came out of the dark like buckshot fired from a double-barreled shotgun. It reminded him of some of the bad trips he had experienced while on drugs.

"I don't like this any more than the rest of you, but what are we supposed to do? Gadarn and Alana's mother aren't about to just go away, and burying our heads in the sand won't do any good. This storm was a long time coming, and I bet if we check we'll find records of storms just like it occurring in conjunction with Morgana's transformations."

"The fifty-year storms," Truman whispered.

"That's right," Cal added. "There have always been theories floating around to explain why the earth is beset by weather cataclysms every fifty or so years. You think this could explain it?"

"What does this storm have to do with my mother?" Alana asked.

"I don't know," Luther admitted. "Maybe nothing. But what Marty said to us back at his shop started me thinking. The one thing that just about every scholar agrees upon is that the Druids were supposed to be able to control the forces of nature. Well, we got Druids, and we got nature up to our eyeballs, and I sure as heck don't believe in coincidence."

"It sounds too fantastic," Alana muttered.

"Oh no," said Truman. "Lute's right. There are many, many references in the literature; one book written in 1625 mentions two magicians who used their charms to cover an entire region with darkness for three days."

"There are a bunch of references to icy Druidic fogs and thunderstorms," Cal added.

"But why?" Alana insisted. "Why all this? What's the point?"

"Who knows how a creature like Gadarn thinks. Maybe this storm is a way of covering his tracks, or maybe it's just the byproduct of his magic."

"Byproduct?"

"Let's face it. Whatever else they may be doing, they're manipulating the very laws of nature, bending them to their will. Those are incredibly powerful forces—incredible power! When you do that, something has to give."

"Yeah," Cal muttered. "It isn't smart to mess with Mother Nature."

"Just look at atomic power," Luther continued. "When it's done properly, you get a steady, controlled release of beneficial energy. When it's done wrong... boom!"

"So that's what you meant by a byproduct?" Alana said. "What they're doing—what Mother is doing to me is—"

"Stretching the bonds that bind the universe together," Cal said.

"Or," Luther added, "they just like doing stuff like this 'cause they can."

"Anton would do that," Alana muttered darkly.

Ungrateful Dead

"He'd destroy the whole world just to show that he could."

"Well, let's pray that your mommy isn't ready for that just yet."

Tru slowed the car. "What if it's something else?"

"Like what?" asked Cal.

Truman was uncharacteristically quiet for several seconds, and looking at his friend's face, Luther got the impression that Tru had just had a thought that was so disturbing he was having trouble putting it into words. "What if they're doing this on purpose?"

"On purpose?" Cal laughed and slapped the seat. "Man, that's the craziest thing I ever heard, and in my line I've heard some doozies."

"Why would they do that?" Luther asked with a smile.

"Yeah," Alana added. "Why?"

"I'm not sure," Tru admitted. "It's just—from when you-all first told me about this, I thought it was too deliberate, too planned. If Morgana is as old as she claimed up in my bedroom, then she hasn't lived that long by being stupid or careless."

"Amen to that," Alana chimed in.

"But what would be the point?" Cal said.

"I don't know that either. I'm just telling you what I feel. That is what you do, isn't it? Listen to how people feel?"

"Yeah," Cal replied under his breath. "And most of them are nuts."

"What if all this serves some purpose? What if we were wrong, that this isn't the byproduct, this was the plan all along—a world of ice?"

Cal peered out the window. "Then they're doing a bang-up job."

"Shouldn't it be right around here somewhere?" Luther jumped in.

They were gliding past rambling two-and three-story mansions, whose faded facades had once represented the grandeur of pre–World War II Memphis. But now, like aging dowagers who had had one too many facelifts, their balconies drooped and their plaster columns and ornate scrollwork were chipped and pitted by time, termites, and neglect. Their rolling lawns resembled long-forgotten European battlefields, where flash-frozen shrubbery took the place of bombed-out chateaus—leafless and dead long before the first killing frost. And yet most of them at least tried to put on a show of respect, to cover up their liver spots and age wrinkles with paint, to trim the bushes. Most . . . save one.

"Hey! Take a look at that driveway," Cal said, pointing to a pair of concrete strips, which started between two antique brick pillars, and vanished behind a stand of tall shrubs. The snow covering the entrance to the driveway was marred by the passage of numerous sets of radial tires. "I bet that's it."

"I don't see a number," Luther said. "Anybody see one?"

Tru shook his head. "No. I'll keep going to the next house and see if it's marked."

But as the car started past the end of the driveway, Luther's thigh suddenly felt as if someone had slipped a red-hot ember into his pocket.

"Whoa! Ow! Damn!"

He bounced up and down on the seat, trying to get his hand into his pocket. When he did, he came out with his key chain—the crystal fob on the end was glowing.

In all the commotion, Tru inadvertently hit the brakes a little too hard and the car fishtailed across the road,

Ungrateful Dead

jumped the curb, and buried its back end up to the rear axle in a snowdrift.

"Damn, man, what's wrong with you?"

"Look!" Alana cried.

Luther held up the chain and fob, but the light had faded. "It was burning the crap out of my leg a minute ago."

"It's that . . . that, whatchamacallit," Alana said in awe.

"Serpent's Egg," Luther supplied.

Luther held the chain by the window nearest the driveway, and the crystal glowed. When he pulled it away, it dimmed.

"My gosh," Cal whispered. "Would you look at that."

"What is that thing?" Tru asked.

"It's just a souvenir, a tourist gimmick. There's a clover inside and it's supposed to bring good luck."

"Where did you get it?"

"Genny gave it to me." He touched the glowing globe gingerly. "Go figure, it's cool now."

"Genny? That's the girl that—"

"Yeah."

"Has it ever done that before?" Tru asked.

"Well . . . yeah, now that you mention it. A couple of times. But never anything like that."

"And you didn't think anything about it?"

He held the fob up and looked at it from different angles. "Not really. I thought it must have a battery or something that went haywire from time to time."

"What does it mean?" Alana asked.

"Uh . . ." He returned the chain and keys to his pocket. "Faulty wiring?"

"Oh, boy."

Tru threw the car into reverse and gunned the engine.

367

The tires spun like crazy, but the car didn't move an inch. He tried putting it in drive with the same result. "Well, whether we're at the right place or not, we're stuck."

"What now?" Alana asked.

"We walk."

They piled out of the car into the driving snowstorm, made their way carefully around to the trunk, and began unloading their water weapons. They were wearing heavy gloves and parkas with fur-lined hoods, which made handling the slippery plastic a chore, but they managed to get everything, including the water balloons, which had frozen, making them easier to transport. In the street, they gathered in a circle and put their heads together.

"Which way?" Tru shouted to be heard over the howl of the wind.

Luther pointed straight up the driveway.

"Shouldn't we go through the bushes?" Cal yelled.

"We might get lost. Besides, in this mess there's no way they're going to see us coming. Just keep your ears peeled for cars. If you hear one, tap the person in front of you, and step off into the bushes til it passes."

Everyone nodded their heads.

They crossed the street and started up the slippery slope in single file, following the path of rapidly filling ruts. Cal, by virtue of being the biggest and the only medical doctor in the group, took the lead. Tru came next, followed by Alana, and then Luther. Alana had on a pair of tan corduroy slacks and a white parka, and Luther had to stay within about five inches of her or risk losing her in the storm. Initially, thanks to the tall hedges lining the driveway, most of the wind passed over their heads, and they made it to the first bend with little problem. Visibility could only be measured in inches, but by trusting their feet more than their eyes, they were able to follow the latticework of tire tracks relatively easily. Once they rounded the bend, however, they were at the mercy of the wind, which pelted their faces with stinging flakes and cut right through their parkas. It was right after the curve, while they were trudging along with their heads down, that Luther heard the man yell.

"All right, Dr. Weinberg, that's far enough!"

Luther looked up. He couldn't see more than three inches past Alana's shoulder, so he figured the man hadn't seen her yet, and without a word, he picked Alana up and tossed her into the deep snowbank at the base of the hedges. She landed without a sound and vanished like a rock dropped into a lake, and Luther prayed she had the good sense to keep quiet.

He felt something hard dig into his kidneys and heard a voice shouting in his ear.

"Just keep right on the way you was going, boyo. You'll be at the house in a minute."

Luther raised his hands and started walking.

"I can't see a damned thing," Rachel said. "You sure we're going the right way?"

"You're doing fine, Mom," Sam replied. "One more block, and we turn right."

They skidded around the corner, but Rachel fought the wheel and righted the car before they hit anything. Halfway down the street, she took her foot off the accelerator and let the car coast to a stop.

"Oh, no."

Truman's car was sitting half-buried in a snow drift, and less than ten yards away was the green van—abandoned.

"We have to go to the police now," Rachel cried.

"No, Mother, we don't."

Rachel turned her head and looked down the barrel of Cal's gun.

"Turn up that driveway," Sam said.

"Samantha! Have you lost your mind?"

"Maybe. Just do as I tell you and drive!"

The girl's eyes were as hard as flint, and the hand holding the gun was as steady as a rock. Her thumb came up and pulled back the hammer. "Do it!"

Rachel looked around wildly, but the world was a white blur, and the only reality was her daughter sitting on the seat beside her with a gun pointed at her head.

"Why?"

Sam laughed. "Really, Mother, don't you know?"

Sam put a finger to her right nostril—it came away smeared with blood.

"Oh Sam, no! Listen to me. You can fight it! I know how it makes you feel, but you can beat it."

"Like you did?" The girl laughed again. It was a harsh and somewhat hysterical sound. "Now move!"

Almost blinded by tears, Rachel eased up the driveway, following the tire tracks and footprints that were rapidly disappearing under a fresh blanket of snow. All at once, a figure came running out of the storm waving its arms like a conductor trying to flag down a train. Rachel screamed and hit the brakes.

The figure ran up to Sam's window and rapped on the glass—it was Alana. Sam lowered the window.

"Thank God I recognized your car. Luther and the others were captured by Anton's men. We have to go for help."

Sam smiled. "Get in."

The men, two Irish thugs from the look and sound of them, ordered Luther and his friends into the foyer. The men had guns—big guns, which they seemed very comfortable with, so there was little argument. Once inside out of the wind, the fat one skinned out of his fatigue jacket, then held his gun on them while his companion took off his coat.

"Drop all that shit here and take off them coats," one thug said. "You ain't gonna need them."

The alcove was piled high with expensive coats—mostly furs and cashmere topcoats, so Luther and the others dropped the water guns, peeled off their parkas, and added them to the heap. As soon as the second man pulled off his ski mask, Luther recognized him as the guy from the parking lot at the University the night he'd met Alana. That seemed a very long time ago. The guy picked up one of the water guns and held it up.

"Hey, Ward, get a load a this." He turned to Luther and grinned. "What was you plannin' on doing with this, mate? It ain't full a piss, is it?"

Luther thought of several snappy comebacks; all of which would have probably earned him a rap in the mouth, so he held his tongue.

The fat guy, the one his pal called Ward, patted them down for other weapons and fished a frozen balloon out of Cal's parka. "Yo, Col, lookie here! They brought decorations for the party, ain't that nice?"

"I'm touched," Colin O'Dwyer replied with a chuckle.

Ward tossed Cal's lighter and penknife onto the pile, but returned his wallet and car keys. When he got to Luther, he pulled the key chain out of Luther's pant's pocket and held it out away from him.

"Yo! What's this thing?"

The crystal fob was flashing like the strobe light on a police car.

"Uh, it's a light so I can see to open the car door in the dark."

Shaking his hand, the fat man tossed the chain back to Luther. "Thing gets kinda hot don't it?"

"It helps when the lock's frozen."

"What won't they think of next?"

"Okay, boys," Colin said. "Right this way."

Colin led them past the main staircase, down a long hallway, and through a banquet-sized dinning room to the kitchen. Like most of the city, the power was out, but there were lighted candles on almost every flat surface, including the floor and windowsills, and big banners hung in the rooms, all printed with some variation of "Welcome Back!" The table in the dining room, and the counters in the kitchen were full of food, and bottles of wine and coolers brimming with ice and cold beer had been placed in the corners.

"Big doings, huh, guys?" Truman asked.

"Aye, you're right about that, boyo," Wardley replied.

"So where is everybody? Or is all this just on our account?"

"You'll be seein' shortly."

The fat man opened the door to the cellar and motioned Luther in with the gun. Luther approached the opening cautiously, pausing just outside.

"You got a flashlight?" he asked the man.

"Sorry."

"But I can't see a thing."

"Leap o' faith time, my friend. The stairs are right there."

Since he had no choice, Luther stepped out blindly with his right foot. At the instant his shoe came down on the landing, the heat and incredible stench hit him like a blast of August wind off the East River, and he put on the brakes so fast that Cal bumped into him from behind.

Ungrateful Dead

"Keep it moving!"

"My God, what's that smell?"

"Go on with you. You'll get used to it."

Luther reached out, found the handrail, and started down the steps. He took as much time as he could without angering his captors, figuring that if Gadarn had wanted them dead they'd be lying out in the snow already. Course, it never hurt to be careful. Halfway down he noticed a faint greenish glow.

"You see that?" he whispered to Cal.

"The glow? Yeah. Where is it coming from?"

"What are you two whispering about?" Tru asked.

"The glow," Cal replied.

"Yeah, I see it."

The stairs seemed endless. The deeper into the dark they descended, the more Luther thought about the history of the place, and he began to wonder if he'd misjudged Gadarn's intentions.

All at once the torches set around the dungeonlike cellar ignited, and the crowd of people in white robes began shouting, "Surprise!" and whirling about like intoxicated dervishes.

Luther blinked at the sudden explosion of light, then opened his eyes and took in the whole macabre scene in an instant. At the bottom of the steps, wearing a Cheshire-cat smile, was a troll with a shock of wild, carrot-colored hair—Luther figured that had to be Gadarn. Across the room—even though he had been expecting it, he was still unprepared when he finally saw it—was the tree. It was huge. It dominated the room like some giant, hulking spider, with limbs, that hung down like jointed legs, hundreds of heavy, softball-size acorns, and waxy, dark, saucer-shaped leaves that resembled nothing less than flat plastic bags full of congealed blood. He saw a man, all shriveled and white, nailed to

373

the tree's trunk in some horrible parody of the Crucifixion and, lastly, he stared at the horde of white robes with their flat, dead eyes and grinning faces. Finally he saw the table at the base of the tree and Morna lying on top of it like a frail, fairy-tale princess waiting in vain for her first wake-up kiss.

"Welcome!" Anton's surprisingly melodic voice boomed out over the sounds of celebration. "I cannot tell you how happ—" He must have noticed there were only male faces among his new guests, for the smile died, and he stared daggers at Wardley. "Where is she?"

The fat man shrugged. "She wasn't with them."

In the meantime, the revelers were still cheering and laughing and dancing around the floor like Rotarians at a Mardi Gras parade. Anton spun around and screamed, "Shut the fuck up!" and the crowd gradually wound down and began milling about, muttering like a herd of sheep that had been attacked by their watchdog.

Anton turned back and glared at Luther. "Where is she?"

"Who?"

After tapping his foot for a few seconds, Anton stalked over to a lever on the wall and yanked it down. The cellar filled with a heavy grinding noise as the steel, watertight doors slowly ground down to seal off the tunnels.

"I don't have time for this shit." He waddled over to the table at the base of the tree and stood over Morna, glowering up at Luther with the fires of insanity blazing in his eyes. "Boyo, if you care one whit about this little bitch, I suggest you quit screwing around. I don't have to have her mother to complete the ritual, but I promised me guests they could watch, and I'm a man o' me word."

Ungrateful Dead

Luther kept tuning in and out of Anton's threats. He was having trouble tearing his eyes away from the tree ... the Dair ... the Temple of Set; those and a hundred other names history had given to something so vile, so horrible that, standing clear on the other side of the cellar, he could feel the malevolence radiating from it like some gigantic dynamo of evil. It was incredible. He'd read about it, seen drawings of it, had imagined what it would look like many, many times. And yet this ... the reality—it was so much more and so much worse than he could ever have imagined. It was intelligent—it was aware! Not intelligence the way the human mind understood it, but something darker, more elemental, and much older than man. Something that for centuries had lurked in the moist, lightless places of the earth, watching with growing envy and loathing as mankind rejected its dark, cold, primordial ocean womb for the warm, sunlit expanses of the land. Was such a being really a god? All Luther knew in that instant of visceral insight was that he recognized it for what it was, and worse—it recognized him.

"Are you daft, man?" Anton screamed.

Snapping out of his reverie, Luther locked his eyes on Alana's daughter. Anton was holding a handful of squirming, black leeches over the girl's face.

"You want to see what me little friends here can do when they set their minds to it? Look at the big ape behind me."

Luther raised his eyes to the man hanging like a side of beef on the tree. It was Grover! His eyes were shut, but his face, though bloodless, was riddled with oozing sores, and as Luther watched in horror, a leech wriggled out of one of the holes in his cheek. The creature didn't care for the world outside, or maybe it was the company; either way, it turned right around and bored through

Grover's lip and disappeared into his mouth.

"Look, Gadarn . . . take it easy," Luther said. He held his hands out away from his sides, stepped down onto the muddy floor and made his way slowly toward the tree. Anton's followers parted without a word and let him pass.

"I don't know where Alana is this very minute. But I know how to find her. Take it easy on the girl, and we'll work something out."

Anton chuckled and raised his hand level with his face. "Amazing the effect me friends here have on people." A leech inched along his finger until it reached the fingernail and then raised its blunt head and peered around. When nothing promising appeared, the creature curled itself around and slithered up under Anton's fingernail. If the dwarf felt anything, he didn't show it.

"I tell you what, laddie. You come over here and whisper in me ear where she is, and I'll send me boy Danny to fetch her for the festivities."

Luther kept walking. "She could be one of three places. She's very paranoid about what's been going on, so she won't be easy to find."

"Aye, like they say, even paranoids have enemies." He chuckled again, and Luther thought the little creep was in a very good mood.

The way Luther saw it, the problem with being a nonviolent person was that when the time for violence came, one rarely knew how to go about it. Should he just walk up to Anton, pop him in the mouth, grab Morna, and hope Cal and Truman weren't so shocked by his actions that they forgot to back him up? He figured Cal could handle an even dozen of the robed weirdos and Tru, if worse came to worse, could talk eight or ten more into a coma. But Anton's thugs . . . He needed something—an equalizer. A baseball bat would be nice. A machine

Ungrateful Dead

gun would be better. Anton was busy gloating and not paying much attention, and Luther noticed what appeared to be a toolbox sticking partway out from under the black sheet covering the table. A hammer? he wondered. But the idea of bludgeoning a man—even Anton—with a hammer, made Luther queasy. He hadn't always been so squeamish. When he'd been on drugs, he'd been a holy terror. Wasn't he the same man he'd been then?

The painful truth was, he wasn't the same man he used to be, and he had no real desire ever to be again. But in about two seconds, he was going to have to try to bean a man half his size with... something, to try and save a girl's life—not to mention his own and those of his friends.

Luther was trying to peek into the toolbox without calling attention to what he was doing. In addition to a screwdriver covered with something that looked like rust, he saw a hacksaw and one of those fold-out rulers that carpenters use. If the nuns had been there, he knew what they'd vote for. As he got closer, he saw what he was looking for—the wooden handle of a hammer jutting out of the upper tray. One chance was all he was going to get. Grab the handle, pop Anton on top of his pointy little head, and boogie. He could do that.

As Luther reached the table, Anton grinned and nonchalantly shoved the toolbox farther under the table with his foot. "Temptation is a fickle lady."

"Shit."

The dwarf laughed nastily.

The door at the top of the stairs opened, and Danny Keats appeared on the landing. He had a .45 caliber automatic in his hand and a wide grin on his handsome face. "Hey Anton! We got more visitors."

He made a motion with the gun, and first Rachel, then

Alana, and finally Sam joined him on the platform.

"Ah!" Anton beamed. "So lovely to see you again, my dears."

Danny marched the trio down to the cellar. Rachel immediately ran to Cal and buried her face in his chest, but Alana walked defiantly up to the table, took Luther's hand, and then glared at Anton. Sam strolled up to the redheaded dwarf and handed Cal's gun to him.

"I brought them, just like she wanted me to."

Alana tilted her head and whispered in Luther's ear. "She's got one of those things in her."

The crowd closed in around them, grinning like spectators at a Tijuana cock fight. Anton placed the gun in the toolbox, then straightened up and stroked Sam's cheek. "Well, now, ain't you a pretty little thing."

"Keep your hands off her, you animal," Rachel snarled.

Sam began rubbing her chest against him like a cat.

"As you can see, darlin', like you, the colleen just can't keep her hands off o' me."

Rachel made a lunge for him, but Cal wrapped his arms around her waist and held on tight.

"Haven't you had enough of your sick little games?" Alana sneered. "Or could it be that Mother wasn't enough for you? Seems I recall you told her she was the only one, the only woman in the world."

Anton sobered so fast it was almost comical. He shot a sneaky glance at the tree and lowered his voice. "And just how would you be knowing what was said between Morgana and me?"

"You forget—Mother and I have been sharing a lot lately. My body . . . her memories. In fact, it wouldn't surprise me if she could see what I'm seeing right this minute."

The white robes let out a collective gasp, and Anton

Ungrateful Dead

shoved Sam away from him as if she had the plague. The girl stumbled and would have fallen if Luther hadn't caught her arm. When they came in contact, the key chain in his pocket sent a spark of white-hot fire shooting down his leg, and Sam yelped, jerked free of his grasp, and stared at him with a confused expression until the mob moved in and spirited her away.

"Enough of this blather," Anton snapped. "Prepare the girl."

Danny went around Luther, unfastened the restraining straps, and scooped Morna up in his arms. Wardley and Colin came out of the crowd with shovels and began digging around the roots of the tree.

"What do you think you're doing?" said Alana. "This is between Mother and me. Let the others go."

"Sorry, darlin', no can do. Your friends here"—he nodded his head toward Luther and the others—"well, the Temple has to eat just like the rest of us. And, before any of you get any funny ideas," he added quickly, "me friends over there are a keepin' a wee close eye on the colleen."

Luther cut his eyes to Cal and Rachel. Cal looked like he wanted to scream, but he only dropped his eyes.

They were boxed in; damned if they tried to fight, damned for sure if they didn't. Even if he could reach Cal's gun under the table—and he didn't shoot himself in the foot—there was no way he could grab Morna and get to Sam before the crazies did something to her. He needed a miracle.

"But why Morna?" Alana insisted. "What if something happens to me? What happens to Mother then?"

"Aye, that would be a pickle. But lucky for us, you're here all safe and sound. And the girl? Buryin' her breaks the bloodline, which is the final step in the ritual that opens the gate. You move out, so to speak, Morgana moves in. Ain't life grand?"

Alana moved around the table until she was opposite Anton. "Those things in the tree . . ." She stared at the hole the men were digging. "Are they this god of yours? Are they Set?"

Anton's eyes followed hers into the hole. "The worms? No. They're what you might call his emissaries. He speaks through them and they report ba—"

The instant Anton was distracted, Alana squatted and reached blindly under the table, fumbling through the awls and wrenches for Cal's gun. Unlike Luther, she had no qualms whatsoever about blowing Anton or anyone wearing a white robe into the next time zone, if it meant saving Morna.

"Hey!" Anton yelled. "What do ya think you're doin'?"

She couldn't find the gun, so she grabbed the first thing she laid her hand on—it was the hacksaw.

Anton lunged across the top of the table, but with his stubby little arms had as much chance of reaching the saw as Luther had of winning the Pulitzer Prize in literature.

Alana backed out of reach and held the rusty blade up to her throat.

"Tell me again what happens to Mother if Morna and I are both dead."

Anton went so pale that his freckles stood out like ketchup stains on a white satin tablecloth. "Now take it easy . . . let's not do anything we might be sorry for."

Alana ran a finger over the saw's jagged teeth. "Feels pretty sharp to me. What do you think? One quick slash across the old jugular? I bet I won't feel a thing."

The dwarf's mouth was opening and closing, but nothing was coming out. Finally he turned and glared at

Ungrateful Dead

Danny Keats, standing beside the hole with the girl poised in his arms.

"Do something!"

Danny frowned. "Just what would you be expectin' me to do?"

"I'll tell you what we're going to do," Alana hissed. "Pretty boy there is going to put my daughter down . . . now!" Danny did as instructed. "Now she and Luther, all of them—including Samantha, are going to leave. Once they are safely out of here, Mother and I can settle our differences."

"I don't suppose you'd be wantin' me to call a taxi for you, too?"

Alana shook her head. "No. I'm not stupid. I know there's no way out for me. Anywhere I go, she can find me. Just let them go. I never should have involved them in this in the first place."

"No way," Luther said. "Cal and the others should go, but I don't leave until you do."

"Ain't this touchin'?" Anton turned and held his hand out to his followers. "We got our very own love story goin' right before our eyes."

While Anton was busy performing for the crowd, Luther had a brainstorm. Assuming everything he'd read about Druid rituals and high priests was accurate, then it was a better than average bet that Anton had been exceedingly stingy with his knowledge of mystical powers. If that were the case, then Anton was the only thing holding them all together, and all Luther had to do was take him out and the rest would probably run.

Yeah, he thought, good plan. All he had to do was take him out. How?

Luther caught Cal's eye and inclined his head toward Sam. Cal glanced in his daughter's direction, then nodded that he understood, and whispered something in Rachel's ear.

Alana smiled sadly at Luther. "Don't be an idiot. Get out of here while you can."

He casually slipped his hand into his pocket and strolled around the table.

"Women!" he said with an exaggerated sigh. He closed his right fist around the keys, holding them like he had in Kevin Carter's apartment—wedged between his fingers with the sharp ends pointed out. Brass knuckles would have been a hell of a lot better, but it was the best he could do.

"Talk to her," Anton implored Luther. "Make her see how hopeless this is."

"Well, that's a problem," Luther replied. "What am I supposed to say? Alana, put down the saw so they can bury your daughter alive and murder all your friends and then let your dead mother take over your body—You've got a lot to learn about motivating people."

Alana was watching Luther closely. He was up to something, but she had no idea what. She looked for Cal and saw that he and Rachel were "allowing" the crowd to squeeze them back toward the opposite side of the cellar, where Sam was being guarded by two men in robes.

"What's it going to be?" Alana snarled.

The little man looked like he was going to have a nervous breakdown. He couldn't afford to let Luther and his friends leave, and he couldn't even imagine what his mistress would do if anything happened to Alana and Morna. He gazed around the sea of vacant faces, all of them staring at him, waiting for him to work his magic against these heretical upstarts. They didn't understand—the magic wasn't his! It had never been his. Morgana was the source. She had showed him a few simple

Ungrateful Dead

tricks—the thing with the dogs for one, but the *real* magic, the *real* power she had hoarded like a miser with his gold.

Do something, you little twerp!

Great! Anton thought. Now he had Morgana's voice screaming at him inside his head. Well, fuck her! Fuck all of them! They didn't know what he was going through. None of them understood. He glanced up at Grover, hanging lifeless and drained like an empty suit on a wire hanger. Grover had understood. But look at him now. The leeches had turned him into a skin sack full of bones and rotting tendons. He reached up and touched the dead man's foot.

"Grover?" he whispered. "Grover, what should I do?"

All at once Anton screamed and backed away from the tree, holding a bloody hand. He couldn't believe his eyes. The leeches had attacked him . . . *Him*! They had come out of the sole of Grover's foot and were burrowing into his hand, and he had never felt such pain in his life.

Now! Luther thought.

He pulled his hand from his pocket, and it was as if the shamrock lodged in the crystal's heart had been miraculously transmuted into a tiny dwarf star, which had suddenly and without warning gone supernova.

Beams of blinding white light shone out of the gaps between his fingers.

Luther let out a yelp of alarm, opened his fist and almost—almost—dropped the key chain. The keys themselves remained jammed between his fingers, but the fob dropped down like a lantern on a chain. Unimpeded by his closed fist, the light flowed out in every direction, illuminating even the darkest nooks and crevices, obliterating all but the most minute shadows.

Bellowing in pain, Anton and his followers threw their hands over their eyes as they stumbled about blindly in the mud. Their discordant cries, though loud and pitiful, were nothing compared to the thunderous, high-pitched keening emanating from the tree. The sound made Luther's teeth ache and his hair stand on end. It was Death given voice, disease given a song, despair in auditory form. It was the screams of a thousand mothers as they watched their children being put to the sword, and it made Luther want to lie down and die.

Fortunately, by that time he discovered his hand hadn't burned to a crisp, and he noticed something even more bizarre—he could see. The light that was blinding everyone else merely made his surroundings appear insubstantial and surreal; he could see quite clearly. He held the fob up and tried to locate Alana, Cal, and the others and finally spotted them stumbling about in the midst of the white robes.

Something else was odd—several of the people—including Samantha, were bent over at the waist as if they were vomiting. Only instead of their dinners, huge, disgusting, chunks of leeches, bile, and blood was spewing from their mouths and noses. He turned to see where that horrible noise was coming from and saw the Temple of Set shaking and swaying like a highrise in a hurricane, its waxy leaves crinkling up and, one after another, its massive roots ripping loose from the mud. Around the roots, the black worms were evacuating the soggy ground like night crawlers during the spring floods.

It was insane—absolutely insane! He was a full professor of Paranormal Psychology; he'd read and studied about things like this all his life. But magic—the occult—they didn't really happen! He peered at the glowing crystal, willing his eyes to penetrate its depths, but

Ungrateful Dead

that was like trying to see into the heart of a volcano. In that instant, he realized for the first time in his life how he had lied to himself—he'd never really believed. The supernatural—the unnatural ghosts and witches and zombies, voodoo and fairies and ghouls—he had reduced them all to stolid homework assignments and hypothetical propositions for dissertations. After what happened to his sister and then Genny, what better way to exorcise his personal demons than to ridicule and analyze them to death under the guise of "scientific" scrutiny. His terror, frustration, and failures were confined in manila folders and defined by neat, multisyllabic words, and meaningless clichés. And now, with the proof of his folly staring him in the face, the best he could come up with was—this is nuts? Things like this just do not happen? Get a grip!

Almost too late, it occurred to him that in addition to being an intellectual coward, he was guilty of playing orthodontist to a gift horse. This was his chance—round up his friends and get the hell out of Dodge.

With the fob dangling from one hand, Luther used his free hand to grab Alana's arm. "It's me."

"What's happening?" she cried. "I can't see a thing."

"I'll tell you later—here." He led her to Morna and placed her hand on her daughter's shoulder. "Help her, we have to get out of here."

He waited while she got control of the girl. She was groggy, but docile.

"Luther?"

"I'm right here. I'm going to lead you two over to the stairs and then go get the others."

"What . . . what about Mother?"

He glanced at the tree. "Fuck her."

Still holding the fob as high as he could, Luther

guided Alana and Morna slowly through the crowd. The people in the robes gave ground, moaning and bumping into each other as if, in addition to the blinding light, the fob emitted some kind of silent, ultrasonic ray that caused them severe pain. A few feet away, Anton was clutching his mangled hand and stumbling around in a circle like his followers.

When they reached the bottom of the stairs, Luther said, "Wait here. I'm going for Cal and the others."

"Where am I?" Alana replied.

"By the stairs, but don't try to climb them by yourselves."

He made two more trips, one to fetch Cal and Rachel, and one to bring Truman over.

"Where's Samantha?" Rachel called.

"Going to get her now."

He found Sam leaning against one of the watertight doors. She was crying and shaking and snorting bubbles of blood and mucous from her nose.

"Sam?"

"Uncle Luther! Uncle Luther, where am I? Where's all that light coming from?"

His arm was getting tired and the strain of constantly looking over his shoulder was beginning to get to him. "Later. We have to go." He took her hand and turned to leave and there, right in front of him, surrounded by an cocoon of shadow, was Genny.

"Hello, Luther."

"Genny?" His mouth was suddenly as dry as sand.

"Uncle Luther, who are you talking to?"

Genny smiled that wonderful smile and held her arms out away from her sides. Her hands were small and soft and delicate, and he ached as he remembered the magic those slim fingers could work. She was dressed in a dark, floor-length gown that clung to her curves and looked

Ungrateful Dead

like stars scattered across a night sky. She moved toward him as if floating on a cloud and in her wake left a trail of glistening slime.

"Genny, what are you doing here?"

"Here? This is my home. I live here. I've lived here since you left me all those years ago."

"I never left you. You . . . you disappeared."

"No, you went away and forgot about me and finally I ceased to exist. Now this Temple is my home and here you are trying to kill me all over again. Why? Please stop. Put the egg down."

"The egg?"

"The Serpent's Egg. It's killing us."

Luther blinked and stared at the crystal fob. It didn't look like an egg. Inside, in the center, he could make out the faint, tri-lobed outline of the shamrock, the outer edges of its leaves glowing like molten gold. He peered past the shamrock, framing Genny in the multifaceted circle.

It wasn't Genny anymore. It was an auburn-haired little girl dressed in a peasant frock of the kind he'd only seen in ancient picture books. She had a pale face, a small, round nose, freckles, and eyes that burned bright with madness. In the crystal she appeared to be standing on a mud bank beside a stream of clear, running water, and in the background was a village of thatched huts surrounded by tall trees whose leafy tops were shrouded in mist.

"Morgana," he whispered.

So this was what she really looked like. Stripped of all the lives stolen over the countless centuries, she was still a little girl, frozen forever in an instant of time by the evil magic of the Druids. Words popped into his head he didn't quite understand. Something he'd read;

something he'd heard; a dream he had sensed in the crystal.

As the shell is about the egg, so is the firmament around the earth. The firmament is a mighty sheet of crystal.

More words appeared in his head and spilled out of his mouth:

"Chosen leaf
 Of Bard and Chief,
Old Erin's native shamrock!
 Says Valor, 'See
 They spring for me,
Those leafy gems of morning!'
 Says Love, 'No, no,
 For me they grow,
My fragrant path adorning!'
 But wit perceives
 The triple leaves,
And cries—'O do not sever
 A type that blends
 Three godlike friends
Love, Valor, Wit, for ever!
O! The Shamrock, the green immortal Shamrock!' "

The firmament is eternal night, the shell of the egg the light. To defeat the darkness one must shatter the egg.

Morgana was almost upon him. Holding on to Sam's hand, Luther began backing as quickly as possible toward the stairs.

Ungrateful Dead

"Where are you going?" Morgana cried. "Don't leave me again!"

"You're not Genny," Luther hissed. "Genny was good. You're the opposite of good. You are like those vile leeches, a parasite, first sucking the life out of your prey and then infesting their bodies. You use corpses like draft animals until they're ready to drop and then abandon them and move on to another. Well, you're not getting Alana, and you're not getting Morna, and you sure as hell aren't getting me!"

Morgana stretched out her hand and a single shadowy tendril coiled out from the tips of her fingers. Dark and diaphanous, it undulated slowly through the air like smoke, weaving and twisting as it made it way toward him. Luther tried to move Sam along, tried to hurry the others up the stairs, but had only managed to reach the bottom step as the wisp of darkness reached him.

Ignoring Luther, it coiled around and around the fob like a snake. He tried juggling the chain to free the crystal, but the darkness clung to it like a stain and when the light abruptly dimmed, Anton came out of his daze, whirled around, and screamed, "Get him!"

Danny and Colin sprinted for the stairs, their bare feet slipping and sliding as they tried to get traction on the muddy floor.

"Let's go!" Luther shouted, and Truman turned Alana and Morna around and pushed them ahead of the others up the stairs.

Luther ran up the first three steps, then whipped around, and kicked Danny square in his perfect, white teeth.

"Oh, Jesus," Luther mumbled. "That had to hurt."

Danny tumbled back into Colin, and both men wound up in a heap in the mud.

"Stop him!" Anton yelled.

Several men in robes raced across the floor, and Luther, in desperation, shook the key chain so hard he almost dropped it, but the darkness refused to budge.

The firmament is eternal night, the shell of the egg the light. To defeat the darkness one must shatter the egg.

"Well, hell," he muttered. "Here goes nothing," and he reared back and hurled the key chain at the tree as hard as he could.

The crystal struck the trunk just above groundlevel and shattered, giving off a tiny blip of light, which quickly dissipated, and scattering glass shards and bits of shredded shamrock among the roots.

In a blink of an eye, the light was gone and darkness and gloom reclaimed the cellar. The tree fell silent, Morgana silently slipped back into whatever dark, shadowworld she had come from, and for almost a full minute everyone else stood frozen in place, staring at each other in the sudden deafening silence.

Then Anton started to laugh.

"Poof! Did you see that my friends? Poof!"

He laughed so hard he had to rest his hands on his thighs to keep from falling over.

Luther glanced up at Alana and then Cal and shrugged. "Sorry, guys."

Anton's glee became contagious, spreading like the flu among his followers slowly at first, but gaining momentum and volume as relief at what they had just survived sank in. As the laughter continued, Luther waved Alana and the others on and began edging up the stairs himself, thinking that if they made it as far as the hall they might be able to lock the door and then make a run for the cars. He kept checking to see if Anton had noticed what they were up to, and that's when he saw the mist.

At first he thought his eyes were playing tricks on him—the torchlight in the cellar wasn't that great to start with, but when he realized the greenish vapor was not only real, but getting thicker, he grabbed Cal by the arm.

"Look!"

"Where is it coming from?"

"Around the tree roots."

"Right where the pieces of your key chain fell."

"Exactly."

The mist was rapidly becoming a fog and beginning to creep along the ground between the feet of Anton's groupies. The first woman it touched grabbed her throat and screamed. At about the same time, the tree, which had been silent for almost five minutes, renewed its high-pitched screeching.

Anton slapped his hands over his ears. "What the hell is going on?"

The mist coiled up around their knees, swirling like heavy surf driven by strong winds. Luther urged his friends on, taking the steps two at a time until they reached the relative safety of the landing. Cal and Tru hustled Alana, Rachel, and the girls through the door, but Cal returned a few moments later with his arms full of water balloons, lining them up along the top of the railing. "I figured we were too far away for the guns."

Luther nodded and they began heaving the water bombs at the tree.

The balloons burst on impact with the side of the trunk, raining the deadly poison down on the roots. In seconds, the leaves began to roll up like dead spiders and fall off. Then, one by one, the acorns dropped to the ground, cracked open, and spilled their squirming seed, along with clouds of acrid black smoke, which mixed with the green fog and added to the Druids' torment and confusion. The leeches paused long enough to feed on their dying brethren in the acorns and then scattered in every direction like cattle stampeding from a forest fire. In their greed to escape the toxic smog, they swarmed up the Druids' naked legs, latched on with their sucking mouths to anything warm and pliant, and then pierced and repierced the soft flesh with their razor-sharp tooth plates—the screams of the dying were horrendous.

A few of the more hardy souls, including Anton and his pal Danny Keats, made it as far as the steps and started up, but their faces, already black from the smoke, were covered with blood and leeches, many of which were already feasting on their victims' eyes. Anton had barely started to climb when the man behind him, in his haste to escape, dragged him down and tried to climb over him—the dwarf was crushed and broken under the weight of his followers' bare feet.

No one made it past the first ten steps.

Below, the Temple of Set began to smolder and then burn. The flames added more lethal smoke to the toxic atmosphere, but by that time everything below the landing was still.

Luther tapped his friend on the arm. "Let's go."

Cal watched until the flames spread to the staircase, and nodded. "God help us."

"Amen to that."

Epilogue

"I wish you didn't have to go," Sam said.

In the three weeks since their escape from the cellar, Sam and Morna had become practically inseparable. They had spent Christmas with the Connelys and New Year's with Luther and Alana in New Orleans. As girls their age often did, they swapped books and cosmetics and clothing... especially clothing. They were in Morna's refurbished bedroom, where she was just putting the last few pieces of clothing into her suitcase. In an hour she and Alana would be boarding a plane to London.

"Me, too," Morna replied. "But we have to."

"I know... the cops."

The local police had been asking questions about a black Z and a badly scarred woman with red hair who had been seen leaving a local bar with a man who later turned up in pieces. Since telling the truth was obviously out, Alana and Luther decided it would be prudent for her to leave the country for a few months, just long enough for Kevin Carter to be pushed out of the headlines by the next grisly murder.

"So why isn't Uncle Luther going with you?" Sam asked.

"You know him. He and Doctor Connely are working on this big paper.

It's all very hush-hush, but Mom told me it was about what happened to us."

"Really? Cool. Will I be in it?"

"I don't think any of us will be in it, by name anyway."

"And he's coming over later?"

"Yes. At least in time for summer vacation."

"I think it's so neat that your mom is giving up her job to come with you."

"Well, finding out Grandma left her all that money didn't hurt." Then Morna added sadly, "I guess, in a way, she was planning on leaving it to herself."

"I know. But I think it's neat. I have a rich friend."

Morna went to the dresser in her panties and bra and held her latest acquisition, a brightly striped silk blouse, up in front of her. "What do you think?"

"Better than that school uniform."

"Oh, you!"

"Do you think it will be warm enough?"

"Well, the weather here's back to normal . . . I think so. I still have my coat."

"What about undies? Lingerie is of the utmost importance! Even more important than your handbag."

Morna lowered the blouse and did a slow pirouette. "What do you think?"

Sam went over to her friend and gave her a long,

Ungrateful Dead

slow, up-and-down. "Not Victoria's Secret, but not Kmart either." She noticed the black mark on Morna's right breast. "What's that?"

Morna followed Sam's gaze. "Oh. A mole."

Sam took a closer look. "I don't remember seeing that before."

"Yeah, I know. I just noticed it myself this morning."

"It got that big overnight? Maybe you should see a doctor."

Morna shrugged and slipped the blouse over her head. "Maybe when we get to London. It's no big deal."

HOWL-O-WEEN
Gary L. Holleman

Evil lurks on Halloween night....

H ear the demons wail in the night,
O ut of terror and out of fright,
W erewolves, witch doctors, and zombies too
L urk in the dark and wait for you.
O ther scary creatures dwell
W here they can drag you off to hell.
E vil waits for black midnight
E nchanting with magic and dark voodoo,
N ow Halloween has cast its spell.

_4083-2 $4.99 US/$5.99 CAN

Dorchester Publishing Co., Inc.
P.O. Box 6640
Wayne, PA 19087-8640

Please add $1.75 for shipping and handling for the first book and $.50 for each book thereafter. NY, NYC, and PA residents, please add appropriate sales tax. No cash, stamps, or C.O.D.s. All orders shipped within 6 weeks via postal service book rate. Canadian orders require $2.00 extra postage and must be paid in U.S. dollars through a U.S. banking facility.

Name_____
Address_____
City_____State_____Zip_____
I have enclosed $_____ in payment for the checked book(s).
Payment <u>must</u> accompany all orders. ❑ Please send a free catalog.

Cold Blue Midnight

Ed Gorman

In Indiana the condemned die at midnight—killers like Peter Tapley, a twisted man who lives in his mother's shadow and takes his hatred out on trusting young women. Six years after Tapley's execution, his ex-wife Jill is trying to live down his crimes. But somewhere in the chilly nights someone won't let her forget. Someone who still blames her for her husband's hideous deeds. Someone who plans to make her pay . . . in blood.

___4417-X $4.99 US/$5.99 CAN

Dorchester Publishing Co., Inc.
P.O. Box 6640
Wayne, PA 19087-8640

Please add $1.75 for shipping and handling for the first book and $.50 for each book thereafter. NY, NYC, and PA residents, please add appropriate sales tax. No cash, stamps, or C.O.D.s. All orders shipped within 6 weeks via postal service book rate. Canadian orders require $2.00 extra postage and must be paid in U.S. dollars through a U.S. banking facility.

Name_____
Address_____
City_____ State_____ Zip_____
I have enclosed $_____ in payment for the checked book(s).
Payment <u>must</u> accompany all orders. ❏ Please send a free catalog.
CHECK OUT OUR WEBSITE! www.dorchesterpub.com

Elizabeth Massie
Sineater

According to legend, the sineater is a dark and mysterious figure of the night, condemned to live alone in the woods, who devours food from the chests of the dead to absorb their sins into his own soul. To look upon the face of the sineater is to see the face of all the evil he has eaten. But in a small Virginia town, the order is broken. With the violated taboo comes a rash of horrifying events. But does the evil emanate from the sineater...or from an even darker force?

___4407-2 $5.99 US/$6.99 CAN

Dorchester Publishing Co., Inc.
P.O. Box 6640
Wayne, PA 19087-8640

Please add $1.75 for shipping and handling for the first book and $.50 for each book thereafter. NY, NYC, and PA residents, please add appropriate sales tax. No cash, stamps, or C.O.D.s. All orders shipped within 6 weeks via postal service book rate. Canadian orders require $2.00 extra postage and must be paid in U.S. dollars through a U.S. banking facility.

Name_____
Address_____
City_____ State_____Zip_____
I have enclosed $_____ in payment for the checked book(s).
Payment <u>must</u> accompany all orders. ❏ Please send a free catalog.
CHECK OUT OUR WEBSITE! www.dorchesterpub.com

SHADOWS

Kimberly Rangel

WHERE TERROR RULES...

In the distant past, in a far-off land, the spell is cast, damning the family to an eternity of blood hunger. Over countless centuries, in the dark of night, they are doomed to assume the shape of savage beasts, deadly black panthers driven by a maddening fever to quench their unspeakable thirst. Then Selene DeMarco finds herself the last female of her line, and she has to mate with a descendent of the man who has plunged her family into the endless agony.
_4054-9 $4.99 US/$5.99 CAN

Dorchester Publishing Co., Inc.
P.O. Box 6640
Wayne, PA 19087-8640

Please add $1.75 for shipping and handling for the first book and $.50 for each book thereafter. NY, NYC, and PA residents, please add appropriate sales tax. No cash, stamps, or C.O.D.s. All orders shipped within 6 weeks via postal service book rate. Canadian orders require $2.00 extra postage and must be paid in U.S. dollars through a U.S. banking facility.

Name_____
Address_____
City_____ State_____ Zip_____
I have enclosed $_____ in payment for the checked book(s).
Payment <u>must</u> accompany all orders. ❏ Please send a free catalog.

ATTENTION HORROR CUSTOMERS!

SPECIAL
TOLL-FREE NUMBER
1-800-481-9191

*Call Monday through Friday
10 a.m. to 9 p.m.
Eastern Time
Get a free catalogue,
join the Horror Book Club,
and order books using your
Visa, MasterCard,
or Discover®*

*Leisure
Books*

GO ONLINE WITH US AT DORCHESTERPUB.COM